Brandy Morehouse

Copyright © 2011 Brandy Morehouse
All rights reserved.
Cover photographed by Steve Steinmetz
Cover designed by Roger Webb

ACKNOWLEDGMENTS

I know that no one ever reads this part of the book anyway, but I feel it is necessary to say a great big thank you to all the people who helped put this project together. It's been a rough road, but we made it! So, thank you to Caitlin Bentley and Tonya Duffy, my editors and cheerleaders, as well as my cover art friends, photographer Steve Steinmetz and graphic artist Roger Webb. Let's not forget Caitlin and our pal Nathan Bingman, who so graciously offered to pose for the cover, and Dave Severt, who provided the "props" for the photo as well. And of course, big thanks to all of my family, especially the grandmas who helped with babysitting and my amazing husband, Jeremiah, who was willing to sacrifice so many evenings as I sat up at night, typing away on my laptop. I couldn't have done it without you all!

Chapter 1

By the time Sarah managed to pry open her bloodshot eyes, the sun was already peeking through Cary's bedroom window. Last night was definitely a mistake. Too much booze and not enough dinner made for one hell of a morning, that was for sure. Her left hand moved to the nightstand beside the bed, desperately searching for anything to make the dull throbbing in her head vanish, while the right groped for something to pull over her eyes to block out the accursed sun. Neither was very successful.

"Feeling better?" The sound of her best friend's voice ripped through her head, bringing tears to her tired eyes. What the hell had she done?

She remembered riding with Cary and Luke to one of the biggest parties of the year, the Back to School Blast at the old Carter farm. No one had lived there for years, making it a great place for local teens to congregate and perform all the unspeakable acts that most adults accused them of anyway. The annual party had become infamous for creating quite a stir about town, especially since there was always at least one visit from the police and usually a few major injuries. While that might not sound like much fun to the older generations, it was a blast for a bunch of kids with nothing else to do on a Friday night.

When they'd arrived at the party, there were already at least a hundred people wandering around the three and a half acres still untouched by the company that now owned the property, and even more inside the old barn that had once housed some of the finest horses in the county. Now, it was little more than a rotting wood heap whose roof leaked when it rained and sounded like it might collapse in even the slightest breeze. Still, it was a bit more private inside those decaying walls, and that was where many a drunken teen had lost his or her virginity. And that had been her goal all along, hadn't it? To find some cute guy who could show her a good time in that barn, or anywhere else they might find along the way.

It had been Cary's idea. She was convinced that the only way to be a healthy, happy, well-balanced teen was to have at least one sexual encounter before graduation. She also believed that sex with random strangers was an acceptable way to fulfill this requirement. For a moment, Cary had even convinced the rest of them that this was something they needed, and poor Sarah, who seemed to feel like a third wheel quite often these days, had gone in search of a mate, at least for the evening.

Alcohol had flowed as water that night, and she had been mighty thirsty. Or maybe she'd just needed that extra bit of courage that only comes in liquid form to get up the nerve to follow through with her plans. Things got a little fuzzy after her third cup of some strange punch that was circulating through the crowd. She remembered a moment when one of Luke's friends from a neighboring school invited her to go to the barn, but she couldn't remember if she'd actually followed through with it or not. Suddenly, the idea of sleeping with someone she'd only known for a few hours seemed a lot less attractive. She couldn't even remember the guy's name! Of all the people to share such an intimate act with, the nameless, faceless stranger from the party was not at the top of her list.

"I didn't do anything stupid, did I?" Even her voice sounded as if it was just not quite ready to begin the day.

Cary laughed. "You mean besides drinking until you puked? Nah, nothing stupid."

She moaned loudly, suddenly realizing that the putrid smell of bile and booze was coming from the hair that lay limply across her face. Worse still, she didn't even have the energy to reach up and brush it away. Cary just shook her head.

"Aspirin?" The very idea of putting anything in her stomach was terrifying, but given the state of her head, it was a risk she was willing to take.

"I'll get you some. Any breakfast?"

And at that, her stomach decided it hadn't quite finished ejecting its contents. She took off down the hall to the bathroom, barely making it to the toilet before the mixture of alcohol and gastric juices left her body. Little was left in her gut, but that didn't stop the muscles from contracting sporadically for nearly fifteen minutes. Finally, Cary showed up in the doorway with a glass of water and a bottle of pills. Sarah tossed back two of the tiny red and yellow capsules and guzzled the liquid. Her insides instantly began to twist and moan in defiance.

Cary placed a cool hand on the back of her neck. "You'll feel better in just a few minutes, I promise."

"I don't think I'm ever going to feel better," she groaned, rubbing her eyes with the heels of her hands. Yet even as she spoke the words, she could feel the tension in her abdomen begin to ease and the throbbing in her head grew softer.

"You can be so dramatic. It's just a hangover, Sarah. Many a human has endured much worse and lived to tell the tale."

"Yeah, well, this is my first time. Cut me some slack."

In fact, this was the first time she could ever remember being sick. She had only ever thrown up once before when she was seven after eating a ton of junk food at a carnival and then braving the rollercoaster. Even as a small child, she'd never been subjected to the standard illnesses like chicken pox or strep throat. She'd never been to a hospital except to visit other people. Generally, her life had been full of blessings in regards to her health. Now it seemed her luck had finally run out.

"Your dad called." Cary wasn't smiling anymore. Talk of Andy was always a bit sobering, especially between the two of them. Cary understood better than most what she faced every day in her home as that madman went on rampages about the smallest things and ran off to feed his addictions for months at a time. As her best friend since grade school, Cary had witnessed all the damage inflicted on her family by the loser that called himself her father.

"What did he want? Written statements from your parents confirming that I was here with you last night?"

"Something like that. I told him you weren't awake yet, but I'd have you call as soon as possible. What are you going to tell him about last night?"

"I'll tell him I stayed up all night with you and some friends, and I ended up crashing at your place." She couldn't help but grin a bit, especially since the misery she'd felt upon waking was now almost completely forgotten. "It would be wrong of me to lie."

"Of course it would. So, about that breakfast?"

"My vote is on waffles."

The two girls walked out to the kitchen, arm in arm, savoring the time without any adult supervision. Cary's parents were out of town for the weekend, so the rest of that Saturday was spent listening to loud music, most selected by Cary who was notorious for her obsession with the Beatles, and lounging around doing absolutely nothing of real consequence. It was a perfect end to a perfect weekend as both girls eventually fell asleep in the living room to the sounds of late night television.

Chapter 2

"Everything alright?" Vanessa asked from her seat on the plush green sofa as he stepped through the front door. Though she tried to keep the tension out of her voice, it was obvious she was concerned. Whenever she waited up for him like this, it meant something was up. Probably just the incident last night. Combat was his specialty, not hers, and reassuring her that he could handle whatever they might throw at him was especially tricky lately.

"Fine. The girls are sleeping and Thomas took over the watch so I could get some rest." The look she gave him confirmed his suspicions. There was more on her mind than his little skirmish.

"You're limping." Her tone was calm, but her eyes begged him to tell her everything that had happened. She wanted more fuel for her argument against this assignment. He refused.

"I'll live. Good night."

As he started for the stairs, a hand landed gently on his shoulder where the fabric of his coat had been ripped open. He knew that if she looked too closely, she would also find that the sleeve of his shirt was torn, as was the skin beneath. The black cloth hid most of the blood that had dried into a stiff, dirty mess while he waited for someone to replace him at his post. At a distance, it would have been easy to hide. Now, between the hardened mess beneath her hand and the slight jerk he gave in response to her touch, it was impossible to deny the injury.

Their eyes locked for a moment, and he saw all the questions, all the worry and the frustration lurking in those emerald pools. He tried to remain as reactionless as possible, though she knew him well enough to pick up even the slightest hint of anxiety.

"Alright," she sighed, removing her hand slowly. "I promise not to lecture if you promise to let me take a look at that."

"Fine."

She shook her head and they made their way to the kitchen where she began cleaning the cut. This one would definitely need stitches. The knife had cut deep, but thankfully there was no serious damage. Once she had finished the cleaning and begun the stitching, he discovered the real reason for her concern.

"The Council wants to speak with you about The Girl." His muscles immediately tensed as she spoke the words he'd dreaded for almost a year now. She paused in her sewing until he relaxed once again, and then went back to her work and her explanation. "Apparently, they found a boy in New Mexico who fits the criteria. They're leaving next week to meet him and find out for certain, but the hunter that discovered him is quite confident…"

"He isn't the one. He can't be."

With a heavy sigh, she asked, "And if he is?"

"He isn't the one," he said again, anger seeping into his voice this time. She took that as her cue to drop the subject.

Once his arm was stitched up and wrapped in a clean bandage, she sent him off to bed with one final bit of advice.

"Your father was a very intelligent man who realized that there is a limit to the wisdom of the Council. Even if they decide to take this boy under their wing, it might be best to continue watching over Sarah for a bit. Whether she is what we believe she is or not, the Others have obviously expressed an interest in her."

"Good night, Vanessa."

Upstairs, he undressed, took a quick shower to rinse off the blood and sweat of battle, threw on clean clothing and crawled into bed. He was asleep before his head reached the pillow.

Chapter 3

The day she decided she truly hated her father was the day he saw the piercing. It was harmless, really. Just a tiny scrap of steel in her navel, covered by her favorite black baby doll tee. Her mother hadn't seen it yet because she'd worked second shift the night before and hadn't gotten home until almost two in the morning. Amy, an avid runner and captain of the cross-country team at their high school, had overheard the entire dramatic story from Cary at practice the night before. The brave best friend was telling one of the other girls about how she had nearly vomited as she watched the whole process. Cary had praised her friend, saying how brave Sarah was and how she'd never even made a sound. Which was true. Sarah hadn't made a single sound as the needle pierced her flesh. She had been too busy passing out.

That night, as the young rebel was climbing into bed, her little sister had knocked on her door and asked to see it. She was more than willing to show off her new jewelry to Amy, who wouldn't necessarily approve, but would at least give the idea a chance.

"It looks so painful," Amy had whispered.

"Nah, I didn't feel a thing when it happened. Besides, who cares? It looks awesome."

"Same old Sarah." Amy had chuckled and asked, "How do you think mom and dad are going to react?"

With a wicked grin, Sarah had replied, "I hope Andy's head explodes."

"You're horrible!"

"He deserves it. Besides, it's an easy piercing to hide. He probably won't even notice until I've moved out."

"You better hope so," Amy had cautioned once again as she left the room to go to bed. And, rolling her eyes, Sarah had settled in for the evening as well, content with her new jewelry.

This morning seemed to be just like every other morning, in that her mother, Angela, was already up and making breakfast before anyone else had lifted an eyelid. The girls were downstairs in the kitchen an hour after their mother first climbed out of bed, gulping down their meal to ensure that there was enough time to finish homework before they left for school. Eventually, Andy made his way to the table, nowhere near ready to start his busy day of job hunting, which usually consisted of reading the classifieds in the morning paper and mailing a few resumes before lazing around on the couch until bedtime. Always the comedian, Sarah commented on his bed head and ratty old bathrobe as she reached for the milk.

"Why, Andy! Is that a new haircut? And a new suit? You must have an interview today!" Her mother gave her a brief but angry glare as a warning to drop the subject. Amy, however, grabbed her arm in another kind of warning.

She looked up to see Andy's cheeks and forehead turning a deep shade of red. His eyes were fixed on her stomach, and the rage she saw lurking behind those blue orbs sent a shudder through her body. He'd seen the piercing. Trying to make a quick escape, she grabbed her bag and her keys from the counter, racing to the back door with the knowledge that if he caught up to her it wouldn't be pretty.

She wasn't fast enough.

"What the hell is that?" he demanded, yanking her arm roughly until she faced him once again. The color had spread to his entire head, and deep blue veins pulsed furiously at his temples.

"Let go of me." The order came out sounding like the deep growl of a cornered animal, which was quite appropriate, given the circumstances. Andy might look like a bum, but in the end she knew he was quite capable of physically overpowering her.

When his hand collided with her cheek, Angela finally tried to intervene. Her slender fingers, still covered in bits of pancake batter, wrapped around the arm that held her daughter. It did nothing except amplify his anger.

Sarah reached up and felt the place where he'd struck her, terrified at the tiny trickle of blood that flowed from her left nostril. Andy had been angry before, and he'd even threatened to kill her a few times, but until now, she had never actually believed that he might follow through with one of his threats. This was the first time he'd ever hit her, and hard enough to draw blood. Who could guess what he might do next?

"I want to know who did that, and I want to know *right now*!" His grip tightened as he pulled her closer, pushing his face into hers as he ranted. "You will not leave this house until I get answers!"

"Leave her alone!" Angela begged. He tossed her aside as she once again tried to separate them, too focused on his daughter to care about the hysterical woman hanging on his free arm.

"Why does it matter? Are you going to track down the culprits and beat the crap out of them, too?" The words were strong and defiant. Inside, though, she wondered just how much provocation it would take before he really did injure her seriously. A busted nose was one thing, but his eyes told her that he was ready to do much worse. All he needed was a reason, and if she didn't watch her mouth, it wouldn't take long for him to find one.

"I've had about enough of your attitude."

He grabbed her other arm, hoisting her into the air and throwing her onto the dining room table with strength that seemed almost inhuman. Breakfast scattered across the room and dishes shattered on the floor as she hit the wooden surface, barely able to stop her body from tumbling helplessly to the floor. Before she could recover, Andy marched over to where she lay, pulling her shirt up with rough hands that seemed eager to connect with her delicate flesh once again. Then, with a smile that screamed murder, he reached down and wrapped fevered fingers around the tiny piece of jewelry that had started all of this.

Screams ripped through the air as the metal was torn from her flesh. Sarah's cry came first as pain finally convinced her that this might be the very last morning she ever saw. Angela was next, once again tossing herself at the madman and receiving her own bruises as she was slammed to the floor. Amy remained huddled in the corner, completely silent as she had been since Andy first grabbed her sister.

"Next time, I suggest you think twice before you start flapping your tongue," he sneered, throwing the steel bar onto the table beside her throbbing face. It made a sound that was both happy and horrible as it collided with the polished wooden surface now covered with spilt milk and coffee.

"Get out!" The shrill noise coming from the floor below her no longer resembled the voice of her mother, but reminded her instead of an angry gerbil.

This thought, coupled with increasing panic, was enough to push her beyond her breaking point, and laughter burst forth from deep within, despite her fear and pain. Or perhaps it was because of the fear and pain that she found she could not stop, not even when she saw the look that Andy shot towards her. It was a look of pure evil. A look that said, *You've finally sealed your fate.*

Long slender fingers wrapped around her neck, yet still she laughed. Even as her lungs begged for air and her lips began to turn blue and she was no longer able to make any sound other than squeaks and gurgles, she continued to smile. Not because of her mother, or her father, or even her frightened sibling cowering in the corner, but simply because there was nothing else she could do. She couldn't fight him. She definitely couldn't scream. She couldn't talk back or get the last word in as she normally did. She was going to die, but at least she could die knowing that Andy had still lost the battle as far as her will was concerned. He could not break her.

Darkness began to creep in around the edges of her vision, slowly seeping into the world until all she could see were those eyes, burning with hatred and fear. Fear that he would not win, not even if he choked the life out of her here in this tiny kitchen where she had eaten the past sixteen years' worth of dinners with him. Yet there was no sign of him letting go.

And then, she was free. Her body began sucking in bursts of oxygen rich air as quickly as possible, coughing and gagging as though she'd nearly drowned. There were hushed voices, and then the sound of the door, but she was too busy worrying about breathing again to care much about anything else. When she finally looked up, Angela was huddled in the corner with Amy, stroking the girl's hair in an effort to calm her.

"Are you alright?" the woman asked, her voice shaking almost as much as her hands.

Without another word, Sarah slowly climbed to her feet, grabbed her bag and stumbled to the front door. No one tried to stop her this time as she left her home. Andy was long gone by the looks of things, though both cars were still in the driveway. Still afraid of blacking out at any moment, the battered girl trudged down the street, away from the stinking mess of a life that waited for her back in that house.

Chapter 4

This was such a mess. How was he supposed to keep her safe and still remain hidden if her own family was a threat? Andy and the girl had been through their fair share of fights, maybe even more than average, but this was by far the worst. He had never hit her until this morning, and while the man outside could not hear the conversation from his place behind the rose bushes, he had a pretty good guess that daddy had just discovered the naval piercing from The Girl's adventures yesterday.

As soon as she hit the table, he moved out of his hiding place, ready to give up his secret if it meant keeping her safe. He just caught a glimpse of The Girl's mother hitting the floor as he sprinted to the front door. It opened easily, much to his relief. Breaking into her house would have definitely drawn more attention than he wanted.

His heart stopped as The Girl's screams echoed through his ears.

Please, just don't let me be too late...

The scene that greeted him was one of pure insanity. Andy had her by the throat, her lips and face already turning a deep shade of purple. Her mother was in the corner along with her sister, and both were clearly worried that they might be next. Blood and milk covered the tile floor below The Girl, along with bits of broken dish. Without another thought, he grabbed one of the pistols from beneath his long black coat, bringing it down hard on the back of the would-be killer's head. Andy immediately released The Girl, crumpling into a pile of useless flesh and bones on the floor beside her.

"Get her to a hospital," he ordered in a voice just above a whisper as he began dragging the lifeless body out the front door and into the bushes nearby.

He pulled out his phone, calling Vanessa mostly for advice on how to handle the situation. As far as he could tell, The Girl had been on the verge of unconsciousness when he'd arrived, which meant she probably hadn't noticed him at all. But if she had, it wouldn't be long before she started looking for answers, and the first person Angela would send her to was Vanessa.

"Hello?" She sounded awfully chipper for seven-thirty in the morning.

"We have a problem," he said quickly. "Andy just tried to kill her."

"What?" Shock and disbelief replaced the friendly tone she'd used to answer the phone. "Andy, her father?"

"Yes. I stopped him, but I can't be sure that she didn't see me. Now I have an unconscious nutcase lying in the bushes between the backyard and the neighbor's fence, and I have no idea what to do next."

"Okay, just stay calm. I'll call in some help. Did Angela see you?"

"Yeah, she and Amy were both there."

"And you said you aren't sure if Sarah saw you or not?"

"I think she passed out just before I came in, but I'm not certain."

There was a brief pause as the woman thought about this.

"Make sure she gets any medical attention necessary. And don't worry about Andy. The cleaners will take care of him when they arrive."

"Son of a…" She was leaving. Despite the gash in her stomach, the broken nose the huge bruises on her throat, and the fact that just moments ago, she'd nearly been killed by a man she trusted, The Girl was stumbling out of her home and down the street.

"What is it?"

"I have to go. Tell the team to hurry."

Slipping the phone back into his pocket, he crept silently out of the bushes and began following The Girl once again, praying that she wouldn't get into any more trouble today.

Chapter 5

"I have to go to school. If I'm late again, they'll suspend me for sure." Another coughing fit broke her raspy voice, and Vanessa placed a comforting hand on her forehead, brushing away a few loose strands of violet hair. She led the trembling girl into the living room, closing the door behind them.

"I think the principal will understand," the woman smiled reassuringly as she eased Sarah onto the soft green sofa.

"Really, I'm fine." But she wasn't fine. Not at all. She could feel her throat swelling shut, and breathing was getting more difficult with each passing moment. Her navel burned as a scab slowly began to form where a tin silver barbell once was.

"Argue with me," Vanessa shook her head, reaching for the phone that sat on the mahogany end table to her right. "You'll pass out soon enough, and then it's my call."

As if it had read her mind, the phone began ringing and Vanessa glanced down at the caller ID screen. Sarah saw it as well, but it only gave a number she didn't recognize. Turning away from the frightened girl, Vanessa held up a finger to silence her as she answered the call.

"Hello," she said calmly, her warm yet still very concerned smile filling the girl with a sense of ease that should not have been attainable given the situation. "Yes, she's with me now. We're discussing the hospital."

"Who is it?" Sarah croaked, but the woman just shook

her head.

"I'll keep you informed. Be careful."

A man. It was a man's voice, no doubt about it. What it was saying remained a mystery, but that deep, rich tone was clearly too masculine to be her mother or sister. So who else knew what had happened? Who else would be calling here to check up on her?

"It was him, wasn't it?" she demanded, jumping to her feet.

"Who?" Vanessa asked nervously, rising with the girl as the receiver dropped to the couch.

"Andy! You told him I was here!" The room was spinning now. Faster and faster it went, making her feel as if she was on some cheap carnival ride. "He'll come here and finish the job!"

"It wasn't Andy," Vanessa cooed, trying to wrap comforting arms around the girl.

She ducked out of reach shouting, "Liar! It was him! You want me to go to the hospital because he's there waiting for me!"

"Stop being so paranoid and sit down."

"I trusted you!" Charging towards the door, she made it about halfway across the living room before crumbling to the ground in a trembling heap. Vanessa was right behind her, rolling the broken girl onto her side and shaking her head.

"Just like your mother," she smiled, placing a cool

steady hand on her forehead. The other hand checked for a pulse on her wrist, and the smile faltered for just an instant as she said, "Time to go see a doctor."

"Please, don't let him hurt me," the girl wheezed as the world began to fade into darkness once again.

"Sarah, I'm not going to let anyone hurt you."

"Promise?" Almost gone. Almost...

"Promise."

And though she had barely enough strength to remain conscious for even a moment longer, she managed a weak smile in the hope that Vanessa would understand. If there was one person on the planet she trusted with her life, it was this woman with the enchanting emerald eyes and a smile that could melt glaciers. Even now, after Andy's betrayal and Angela's lack of concern, she felt almost safe in the arms of this woman.

Almost.

As everything disappeared, she could barely hear the sweet sound of Vanessa's voice on the phone with the EMT's. They were discussing her condition, all very professional. Except somehow it wasn't. There wasn't enough time for her to consider it, though, as darkness took hold and Sarah finally lost consciousness.

Three hours later, she gazed through the one eye that hadn't swelled shut at the woman in the blue suit. When she'd regained consciousness, Vanessa had been sitting at her bedside, talking in hushed tones with this woman and a man whom she assumed was a police officer due to the slight bulge under his jacket. Probably a gun. There was plenty of time to ponder such things before they noticed her staring.

"So good to see you're awake," Vanessa greeted her warmly, but her concern was hard to hide. "We were all very worried."

"Where's mom?" The silence was all the answer she needed. "Still too busy worrying about Amy, huh? Well, I guess that's to be expected."

"Sarah, your mother and sister have been taken into protective custody by the police. Andy has disappeared. No one knows whether or not he's planning to come back and…"

"Finish the job?" Vanessa moved her eyes to the floor, gnawing at her lip as she tried to think of a way to respond. "I suppose these fine people would like for me to tell them what happened. Maybe even press charges against the man who did this. Is that right?"

"Yes."

"We can wait until you've had a chance to rest," the woman in the blue suit said nervously.

The man interjected, "Like hell we can! Sarah, if we're going to catch this guy and punish him for what he's done, we need a statement from you. Now."

"Well, I'm afraid that isn't going to happen. To tell you the truth, I can't even really remember what happened this morning." Her answer was obviously not what the man wanted to hear, yet he didn't seem all that surprised by her response. Definitely a cop.

"Look, I have to get back to work," he told the blue suit woman. "See if you can't get her to change her mind."

The man left and Vanessa excused herself for a moment to use the ladies room. Sarah was all alone with Blue Suit Lady now. Finally, the woman introduced herself.

"I'm with social Services, Sarah. My name is Theresa, and it's my job to make sure you don't have to live like this anymore." All in all, she seemed like a nice lady, although very nervous. *This must be one of her first solo cases*, Sarah thought with a grin.

"Something funny?" the woman smiled weakly from the edge of the bed.

"Just this whole situation. Do you really think I'm going to change my mind about any of this?"

"Well, I certainly hope so. It would be a shame to see such a pretty girl spend most of her youth in this place, wouldn't you agree?"

"What about my mother? Or my sister, Amy? Why don't you convince them to tell you what you want to hear?"

"Neither one remembers anything about this morning. They're convinced that you and your father got into a shouting match and then you just ran off." She paused for a moment, giving Sarah a chance to jump in and explain before proceeding.

It was a very long, very awkward silence. Finally, Blue Suit Lady pushed on, "I'd say by the look of your face and throat it was a little more than yelling."

"I really don't remember."

Liar. She's trying to help you, but instead of letting her do her job, you're protecting the monster that did this.

Guilt suddenly overwhelmed her. Why was she doing this? Why was she being so difficult? Sarah shifted her eyes to the colorless world of the hospital blanket draped over her lap, picking absently at the coarse material. And that's how they remained, the woman perched on the bed by her feet as she sat in silence until the door finally swung open and in walked Vanessa with two bowls of delicious smelling soup.

"I'm sorry," she apologized to the woman in blue. "Were you two still talking?"

"No, actually, I was just leaving." The woman stood, placing a small white piece of paper on the bedside table. "If you change your mind…"

"It's been a blast, but I don't think we'll be seeing each other again anytime soon." Sarah gave the woman the most insincere smile she was capable of before Blue Suit Lady quickly rushed out of the room.

"I take it that didn't go so well?" Vanessa sat a bowl in front of the now ravenous teenage girl.

"I told them I didn't remember what happened this morning," she shrugged, grabbing her spoon and practically lunging at the food in front of her. Vegetable. Her favorite.

"Do you?"

There was a brief pause in her slurping as she considered how to answer this question. Vanessa had been a friend of her mother's since before she was born, and while it was possible to keep some things secret from her parents and even her sister, Sarah had never been able to keep a secret from Vanessa. Somehow she always seemed to know everything there was to know about her. At times like these, that ability to see through her was frustrating, but oddly comforting as well. Lying to the police was one thing, but trying to lie to Vanessa felt like an insult to the woman's intelligence. Besides, it was nice to know there was someone she could talk to about this that wouldn't necessarily pass judgment, unlike her mother or sister or the police.

"I do." Suddenly, she wasn't quite so hungry.

"So I guess the real question is, why did you lie?" Vanessa's eyes never left her own bowl as she daintily scooped tiny spoonfuls of soup into her mouth.

"I guess it's because, no matter what, Andy is my father. He's a psycho and a slob, and he's completely useless, but he's my father." There was a deep sigh and then came the real reason. "Besides, I deserved it."

"Did you?" Still no eye contact. Still no hint of shock or judgment.

"If I hadn't gotten my belly button pierced, none of this

would have happened. And if I'd just shut my mouth and let him get it out of his system, I'd be sitting in math class right now, struggling over some stupid trig problem."

"Hmm, that's interesting." Finally, the beautiful woman with the copper curls placed her dish on the nightstand just beside the business card and turned her deep emerald eyes to the girl in the hospital bed. "So, you're saying that if you hadn't gotten that piercing, then Andy wouldn't have snapped and tried to kill you?"

"Y-yes." And now the logic seemed flawed somehow.

"Then perhaps it's Cary's fault for driving you there last night, or perhaps the one who did the piercing is to blame."

"Vanessa, that's ridiculous."

"So is blaming yourself. If it hadn't been the piercing, it would have been something else. Andy was on the edge because of a series of poor choice that *he* made. Andy is to blame for everything that has happened in his life, Andy is to blame for his breakdown this morning, and Andy is to blame for your impromptu visit to the hospital." Never once did Vanessa's voice rise to show her outrage, but her eyes were shimmering pits of fury.

"Vanessa, I…" She couldn't finish. The tears came, and the woman who had been there for her more than anyone else her entire life scooped the sobbing girl into her arms as the fear and anger boiled up from deep within. Time slipped by silently, and when she was all used up, Sarah lay her head back down on her pillow and slept with the deep peaceful dreams of a child as Vanessa sat patiently beside her.

Chapter 6

She entered the house at quarter to ten, dragging her weary body into the living room where he waited patiently. Two hours had passed since her last phone call, and she'd told him that she was staying until visiting hours were over. Still, he couldn't help but worry about her being out on her own so late. Any number of things could have happened to her on the way home.

"You didn't have to wait up," she sighed, flopping down on the couch beside him.

He stood and walked out into the kitchen to make her some tea. She looked like she could use it.

"She's going to be fine," she called, and immediately he felt as if a weight had been lifted from his chest. Nothing to worry about. The Girl was safe. "Doctors say she can go home tomorrow. Angela and Amy are with her now. That was one hell of a mess, though. I can't believe they would just leave her like that. They didn't even show up to the hospital until just before nine. I don't think Angela wanted to be there at all, but Amy convinced her."

"Who else is there?" There was a slight pause before she replied, and he could just imagine her face at that moment. Smiling that knowing smile, the one that said, *Do you ever think of anything else?*

"Thomas." Good. At least it was someone who could

handle things if the situation got too rough. "He's been there since just before she arrived. Said he was surprised you didn't hitch a ride in the ambulance and pose as one of her doctors to keep an eye on her."

"I'll go relieve him in a few hours."

It was difficult to stay away that long, knowing that things had begun to escalate and that anyone could be considered a threat now. His entire life since his father had died almost five years ago had been keeping The Girl safe. But then, things hadn't gotten completely out of control until just before the school year started. Up to then, he'd dealt with this assignment solo. These days, it seemed he was calling in backup every weekend. Sitting here when she could be in serious danger felt completely wrong. Still, he had to sleep. It wouldn't do anyone any good if he couldn't keep his eyes open while he was on guard duty.

"So, what happened to Andy?" she asked as he handed her the steaming mug. She'd already removed her shoes and was lounging lazily on the soft green couch cushions. He sat down in the chair beside her, his elbows against his knees with his hands hanging between his legs.

"We put the fear of God in him and sent him off to Phoenix. Shouldn't have any more trouble with that one."

"Good. God, if you could have seen how much he hurt her." He had seen, but he had a feeling that wasn't what she was talking about. Being almost strangled to death by your father was bound to have some psychological repercussions.

"I'm going to go take a nap before I go back on duty. You should get some rest, too. Tomorrow is bound to be a busy day for all of us."

"That's usually my line," she smiled, sipping her tea as he made his way up the stairs to his room.

Andy had been a completely unexpected threat, one that no one had ever anticipated. Still, an overwhelming sense of guilt seemed to coat his thoughts as he slipped off his boots and sank into bed. He should have seen it. He should have watched her more closely. It was his job to keep her safe and he had almost lost her. People don't just snap like that. It must have been building for weeks, maybe even years. There must have been signs. How could he have missed this?

It didn't matter. Andy was gone now. She was tucked safely in a hospital bed for the night. Thomas was watching over her. He couldn't ask for a better replacement. Right now, he just needed to get some rest and get back to his post. Even without Andy in the picture, there were plenty of dangers to deflect. Tomorrow would be no different.

Despite all this knowledge, though, he couldn't quite clear his conscience. Eventually, he did manage to sleep, though even his dreams could not help him escape the weight of his thoughts.

It was a very long night.

Chapter 7

"So, you and Jacob have been seeing each other for quite a while now."

The sly look Cary shot her way was enough to make her blush. She was getting ready to go out with her latest boyfriend, Jacob, to endure yet another ridiculous horror movie. He loved them, but she found herself wondering if maybe there was something better she could be spending her time doing, like maybe trimming the hedges in the front yard with a pair of nail clippers. Still, a dark movie theater was an excellent place to fool around. If she could distract him from all the carnage on the screen, that is. Recently, that was becoming less and less of a problem, which was beginning to create a new set of issues that needed to be dealt with soon. For instance, she would not give up her virginity in the back of a pickup truck to someone she'd only been seeing for a month.

"Yes, we have, and no, we haven't." Cary shook her head at this last statement, as Sarah continued. "I've thought about it, but in the end, it just doesn't feel right. Not yet."

"If you keep waiting around until it feels right, you might never feel it at all." Cary tossed her books into her locker and pulled out her jacket. The weather had finally begun to shift from the hot, humid days of summer to the cool breezes of autumn, and since Sarah wasn't planning on going home on a Friday night until long after the sun had set, a jacket would have been an excellent idea. Too bad she'd left hers on the living room couch.

"Just because I'm not as easy as you…" She gave her friend a playful shove.

"Joke if you want, but I'm serious. You're only young once, Sarah. Enjoy it while you can. Besides, if tragedy strikes tomorrow and you're suddenly a blind quadriplegic mute, who's gonna want that?"

"Thanks for the uplifting images. So, are we still on for after the movie?"

"Yep. My place, eight-ish, tons of young able-bodied lads who'd love to get their hands on an angel like you. Who knows? Maybe you'll meet the man of your dreams tonight and you can dump that loser you're with now."

"Jacob is not a loser," Sarah insisted, but the truth was, she really didn't want to stick with this relationship much longer. Jacob was a nice guy, but there was something about him that was a bit off. It wasn't anything he said or did, just a feeling she got whenever he was near her. Like someone else was there, watching them, waiting for…well who knew? It was silly anyway. Still, she couldn't shake the feeling.

"Please, spare me the lecture. I know he's a good guy, but you really could do so much better." Cary tossed a quick glance at her watch before sighing, "I have to get out of here. Lots to take care of before the big bash tonight."

"Don't most people wait until *after* the homecoming

game for a victory party?"

"Cary rolled her eyes and replied, "Consider it a pep rally. We cheerleaders have to get the team excited somehow."

"Don't work too hard. It'll be trashed by morning anyway."

"Such pessimism! See ya 'round eight. And try to ditch your little pet Jake. He's such a downer."

Cary took off at a steady, determined pace for the parking lot, while Sarah made her way to the science lab to meet Jacob. Maybe she could fake an illness or something to get out of this whole evening with him.

That's lovely, Sarah. Not even a month with this guy and already you can't stand to be around him for more than an hour. And you were actually considering sleeping with him?

He was already waiting for her in the hall, talking to a few of his buddies from the football team. Jacob wasn't one of the star players, but he did get plenty of time on the field, and he wasn't half bad at the game. Unfortunately, his grades had begun to slip due to an increase in the amount of time spent on extracurricular activities. Sarah had not made that mistake, choosing instead to excel in her studies and leave the sports to those who could play. For this reason, she had been a perfect candidate to tutor Jacob in his biology class, eventually leading to a slightly less professional relationship outside of school.

"Hey, Sarah!" Danny, one of Jacob's teammates, rolled his eyes as she approached. "I was wondering where you were.

Figured you'd be stuck to our buddy Jake here the moment you heard that bell ring."

"And I'm glad to see you've stopped salivating at the sound of that bell," she replied smugly.

"Okay, guys, take it easy." Jacob hated being caught in the middle of these verbal battles. His teammates were not the wittiest individuals on the planet, and Sarah's sarcasm had a tendency to cut deep. Eventually, every heated debate turned into a barrage of name calling and enraged threats if Jacob did not mediate.

"So Jake, you coming to the party tonight at Cary's house? Bet it'll be a blast, and there's bound to be lots of pretty girls there, most of which will actually put out." The look on Jacob's face, coupled with this last comment from his friend, was the final straw.

"Excuse us, Danny. Jacob and I have plans for this evening that don't involve scratching ourselves or playing fetch." She grabbed Jacob's arm and quickly led him down the hall, moving silently towards the parking lot where his old Ford was waiting to take her home. Why hadn't she just left with Cary? Hell, just a more comfortable pair of shoes so she could walk home would have been better than this. But now he was her only ride home, which meant that a confrontation was inevitable.

When they reached the rusted red heap, she spun around on him with such force that he took a frightened step back. Trying her best to keep her emotions under control, she found her voice remarkably steady as she initiated the argument.

"What the hell, Jacob?" she demanded. The look he gave her was one of shock and terror, much like that of a cornered rabbit. "I can't believe you! I thought you were different from other guys!"

"It's not like that..." he began. She quickly cut him off, not willing to give him a chance to explain all of this away. Sarah might be a lot of things, but a whore was not one of them, and she wasn't about to let her own morality be used as a weapon against her.

"Isn't it? You told those apes about some of our most private moments! How can I ever trust you again?"

"I didn't tell them anything!" he shouted, finally overcoming the fear with his own anger. Sarah stopped suddenly, unsure of how to continue. "I didn't tell them about us, Sarah. Danny just said that because he was trying to piss you off. Yes, the guys did start talking about girlfriends, but I kept my mouth shut because it's none of their business."

"You're damned right it's none of their business." Her words were strong, but her voice had lost its firmness thanks to the embarrassment she now felt welling up inside of her.

Jacob wrapped his arms around her, surrounding her with his warmth, and she wondered if she was supposed to be feeling what all those romance novels and movies described when a woman fell into the arms of the man of her dreams. It should have felt magical, or comfortable, or at least safe. She felt none of these things. Instead, a knot slowly began to form in the middle of her stomach. It reminded her of the feeling just before she gave her presentation on origami to her English class. That feeling, that knowledge that something is about to happen and there's no way to avoid it or stop it or even slow it down, was creeping up on her again.

Ever since her visit to the hospital last month, she'd felt as if there was something going on just outside her view. As if some outside forces were conspiring against her, trying to break through the bubble of her reality. The doctors said it was a normal reaction, since her father, a man she should have been able to trust, had nearly killed her. And while everyone around her agreed with this opinion, she still found herself wondering if maybe there wasn't something more.

Jacob finally let go and climbed behind the wheel of the old Ford. Sarah started to open the passenger side door, then stopped as something caught her eye. Movement, just behind the school in a group of knotty old pine trees. She waited for a moment, staring into the tiny grove in the hopes that she would see it again. Nothing happened, and when Jacob called to her impatiently, she shrugged it off. Just a bird or squirrel, nothing to worry about. Still, as she climbed into the truck beside the brawny football player, she couldn't help but notice that the knot in her stomach had gotten just a little bit bigger.

Chapter 8

"You can't keep her safe forever," the thing in front of him hissed. Mousy brown hair now highlighted with streaks of deep crimson and damp with sweat hung down in front of its face, masking most of the damage he'd already caused.

"Why are you here?" he demanded. It wasn't unlike them to check up on The Girl, but since her trip to the hospital a month ago, they had begun popping up all over the place. They would show up, follow for a few hours, and then disappear. This time had been different. This one had posed as a substitute teacher for the last two days in The Girl's biology class.

"The same as you," it replied, and he could hear the amusement in its voice. "We must protect what is ours."

"She doesn't belong to you."

"She will."

It was stalling, and he was too busy trying to collect information to notice the small black object that slipped out of its pocket and into the palm of its left hand.

"You're sending someone to the party. Who?"

The smile was just barely visible through the mat of hair and blood, but it chilled him all the same. Just before its hand shot towards him, releasing the projectile into the air, he dove to his right, drawing both of his pistols and putting two bullets through its face. Even with the silencers, every bird and chipmunk scrambled to escape the sound of danger. When he turned around, he saw a small splatter of black goo on the trunk of the tree just behind where his head had been. Already, the area around the splatter was beginning to turn gray and crumble.

So much for his interrogation. That was the most information he'd been able to get out of one of them so far, and all he'd really done was finally confirm his suspicions about the party. Well, at least he had enough to convince the Council to send a team to back him up tonight. Whatever they had planned, he hoped a team of six would be able to handle it. No way would they give him more backup. Not without some serious intel, and that was something he didn't have despite a week of attempts.

There was shouting coming from the parking lot. He recognized the voice at once and his muscles immediately tensed in preparation for another battle. A few moments were enough for him to realize she was in no real danger. Just a little spat between The Girl and her boyfriend. Maybe she'd finally dump that loser.

When the boy hugged her and got into the truck, he relaxed enough to slip his weapons back into their holsters. Nothing to worry about here. The Girl suddenly turned, her gaze fixed directly on him. For a moment, he couldn't breathe. Had she seen him? Impossible. The trees and the building and all the cars, they should have been enough to keep him hidden. Still, she seemed to be staring right at him. A tiny shiver tried to creep up his spine, but he suppressed it quickly. She was just a girl. Just a scrawny little girl. And she wasn't looking at him.

Couldn't be.

    Still, he couldn't help feeling relieved when she finally turned and climbed into the truck. That was far too close.

    Once the truck was gone, he pulled out his phone and called in the cleaners.

Chapter 9

He seemed really nervous. The movie was one of those old black and white horror flicks, and she was completely bored through the entire hour and a half. Jacob obviously wasn't paying any attention to the movie, glancing around the theater every few minutes rather than looking at the screen. When she tried to put her hand over his, he nearly jumped out of his seat. He wouldn't touch her at all, and he refused to look at her even after they left the theater. Apparently, her little tantrum earlier had upset him more than he'd let on.

Finally, they got into his truck and her curiosity got the best of her.

"Are you upset about earlier?" she sighed, not looking forward to yet another confrontation today. Two fights in two hours. That had to be a new record.

"What do you mean?" he snorted, shaking his head. "Why would I be upset?"

"I don't know. You just seem kinda...weird."

"Thanks," he sneered, and she quickly tried to explain.

"I just meant that you aren't yourself. You hardly watched the movie, you're all jumpy and irritable, and you haven't even looked at me since the scene in the parking lot. Jake, I'm sorry if I upset you, but I just thought..."

"It's not that," he interrupted. "I just...I have a lot of stuff going on at home right now, and it's sorta hard to focus."

"What's up? Is it Adam? If that little brat is causing trouble, I can talk to him. Maybe a good thrashing is even in order."

"Nah, it's not Adam. Just some family stuff. Nothing to worry about." Somehow, she just wasn't convinced. Maybe it was the tremble in his voice or the absolute defeat in his eyes. Whatever was going on, it was important. Still, Jacob wasn't the kind of guy to share this sort of thing openly.

"You know if you need anything, I'm here."

"Yeah, thanks." His voice was empty and cold as he spoke, and she decided to drop it for now. Maybe later after the party when he was nice and sloshed she could try again.

"So, I'll see you at the party later?" she asked as they pulled up outside Cary's house.

"Yeah, I'll be there," he replied, looking away from her and focusing his attention on the stray cat that was inching its way up the street instead. Sarah shook her head and opened the door, jumping out of the vehicle with a sigh.

"Look, I know I overreacted earlier, and I'm really sorry, okay? Can we just forget about it and try to have a little fun tonight?" Okay, so maybe she wasn't quite ready to give up on Jacob just yet.

Finally, his eyes fell on her, though not her face and not for very long.

"You're right," he told her neck. "Tonight should be about having a good time."

"So I'll see you here at eight?"

"Wouldn't miss it," he said as she slammed the door. He was gone in a flash, and Sarah turned her attention to more important things. Like what was she going to wear?

Chapter 10

The thin, nauseatingly sterile smell of the hospital was bad in the hall, but it was nothing compared to the stench of her room. The hospital smell still lingered, but it had begun to mix with the stale smell of old sweat and urine. It was the smell of death, and it had done what none of the kind words offered by the doctors and specialists could.

Up until now, he'd hoped that none of this was real. He had almost convinced himself that the past three months had been one terrific nightmare and that any minute he would wake up and find things all just as they once were. She would be out in her garden, weeding or harvesting the latest crop of herbs and vegetables, singing in her sweet yet slightly off-key voice. He would run up to her and wrap his arms around her in a giant bear hug, trying to show her in that one gesture just how much he really loved her and finding that he still came up short.

"Silly boy," she would laugh, and the sound would be music to his ears. A sound so full of life and joy that it would seem ridiculous to have ever imagined the scene that greeted him now.

But with the smell of decaying soul surrounding him, it was impossible to deny the truth. This was not a dream. The sound of her beautiful voice, the feel of her soft hand pressed against his cheek, those were all in his head. Memories of the way things were before. The truth was that she was dying. The truth was that she was being eaten alive from the inside out by a mutated form of her own body. The truth was it was one of the most excruciating ways to die, and all he could do was watch as the woman who had given him life slowly lost the battle for her own.

His father sat beside the bed, gently stroking a frail hand. He didn't look up when the boy entered the room, but it didn't matter. He wasn't there for his father. Not today. Today, he needed to talk to her. Alone.

"Jacob!" his father exclaimed as the boy placed a hand on the man's bony shoulder. What had happened to the youthful, carefree parents who had raised him? What happened to the man who taught him to play football in their backyard or the woman who always made an extra batch of oatmeal raisin cookies because she knew he loved them so much? Could these two skeletons really be all that was left?

"Where's Adam?"

"Probably still playing basketball with his friends. He should be by soon. Why don't you go get some coffee or something?" At first, he thought the old man might try to argue, but something about the look on the boy's face must have changed his mind.

"Okay, I guess I could use a little break. I'll be back in ten, though."

"Make it fifteen," Jacob suggested, helping his father stand.

Moving stiffly, the old man made his way to the door, glancing back only once at the woman lying lifelessly beneath the thin hospital blankets. Through it all, he had stuck with her, and even now when things seemed hopeless, he almost never left her side. Jacob could only hope that he would one day find a woman whom he could love like that and who would return his affections with the same enthusiasm.

After his father was gone, Jacob sat down on the side of the bed, leaning over his mother's pale, sunken face until he could smell the sour breath leaving her mouth. This wasn't fair. How could something like this happen to such a wonderful person? And now, he had a chance to save her. The woman at football practice had given him that chance. All he had to do was one simple little favor for this woman, and his mother would be saved.

"Hey, ma. Lookin' pretty good. I bet all the doctors wish dad would take a hike so they could have a shot at you."

The corner of her mouth twitched just a bit, and then she was still again.

"Listen, I met this lady who says she might have a way to cure you. The price is a little steep, but I figure for you, nothing is too expensive."

Slowly, her eyelids began to flutter, and for the first time in two weeks, he was staring into two big blue pools of light. She was conscious, and by the look of pain and concentration on her face, she was trying to say something.

"No," she finally wheezed, her whole body trembling with the effort of that one word. "Don't."

"But ma, I can save you! Please, you have to understand…"

"No," she said again, a little more firmly. "Not…for me. Too late…"

"It's not too late."

She shook her head, gasping as another agonizing pain engulfed her, sending her body into a series of spasms that made his heartache. Finally, she opened her eyes one last time, obviously exerting a great deal of energy to do so, and stared deeply into his face. Those eyes said it all. *Don't give up your soul to save an old woman*, they said. *I won't let you make that mistake.*

She knew. The woman had said no one would ever know, but somehow his mother did. He might be able to save her life, but things would never be the same between them. Because she would know.

"Mom, I have to do this. For you. For Dad."

For yourself, her voice whispered inside his head, and he knew there would be no convincing her. He could never lie to his mother, and even now, while she lay here dying, she would not let him lie to himself.

The woman's eyes slowly slid closed, leaving him alone in the still, sterile hospital room once again. His father returned a few moments later to find his son standing beside the window, looking out over the parking lot as the woman that they loved lay quietly in her bed, oblivious to the world around her. He tried to place a comforting hand on the boy's shoulder only to have his hand brushed away as Jacob quickly exited the room, wiping away the few renegade tears that had managed to escape.

Climbing into his truck, he thought back to the night before. He'd been practicing along with the rest of the team. They'd been so absorbed in their drills that no one had noticed the woman standing in the shadows of the bleachers, watching them with silent interest. No one except Jacob. But she had only been there for a moment, and then she'd disappeared like a shadow in the noon day sun. Convinced he'd been mistaken, Jacob continued to practice with his team until the coach called an end to the session. After everyone was off the field, showered, and on their way home, Jacob had stayed behind to speak with the coach about possibly missing a few practices because of the situation with his mother. The coach, Mr. Bronan, had been very sympathetic and told the boy he understood completely how he felt since his own wife had died just a few years ago of cancer. Though it was little comfort to the boy, he had accepted his coach's condolences and a reference to a good therapist before leaving the office.

As he was exiting the building, he'd noticed someone standing next to his truck. She had been dressed in a very expensive looking suit, but it had been the hair Jacob noticed first. It was completely unnaturally, sort of like the black holes he'd seen in an eighth grade science video. The void was so intense, it even gave the appearance of draining a bit of the color from surrounding objects. The woman had waited patiently for him to arrive next to the vehicle, and then offered a friendly smile.

"Jacob Cannon?" she'd asked, and her voice had been like silk.

"That's me." He'd tossed his gym bag into the passenger seat before turning his full attention to the stranger who had somehow known his name.

"I've come to make you an offer."

"Look, if one of the guys put you up to this…"

"This isn't a joke. I want to help. You see, I heard about your poor mother, Cynthia. Such a lovely woman with such a tragic illness. I've come here to offer my services to aid in her recovery."

"Okay, this is so not funny. How did you find out about my ma?" He hadn't told anyone except the coach, and even he didn't have all the details. When the woman's only reply had been a sympathetic smile, his anger had immediately taken control. Feeling the rage burning in his face, he'd barked, "Why don't you get the hell out of here before I go call the cops?"

"I know, I know. Seeing is believing, right? Well, allow me to demonstrate."

The woman had pulled one of her hands out of her pocket. In it, she'd clasped a rather large knife which she had then quickly thrust into the boy's stomach. Jacob had gasped in surprise at first, and then the pain had hit. It had radiated from the wound in white hot ripples, coursing through every inch of his torso and even extending into his limbs.

"Now that the fun part is over…" she'd grinned, and there had been something about that look that had turned his blood to ice as it poured from his body to pool on the asphalt below.

The woman had placed her hands on either side of the stunned boy's face just before his knees had begun to buckle. The knife had vanished, probably dropped on the ground in the confusion. More pain had filled his body, but this new pain seemed to originate at his cheeks where the woman's hands met his flesh. It had also seemed a hundred times worse than anything he'd ever experienced in his eighteen years of life. His vision had blurred with tears as the agony grew more intense. And finally, just when he'd been certain he would pass out, the pain had vanished. He'd looked down and discovered that his shirt was torn and bloody where the knife had entered, but a closer inspection had revealed that there were no marks on his body from the weapon.

"Now, I am willing to do the same thing for your mother. Well, not exactly the same, since she's dying of cancer and you were dying from a stab wound, but you get the idea. And all you have to do in return is take care of a little problem for me."

"What problem?" This was it. This was the miracle

they'd been waiting for. If only it hadn't felt like he was selling his soul to get it.

"Your girlfriend, Sarah Goode. She's become a bit of a problem, and I need someone to help me deal with her. You are the most logical candidate for the job."

"You want me to kill her?" He couldn't believe it. He and Sarah were far from close, but to kill her? How was he supposed to do that when he wouldn't even go deer hunting with his father?

"He was definitely right about your wit," the woman had chuckled, and her smile had reminded him of a hyena's grin, menacing and evil. "No, I don't want you to kill her. Just bring her out to the old farm house tomorrow night. Make sure you're alone, and don't tell anyone where you're going. Once that's taken care of, I'll make a special stop at the hospital. Before you can drag your weary bones from bed the next morning, your 'ma' will be good as new."

"And if I don't?"

"Then I'll hunt you down and kill you. Slowly. So, do we have a deal?" The hand that had held the knife was then extended towards him in a very different kind of gesture. He'd hesitated for a moment, wondering if this was a good idea. Maybe there was something else that could help her. Some new medical breakthrough that could save his mother's life. But there was no such cure, and deep down he'd known that this was the only way. So, with a heavy heart, Jacob had taken the woman's hand and sealed the deal.

And now, pulling up in front of his home so that he could change for the party, he was beginning to wonder if he actually had the nerve to go through with it. He loved his mother with all his heart, but something about this just felt wrong. And did he even have a choice? The woman had said that if he didn't follow through, she would kill him as well. And what about his father? That poor man had suffered so much already. If he lost both his wife and his son at the same time, what would happen to him? With no parents and no big brother, how would Adam survive? They had other family, of course, but none in this part of the country. And would any of them even be able to take in another mouth to feed? His mother's life wasn't the only one at stake. So now there was only one real question left to answer. Was the life of one girl worth more than the lives of Jacob and his entire family?

He was still trying to answer this question when he arrived outside Cary's house a few hours later.

Chapter 11

By eight-thirty, Cary's house was packed, and many people were already moving out to the backyard where there was more room to mingle. Everyone brought his or her own contribution to the party, whether it was music, food, alcohol, or other mind-altering substances. The last of these, Sarah and Cary made it a point to avoid, but everything else was fair game. When Jacob finally arrived at a little past nine, his girlfriend was well on her way to being completely trashed.

"You've been drinking," Jacob scolded when he finally found her out back dancing with one of Cary's male friends from out of town. The dress she was wearing was strapless and hugged her body so tightly it seemed almost painted on her skin. A wave of jealousy swept over him with surprising intensity.

"Only a little," she smiled sweetly, not actually aware of how much she had already consumed.

"Sure doesn't smell like just a little."

"So I've had a few shots and a couple of beers. I thought tonight was about having fun."

"What the hell were you thinking? What if your mom finds out about this?"

"Who's gonna tell her? You?"

"No, but someone might." His argument obviously wasn't getting through.

"Are you trying to threaten me? You're still mad about

earlier, and so you're gonna run and tell my mommy that I've been a naughty little girl, is that it?"

"Sarah, that is not what I'm saying!" Their voices were growing louder with each passing moment, and it was clear to those nearby that things were about to get ugly.

"You know what? You go right on ahead and tell her! I'm sure she won't care much that her daughter is out drinking herself stupid! In fact, she's probably expecting it!"

He started to reply, to tell her that she was being ridiculous, but she didn't give him a chance. All the color drained out of her face in an instant and the crowd watched in horror as the lovely girl in the skin-tight black dress spewed forth a cocktail of liquor and cafeteria pizza all over one of the best football players the tiny town had ever seen. Or at least that's how they would describe it later, embellishing on the details as it traveled until it had achieved that unreal quality of true urban legends. And, like all good urban legends, this one would end in tragic events that none of these young party-goers could have foreseen.

Cary and Jacob both helped the nearly unconscious girl upstairs to the bathroom where they did their best to clean up the mess. Cary let Jacob borrow some of her dad's clothes and they dressed Sarah in the clothes she'd been wearing earlier that day.

"What is that?" Jacob asked, pointing to the tiny pea-sized white spot just below the waist of Sarah's panties.

"Don't be such a perv," Cary slapped his hand away. "It's just a birthmark. She's had it forever."

"Weird. I thought birthmarks were supposed to be dark." He managed to wiggle her into the skirt as Cary slipped the black tee over her head. Through it all, she remained oblivious. "It's got kind of a funny shape, too. Almost like a hummingbird or something."

"That was one of her favorite dresses," Cary shook her head as she stuffed the party gown into a plastic bag. "Trashed now, though."

"I think I should take her home," Jacob volunteered. "She needs to get to bed."

"Her mom's going to pitch a fit."

"Maybe, but I think she's working the night shift at the grocery store tonight."

"Lucky break. I'll help you get her to the car."

They managed to drag the lifeless girl back down the stairs and out to Jacob's truck. Cary grabbed his arm as he closed the passenger side door. Her fingers were icy cold, but the look she gave him was even colder.

"I think tonight might be a good time to take Sarah out to the farm. It's very quiet, and private. Perfect for a couple of teenagers looking for some time alone."

The farm. She had told him to take Sarah to the farm. Somehow, this silly little blond knew about his deal.

Grabbing Cary's arm, he demanded, "What do you

know?"

"I know enough. Do what you're told and no one gets hurt."

"Liar. What about Sarah?"

"She's not the one they want. Take her to the farm or they will kill you and your family."

"How do you know that?"

The smile she gave him sent a shiver down his spine. "Because I know. Just do it."

He hesitated, thinking back to last night when he'd met the woman who'd promised him a miracle. Could she really live up to her end of the bargain? Could anyone save the woman who had once taught him the names of all the herbs in her garden? Was it possible to take the twisted, malignant lump of flesh that he now called mother and turn her back into the vibrant woman he remembered from his youth? And, more importantly, was that woman's life worth the life of the girl now lying in his truck?

"Yeah, I guess you're right," he finally mumbled, practically running to the other side of the vehicle. He wanted this whole nightmare to be over. He wanted his life to be normal again. But mostly, he wanted to be away from her. Those eyes…

A twist of the ignition and off they sped into the night, Jacob's head still full of doubts and Sarah's full of nothing.

Chapter 12

"Follow them," the man in black ordered, hopping into the van parked just down the street from the party. They had been watching the whole scene as The Girl puked all over the boy, but once she was moved inside, he had been the only one lurking in the shadows. How he'd managed to avoid being noticed was a mystery to everyone. Still, he'd followed until they left the building, and the moment The Girl had been placed in the truck, he'd called the team back to the van. Now they were driving away from the chaos of drunken teens and into a new set of problems.

"Where do you think he'll go?" Thomas, the giant man behind the wheel, asked.

"Someplace private." How many places could a couple of kids go, especially if they didn't want to be seen?

"That old farm?"

"Let's just follow him and see what happens."

Thomas had a real knack for guessing the next move of most targets, but right now the man wasn't about to take a risk that big. They could try to get there before the boy, or send another team in ahead of them, but in the end they might be wrong. And if they were wrong, then it would mean the end of this particular assignment.

They drove in silence for a few moments, and then Thomas just couldn't keep his mouth shut any longer. It was one of the most intriguing qualities of the young hunter. Most of the people in this line of work tried not to form strong bonds with those around them, and so there was very little communication amongst them on a personal level. Anything that needed to be said to protect lives or meet objectives was said. Small talk was avoided at all costs. Except when Thomas was around.

"So, who's up for a rousing game of 'I Spy'?" No one answered. "Okay, I'll go first. I spy with my little eye something black." Still nothing. "I know it's a hard one, but you'll never know unless you start guessing. Come on!"

"Is it your coat?" one of the men in the back, Gregory, called. Thomas shook his head.

"Good try, but wrong. Anyone else?"

"It's the steering wheel," the man said flatly. "And we should really try to focus on the task at hand."

"It's like you're psychic or something!" Thomas shouted, ignoring that last comment.

"Just observant."

"Very clever, oh wise one. Too bad The Girl isn't here, or I could say I spy something green and ugly."

"What's that supposed to mean?"

Thomas shook his head again, "I saw you when you came out of that house tonight. You would have given anything to be the one taking her out of that dress."

"Did you *see* her?" Gregory asked with a laugh. "Any man who wouldn't want to undress that *couldn't* be straight."

"Enough." The man's voice was steady, but the waves of anger and embarrassment that washed over him made it difficult to maintain his normal level of control.

"You're right," Thomas agreed. "I shouldn't have said it. But I do worry about you."

"There's nothing to worry about. The Girl is just another assignment."

"And what an assignment she is."

With a sigh of frustration, the man sat back as Thomas pulled in behind the red pick up just outside the old barn that sat next to the brand new Whispering Pines housing development site. The vehicle was empty, but they hadn't been following too far behind. The boy must have already taken her into the barn, though there hadn't been enough time for him to finish the job yet. At least, he hoped it hadn't been enough time.

"Well, boys and girls, time to go back to work," Thomas sighed. And with that, the team crept quietly out of the vehicle, surrounding the building like a pack of wolves. All around them, the normal night sounds suddenly fell silent as if the entire world was holding its breath to see what would happen next.

Chapter 13

She was much heavier than she looked. Perhaps the added weight of his conscience was what made the walk from the truck to the barn so difficult. Or maybe that was just a convenient excuse for him to quit now before it was too late to turn back. He placed her as gently as possible onto the dirty straw lined floor, and she began to stir. At the sound of her soft moan, he lost all of his nerve. He could not do this to an innocent girl, no matter what was at stake.

"You really are so predictable." Jacob spun around to see long black hair and hateful muddy brown eyes lurking just behind him. She smiled wickedly as she approached, and it suddenly became clear that she was not human. No human could ever produce such an empty, terrifying stare. No human could look upon these two helpless teenagers with such cold indifference. He tried to say something, to explain to the creature that he couldn't let her harm this girl, not even to save his family.

When he opened his mouth, no sound came. The look on the creature's face was one of amusement, but it did not seem shocked that the boy kneeling here in front of it would change his mind and try to back out of their agreement. And suddenly Jacob's stomach twisted in a knot. He had been used. This thing had known he wouldn't kill her, which was why it hadn't asked, but it also knew that he would be more than willing to bring her to something that would if it meant he could have his mother back. He could try to stop this, but it would do no good. Sarah was going to die tonight because of his greed.

"You really aren't very bright, are you, boy?" The thing shook its head as Jacob glanced around the barn, finally realizing that there were others here as well, hiding in the darkness, waiting to strike. Another car pulled up outside, its headlights casting wicked shadows on the walls and briefly illuminating the silhouettes of the creature and her companions. She laughed, saying "Our other guests have arrived."

"It was a trap?" His voice was so small and weak it made him sick. And the idea that he had fallen for their little trick only made that feeling of nausea grow.

"Oh, not for you. Or for her." The thing pointed a long slender finger at the girl on the floor. "The truth is, we don't want her to die. Not just yet. The ones that followed her here, however, are a very different matter."

"What about my mother?" Such a silly question, yet so important to him even at this dark moment.

"I told you to come alone." Jacob screamed as a searing flash of pain tore through his stomach. He looked down to see that his shirt just in front of where he'd been stabbed last night was beginning to change from navy blue to dark maroon. "Undoing those repairs is just as easy as creating them."

Jacob stared at the stain spreading over his torso, feeling a deep cold creeping through him slowly, methodically, destroying him one piece at a time. His vision began to blur, and then he was falling forward. The boy lost consciousness just before his face smacked into the dirt floor, and a few moments later, Jacob drew his last breath.

"Now for the real fun." The monster stepped back into the shadows, waiting for the battle to begin.

Chapter 14

It was impossible to tell just how many of them were inside, but his guess was at least ten, maybe fifteen. And one of them was not your average minion. The way it had killed the boy and the look on its face only helped to drive this point home. What had they done to warrant an attack from such a powerful creature?

"I think you must have really pissed them off, oh fearless leader," Thomas radioed. Now was not the time for jokes, which meant Thomas would be full of them.

"We need more men," the man in black replied, not liking the knot that had begun to form in the pit of his stomach. This situation had gotten completely out of hand and much too quickly.

"Well, if we sit around and wait for backup, there won't be anything left to save. They know we're here, and if we don't make a move soon, they'll find a way to make us." Thomas had a point. Those things wouldn't hesitate to begin torturing The Girl if it meant forcing the team out into the open.

"Then I guess we'll just have to surprise them somehow. Catch them off guard."

"And how are we going to do that, leader-boy?"

"We're going to walk right through the front doors. Thomas, call in anyone available."

"So, we're just going to forget about that whole Council

authorization thing again, huh?"

"Do you have a better idea?"

"So I guess I'll call in the closest team. Then what?"

"Then we stall."

"That's it? That's your big plan? Man, your luck had better be as good as it was back in the old days, 'cause your plans are getting weaker by the day." Thomas didn't sound convinced.

"Just do it. When I give the signal, we all move to the front of the building. Got it?" He listened as everyone confirmed the orders, and then waited for Thomas to check in on the backup situation. Once everything was in place, the team moved into position.

"Are you sure about this?" Thomas asked as they approached the front of the barn. "It's awfully risky."

"Better to take a chance than lose The Girl," he replied.

"Is that you speaking professionally, or is this personal?"

There was a pause as he forced himself to remain calm. The last thing they needed was to start fighting each other here where all those inside the barn could see. What they needed was a distraction, something to lure the monsters out of the barn and away from The Girl.

"Thomas," he sighed, "I have an idea."

"I don't like the sounds of that," the giant responded.

"You remember the Cali Campus Raid?"

"Hard to forget it. You really think that'll work this

time?"

Taking a slow, even breath to steady himself, he replied, "Yeah, I do."

"Alright," Thomas agreed. "I'll take first entry. Greg, you and Erin come in behind."

"I'll take rear position," the man volunteered. "Chris and John will play cleanup."

"Moving into position," Thomas told them, and the rest of the team quickly took their places as they prepared for this very dangerous dance. The silence was nauseating, building the tension in him as he waited for the words that could lead to the end of the entire team. Finally, just when he was about to call it all off, Thomas radioed, "On my mark."

"Roger that," the man breathed, hoping he didn't sound half as nervous as he felt. If this went badly, it would be his fault. He had made the call. The entire team was depending on him.

"Ready…" Thomas whispered, and he could see the giant man's silhouette inching along the side of the barn towards the front door from his place among the trees. "Set…Go!"

Bursting through the door, Thomas charged into the building, pistols drawn and ready for battle. The only light inside was the few stray moonbeams that managed to squeeze through the cracks in the walls and the holes in the roof, but it was enough to see nearly a dozen figures darting from their hiding places.

"I've got four on the left and five on the right," Thomas called, and immediately the two hunters that had been waiting at the edge of the building were racing in to help.

"Chris and John, move to the rear and pin them down," the man ordered, and two more shadowy figures crept silently to the back of the barn. A chorus of battle chatter followed as each team member called out their kills and gave new counts.

"Thomas, on your ten," the man directed, and Thomas took out one of the targets that had been hiding behind a rusted old tractor on the left with his pistols. "Gregory, you've got two straight ahead," he called, and Gregory quickly put a few rounds through the targets.

He didn't catch the one above in time, and it dropped from the rafters and attacked Erin. She managed to impale it with a pitchfork before it could cause any serious injuries. As the initial entry team drew the attention of the final five, Chris and John came in from the back and took them all by surprise.

"Friendlies coming in from the rear," the man warned. "Moving into southeastern and southwestern corners."

"Got em," Thomas replied. "Let's give each other some breathing room."

The team members staggered themselves, leaving plenty of space to engage the enemy without injuring each other. In a flurry of bullets, the team managed to destroy what was left of the enemy soldiers and begin surveying the damage.

"We're missing the boss lady," Thomas radioed, and

the man felt his stomach clench.

"No one made it out," he responded, quickly pulling his pistols and starting towards the barn.

"I've got the hostage, but the other one is long gone."

"It's not gone," the man told the team. "Stay alert. It's going to take all of us to keep that monster busy long enough to grab The Girl and get her out of here," he called as he began searching outside the building. "Do what you can to distract it, and if you see a chance take it, but remember our primary objective is to rescue the hostage. Clear?" His speech was followed by a chorus of agreement.

The shadows near the tree line suddenly began to swirl and shift, and out marched the creature, her face a shadowy mixture of joy and rage. The lack of good lighting probably prevented the hunter from fully appreciating just how terrifying this monster could be, but even so, he stopped dead in his tracks the moment it stepped out into the open.

"What did you do to The Girl?" he demanded. The night air trembled with the creature's wicked laughter.

"I did not come here for her," it replied, stepping closer to the young man who had already seen more bloodshed in his short lifetime than most war veterans. He fought the urge to take a step back and won. Barely.

"Then why did you come here?"

"Do not waste time with questions for which you already have answers, boy."

The others had already secured The Girl, but it was clear that they needn't worry much about her at the moment. She was not the one caught in the deadly gaze of this monster. She was not watching in horror as it slowly crept through the stillness of the cool October evening, inching its way closer to its intended victim. No, she was in no real danger tonight.

"Your little friend has been digging in her books again," it growled, and the sound of its voice made his stomach clench so tightly he thought he might vomit. "We warned her once before about meddling in our affairs, but I guess she just didn't learn her lesson."

"She's close, then, isn't she?" It stopped moving just a few feet in front of him. Close enough that if it wanted to, it could reach out and wrap its hands around his throat.

"If she was, we wouldn't bother with you. Still, we've found that it's better to stop these kinds of problems before they get out of hand. Much like we did with your father."

An image of his father popped into his head, crowding out all logical thought and replacing it with the sound of his deep baritone voice as he explained the basic principles of The Society to the five year old boy sitting next to him at the dining room table. It was so real, that picture. The smell of his father's latest attempt at cooking something that vaguely resembled chili. The soft, gentle hand patting his back when he began asking the really important questions like why they had to keep so many secrets. It was as if he had somehow been magically transported back in time, before the world went mad.

Suddenly, this memory was replaced by a much darker one. One which he had tried so many times to forget but still, it came back to him in dreams and nightmarish moments like this. He had found the body in front of the bar, mutilated and almost unrecognizable as human. Almost. Hanging there from one of the light posts was his father with a message carved into his chest.

"Decide," he whispered.

That was the message, directed at Vanessa as much as the Council, but they had taken it as a direct threat to the whole organization. Decide. Decide what was more important, the Prophecy and the truth, or The Society and the lives of loved ones. Vanessa had chosen life, but lately she had been spending more and more time in their private library, and just last week someone had delivered a special package for her from the Council's vaults. Could she have started back into her research, and if so, why had she not discussed it with him?

"Yes, and it appears that her decision was not in your best interest."

The creature's eyes met his, and he was falling into those deep brown pits of hate. Trying to look away only resulted in a strange sort of vertigo where his stomach began to shift uneasily and his ears rang with the sound of his own heartbeat. Something wrapped around his upper arm, and it felt as if a swarm of angry bees had landed there. Even through the layers of heavy material he could feel their stings, hot and full of poison that raced quickly to the rest of his body.

"I would really love to take my time with you," the thing said, but its voice was fuzzy and dim. "Unfortunately, I have other business to attend to this evening. Such a shame, too. You would have been fun to break."

"NO!" someone shouted from miles away. He barely heard it as he tumbled closer to the bottom of the dark, empty wells. And once he reached the bottom, he would never find his way back out.

Chapter 15

There were loud sounds that reminded her of firecrackers and then nothing for what seemed like an eternity. Her eyelids felt as if they had suddenly transformed from normal flesh to lead curtains, and it took all her strength just to pry them open. Once she did, though, the fear that suddenly gripped her was enough to keep them from closing ever again.

Dark shadowy figures rushed towards her in a place that smelled like old hay and stale beer. What the hell had happened? She could remember arguing with Jacob, and she thought she remembered sitting in Cary's bathroom, but that was as much as her tired mind could piece together. One of the shadow creatures knelt down beside her and placed a hand over her mouth, muffling her scream before she even knew it was coming.

"Be very quiet and do exactly as I say," a voice whispered. It sounded like it might be male, but she was too frightened to care much about voice analysis at the moment. "I'm going to take my hand away from your mouth, but you have to promise not to scream. There are some very bad people here who want to hurt you, but I promise I'm not one of them. Nod if you understand."

She bobbed her head quickly up and down and the hand disappeared back into the shadows. Oddly enough, she found herself wanting to believe this stranger's story, despite the fact that she had no idea where she was. Or perhaps it was because she didn't know what was going on or what had happened while she was unconscious that she found herself desperate to trust this gentle whisper.

"I'm going to help you up, and then we're going to move quickly through the doors to the van waiting outside. Do you think you can run?"

"I don't know," she whispered, honestly unsure of what she might be capable of at this point. Her legs seemed fine, but maybe that was just because she wasn't trying to use them yet. What if something was broken or dislocated or something? It was too dark to see, and shock could make it impossible to feel pain, right?

"One step at a time, then," he replied, and she could have sworn she heard a hint of amusement in his voice.

Strong arms slipped beneath her armpits, hoisting her up with little effort. They remained until the shadow man seemed satisfied that she wasn't going to collapse back onto the ground. Then one enormous hand engulfed her right arm above the elbow, and she heard the sound of several pairs of feet beginning to scurry towards the doorway in front of them. A thin beam of moonlight finally crept from behind a cloud as she began moving, and from the corner of her eye she caught a brief glimpse of a dark blue letter jacket soaked in blood, still wrapped around its owner.

Her knees started to buckle as the scream rose up in her

throat once again. The hands supporting her didn't stop moving, dragging her from the ghastly scene as quickly as possible, and somehow she managed to suppress the cry of horror that had sprung up so suddenly. What was going on? She finally realized that she was in the barn at the old farm, but why? How had she gotten here? Who had killed Jacob?

"I don't understand," she mumbled, but the man hushed her before she could voice any of these questions aloud.

"We'll explain later. Right now, we need to..."

And suddenly he stopped just outside the doorway. Before them stood a woman with hair the color of midnight, her right hand wrapped around the opposite arm of a man dressed in all black. Even in this lighting, the look of pain on the man's face was unmistakable.

"NO!" the man who had been holding her screamed, and all the other shadows from inside which now had the tiniest hints of faces, began charging forward. Her own protector ran blindly into the fray as well, leaving her to watch with dawning horror as the other figures dropped to the ground, clutching at their throats and desperately trying to regain the air that had been mysteriously stolen from them.

"Such silly creatures," the woman smiled, and Sarah realized that she wasn't a woman at all. She was something far more dangerous. And if she stepped anywhere near that monster, it would probably do to her what it had done to the others.

Yet her instincts told her that this was not the case. It would not kill her. In fact, it probably didn't even realize she was there just yet, and if she could find a way to stop that thing from hurting the others before she was noticed, maybe she could save some lives. Her senses immediately cleared, and her night vision, which had always been remarkable, kicked in. There, laying there on the ground just a few steps away like some sort of sign from above was a pistol. She wasn't sure if trying to shoot this monster was such a good idea, considering she'd never fired a weapon in her entire life, but what did she have to lose? There were two vehicles nearby, one of them a black van and the other Jacob's pickup, but she didn't have the keys for either, and she didn't think she could get them without being discovered. They were miles from any other people, so running was out of the question. This was her only chance.

Taking a deep breath, she quietly slipped from the safety of the barn, reached down, and wrapped her trembling hand around the cold hard metal. It didn't look too complicated. Just aim and pull the trigger. Still, what if she missed and hit one of the others nearby? Or what if one of the ones lying on the ground decided to take one last swing just as she fired the shot? And then the big question. Could she actually bring herself to shoot another living thing? Especially if her goal was not to immobilize, but to kill? Because if she didn't kill this creature, she would be its next victim.

Stop thinking about it and just do it.

She raised the gun, wrapping both hands around the grip and locking the elbow of her right arm. As her finger slid down onto the trigger, she remembered something her old friend Alan had told her about his experiences deer hunting. He'd graduated over three years ago, but his wisdom lived on in her head, filling her with the confidence she needed to finish this.

Aim for the chest first. It's the bigger target. Then, if it doesn't stop moving, step up and shoot it in the head.

Sarah wasn't sure if that same logic applied to killing other creatures as well, but it was the only bit of encouraging advice on the subject that her tired mind could locate. Dropping the barrel until it was even with the thing's back, she pulled in a deep breath and let it out slowly as she squeezed the trigger back.

Please don't let me miss.

There was another loud popping sound as her hands jerked back a fraction of an inch. Everyone went completely still, and for an instant, it seemed that single shot had actually stopped time. Finally, a thick, agonized howl of pain rose up from deep within the black-haired monster, shattering the stillness of the night with its fury. It dropped its prey and spun around to face her, clearly outraged. With almost inhuman speed and unimaginable accuracy for a novice such as herself, Sarah shifted the barrel to the blazing brown orbs that had locked on her. Without a thought, she pulled the trigger again, hitting its forehead just above its left eye.

All the rage that had twisted what would have normally passed for very feminine features into a nightmarish image of evil slowly melted into confusion and shock, and then that faded as well, leaving only a blank, empty expression as the beast fell to the ground in a lifeless heap. The gun slipped from her hands as her whole body began to tremble violently, and she dropped to her knees to vomit for the second time that evening.

The next few moments were a blur as those around her finally began to sound a little less like they were asphyxiating. At one point she realized that she was no longer wearing her black dress, and she wondered how she had been able to change while she was unconscious. The obvious explanation was that she hadn't, that someone else had changed her clothes while she slept. Had it been Jacob? The thought brought back the image of the dead body lying inside the barn, causing her stomach to tighten once again. There wasn't enough force to induce more vomiting, but it was pretty close.

A hand fell softly onto her shoulder and she jumped to her feet so quickly that she nearly passed out. The man standing next to her had a body that would intimidate a professional wrestler. His big, broad shoulders and muscular frame made her think of all those old fairy tales from her childhood involving giants. The big goofy grin on his face, however, convinced her that he was not a mythical beast that wanted to grind her bones to make his bread, and she relaxed a bit in spite of the circumstances.

"Nice shootin', Tex," the man smiled, and she couldn't help but return the gesture. Their smiles faded quickly as one of the others began to shout at the giant.

"Thomas!" A woman yelled, and there was a clear sense of urgency in her tone that forced the giant's attention to shift away from the still frightened girl. She followed his gaze, and just before he took off at a dead sprint across the clearing, she saw a crowd of kneeling figures gathered around something lying on the ground.

"Is he still breathing?" the giant, Thomas, shouted as he approached the group, and the woman who had spoken before nodded.

"Barely. I don't think there's anything that can be done for him, though. He's too far gone."

Their voices were hushed whispers now. She could only make out a handful of words, but they were enough for her to grasp the gravity of the situation. Someone, probably the man who had been the deceased woman's original target, was dying. And it was a painful death he was facing, by the sounds of things. Slowly, not even sure of what she was planning to do but knowing that she had to try to help these people who had risked their own lives to save hers, she slipped over to the crowd of grim faces.

"Let's try to make him as comfortable as possible," she heard Thomas sigh softly, and the sense of pain and loss that radiated from his solid frame broke her heart.

"What's wrong with him?" she heard herself ask. Her voice was so much steadier than the rest of her that she almost didn't recognize it. Thomas took a quick swipe at his cheeks before turning to face her.

"It's nothing that you need to worry about just yet," he answered, trying to steady his voice.

"He's your friend?"

The man chuckled. "Yeah, something like that."

Not really certain what she was doing or why, she knelt down beside the dying man, brushing away a clump of dark, damp hair from his forehead. The muscles in his body jumped and twitched in violent spasms that were mirrored by the agonized expression on his face. His eyes stared blankly into the starry sky, dull and vacant as if the life that had once been housed in this vessel had already moved on.

"What's his name?" she asked, leaning in closer to gaze into those empty black eyes.

Thomas hesitated before finally deciding that it really couldn't hurt anything to tell her. The man was dying, after all. So what if she knew his name?

"Elijah," he replied in an uneven voice, and she could feel the tides of grief finally break through the man's defenses, releasing a flood of anguished tears that only a long-time companion could shed.

Staring into empty eyes, she whispered his name. When her hand landed on his trembling chest, there was a spark of life in those pits of nothing. She said it again, and again, and again, a bit louder and stronger each time until she sounded as if she were commanding him to return to this frail frame.

And then it happened. His whole body suddenly tensed and a huge flash lit up the solemn darkness that surrounded them. She felt herself being pushed away from the man's body, but she fought it until she was sure. Until she saw the determined gleam light up those corpse's eyes and a shriek of agony escaped his pale lips.

"What the hell was that?" she heard one of the others ask, but she could not have explained what had just happened even if she had known herself. The world around her faded into nothing and she found herself trapped in darkness once again, except this time she could feel something far worse than shadow men lurking nearby.

Chapter 16

By the time they made it to the hospital, he had finally stopped shaking, though there were still occasional tremors that rocked his aching body in fits that were more frustrating than painful. Thomas had wrapped him in blankets and helped carry him to the van. The Girl lay on the floor in front of him, out cold but still alive. No one said a word about what had happened while he was out, but it obviously hadn't been good. Still, they hadn't lost any team members, and they had achieved their primary objective, so he considered it a successful mission.

Vanessa was waiting in the emergency room parking lot, along with a handful of the best doctors in Wisconsin. Gregory took The Girl inside, but Thomas kept him in the van until the docs had given him a clean bill of health.

"Well, you don't seem to be experiencing any of the ill effects of their poison," the chief physician shook his head. He pointed to the patient's arm where a hole the size of someone's palm had been created in both his coat and shirt by some sort of corrosive material. The skin beneath appeared to be irritated, but nothing more dramatic than a bit of redness and swelling. "I'd say you got off lucky that time, my boy."

Thomas had been standing outside the van, speaking with Vanessa in hushed whispers. When the doctors began to exit the vehicle, the conversation stopped abruptly. Elijah's suspicion that there was something about the events of that evening they didn't want to discuss in front of him grew stronger still, making his muscles tense. Another round of tremors rocked him, and he cursed softly to himself.

"So he'll be alright?" Vanessa asked, completely unable to hide the relief she felt at the sound of the doctors' words.

"With a bit of rest and a good meal, I think he'll be just fine," the chief physician answered as he patted her on the shoulder.

"I can't tell you how much we appreciate you coming out here in the middle of the night like this," he heard the woman saying as he forced his stiff body to crawl from the van and make his way out into the cool night air. Thomas saw him coming and offered a welcome hand.

"Anything for you, dear." The doctor, who must have been at least twice Vanessa's age, leaned down and planted a kiss firmly at the corner of her mouth. His muscles immediately tensed as a blinding rage threatened to take control. This instinctual reaction caused his tremors to become more violent, making it all he could do to stay on his feet.

"Easy," Thomas said softly. "She's got it under control."

The old man walked out into the parking lot, the other doctors trailing immediately after. He saw the large red patches burning on the woman's cheeks, but he managed to keep his mouth shut for now. She seemed embarrassed enough. No need to push it right now, especially given his current condition.

"Sorry about that," she shook her head. "One cup of

coffee and suddenly he thinks we're an item." There was a moment as she tried to pull herself together, then she turned and wrapped her arms around his neck in a warm embrace. "If you ever scare me like that again, you won't have to worry about dying in battle, that's for sure!"

"So, when are you going to tell me what happened back there?" he asked calmly, though his head was full of questions that demanded immediate answers.

"Not out here. It's much too cold to stand around outside and talk."

"Inside, then. Where I can keep an eye on The Girl." He started to step towards the hospital, but Thomas stopped him.

"I don't think so. You need to go home and rest. I'll take over the assignment until you're feeling better."

"Thomas, I feel fine. Now let me pass."

"No way," Thomas replied, looking to Vanessa for support and finding plenty.

"He's right," she agreed. "You need to go home and rest. You'll be no good to Sarah if you're too weak to fight off the Others."

So it was settled. He would go home with Vanessa, and she would explain what the big secret was. Still, it felt wrong to leave The Girl like this, especially after such a nasty confrontation.

"Alright, I'll go home, but only if Thomas agrees to call in the morning with an update on her condition."

"Done," Thomas clapped him on the back and ushered him to Vanessa's car.

Before they left, Vanessa gave Thomas a big hug, thanking him again for some unknown favor. Thomas simply nodded, tossed a quick wave at the man sitting in the passenger seat, and then headed into the hospital. As they sped off into the approaching dawn, he couldn't help but try to think back over the past few hours. In the end, all he could remember was the thing telling him that The Girl had been in no real danger, that he was the real target. And then there was the voice. The beautiful, angelic voice that had called to him as he began to regain consciousness. Had it been real, or had he imagined that voice? Did it really matter? Something in his gut told him that it did, and he was almost certain that it was connected to the secret that Thomas and Vanessa were trying to keep from him.

By the time they arrived at the house, his head was swimming in questions. Vanessa refused to answer any of them as she silently led him to the living room couch. As she stepped towards the closet near the front door to gather some blankets, his patience finally broke.

"Dammit, Vanessa, what happened?" he barked, and she flinched as if he'd struck her. They both knew it took a lot to get to him. Of course, seeing The Girl in such a state was always enough to tie his stomach in knots.

With a sigh, she turned and told him, "You almost died. That thing was after you, not Sarah. They used her as bait to get to you."

"Why?"

"Because I've been looking at the Prophesy again. After the boy in New Mexico, the Council asked me to resume my work." She refused to make eye contact as she sat down across from him.

"Why didn't you tell me?" he asked flatly.

Picking at a stray thread on one of the blankets, she answered, "Because I didn't want to upset you."

"You didn't trust me."

"No!" She finally looked at him, grasping his hand in hers. Those big green eyes were full of tears, and he felt himself soften. "I just...I know how hard it was for you when your father passed, and I didn't want you to start reliving any of that."

"Well, now I know." And that was all he could think to say. Strangely, it seemed enough.

With a smile and a nod, she handed him the blanket. Then, she stood and slipped silently upstairs to her room. So she was working again. That meant more interference from the Council. It also meant more problems, especially since the Others would be watching them. They had already tried to kill him once. As soon as they realized he was still alive, he would become a major target.

And he still didn't know what had happened to The Girl. What could they have possibly done to her that she had survived? Thomas was there. He could explain it tomorrow.

Now, it was time to rest. Wrapping the blanket around him, he curled up on the couch and slipped into a deep sleep.

Chapter 17

She heard the voices long before she dared open her eyes. Something bad had happened, but she couldn't remember what. The throbbing pain that sprang up just behind her eyes whenever she thought about it for too long was enough to discourage such behavior. Amy's was the first voice she heard, followed by her mother's. Both seemed to be quite worried about her, but neither gave any details about what had happened.

"What was she doing out there in the first place?" her mother sobbed. She could just imagine Amy putting a comforting arm around the distraught Angela and leading her to a chair where she could rest.

"I guess we'll just have to wait and see what Sarah has to say about it when she wakes up," Amy replied calmly.

Pride welled up inside Sarah as she listened to her sister's steady voice. The young girl would keep her cool for as long as her mother couldn't, which was exactly the kind of level-headedness necessary in this sort of situation. It was good that she was keeping their mother from panicking too much. The last thing Sarah needed right now was to know that Angela was a basket case because of something stupid her rebellious teen daughter had done. Of course, she had no idea what that act of stupidity might have been, but it would surely come back to her in time. Another blinding pain crept into her head, and she quickly shifted her thoughts back to the conversation going on beside her.

"I just can't believe that something like this could happen to us." Us. Not Sarah, not her daughter who was lying in what smelled like a sickeningly sterile hospital bed. Us.

"Mom, it's going to be okay. The doctor said she just has a little concussion. She should be fine in a few days. Please, you have to calm down, okay?"

"How can I calm down? I'm sitting here in a hospital when I should be at work making sure we have enough money for food and bills."

That's right. She was just one big inconvenience to everyone around her. Even now, when she could be dying for all they knew, her mother's chief concern was missing time at work. Rage welled up inside her, gnawing at her sanity until she was certain she would go completely mad.

"Why don't you go down to the lobby and get some coffee," Amy suggested. A few moments later, a door closed and a tender hand wrapped around hers. "She didn't mean that, you know. She's just upset. You really scared us this time, Sarah."

"She certainly did," Vanessa's voice chimed in. The hand tensed for a moment, then relaxed as its owner realized who had spoken.

"Hey, Vanessa," Amy sighed. She sounded relieved that someone else was there to help take care of things.

"So, I hear she's going to live." There was a hint of amusement hiding in that voice, but it sounded like it might be masking yet another deeper emotion. Fear, perhaps?

"Yeah, well, that depends on mom's reaction to her side of the story. So far, all we know is that she and Jacob were out at the farm and she's the only one that came back alive."

A hint of some distant memory tickled at the back of her mind, but she pushed it away quickly. Better just to wait and remember later when it didn't make her head feel like it might explode.

"Oh, I'm sure she has a good reason for being there. Sarah is a very intelligent girl, and I'm certain that she wouldn't do something as foolish as running off to an abandoned farmhouse in the middle of the night without a good reason." Why did those words seem so very patronizing? Probably because even Vanessa was questioning her behavior this time. Fantastic.

The door squeaked open and footsteps approached the bed. There was a brief pause before she heard the sound of her mother crying again. Vanessa tried to soothe her, but it took several minutes before she was calm enough to speak.

"I just don't know what to do anymore," the woman choked out between sniffles. "I know you said we would have to deal with some unusual situations, but I don't think I can take any more of this."

Unusual situations? What was her mother talking

about? Perhaps the stress had finally gotten to her.

"Be strong, Angela," Vanessa soothed. "Soon she will know the truth and your job will be over."

"I'll always be her mother. And I'll always worry about her, *especially* after she knows the truth."

Finally, she had heard enough. It took a great deal of effort, but she managed to pry her tired eyes open so that she could see her surroundings. Definitely a hospital room, and there were the three visitors gathered beside her, their faces full of despair. Except for Vanessa. Even now, she seemed completely calm. She was also the first to notice that Sarah was awake, but she said nothing. Instead, she gave the girl in the bed a quick wink when the others were not looking and continued with the discussion. It took three tries before she found enough voice to get their attention.

"So, who wants to explain to me what this truth is?" she asked hoarsely. Amy and her mother exchanged an uneasy look, and then turned to Vanessa, whose smile hadn't faltered at all.

"Good to see you again, dear," the beautiful red-head replied. "I'm afraid you must have gotten quite a knock on the head. How do you feel?"

"Like I've been run over by a bus. Twice. Now, about this truth of yours."

"Now is not the time, Sarah. You are still recovering from a nasty concussion, and you're confused enough."

"Stop treating me like I'm five!" she shouted,

immediately regretting it. Vanessa's argument made perfect sense, and to be fair, this woman had never treated her like a child, even when she should have. Still, Vanessa's response was not anger but relief.

"Same old Sarah," she chuckled. "We can discuss all of that another time. For now, let's focus on what happened to warrant a trip to the hospital."

Amy found her voice and asked, "Do you remember anything about last night?"

Sarah shook her head. "I was at Cary's house. She was having a party, and Jacob was supposed to meet me there. I remember I was wearing a black dress, and when Jacob and I started to argue, I think I threw up on him. And then I woke up here." There was more, she knew there was, but trying to retrieve that information created another bolt of pain that shot through her head and made her wish she would just pass out again. Vanessa sensed her pain and frowned.

"Perhaps now isn't the best time for interrogations. I think we should let Sarah get some rest." Vanessa began to move towards the door, followed by her mother and sister.

"Wait!" Sarah exclaimed. Were they really planning to leave her here alone?

"We'll be back tomorrow," her mother reassured her.

"Speak for yourself!" Amy cried. "I'm going to the bathroom and I'll be back in just a sec." Sarah breathed a sigh of relief, but her mother did not looked pleased. Being left alone here all night scared her more than she could ever explain to these people. Hospitals always gave her the creeps. Something about them seemed to drain her, like the presence of all those sick and injured people just sucked the life out of her. Plus, it would be a lousy place to wake up and realize the zombie apocalypse had struck.

"Amy, you have basketball tryouts tomorrow morning. You need to be well rested," her mother lectured. She knew of Sarah's phobia but wrote it off as silly childhood drama.

"I need to be here with my sister, especially since you aren't going to be." That one stung, just as it was meant to. Amy might have been Sarah's polar opposite in many ways, but in the end they were sisters, and sisters looked out for each other.

"I have to work," Angela almost whined. "I have to support our family. Why can't anyone understand that?"

"I do understand," Amy argued, "but I honestly don't think missing one day of work is going to break us. You do what you have to, and I'll do the same."

And with that, Amy left the room. Sarah's mother stood in the doorway for a moment, silently weighing her options. Finally, she turned back to Sarah long enough to say, "I'll be back tomorrow afternoon," before leaving. Vanessa, who had watched all of this drama in silence, finally spoke up.

"It must be very difficult for someone who has battled financially for as long as your mother to realize when the war has finally ended."

"Alright, Confucius. I understand her concerns, but it still hurts to know that work is more important than her daughter's life."

"Don't be so dramatic, dear," Vanessa laughed. "You're far from dead. In fact, the doctors will probably send you home long before your mother gets away from her other commitments."

She was right. Things could have been a lot worse. A few bumps and bruises were nothing to get worked up over.

"So, any idea what happened?" Vanessa asked patiently.

"I already told you what I remember." But there was more. Something else that was bothering her, lurking in the back of her mind. A name.

"Of course," the woman nodded. "I'm not accusing you of anything. I just thought maybe you left some details out because of your mother."

"No, nothing like that." Then, taking a deep breath, she decided it was time to ask. "Well, maybe one thing."

"What is it, dear?"

"A name. Elijah. It's like it's stuck floating around in my head, but I'm not sure what it means. Any ideas?"

"I'm afraid not. The doctors in the E.R. did say a man dropped you off, but he didn't give his name. Perhaps that's where you heard it?" She was hiding something, but now didn't seem like the time to push.

"Yeah, I guess," she agreed. For now, she just wanted

to rest, and it looked like Vanessa felt the same. "Go home and get some sleep. I'll be fine"

"I know you will."

Amy returned and Vanessa nodded goodbye to the girls as she exited the room. Grabbing an extra blanket from the closet, Amy made herself as comfortable as possible in the chair beside the bed. As the two girls settled in for the evening, an alarm began to sound down the hall. Sarah barely heard the sound of doctors and nurses rushing past her door before she drifted off to sleep.

Chapter 18

The man that stepped into the room was definitely not a doctor. His charcoal suit complete with scarlet tie stood out like a festering sore in the stark whiteness of the hospital room. Atop his head was a perfectly groomed set of flames that seemed to make the green of his eyes that much more intense. Those eyes scanned the room in a flash and finally settled on their target as if he had known exactly what he was looking for before he arrived.

"You must be Adam," he smirked as he approached the youngest of the trio. Adam and his father were both huddled around a frail wilting creature in a hospital bed. "So nice to finally meet you."

"Who are you?" the boy's father demanded, stepping forward without releasing his grip on the skeletal hand made even more grotesque by the tubes protruding from it.

"Jacob was not strong enough," the man continued as he placed a well-manicured hand on the boy's shoulder. "You, though…"

"How do you know Jacob?" And suddenly, his father's face contorted in a mixture of grief and pain as it turned a terrible shade of gray. The moment he collapsed to the floor, alarms began to sound all around them.

"I knew she would fail," the man shook his head. The boy, though horrified at the sight of his parents' deaths, could not pull his gaze or his thoughts away for more than an instant from this man.

"My dad…" he whimpered, but the man simply shook his head once again.

"We should go. There is much to discuss and little time left before the doctors arrive with all their questions."

"But what about them?"

"What about them?"

"We should help them."

"Their lives are lost," the man replied, and though his tone was full of sadness, there seemed a hint of excitement there as well. "We cannot save them. But we can make the responsible parties pay."

"What do you mean?"

"Come with me and I'll explain." Wrapping a comforting arm around the boy's shoulders, the strange man led him through the doors and past the stampeding herd of doctors rushing to the room. Behind them, the two withered corpses remained, their hands now locked in a sign of eternal devotion.

Chapter 19

She went to the funeral a few days later. Jacob and his parents were being buried in three consecutive plots at Willow Ridge Cemetery. While his parents' life insurance paid for all their needs, Jacob had to rely on the community to pay his expenses. And they did so with heavy hearts, since the school's dream of making it to the playoffs had died with Jacob. Or at least that's what the coach kept telling everyone at the reception afterwards.

Sarah received all of the condolences since the only members of the family in attendance were those being returned to the earth. Adam, the youngest of the family, was now missing, and, as Jacob's girlfriend, she was forced to take on the role of next of kin during this ridiculous ritual they labeled a funeral. Still, it wasn't as bad as she'd expected. The actual service lasted about an hour, and the reception at the family's church was full of bad food and obnoxious people, but she was able to sneak out after only an hour and a half. That left her with an entire afternoon to reflect on the whole mess.

Fragments of her memory had tried to surface, but chasing them down proved to be an almost impossible task. The only thing she had managed to remember about that evening was that after vomiting on the now deceased Jacob, he and Cary had taken her upstairs to change her clothes. She also remembered that Jacob had borrowed some of Cary's dad's clothing, which helped eliminate the only suspect the police had. So what was missing? What had happened during that big gap in her memory?

She found herself wandering into the park where she had played as a child. Things here were just as they'd always been. Children buzzed around frantically, playing whatever energy absorbing games they could think of and shrieking at the tops of their lungs. Smaller children sat with parents eating picnic lunches and playing counting games with blocks. The jungle gym was covered by swarms of little people, eager to expend as much energy as possible before being confined to their homes for the winter. Far from peaceful, true, but still better than listening to insincere people talking about how well they knew the boy who had sat on the opposite side of the cafeteria for lunch and how much they would miss him even though the only name they knew him by was the one printed on the back of his jersey.

The vision came quickly with all the force of a tsunami. Her whole world suddenly faded away and was replaced by the old farm. The same farm she had been to a dozen times before as her schoolmates sought out any reason for a little party. So dark she could barely see her hand in front of her face, the smell of musty old hay filling her nose, she discovered that she was terrified of what might be lurking in the shadows. Groping frantically for anything familiar, her hands fell on harsh wool soaked in something warm and wet. Finding a tiny sliver of moonlight that had snuck through the cracks of the crumbling barn surrounding her, she brought the object into the light only to discover that she was holding the blood-soaked letter jacket of her now deceased boyfriend.

    This horrific image left her just as quickly as it had come, and she found herself back in the park, unable to fully grasp what had just happened to her. She found a place hidden within the trees that marked the edge of the park, and here the tears came easily. They had been trapped these past few days by her fear that others might see her in such a weakened state, worried that her tears might trigger those of others around her. Already she felt as if she'd caused those that she loved a great deal of suffering. To cause them any more grief would be unforgivable. Leaning back against the bark of a strong, sturdy maple, she let herself have a moment that was hers and hers alone. This was not just about the boy who had died, though. Hidden in the shadows of the towering woods, Sarah grieved for her innocence.

Chapter 20

The man in black watched her from the shadow of a nearby spruce. If anyone could understand what The Girl now felt, it was this man who had witnessed the murder of his own mother at the age of three and had been taken under the wing of the Council at ten. One of the youngest hunters in the history of their organization, and also one of the best. However, the loss involved was much greater than any would have guessed, and it had nearly killed him.

The girl wept, and he waited, wishing he could comfort her and knowing that to do so would only make the situation worse. Still, after what she had done for him…

When Vanessa had told him the tale of that night at the farm, it had been nearly impossible to believe. Thomas had confirmed the story, though, offering more details that just led to more questions. That this girl was special he had no doubt. All of the research begun by his father and followed up by Vanessa after his death had only confirmed what they already knew. Never in any of this research, however, was there any mention of special abilities such as saving those on the brink of death. And for her to have helped him was even more illogical. Why hadn't she just left? She could have escaped. The team was too busy worrying about the death of its leader to notice her running off into the night. So why had she stayed?

And what a lucky break for all of them that the

memories of these events were lost to The Girl. Had she remembered what went on at that farm, she would not be standing here now, mourning for her boyfriend. She would instead be proving herself to the Council, a feat which he no longer doubted her capable of doing. But even with her new-found abilities, would the Council actually accept that she was the being described in the Prophecy? And if they didn't, then what would become of her?

That was a silly question. When the five year old boy they had tested had turned out to be nothing of importance, they had executed him. The same would happen to any outsider who caught even a glimpse into their world unless they could be of some use to the organization as a whole. And at her age, that was highly unlikely. New recruits usually ranged from three to seven years of age when they were chosen. The Girl was much too old.

And if the Council did decide that she was who they believed her to be? Then what? Would they use her long enough to fulfill her destiny and then cast her aside like an old boot, or would they kill her then as well? His right hand slowly moved up his left arm until it rested upon the spot where now there was only a faint discoloration the size of a pea. The world was an awful, scary place. To kill someone with the ability to change that seemed like a terrible waste.

Chapter 21

"Wow, this place looks fantastic!" Vanessa stepped through the front door, shrugging out of her long, forest green coat. Sarah snatched it with a grin and dashed off to put it in the closet while Angela remained by the tiny red-head's side.

"The girls worked really hard to get it all done by tonight. They've been so excited these last few weeks." Angela's pride managed to sneak past her usual defenses and make a brief appearance as she gave her friend a quick tour of the holiday trimmings.

"So she really can smile," Sarah snorted.

"Don't start," Amy cautioned, giving her sister what was supposed to be a stern glare. It only made them both chuckle. "Seriously, you know she loves us. She's just had a lot to deal with this year."

"Yeah, yeah," Sarah rolled her eyes.

"I'm serious. Give her a chance tonight."

Just then, the doorbell rang and Sarah raced over to answer it. Anything to get away from the heart to heart her little sister seemed determined to have this evening. It had started the minute their mother returned from work. Apparently, grocery store cashiers were required to put in a few hours on Christmas Eve, despite family plans. Or perhaps she had volunteered for the extra shift for the holiday pay. Either way, it was frustrating. Rather than being at home helping them get ready for their big dinner, Angela had spent most of the day ringing up groceries and forgetting to grab the last minute supplies that the girls had requested.

"Happy Holidays!" The blond man at the door smiled, handing her an expensive looking bottle of wine. Confused, the girl stepped aside and motioned towards the kitchen where the rest of the dinner party had gathered.

She invited her divorce lawyer?

Shaking her head, Sarah trudged out to put the wine on ice. At least he had good taste in booze. The sounds of merry chatter buzzed all around her, leaving a warm feeling in the air that wrapped around her, smothering her as she tried to make sense of it all. They might be a small group, but there was enough joy to fill the whole house. And yet, she still felt like an outsider. Everyone else was smiling and happy. Everyone around her belonged. Holidays were never this peaceful in her home. It probably had something to do with the absence of that worthless piece of trash Andy.

Just the thought of that nut job made her stomach twist in furious knots. Ever since that morning when he'd...God, no one had ever made her feel like that. She'd been so helpless. That stupid creep had left a wicked memory, and now she caught herself flinching at shadows.

"Sarah?" She realized Vanessa was beside her, staring at her hands. They were wrapped so tightly around the back of the chair in front of her that the knuckles were snow white.

"Yeah," she nodded, forcing her fingers to release the poor chair. Her mother came over to scold, laughing in that annoying *I'm-embarrassed-to-be-seen-with-you* way that set the girl's nerves on edge.

"Vanessa asked about school, dear." That patronizing look just enraged the teen that much more.

"It's peachy," Sarah spat, storming into the living room. Over her shoulder, she called, "I'm gonna get some air." Behind her, the sound of hushed apologies made her want to scream.

"She's been working on this party all day," Amy told them, and even she sounded like she was making excuses. "I think the pressure just got to her. She'll be fine."

"I just don't know what to do with her anymore. No matter what I do, it's never good enough. She's spoiled, that's what it is."

Yeah, that was it. Spoiled rotten by a father who'd tried to kill her and a mother who could care less. Cary would barely talk to her since her decision to lay off the partying. The only serious boyfriend she'd ever had was murdered. Yep, definitely the life of a brat.

Snatching her coat from the rack beside the door, she stomped out into the icy night. Cold was good. She needed to cool off. Flopping down on the porch step, she took a few deep breaths and tried to keep her anger in check. Blowing up at them would only lead to more problems.

She heard the door and soft footsteps coming towards

her. Probably Amy coming to coax her back inside. She would turn those sad little puppy dog eyes on her, and it might work. It might make her feel guilty for ruining everyone's evening and she might go back inside to apologize. Or she might finally snap and release the flood of emotions that had plagued her for months.

Am I a killer?

It was the question she'd wrestled with since waking in that hospital room to learn of Jacob's death. Had she killed him? Was she capable of something like that?

"Kind of chilly out here," Vanessa whispered, and the girl spun around in surprise. The fiery red-head just smiled and shook her head.

"Scared me," Sarah muttered, turning her eyes back to the road.

"Who were you expecting?" She sat down on the step next to the shivering girl.

"Doesn't matter. I'll be back in soon."

"Hmm," Vanessa nodded. "You know, I've missed you lately. Did I do something to offend you?"

She shook her head and said, "Just busy."

"School trouble?" Another shake of the head. "Angela said she got a call the other day. Seems you forgot it was a school day."

"I didn't forget."

Vanessa sat there, silent and staring at the evening sky.

She wasn't angry like Angela or disappointed like her teachers. Then again, her calm patience seemed worse somehow, like trying to explain her recent behavior would only insult both of them. There was no excuse for the way she had been acting, but it hadn't really mattered until now. When it had just been a nuisance or an embarrassment to her family, she had ignored the effect her actions had on the people around her. With Vanessa, though, it was different.

Finally, she let out a sigh and said, "I know, I know. How terribly irresponsible, right?"

"I didn't say a word," Vanessa shrugged.

"You didn't have to." Casting a wicked glare back at the house as the muffled sounds of her mother's lecturing drifted into the calm surrounding her, the girl spat, "Angela says plenty."

"It's her job to worry about you."

"Yeah," Sarah sighed, turning back to stare at her freshly polished boots. The light from a nearby street lamp reflected back, making it seem like her shoes were made of inky black liquid. Like oil or…

For an instant, her mind flashed back to darkness. She could smell straw and old alcohol. Before her lay a familiar school letter jacket, but it was covered in big, dark stains. She wanted to scream, to call for help, but there was no time. Something was pulling her away. Something big and strong…

Pain tore through her head as the images were ripped

away. Her hands shot to her temples as she fought the waves of nausea that came with the white hot poker in her brain. Another pair of soft, cool hands wrapped around hers, and tears spilled down her cheeks.

"Sarah, what is it?" Vanessa's voice was calm but still clearly concerned. It only made her feel that much worse.

"What is happening to me?" she sobbed, and the tiny red-head pulled her into a warm, comforting embrace. "What's happening to my life?"

"Shh," Vanessa hushed. "Everything will be okay."

"No, it won't! Jacob is dead and I *know* it's my fault!"

"How could his death be your fault?"

"I don't know! All I know is that I was there that night and I'm still alive. There had to be something I could have done to save him. If I hadn't been so drunk…"

"Oh, sweetie," Vanessa sighed. "You can't possibly believe that you could have done anything differently when you don't know what events took place."

But she did. She believed that by surviving, his death somehow was her responsibility. If she had just been as concerned with his survival as hers, maybe they would both still be here. Maybe she would still see him in the halls at school. Maybe he would still insist on going to see those cheesy old horror movies every weekend. Maybe he would be parked somewhere in his truck with her right now instead of buried in the neighborhood cemetery while she sat on her front porch bawling like a big baby.

"You listen to me, young lady." Vanessa pulled away and forced her face up to look into those deep, emerald pools. "You did not kill Jacob, nor is his death in any way your fault."

"How do you know?" Though meant to be tough and accusing, her words lacked any real bite.

"Because I know."

"But you don't…"

"Yes, I do." So final, those three little words. Coupled with the fierce compassion and love in those eyes, Sarah could not deny that she had at least one ally left in this crazy world. "You are alive, and I thank God every day for that miracle. Never feel guilty because you are a survivor."

"How can I not?"

"Sarah, some people in this world are destined to wander through life hoping to be saved. You have never been one of them. For people like you, a greater destiny awaits. That hard head of yours has gotten you through a lot so far. Don't give up now."

"Alright already," Sarah smiled, carefully wiping away the tears as she tried not to smear her makeup. "Enough with the heartfelt speeches."

"I have more, if you like," Vanessa shrugged. "I even have one on the evils of underage drinking."

"Maybe another time." They sat in the glow of the streetlight for a moment, quietly pondering the stillness around them. Things felt so peaceful out in the brisk winter evening. Inside, it would be more nagging and putting on happy faces to please guests, but out here, no one cared if she blew up. No one cared if she had an emotional meltdown. This was a place to just be Sarah, baggage and all. There was only one other place where she felt this open and free to just be.

Vanessa was right. She had been avoiding her pseudo-aunt for far too long. Maybe she'd just been scared of how this strong, independent woman would react to her feelings of guilt. Such weakness was only amplified by Vanessa's contrasting strength. Yet now, it was clear there was nothing to fear. If anything, Vanessa was a solid shoulder to cry on. She was a rock to cling to during this emotional hurricane. She should have insisted on spending every moment with this woman since the incident. It would have been better than lying in her room every night, crying and hoping the nightmares would leave her a moment of peaceful sleep.

"Vanessa?"

"Hmm," the woman replied absently, her gaze locked on a tree just down the street.

"Do you think I need a shrink?"

The woman turned to the girl, an amused expression on her face as she asked, "Do you?"

"I dunno," Sarah shrugged. "I just thought maybe they could do some kind of mumbo-jumbo hypnosis stuff and help me remember."

"Or you could spend the rest of your life wandering around squawking like a chicken whenever you hear a bell ring." The woman was fighting hard not to laugh, which just made Sarah feel that much sillier.

"Ha ha," the girl rolled her eyes. "It was just an idea."

"If you think it will help, we can try to arrange something. I don't know how Angela might react to such an idea…"

"No way! She doesn't need to know. If she finds out I'm screwed up enough to need a shrink, she'll kick me to the curb in a heartbeat."

"Oh, I seriously doubt…"

"Vanessa, please," Sarah begged, "you can't tell her about this. Any of it."

Those cool, green eyes stared into her, digging down into the depths of her soul as the woman decided how to respond. There were times when Sarah could be incredibly dramatic, and she was willing to admit to such extreme reactions. This, however, was not one of those times. Angela had been itching for an excuse to be rid of her troublesome older daughter. A declaration of mental illness might give her all the leverage she needed to get rid of the problem once and for all.

"Alright," Vanessa finally conceded, "but on one condition."

"What's that?"

"Come spend Christmas Eve with me."

"What about the party?" The request was odd, even by Vanessa's standards. She never invited anyone to her home on holidays. Everyone just assumed it had something to do with her late husband, Michael, but no one was brave enough to ask.

"After the party, of course. We can stay up watching silly Christmas movies and snacking on every unhealthy thing in my kitchen."

"I dunno if Angela…"

"I will deal with her," Vanessa interrupted quickly. The excitement and anxiety that flashed in those big, green orbs was even more startling than her invitation.

"Yeah, sure," was all the girl could manage. A smile lit up the woman's face, and she stood in the frigid night air.

"Excellent. Now, let's get inside before we freeze."

The two ladies entered the house to the sounds of playful laughter in the kitchen. Sarah was surprised to discover that Angela was the source of this merriment. Their only male guest, the lawyer who had finalized the divorce just a few short months ago, seemed to be the reason for the woman's jolly attitude, which made Sarah cringe. Was her mother seriously dating her divorce lawyer? How tacky.

"Finally decided to check your attitude?" Angela asked, her smile turning into a scowl as Sarah entered the room. Was she really such a wicked creature that she could bring everyone's good time crashing to a halt by simply being present? Did she really cause that much frustration? Did they all really hate her so much?

As her eyes started to well up with tears, she felt Vanessa's delicate hand wrap around hers.

"Come on, Angie," the lawyer soothed. "Sarah's a good kid. Just let her be."

"Alan's right," Angela declared, plastering a smile across her face and forcing it to stay. She hated it, though. She hated the idea that they were all here, forced to spend time together as a family when all she really wanted was to be alone with her new boyfriend. And now, with him defending Sarah's outrageous behavior, she hated this all just a little more. But she especially hated Sarah, as was made apparent by the look she cast towards the girl as she began pouring the wine.

"You know what?" Amy finally spoke up, snatching the already carved turkey from the counter. "I think it's time to eat."

"Perfect," Alan nodded. "Let me help." He, too, began placing food on the tiny table as Sarah and Vanessa took their seats near the wall.

"Vanessa, I think the girls were going to sit together," Angela instructed, and the icy look she received in return made her fake smile falter just for a moment.

"I'm sure Amy won't mind," Vanessa answered coolly. "It's been ages since I've seen my little Sarah, after all."

"It's fine, mom," Amy chuckled, sitting down across from them.

"Fine. Let's eat, then." Clearly, the carefree façade was slipping. Maybe if she just kept her mouth shut for the entire meal, she could escape the moment it was over.

Dinner progressed uneventfully, with everyone but Sarah making idle chat. Amy tried to pull her into the conversation a few times, but Vanessa skillfully drew the attention away from the timid girl. Eventually, dessert was served. Sarah had baked a store-bought frozen apple pie. Angela, of course, had to comment on how pumpkin would have been more appropriate.

"If your father was here, he never would have allowed it," she blurted out, and Sarah found herself struggling not to smash the pie into Angela's face.

"Mom," Amy cautioned, with a nervous giggle. Her eyes darted frantically from the oblivious Angela to the furious Sarah, waiting for disaster to strike. Vanessa intervened before anything too intense could happen.

Placing her napkin on the table, Vanessa told them, "It's getting late. I really think we should be going."

"Oh, I don't have anywhere special to be," the lawyer spoke up, sipping his wine.

"Stay a little longer, Vanessa," Amy pleaded, again casting nervous glances at her sister. "It's only seven."

"I would love to, Amy," the woman replied kindly as she rose from her chair. "Unfortunately, Sarah and I have plans."

"I don't think so," Angela shook her head. "After the way she's acted tonight, Sarah will be lucky to leave this house for graduation."

"She'll be with me, Angela. What trouble could she possibly get into at my house on Christmas Eve?"

"I said no!" Angela stood, trying to stare down the woman who remained completely unimpressed.

"She needs this." Vanessa's tone remained as flat and emotionless as her face. Angela, however, was furious. Her cheeks turned deep scarlet with rage, and her words came out as a dark, violent whisper.

"She needs discipline."

"Angela," Vanessa argued calmly, but there was nothing calm or rational about Angela.

"Go home, Vanessa," the furious woman spat. Then, turning to the girls, she said, "Amy, clean up this mess. Sarah, go to your room."

"Are you serious?" Sarah finally bolted up out of her chair, outraged at being punished for no apparent reason. "I haven't done anything wrong!"

"You've done plenty."

And suddenly unable to control her fury any longer, Sarah unleashed all the pain and rage she'd been living with for the last few months.

"And you've done nothing!" the girl screamed, pushing towards Angela in a violent frenzy. Vanessa stepped between them, restraining the tiny child as best she could. "Everything that's happened, all the stuff I've been trying to sort out, and you do nothing! My life went from boring to complete crap in the blink of an eye, and every time I try to talk to you about it, guess what you do? You blame me and send me to the room so that you can do ABSOLUTELY NOTHING!"

"What about us? Do you think Amy and I are happy with things the way they are? If you hadn't gotten that damned piercing…"

"No! This is *not* my fault! Don't you dare try to blame me for that lunatic you married!"

"Shut your mouth, you selfish little brat!"

"You're a worthless waste of space!"

"And you're not my daughter!" Everyone froze for a moment as Angela stood glaring at the stunned girl. At first, she thought it was just Angela finally disowning her as she'd feared since Andy left, but then, Angela's mouth twisted up into a satisfied grin and her entire world fell apart. "You are not my blood, and I thank God every day for it. Andy and I adopted you back when we thought I could never get pregnant, and we both regretted it from the moment you entered this house. You are an evil, awful child. Is it any wonder your parents abandoned you?"

"Angela, that is enough!" Vanessa stepped between the feuding females and told Sarah, "Get a bag and let's go."

"If you take her out of this house, do not bring her back," Angela warned.

With eyes that blazed, Vanessa told Angela, "I think you two need a break from one another. Let me take Sarah home…" Sarah raced through the living room and was halfway up the stairs before Angela replied.

"This is her home, Vanessa, whether you like it or not!"

From the second floor, Sarah could hear Vanessa speaking calmly, but her words were not clear. The edge of anger in that rational voice was unmistakable, but it was clear that Vanessa's rational tone was the only thing keeping this from turning into a domestic violence call for the police.

Not wanting to see what Angela might do if she stayed much longer, Sarah grabbed some pajamas and a change of clothes before racing back down to the front door. Vanessa was already there waiting for her, but Angela was nowhere to be found.

"Ready?" the woman smiled, but it wasn't the typical comforting smile she was used to seeing on that lovely face. In her eyes burned all the rage she'd been keeping in check as she tried to reason with Angela just moments ago.

Sarah gave a quick nod and dashed out the door, Vanessa struggling to keep up as the confused girl raced down the street.

Chapter 22

She arrived at the house moments later, shivering with cold, anger, and fear as she waited on the porch for Vanessa to catch up. The things Angela had said were almost as cruel as Andy's attempt on her life. How was she supposed to react to that kind of attack? Should she storm back there and pound Angela's face in, or should she choose the moral high ground instead? And what was she supposed to do now that the only mother she'd ever known had kicked her out and told her there was no room for her in that family anymore? Angela had made it sound like she and Andy had taken her in like a stray dog, and she'd turned out to be rabid.

Everything was wrong. This situation, this place, this life…all of it was crashing down around her and there wasn't a single thing she could do about it. She wanted to scream, to punch something until all the pain was gone, but she knew it wouldn't do any good. Most likely, she would just end up with a broken hand and sore throat to go with all the rest of her complaints.

Vanessa finally stepped up to the door, unlocking it so that Sarah could duck inside as fast as possible. Throwing her bag into the corner near the coat closet, she stormed over to the couch where she absolutely could not sit down. Instead, she began pacing between the coffee table and the television as Vanessa calmly hung her coat and locked the door.

"Sarah…" Vanessa started with that soothing tone that always seemed to make the world look a little less dismal. Tonight, though, Sarah wasn't interested in rainbows and grins. She wanted blood.

"No!" the girl barked, refusing to make eye contact or stop moving even for a moment. If she did, all this hate might swell up inside of her until her head popped off. "Don't you dare try to calm me down!"

"And why shouldn't I?" She could feel those cool, green eyes watching her strut back and forth, her hands clenched into fists at her side.

"Because I have every right to be upset!" she yelled back, finally making eye contact. "That woman…" Her words trailed off into a frustrated blend between scream and growl that made even Vanessa cringe just a bit.

"What Angela did tonight was inexcusable." She stopped moving and glared at the woman as she tried to calmly explain the situation. "We have been discussing the idea of telling you about the adoption, but we both agreed that after Andy and Jacob, you didn't need the added stress…"

"Stop talking," she interrupted. One more betrayal, one more lie, one more person who wasn't who she claimed to be. No big deal, just a little secret between friends. Of course they didn't want to trouble her with this information. Just let little Sarah go on with her happy little life, oblivious to the world around her and marching along to the beat of the drum we choose.

"Silence is what got us into this mess," Vanessa countered softly, and it was the last straw. She could feel the walls closing in on her as the air was sucked from the room.

Pushing past Vanessa, Sarah snatched her bag from the corner and fled into the cold, dark December evening.

Chapter 23

Well, this wasn't exactly how he'd planned to spend Christmas Eve. After wandering all over town and beyond for hours in below freezing temperatures, even he was beginning to feel the wear on his body. How on earth was she still going? She had no gloves, no hat, not even a heavy winter coat. Given the conditions, it wasn't surprising that she seemed to gravitate to the tiny bonfire that some of her classmates had formed in the park. Had she known it was there, or had it just been a happy coincidence? At this point, it didn't matter much. At least she was less likely to get frostbite.

He watched her wander over to the group and take a seat in the bed of someone's pickup truck. Cary was there, drinking and flirting with half a dozen guys, and The Girl seemed almost relieved to see a familiar face. After the night she'd had, he couldn't really blame her.

"So," Cary said as she stumbled over to the truck, "look who finally decided to grace us with her presence."

"You're the one who never returns my calls," The Girl countered fiercely, and he thought for a moment that she might finally decide to release all the tension she'd been carrying around by starting a drunken brawl.

"Easy, Sarah," Cary chuckled with a crooked smile. "You know you're always welcome here."

"Yeah," The Girl chuckled, a half-hearted smile at the

edge of her lips.

"Want a beer or something?" one of the boys asked. He didn't recognize the kid as being from her school, but Cary had probably already slept her way through all of those and branched out into neighboring communities by now.

"Are you kidding?" Cary cried, snatching the bottle from the boy's hand before he even had much of a chance to offer it. "Of course she'll have a beer!"

And with a look of fierce determination on her face, The Girl took the drink and popped the cap off using the side of the truck bed. As she began chugging the contents of the bottle, Cary gave a loud cry of victory. Her companions echoed her shouts, and in a flash, The Girl was tossing the empty bottle to the ground, a triumphant grin on her face.

"Still got it," The Girl grinned, and the boy handed her another as Cary began rambling about her life in The Girl's absence. It didn't take long before the hard liquor made an appearance, and soon, they were all trashed.

So much for that no partying rule.

He remained hidden in the shadows of nearby trees while the teens celebrated the holiday in the way they knew best. They all got blackout drunk and passed out in various positions around the fire. The Girl was one of the last to lose consciousness, and just before she did, she sent a few text messages from her phone.

It was no shock, then, when his own phone began to

vibrate gently in his pocket. Despite basically being the only person here in the park, he was careful to take a few steps farther into the shadows and away from the party before answering.

"She's fine," he said as soon as he put the phone to his ear, and he heard Vanessa sigh with relief.

"I've been so worried," she told him. "Amy called and said Sarah sent her a few texts, but they didn't make a lot of sense."

"She met up with Cary and some friends at the park. They all got wasted and passed out."

Silence stretched out between them until Vanessa finally told him, "Stay with her. Keep her as safe as you can without giving yourself away."

"You sure?" It was awfully cold out here in the open. What if she ended up with hypothermia or something? Everything in him was screaming to just snatch her up and carry her back to Vanessa's house. They might have some explaining to do later, but at least she would be warm.

"She will come back to us when she is ready. For now, let her be."

"And what about Angela?" Even if The Girl wanted to go back home, she didn't believe she was welcome there. After the things her parents had said and done, it wasn't really surprising that she had run off. Would she ever even want to go back to that? Could she ever forgive the people that had lied to her and treated her like a second class citizen in her own home?

"I'll talk to her."

"Are you sure…" he started, but she cut him off with a voice far colder than the night air surrounding him.

"I said I will handle it. She has to go back to Angela for now."

He felt his own frustration growing, but he managed to keep it in check as he replied, "Yeah, alright."

She started to say something else, but he hung up without really listening. It had already been a long night, and now that the sun was beginning to peek over the horizon, he had a feeling the day wouldn't get any better. So, huddling behind an old oak tree with his hands tucked under his arms, he waited and watched, hoping that she would wake soon and find someplace warm to sleep.

Chapter 24

Once again, Sarah found herself waking in Cary's room, not entirely sure what had happened. The last thing she could remember was wandering into the park and discovering Cary's entourage. So much for her rule about not partying. Pushing her aching body off of the super soft mattress, she realized she was still wearing the black and red dress she'd bought for her big Christmas Eve dinner. The same dinner she'd worked so hard to make perfect but had ended in absolute disaster. It seemed these days, everything she touched withered and died.

What was she supposed to do now? Vanessa had lied to her, Angela didn't want her... Who else was there?

"Rise and shine, cupcake!" Cary poked her head in the door with a brilliant smile on her face and said, "Merry Christmas!"

"Yeah," she mumbled, running her fingers through her hair in an effort to tame it quickly.

Stepping into the room, Cary sat a tray of eggs and bacon in front of her and said, "Made us breakfast."

"I'm not really hungry," Sarah told her, casting a disinterested look toward the plates. Cary wasn't buying it, though.

"Oh, come on!" the cheerful girl urged, giving Sarah a playful shove. "It's Christmas and we have lots to do."

"Like what?"

"Like head over to Monica's place. Her parents left her at home while they spend Christmas with relatives in New York. She's having a big holiday bash and we're going."

"I don't think that's such a good idea."

Honestly, she was more concerned with how to handle the homeless orphan bit. Somehow, she was going to need a way to survive on her own, which would mean a job and a place to live. And she would need a car. This tiny town hadn't even heard of public transportation, so the only way to get around was to either walk or drive. Since most of the jobs were outside this sleepy suburb, a vehicle was mandatory.

"Oh, Sarah," Cary rolled her eyes. "Why are you being such a baby about everything? It's just a party! It'll get your mind off of whatever's bothering you."

"What's bothering me is that Angela just kicked me out and told me she isn't even my real mom." With a weary sigh, she stood from the bed and rubbed her puffy eyes. "If I don't figure something out, I'm gonna end up on the streets living out of garbage cans."

"So stay here," Cary shrugged.

Sarah turned to her, mouth agape at the offer. It had been months since Jacob's death, and Cary had barely managed to find the time to say hello in passing from time to time. Now, suddenly, she was offering to house little orphan Sarah?

With a nervous chuckle, Cary said, "What, you think I'm joking? I'm totally serious, Sarah. We have three guest rooms. My parents won't care. They're barely home enough to notice."

"It's a nice gesture, Cary, but I can't…"

"Of course you can!" the girl interrupted, hopping up to stand beside the stunned Sarah. "Come on. What kind of best friend would I be if I let you become a teen runaway? Besides, we'll have a blast! It'll be almost like we're sisters!"

Sisters. Like Amy.

"Cary, I really think we should talk to your parents first. What if they don't want me here?"

"Oh, please," Cary waved the thought away and wrapped her arms around Sarah's shoulders. "You know they both love you. Come on, Sarah. Just say yes."

And as much as she wanted to argue, there didn't seem to be any other solution at the moment. She couldn't go back to Angela, and she wouldn't go back to Vanessa. Until she had some income and could afford room and board somewhere else, this was it. Closing her eyes, she breathed a sigh of defeat.

"So, when is this party?" Sarah muttered, and Cary gave a squeal of delight as she once again threw her arms around her friend.

Chapter 25

Days came and went, but it didn't really matter. Sarah couldn't remember half of what had happened thanks to an overwhelming amount of alcohol. In the brief periods where she'd found herself sobering up, she had wondered about the future, but those moments were fleeting as Cary found another friend's house with a liquor cabinet to raid. While this whole rock and roll lifestyle was far less painful than living with the memories of Angela's hateful words or Vanessa's betrayal, and it sure beat spending night after night tossing and turning thanks to Jacob's death, by New Year's Eve, she was beginning to wonder how long she could really go on like this. School would be starting once again in just a few days, and she was pretty sure Cary would ease up a little once it did. Then again…

Cary and Sarah pulled up to the enormous mansion on the hill only to discover that half of the county had already beaten them here. Music blared from some ridiculously overpriced sound system, and swarms of drunken youths stumbled about wildly, howling at the moon like a bunch of crazed hyenas. Sarah's stomach clenched in fear, but she closed her eyes and took a deep breath. Once she got a few drinks in her, all these people would just fade into the scenery and it wouldn't matter anymore.

"You comin'?" Cary called as she slipped out of the car, a huge grin on her face. Gritting her teeth, she managed to climb out of the vehicle and follow her friend through the chaos and into the much louder, crazier interior.

Jesus, who were all these people? Where had they all come from? Based on her experience, the entire population of Wisconsin wasn't this big. Strange faces swam around her, staring and stuttering as she tried desperately to keep up with Cary. Just when she was beginning to think this was a bad idea, her friend arrived with a few shots of cheap vodka.

"Cheers!" Cary called, but her voice was lost in the din of the party. It didn't matter, though. Sarah tossed back the drink and instantly began to feel the tension slipping from her shoulders. A couple more and she wouldn't even remember why she was so nervous.

Cary led her to the kitchen where bottles of booze lined the counter beside the sink. With a wicked wink, Cary poured another round and the girls drank up. By her third drink, Sarah was beginning to think this party might actually be fun. She tried to excuse herself from the kitchen, and Cary handed her a plastic cup with some sort of red punch in it. Patting Sarah on the shoulder, Cary sent her off into the crowd, alone and drunk.

The living room was enormous, with vaulted ceilings that seemed to stretch for miles. The openness was only emphasized by the skylight above, and Sarah stood for a moment in awe of the cosmos. She didn't even notice the figure stepping up behind her until he spoke and nearly scared the drink right out of her hand.

"Beautiful night," he called over the music, and she spun around quickly to find herself staring into big, blue eyes. Familiar blue eyes.

"Alan?" she gasped, and his face lit up with a brilliant smile. Sarah forgot about her drink and threw her arms around him, nearly soaking his leather jacket in punch. She quickly took a step back, but he just laughed.

"Good to see you again, Sarah." Taking a moment to quickly scan her attire, he added, "Seems not much has changed around here."

"Aren't you supposed to be playing child prodigy in college or something?" she grinned stupidly. He seemed to be straining to hear her, so she repeated herself, though she wasn't sure it came out exactly the same way the second time around.

Slipping the drink from her hand, he sat it on a nearby table and said, "Why don't we get some air?"

"Okay," she agreed with a nervous giggle as he took her by the elbow and led her through the swirling masses to the front lawn.

Once they were out in the sharp, winter air, she found herself wishing she'd remembered a warmer coat. Or maybe just more clothing. This was definitely not the kind of weather for miniskirts and halter tops, and the thin red jacket she'd borrowed from Cary was doing nothing against the icy wind that whipped around her.

"You alright?" Alan asked, still smiling that gorgeous

smile that made her heart melt.

She'd had a crush on him when she first started high school. He had been a senior, but he was only really a year older than her. His amazing intellect had propelled him through school, sending him off to New York to attend some prestigious university and study medicine. It had been almost four years since she'd seen him, and now, he was back.

"Yeah," she mumbled, wrapping her arms around her chest in the most casual way she could manage. "Just a little chilly out here."

"Hmm," he nodded, slipping his hands in his pockets and turning his gaze to the ground. Suddenly, she found herself wondering if his question had been more general.

"You been in town long?" she asked, trying not to sound as nervous as she suddenly felt.

"Since Christmas," he nodded. Her heart leapt into her throat as he added, "My father and I had dinner with your mom and sister the other night. They seemed pretty upset. Said you'd run off."

"Something like that," she agreed, anger burning in her cheeks.

"Right." With a heavy sigh, he turned his eyes to the sky and said, "It really is a beautiful night."

"I'm not going back," she told him. "I will not go back to a house where I'm not wanted."

"I completely agree," he smiled, finally looking at her

again. "You shouldn't go back to a house where you aren't wanted. You should go home to your family."

"My family?" she spat, stomping into the darkness and away from the merry masses. He followed as she continued to rant, "Angela is not my family! She kicked me out, told me I was adopted and that she didn't blame my parents for getting rid of me! If she could go back and do it all over again, she would never sign those papers!"

"I think you're wrong," Alan called, but she was trying hard not to listen. Unfortunately, the farther she got from the party, the easier it was to hear his gentle voice arguing reason in the face of extreme emotions.

She stumbled and fell on the frosty, snow covered ground, instantly chilling her to the core and chasing away any buzz she might have had going. Alan stepped up beside her, helping her to her feet and wrapping his leather coat around her. Staring up into his eyes, she felt more vulnerable than ever, and it made her ill.

"You're gonna freeze out here," he smiled, shaking his head. "Come on. Let's take you someplace warm where you can change."

"I won't go back there!" she pouted.

"Then how about my hotel room? I've got some sweats and a t-shirt you can borrow until those…clothes dry."

Perfect. She was drunk and feeling completely alone. Now was not a good time for the man of her dreams to invite her back to his hotel room. Nothing good was going to happen here. He would be going back to school in a few days. The last thing she needed was to form another emotional bond with someone who was going to leave her.

"I think I'd rather just go back to Cary's," she argued as he continued to lead her to the parking lot.

He laughed and said, "Yes, look how far a life as Cary's sidekick has gotten you."

"Better than a life with a mother who hates me." Tears welled up in her eyes, but she brushed them away before they could leave their icy trails down her cheeks. "Look, I get that you are trying to help, but…"

"Sarah," he sighed, stopping beside a very expensive silver sedan, "I am not doing this for your mother. I'm not doing this for my father or for Amy."

"Then why bother with some stupid kid who can't seem to get her life together?" Okay, so she was definitely whining at this point, but whining was okay given the circumstances, right?

"Let's just say that damsels in distress are my specialty," he winked, tilting her head up to look in her eyes. "Besides, I owe you for that night at the park when…"

"When you got so drunk you thought it would be fun to strip and run past the police station?" Sarah managed a tiny smile, but the one she got in return was thirty times brighter.

"Thank God you were there to talk some sense into me," he laughed. "Now, it's my turn."

In a much more sobering tone, she told him, "You can't just wave a magic wand and fix everything."

"Good," he nodded, opening the passenger side door for her, "because I'm not in the mood to mug any fairies tonight."

She hesitated for a moment, still unsure of her valiant knight. Was this really the best plan? Hopping into a boy's car so that she could go hang out with him in a hotel room with no adult supervision? Isn't this how all those date rape movies started? And then there were all the horror movies and tales of creepy stalkers and serial killers…

"Sarah, this is your decision," Alan told her, his face still gentle despite the seriousness in his voice. "Will you stay here and spend the rest of your life in a sea of drunken debauchery, or will you trust me enough to let me help?"

He was right, of course. She couldn't live like this forever. Eventually, she would need to grow up and face reality. But did it really have to be right now? Couldn't she act grown up when she was…well, grown up?

Making her decision, she slid onto the leather seat and said a quick prayer that somehow, this night would turn into rainbows and sunshine. More likely, it would be a night of tearing open old wounds and crying. Lots and lots of crying. As Alan quickly closed the door and hopped in the driver's seat, she felt the knot in her stomach slowly ease. It was time to deal with her problems rather than running away like some scared little girl. Besides, Alan's hotel room was sure to have a mini bar, right?

Chapter 26

The car ride over had started off awkward and completely silent. Eventually, though, Alan had started reminiscing about the old days, and Sarah had finally given way to the nostalgia. They'd talked about old friends that were still around and those who had moved on. Alan had brought up a few very memorable moments at the farm, but before any of the dangerous feelings about that place had a chance to surface, he'd made her laugh as he told a story about a friend at college that had ended up passed out on the front lawn of a professor's house in nothing but a pair of ladies' thongs. It was quite entertaining. Apparently, Alan hadn't really grown up much at all.

At the hotel, though, things took on a much more serious tone. Alan had offered her a pair of navy blue sweatpants and a soft gray t-shirt, and she had quickly changed out of her soaking wet party clothes. As she stepped past the mirror in the bathroom, she realized just how different she actually looked. Thick makeup caked her face, making her skin even paler than usual and circling her eyes with black rings of powder and gunk. This wasn't her. Cary had done this, just as Cary had picked that pathetic excuse for an outfit. Sarah was no prude, but there was a fine line between sexy and trashy. Clearly, Cary had no idea where that line was.

Time to start over, right? Flipping on the faucet, Sarah

used the bland hotel hand soap until every inch of her face was free of cosmetics. The plain face that stared back at her now was a bit disappointing. Still, it was better than trying to be something she was not. She might be homeless, but she was not a whore. She was just…Sarah.

"Ah," Alan smiled from the twin bed closest to the door as she stepped out of the bathroom, "much better."

"You're lucky," she grinned, trying to run a hand through her stiff, product-laden hair and failing miserably. With a sigh she flopped down on the other bed and told him, "No other man has ever seen me in sweats with no makeup and lived to tell the tale."

"Please," he scoffed, "I've seen you covered in your own vomit. This is nothing."

"Hey, that's only happened three times!"

"Three? I only knew about the first time!" he laughed, and she couldn't help but echo the sound. "You *have* turned into the party hound, haven't you? Angela mentioned something about your recent lifestyle choices, but I thought she was talking about a new girlfriend or something."

The mention of Angela brought the good times crashing to a sudden halt. Instantly, her chest felt heavy and her eyes filled with tears. Where was the booze when she needed it? And why did she suddenly feel like she might be headed down a path that would eventually lead to regular AA meetings?

Clearing his throat, Alan said, "So, now that we've

entered the awkward phase of the conversation, how about you tell me what happened?"

"Not much to tell," she shrugged, lying back on the bed with her hands behind her head. "Andy tried to kill me, Angela blamed me for the whole thing, and then when Jacob died…"

"Jacob?" Alan interrupted, obviously quite shocked. "Jacob Cannon?"

"Yeah," she choked, pressing the heels of her hands against her eyes to hold back the flood of tears.

"How did he die?" Alan whispered, still clearly stunned by this news. It was so nice to be the one to deliver it, too. Sarah forced herself to breathe through the pain that shot through her head as she tried to explain.

"We were at Cary's homecoming party," she managed, just barely keeping it together. "I got trashed and puked on him. Next thing I know, I'm waking up in a hospital room and Jake is dead. The police said they found him at the old Carter farm with a stab wound in his abdomen. Some stranger brought me into the hospital, but I think I was at the farm that night. I just don't remember what happened or why we went there."

Finally, she had done it. She had told someone the story without breaking down or lashing out. Score one for Sarah.

"Well," Alan said, a tiny quiver in his voice, "I suppose that changes things a bit, doesn't it?"

"How?" she asked, refusing to drop her hands for fear that they might be the only things holding her sanity together.

"Your mom…"

"She's not my mom," Sarah interrupted fiercely, and Alan didn't even flinch.

"Okay, Angela, then," he corrected. "Angela said that you were behaving strangely, skipping school and staying out all night. She said you were distant and moody. Honestly, I think she believes you're a junky."

"Clearly, I'm just a drunk," Sarah snorted, finally courageous enough to slide her hands down to her chest. See? No tears. All better.

"I don't think you're either." Moving over to sit on the edge of the bed beside her, he wrapped a hand around hers and smiled softly. "I think maybe you're just grieving for a friend."

Damn. The tears broke loose and she rolled onto her side, burying her face in her hands as she sobbed. Alan gently stroked her hair, offering soft reassurance as she purged all the pain and fear she'd felt for the last few months. This is what she needed. All it had taken was a friendly face and a chance to tell someone her side of the story. Why hadn't Angela given her this? Why hadn't Amy been there for her when she needed a solid shoulder to cry on? The answer was simple and horrible. She reminded them of Andy. All her ridiculous outbursts and emotional instability, the partying and skipping out on her responsibilities. It was just like him. No wonder Angela had kicked her out. No wonder Amy had refused to spend any time with her since Jacob's death. No wonder Vanessa had kept her distance.

"I've been such a jerk," she bawled, and Alan was right there with her, telling her exactly what she needed to hear when she needed to hear it.

"No one's perfect," he told her, and she peeked out from behind her hands to see that same gentle smile hovering over her. "You acted a little crazy, but so did Angela. It seems to me that there were no innocent parties in this situation."

"What am I going to do? I can't go back. I can't stay with Cary."

"I agree with not going back to Cary. She's definitely part of the problem." Brushing the hair from her cheek, Alan offered, "I guess the only thing left for you to do is go apologize and hope that Angela does the same."

"She won't take me back." Forcing herself into a sitting position beside her friend, she sniffed, "She hates me."

"Then why is she so worried about you?"

Sarah turned to look into that handsome face and knew that something big had just happened. Some life-altering, world-shattering revelation was getting ready to crash over her. This was one of those strange defining moments that would change everything she knew about herself and her world.

Before any of that could happen, though, Alan gave her a big grin and a pat on the back as he said, "I'm starving. How about some pizza?"

"Really?" she asked, and she couldn't help but smile as

all the tension melted away.

"Yeah, really. I wasn't about to touch the hors d'oeuvres at that party. Now that I know you're such a lightweight, I feel pretty confident that I won't ever touch party food again, especially when you're around. Who knows when you might blow chunks all over the place and contaminate everything."

Giving him a playful punch in the arm, she told him, "You better watch it, Alan Grove, Jr., or I'll tell your daddy about how you like to party with underage drinkers."

"I'm terrified," he chuckled, pulling out his cell phone. "Pepperoni?"

"I'm game for anything that isn't olives or mushrooms," she shrugged, wiping the last bits of moisture from her cheeks.

"So anchovy and pineapple it is."

"Ew, gross!" she exclaimed. "You'd seriously eat that?"

"If it means making you vomit, then absolutely." With a wicked twinkle in his eye, he turned his back and began punching buttons on his obviously expensive smart phone.

"Jerk," she muttered, propping herself up against the headboard with some pillows and settling in for a relaxing evening with an old friend. It might not be rainbows and sunshine yet, but things were definitely looking a little brighter.

Chapter 27

He heard the doorbell ring and was instantly on his feet. Thomas had taken over his post for a few hours, and he had come home to some much needed rest. Following The Girl through the last few weeks had proven almost impossible. Watching silently as she grew more and more reckless in her behavior had pushed him to his limits, and the man in black had given Vanessa an ultimatum for the first time in their entire relationship together. Do something, or be prepared to tell The Girl the truth. Thankfully, it hadn't come to that, but his refusal to stand idly by and watch her spiral into oblivion had definitely put a strain on his relationship with Vanessa.

Creeping silently to the top of the stairs, he could hear voices. One was clearly Vanessa, and the other was Alan Grove, Angela's divorce lawyer. The third made his muscles tense and his jaw clench in rage.

"…settled in and doing well," the lawyer said, his tone polite and pleasant as always. "Things may still be a bit tense for a few weeks, but I think everything will be fine."

"I can't tell you how much I appreciate your help," Vanessa told them sweetly. "If she hadn't come home soon…"

"Vanessa," the lawyer soothed. "No sense getting all worked up again. Sarah is safe and sound."

"Can I just interject her for a moment?" the boy chimed in, and it took every ounce of willpower in the young hunter not to charge down the stairs to pound the life out of him.

"Alan," the lawyer warned, but there was no stopping this boy from speaking his mind.

"Dad, don't. Sarah is far from safe and sound. She needs someone she can trust, someone to talk to who doesn't patronize her like Angela or avoid conflict like Amy. The best person to keep her on the path to recovery right now is you, Vanessa."

Vanessa spoke up again, clearly irritated at being told what to do by someone as young as the aspiring doctor. The man listened from his perch, ready to intervene if things got too intense.

"I will help Sarah in whatever way I can," Vanessa tried to reassure the boy, but he didn't seem convinced.

"Not good enough. She hasn't actually forgiven you for lying to her all these years, and that sense of betrayal will be difficult to overcome. You need to start rebuilding your relationship with her. She's going to need you."

"Again, Alan," Vanessa said in that all too sweet tone she reserved for dealing with irritating children, "I will do whatever I can to help Sarah, and I do sincerely appreciate everything you did to talk her into coming back to us."

"Son, I believe it is time for us to go," the lawyer prodded, but the boy still had one more bit of advice to give.

"Fine," the boy agreed, "but right now, she is beyond frustrated. If you leave her to sort this out alone, she is going to discover whatever it is you're hiding from her."

"Alan, that is enough!" the lawyer commanded, and the man at the top of the stairs heard the screen door bang against its frame. With a heavy sigh, the lawyer said, "I apologize for my son. He doesn't always think before he speaks."

"You acted the same way at his age," Vanessa chuckled. "He's right, though. It's going to take time and a lot of hard work to repair the damage that was done."

"If you need anything, just call."

"Thank you, Alan," Vanessa sighed.

"What is family for?"

Footsteps were quickly followed by the front door closing. After a few moments, he finally crept down the stairs to find Vanessa resting quietly on the couch, her feet propped up and an arm over her eyes.

"Sit down," she said, waving to the chair near her feet. "I know you heard all of that."

"Do you think she'll forgive you?" he asked softly, and the exhausted woman gave a harsh laugh.

"Of course she will. The real question is, should I let her?"

"I don't understand."

Pushing herself up to a sitting position, Vanessa turned dark rimmed eyes to him and said, "If I let her go now, she might not have to know about any of this. She could go on with her life, get an education, have a family…"

"The Council wouldn't allow it."

"I could talk the Council into letting her go. It would save them resources, limit their exposure, and eliminate the need to kill an innocent girl."

Oh, how he wished it could be that simple. Unfortunately, even if the Council lost interest in this particular assignment, the Others never would. They had set their sights on The Girl, and now, nothing would stop them from getting what they wanted. She had already demonstrated superhuman powers. The Council wouldn't let that go easily, and the Others would never give up until every one of them was dead.

"She needs you," he finally managed to spit out, though it felt like he was somehow condemning The Girl to the same hell he'd endured for most of his life.

Vanessa stared at him for a few moments, her red, puffy eyes searching his face for any hint of hesitation. He gave her none. Finally, the woman stood on weary legs and began walking towards the stairs.

"It's been a long holiday," she called over her shoulder. "We should both get some rest."

Following her up the stairs, he made his way to his room. Despite his fatigue, though, it took a very long time for his conscience to finally stop screaming and let him sleep.

Chapter 28

"Stop staring at yourself in that damned mirror and let's go!"

Angela's frustrated shouts echoed up the stairs to the nervous girl's tiny room. Sarah simply rolled her eyes and made a few more last minute adjustments to her hideous white gown. It made her normally pallid complexion seem even more faded and sickly. And it did absolutely nothing for her figure, which was already lacking in curves. How was she going to make it through the next few hours in this hot, scratchy abomination?

"Sarah, this is your last chance! Amy and I are leaving, with or without you!"

Grabbing the equally repulsive cap with the gold tassel dangling from the top, she dashed down to the living room where her mother and sister were both gathering their things. Flashing them a smile to melt even the iciest heart, she raced out the door and hopped in the backseat of the tiny Taurus. The others joined shortly after, her mother shaking her head with a reluctant grin.

"I know you're excited," Angela told the girl as she carefully backed out of the driveway, "but remember that before you take off with your friends, I want lots of pictures. Think you can do that?"

"Yes, ma'am," Sarah laughed. The truth was, she was feeling a bit nervous about all of this. As class valedictorian, she had been expected to prepare a speech which would be given to the graduating class at today's ceremony. Unfortunately, every time she sat down to write it, her mind began to wander and eventually, her thoughts settled on the strange dreams she had been having for the past four months.

Her sleep had been choppy and far from restful for long enough that she was beginning to wonder if she would ever get a good night's sleep again. She didn't even wish for good dreams at this point. No dreams would have been perfectly welcome, as long as she didn't see the frightful images that seemed to greet her every time she closed her eyes.

So, here she was, deprived of sleep and still without a commencement address for her class as she made her way to the graduation ceremony. Could there be any way to make the situation more stressful?

This question was answered the moment they pulled into the parking lot and saw him. He was leaning against a shiny new red sports car that exactly matched the dress of his short, rail thin escort. Only one person would show up to a high school graduation ceremony with his latest bleached blonde bimbo. Then again, only one person would have the gall to come to any kind of event celebrating a milestone in a life which he had almost ended just a few months ago.

"Daddy!" Amy screeched as she jumped out of the car. Racing over to him, she threw her arms around his neck and laughed as she held him in a joyful embrace. The blonde just smiled stupidly at the elated girl.

"Hey, sweetie," Andy grinned. "How's my girl?"

"I missed you. Why haven't you called?"

"Busy," he motioned towards the car. "New job. How about you? Anything new?"

Amy began rambling on endlessly about nothing in particular. Angela took a few timid steps toward the scene as Sarah was climbing out of the car. She, too, began pitching in bits of information as the conversation continued. The older girl, however, refused to take part. Marching past them and into the school, she could hear the discussion turning towards her and the attitude she had towards her dear "father." But none of that mattered. This was her day, and there was no way she was going to let that jerk screw it up.

Inside, she found Cary and some of her other friends standing around chatting about all of the parties that were going to take place in just a few hours. Naturally, one of the biggest celebrations would be at Cary's house. Most years, the entire graduating class would go out to the old farm and have one last bash together, but most of the class had joined the Jacob Memorial Club and refused to set foot there. Cary's family owned almost as much land, though, and her parents wouldn't be home tonight, anyway. They understood that graduation was a big deal, and because Cary was a mature, responsible adult now, they trusted her to keep it under control. In all likelihood, there would be a few visits from the police, who would then be bribed into letting the event wrap up on its own.

"The party starts at three," Cary was saying as Sarah approached. "Make sure you remind *everyone*. Especially if they don't usually get invited to these sorts of things. This is supposed to be a celebration for the entire class."

Sarah arrived just in time to see one of Cary's other friends from drama glaring as she whined, "I don't understand why you want the losers from the science club or debate team to be there. What are they going to add to the experience?" Clearly, the look on the aspiring actress's face meant that Sarah was being targeted as one of the less than worthy.

"Now, Donna," Cary smiled, and the condescension in her voice was clear even to its target. "If we exclude them, what's to stop us from excluding you as well? Besides, I want this to be an unforgettable night for all of us. People will be talking about this graduation night for the rest of our lives. If all of our classmates show up, then the memory of tonight will live on that much longer."

"Leave it to you to make something as simple as graduating into an opportunity for immortality," Sarah chuckled. But even she had to agree with Cary's logic. Since before anyone could remember in this town, the lines of segregation had been drawn. Until Cary had arrived at the high school, parties were designed for specific groups only. Now, as her final hoorah, she was planning to integrate the entire senior class before everyone ran off to college or work or whatever they had planned. It was ingenious.

Teachers began calling for everyone to take their places in the processional. The tiny gossip ring broke up as they all made their way to the growing lines of blue and white gowns. And the overwhelming sense of anxiety she had felt just hours before was suddenly gone. She knew that she was going to get up in front of these people, give an amazing and incredibly memorable speech, and then go party with all of them at Cary's house one last time.

And that's exactly what she did. Once the administration had its say in the opening ceremonies, they called her up to the podium. With no notes, no index cards, and no real clue what it was she was about to say, she stepped up to the microphone. The adults that were sitting behind her passed a few nervous glances to one another, but she gave them a reassuring nod as she walked by that seemed to put them at ease.

Whatever she said to her classmates won her a standing ovation, but she certainly couldn't remember what it was once it was over. It was as if some force took control of her body, and she just disappeared for nearly fifteen minutes. As terrifying as a blackout like that might seem, it happened so quickly and the results were so surprising that she didn't exactly have a chance to worry about it until long after it was finished.

She was so wrapped up in the moment that she didn't notice the man in black slide back into the shadows as she left the stage and returned to her seat. He noticed her, though. He especially noticed the bizarre look on her face as the crowd began to applaud. And he could not forget the incident quite so easily.

Chapter 29

"Well," Vanessa sighed as she sat down at the table, "that was a lovely ceremony." She took a sip from the steaming mug in her hands and smiled. He was not fooled, though. She had noticed it, too.

"Nice speech," he grunted, his eyes fixed on her face. "All that talk about destiny and rebelling against the leadership of the world...riveting."

"Yeah," she agreed, much more somber now. "It didn't really seem all that strange coming from her, though."

"No," he agreed. "That's what makes it dangerous."

"She is a natural when it comes to public speaking. I agree, it could be a problem if the Council finds out."

"Do you think she planned that speech?" he asked, but she gave a strained smile.

"How should I know? She barely talks to me anymore." He heard such heartache in that voice, but there was nothing he could do. Since Christmas, Vanessa had been trying to patch things up with The Girl without much success.

"Maybe you should invite her out to a graduation dinner?" he suggested, incredibly uncomfortable discussing this topic but doing his best to hide it. She knew him too well, though.

Taking another sip of tea, she quickly changed the subject by asking, "Shouldn't you be getting ready for the big party?"

"Anthony should be here soon. We'll leave together." Another problem. Anthony was the nephew of Councilor Claire Marcum. She'd sent him in as an apprentice to partner with the most infamous hunter in the Society, claiming she wanted him to complete his training with the best. In reality, it seemed a clever way to spy on the two most questionable members of the organization.

"You think they'll make a move tonight?"

He shook his head and answered, "Not likely. There will be too many people, and the chances of luring her away again are slim. Besides, she doesn't drink to unconsciousness anymore."

"Thank God for that," Vanessa agreed. With a sigh, she told him, "Just be careful."

"Always am."

The doorbell rang and he dashed off to answer even though he already knew the identity of their visitor. The truth was, he was eager to get back to his post. The Others had been quiet for quite a while, leading him to believe they were planning something big. Every moment he spent away from The Girl was full of anxiety and anticipation as he waited for Thomas to call. Add to this her performance at the graduation ceremony, and a knot began to twist in his stomach.

Had they gotten to her already? Could he have missed something? Was it possible that they had crept into her life one night while he was at home sleeping and convinced her to sign up?

"Ready?" the young hunter asked as his mentor opened the door. He gave a quick nod and stepped out, leaving without even so much as a goodbye. Vanessa would understand, though. He had work to do. The Girl had to be protected.

"Everything okay?" the boy asked, but he didn't respond. Instead, he marched silently on to his familiar hiding place in the roses to keep an eye on her while she prepared for the celebration.

Chapter 30

Cary's party was a success. Every member of the graduating class showed up, and even some of the underclassmen. She didn't turn anyone away that night, knowing perfectly well that to do so would mean one less mouth to run all summer about how amazing she was.

The Girl came wearing her most extreme knee-high boots and a dress that would have given Angela a massive coronary. And of course, she drank. She drank until most others would have been hospitalized for alcohol poisoning. She drank until it seemed she was incapable of holding a coherent conversation with anyone, though she made her way through the crowd with relative ease despite her inebriation. The last time he'd seen her consume this much alcohol had been the same night she'd saved his life. However, this time, she didn't seem to be nearly as helpless as the night her boyfriend had led Elijah's team to the old farm and into the hands of one of the most dangerous creatures on the planet. The grace and speed she used as she maneuvered silently through the crowd would have been impressive for someone who hadn't downed an entire liquor cabinet in the last few hours. It almost seemed like she was trying to avoid everyone, and it wasn't difficult to see that there was something bothering her. Cary, however, was far too busy with her other guests to worry much about the girl who eventually wandered out to the backyard to gaze drunkenly up at the stars as tears streamed from her dark ringed eyes.

"You okay?" The surprise on her face was almost comical as she turned to face the young man who had spoken. For a moment, Elijah thought he saw a look of recognition begin to surface, but then she shook her head and laughed. No, she hadn't recognized the boy after all.

"I'm fine," she smiled, and her words were barely slurred. Even Thomas didn't have that kind of tolerance, and he was at least four times her size.

"You don't look fine. That's not what I meant. I meant, you look sad. Damn, I'm drunk!" She looked at the smiling boy and laughed, clearly charmed by his awkwardness. "So, what's bothering you?"

"What makes you think I'd tell you?" And the sly look she gave the boy confirmed Elijah's suspicions. She was far from drunk, though she definitely wanted people to believe the opposite.

"Because you look like you need a friendly ear, and because I'm too trashed to remember anything you say to me right now." That brought another chuckle from her. "Come on. I promise I won't tell."

"You know, I don't really remember seeing you at school. What's your name?"

"Tony," the boy answered. "And I'm just here with some friends from baseball. I actually graduate next year." Nice cover, but sloppy. She knew his name now, and if she checked into it, she'd find no one here had a clue who he was. Thankfully, she didn't check.

"Nice to meet you, then, Tony. I'm Sarah." She reached out and shook his hand as they both giggled drunkenly.

"So, why the long face, Sarah?" Hearing her name on the boy's lips sent a wave of anger coursing through the hidden hunter. How could this boy just walk up and introduce himself while the man who had spent years protecting her from the monsters had to stay hidden in the shadows? Hadn't he earned the right to be the one at the party? Hadn't he done enough to be the one to touch that soft, silky skin? Forcing these ridiculous thoughts away, he turned his thoughts back to the scene before him.

"I was just thinking about a friend," she sighed, looking down at her boots as if there might be something of interest there. "He should be here celebrating with us right now."

"Where is he?"

"He died." The finality in those words kept the boy from pushing. There was a moment of silence before she lifted her eyes back to the young hunter's face and forced a smile. "I don't know why I'm worrying about that right now. We're supposed to be having fun, right?"

"Yeah," the boy agreed, but his mood was a bit more somber now as well. "I say we go back inside and drink a toast to fallen comrades. Wadda ya say?"

The girl hesitated for a moment, studying his face once

again as if she might have seen something familiar there. Brushing this thought away once again, she wrapped an arm around his and let this strange boy lead her back into the party where she continued to drink until the wee hours of the morning. Elijah stayed close, but it somehow felt safer now that she was inside with the others. At least she was less of a target in there.

The boy helped her home that night, since she insisted on walking back to her house. And once she was safely inside, the boy found his mentor waiting behind the rose arbor near the garage. The young apprentice was clearly exhausted, but there was a faint hint of a smile lingering on his face. The Girl had obviously left her mark on this one as well.

"She's pretty messed up," the boy told him.

"She'll be fine."

"Are you sure? She was really upset."

"And you calmed her down before she did something stupid. Just don't do it again. She nearly recognized you this time. Next time she *will* remember your face."

With a laugh the boy replied, "Did you see how much she drank? That girl will be lucky to remember her own name when she wakes up tomorrow."

"Go home and get some rest. We'll talk in the morning." If there was one thing Elijah had learned over the years, it was to never underestimate The Girl. She would recognize Anthony because she hadn't been nearly as trashed as she had let on. The boy would learn in time, though.

"Yes, sir." He turned to leave, then paused for just a moment. Turning back to face this almost infamous mentor, he asked, "Is she always so charming?"

"No," he answered honestly. "Most times, she's an absolute nightmare."

"I can see why you like her." And though he should have reprimanded the boy for such a comment, Elijah let his apprentice walk away into the darkness while he stayed behind to keep watch over The Girl. No sense causing a scene out here on her lawn. Or at least that's what he told himself.

Anthony was a good kid, and one day, he would be an excellent hunter. First, though, he was going to have to learn not to question authority so much. But he was young. He still had plenty of time to learn how things worked within their organization. And according to the local gossip, he was learning from one of the best. The Council had never given anyone under the age of twenty an apprentice until now. It was quite an honor for both parties.

The light in her room finally illuminated her window, and from the sounds of shouts and slamming doors that followed, he guessed her mother was home. Angela would not be happy to see her daughter returning so late, especially if she smelled as intoxicated as he imagined she might, and The Girl would definitely be in no mood to let an argument drop without a fight.

The Others

The sound of loud angry music drifted from her room, and he couldn't help but sigh. It was going to be a long night.

Chapter 31

Standing inside the crowded, mind-numbing mall for the past three hours was not the way she'd expected to spend her first day as a high school graduate, but there were worse things she could be doing. Like mowing the lawn, for instance, or counting the number of rednecks at the classic car show that was taking place downtown. Cary had brought a few friends of hers along, one of which could not keep his hands to himself. He was the standard Cary type; handsome, well-built, and dumb as a rock. The other was Jaime, Sarah's arch nemesis since grade school. If one were to look up the word skank in the dictionary, Jaime's picture would be found just below. Or at least that's how it was in Sarah's library.

"Why are we still here?" she moaned, wishing she would feel as little guilt over leaving them here as they had about leaving her at the graduation party the night before. Turns out, Cary and her crew had left around ten to visit the old farm. Sarah hadn't been invited because they knew she wouldn't go anyway. Still, it hurt to know her best friend had abandoned her for these people and a few extra kegs.

"Because we are not going to leave this building until we find a cute guy for you to spend your last few months in Wisconsin using and abusing as you see fit." Cary giggled and stroked her fling's cheek. "Besides, what else is there to do in this wretched town?"

"Go to the park? Maybe a swim? See a movie? Stop in at a restaurant for a bite to eat?"

"It's too hot for the park, I don't have my bathing suit with me, there are no good movies playing, and if you're hungry, the food court is right around the corner." It seemed Cary had thought of everything.

"Fine, then can we at least switch up the stores? I'm tired of looking at clothes I can't afford and would never wear anyway."

"You couldn't fit your bony butt into most of these clothes anyway," Jaime chuckled, shaking one of her many shopping bags in Sarah's face. Sarah shot her a look that would shatter glass and began walking towards the music store. It wasn't big, nor did it have much of anything other than country, rap, and Top 40 artists, but it was better than trendy clothing stores. Or at least that's what she tried to tell herself.

By the time she got to the store, her friends had been distracted by some sort of special at the nail salon. It would be hours before they came out of there, and by then she would be long gone. A brief glance at the music selection confirmed her earlier suspicions. As she stepped through the exit and into the main mall walkway, she slammed directly into someone who seemed to be headed into the shop.

"Excuse me," she apologized, glancing up at the man. Suddenly, her entire body went numb. He was wearing sunglasses, which was particularly unusual considering they were inside, but what was even more unusual was the immediate feeling of déjà vu she felt as she stared up at that emotionless face. The last time she had looked into that face, it had been twisted in torment.

For the longest time neither of them seemed to be capable of movement, and then there was a loud crack, like the sound of thunder from somewhere inside the building. And close, too, from the sound of the accompanying screams. The man turned his head just long enough to catch a glimpse of the frightened masses scurrying towards them, and then his attention returned to her.

"Run," he ordered in a voice that was more mechanical than masculine.

When he stepped away from her and into the wave of frightened faces, she suddenly began to remember bits of what had happened at the farmhouse almost a year ago. Pain ripped through her skull, but this time, the images came anyway. It was as if the dam that had been holding back the flood of memories had suddenly crumbled, and it left her on her knees gasping. Jacob's jacket soaked in blood, a woman with raven hair, gunshots, chocolate eyes full of nothing… She had seen this man that night, and she had saved his life. Perhaps this was his way of returning the favor.

Without another thought, Sarah joined the crowd of fleeing shoppers. She made it back to her car and all the way to the driveway of her home before her entire body started trembling and she dropped to her knees just in front of the porch steps. There she knelt, sobbing and remembering all the things her overwhelmed psyche had tried to keep from her. Once the levy broke, the memories that followed were so intense, so real, that she seemed to be reliving every moment of that night at the farm. Waking in the barn to find herself surrounded by shadowy silhouettes, the figures in the moonlight locked in some sort of battle of wills, the sight of all those people clawing at their throats as the air was sucked from their lungs. She'd found a gun lying in the grass and shot the thing that looked like a woman, once in the chest and once in the head.

Nice shootin', Tex.

Then there was the man from the mall. He'd been almost dead when she knelt down beside him, but something had happened. She had called to him, brought him back somehow. Such a silly idea, calling someone back from the dead. But he hadn't been dead. Not quite. And she had managed to not only stop the process that was slowly sucking the life out of him, but to actually reverse it.

I know you said we would have to deal with some unusual situations...

Angela and Vanessa had a few more skeletons in their closets. Maybe tonight she could find answers to some of the questions floating around inside her weary head.

Chapter 32

How had he missed it? Her best friend since grade school, for God's sake! It was a perfect setup, and he'd missed every warning sign. Thinking back, it was so obvious that most people would have overlooked it. But he wasn't most people. His job was protecting The Girl. He should have seen this coming from a mile away.

Vanessa was waiting at the door with Dr. Trubal when the car pulled into the driveway. The boy in the backseat moaned softly as he was gently lifted and carried into the house. The doctor immediately got down to business while he and Vanessa discussed the incident.

"How bad was it?" she asked, her voice as steady as if she were asking about the weather. He looked down at his blood stained hands before replying.

"Bad. It was a setup, but this time they were after The Girl."

"How many?"

"Three, but one of them wasn't human."

There was a long pause as she considered this. "And did you *choose* to engage them in a crowded shopping mall?"

He shook his head, "They attacked. The Girl broke away from the rest of the group just before one of the girls she was with spotted us. I think her name was Jaime or Jenny...not really sure. I left to follow The Girl and Anthony stayed behind to watch the others. I figured he could handle it, especially since it was a public area with lots of people."

"So how did you see that she made it out safely and still get the young one out alive?"

"I told her to run." He waited for the reprimand, knowing full well that he was not supposed to speak to the target. In no way was she supposed to know that he even existed. The night at the farm had been close enough, and luckily she didn't remember any of it. Today, he had been faced with a choice he could not make, and so he had done what was necessary to make sure everyone made it out of the building alive. Unfortunately, his efforts seemed to have been in vain.

The doctor came down the stairs, slowly removing gloves soaked in red liquid from his wrinkled old fingers. The look on his face told them everything they needed to know. The boy, Anthony, was dead. This had been his first training exercise that wasn't just some simulation, and it turned out to be his last. One bad call and the boy had paid for the mistake with his life.

"I've called someone to come pick up the body," Dr. Trubal said solemnly. He took Vanessa's hand in his and gave it a quick squeeze before grabbing his coat and leaving. The woman's eyes filled with tears, but she brushed them away quickly. Now was not the time to weep. That would come later. Now they needed to decide what to do about The Girl.

"Well, I guess she knows there's something strange going on by now, and I'm sure she's got plenty of questions that need to be answered. I expect she'll be here any minute."

"I'll go make the bed downstairs," he nodded, but she shook her head.

"No need for you to hide out in the basement this time. I have a feeling she'll need you around to keep her safe no matter where she is now, and since she's already seen you twice, I don't think it will hurt for you to be here when she arrives."

"Are you sure?" The last thing he wanted was to frighten her away, and seeing him again with Vanessa might seem like another betrayal.

"Positive. Now, tell me about this creature."

Chapter 33

The moment Amy saw her sister's pale, dazed face, she jumped up from her seat in front of the television where she'd been watching a news report about an attack at the local mall, rushing to Sarah's side. From there, the two of them stumbled to the couch, flopping down noisily while the news reporter continued to relay the details of the grisly scene.

"Police are still searching for any information as to the identity or location of the gunmen who attacked a group of teenagers less than an hour ago, killing one and kidnapping the other two." The reporter's face disappeared, replaced by the faces of Cary St. James and her boyfriend, Joseph Delancy. Sarah looked as though she might throw up at any second as the reporter's voice continued to speak, asking anyone who might have information as to the whereabouts of these two people to please contact the police immediately.

"I don't understand," the shaking girl mumbled, looking up into her sister's worried blue eyes. She was reminded of another set of eyes, these a deep chocolate brown, and the tears came back with all the fury of a hurricane.

"Calm down," Amy cooed, resting her elder sister's head against her chest and gently stroking her hair. "Tell me what happened."

"I don't know. I went to the mall with Cary and some of her friends, and then there was a loud noise and shouting, and he told me to run, so I did…"

"Who told you to run?" But Sarah just shook her head. "Sarah, do you know what happened to Cary and Joseph?" Again, she shook her head, but there was clearly something she was trying to hide.

"Where's Angela?" Sarah suddenly demanded, her eyes filled with an intensity that made Amy's pulse quicken.

"She's upstairs taking a nap," Amy tossed a glance at the top of the stairs, clearly wishing that her mother would somehow sense what was happening and hurry to her rescue. Sarah tried to push the other girl aside to march up to her mother's bedroom, but Amy grabbed her arm. "You need to calm down. Mom had nothing to do with whatever is going on right now."

"She knows something, Amy!" the angry girl snarled, flinging an accusing finger towards the stairs.

"That doesn't even make any sense! She's been asleep for the past two hours!"

With a furious glare, Sarah yanked her arm free and dashed off to confront the sleeping woman upstairs. Amy, recognizing that another ridiculous battle was about to begin, fled the house, deciding it was a perfect time to go get some ice cream at the dairy mart down the street. By the time she got back, the argument would be over, and though she would still have to deal with the aftermath, at least she wouldn't have to be present when furniture and foul language started flying. Sarah was too busy storming into Angela's room to care much about what her sister was doing, though.

Sarah found Angela sound asleep, just as Amy had said she would be. The confusion she had felt earlier now twisted itself into a blind rage. How could this woman lay here so peacefully while Sarah tossed and turned every night, plagued by nightmares that were forgotten even before she woke? How could she keep secrets that could potentially put the young girl's life in danger? And Sarah was certain that's exactly what was happening here. Angela knew something that she either would not or could not share with anyone, including Sarah, and now the decision not to share this information was destroying their lives.

"Get up," she growled, and Angela's head shot up from the pillow, her face a mix of bewilderment and fear. The girl stormed over to the television in the corner, nearly knocking it off its stand as she struck the power button. The reporter was back, her thick black hair now tied back loosely from the soft coffee-colored face. She was interviewing a police officer at the scene, but what she really seemed to be doing was inching her way closer to the body of the dead teen so that her camera operator could get a good shot of the grisly sight.

"What is going on?" the groggy woman asked, trying to rub the sleep out of her eyes without smearing her makeup.

"I was hoping you could tell me."

"I don't know what you're talking about…" But her

words fell short as she saw the faces on the television. The reporter was once again pleading for anyone who might know where the missing children were to please let the police know right away.

"What are you keeping from me?"

"Maybe we should call Vanessa," Angela suggested, but the idea only fed Sarah's anger.

"You are not going to hand this off to someone else or try to stall until I've calmed down! Now tell me the whole story or so help me…"

"What? Are you going to hurt me?"

"Of course not." But the girl's voice faltered as she considered exactly what might have completed her threat. Would she hurt Angela? Did knowing more about this nightmare really mean that much to her?

"Sarah, I know you're frustrated, but I don't have all the answers. Neither does anyone else, for that matter. It would be best if we all just sat down and discussed it together."

"Fine. Get her over here, *tonight*, and we can talk. Fair enough?"

"Fair enough."

And so Angela picked up the phone and dialed that old familiar number.

Chapter 34

The thoughtful silence was shattered by the shrill sound of a ringing phone. Vanessa slowly rose, choosing to take the call in the kitchen. It was probably the Council, wanting to know how Anthony had done on his first day in the field. Normally, they wouldn't care much about such a mundane event, but this was the nephew of a Councilor. It was no secret that Councilor Marcum had always wanted a son, and since that was impossible due to a work-related injury, Anthony had filled that void with little protest. Now, Vanessa would have to relay the dreadful news of his death to them, potentially sealing her fate as well as Elijah's. The Council had heard the old adage, *Don't shoot the messenger*, but most times they chose to ignore such advice, instead taking the view that failure of any kind was a sign of weakness and must not be tolerated.

"Hello," she answered, afraid her voice would give away the fear she was desperately trying to keep in check. The moment she heard the voice on the other end of the line, the tension melted away and a relieved smile lit up her face.

"Vanessa," Angela's trembling voice replied, "Sarah would like to sit down with us and have a little chat."

"I'm sure she would." The immense relief she had felt just a moment ago quickly retreated as another kind of fear surfaced. Eighteen years and now the time had finally arrived. Would the girl actually believe what she had to say? Probably not at first, but then again, she had been surprising everyone quite a bit lately. Would she do so this time as well?

"Are you free for dinner?"

"I'm afraid I have some other business I have to attend to at the moment." She was thinking of the dead boy upstairs and his angry aunt who wielded the power of life and death. "Can she wait until tomorrow morning?"

"Morning? I suppose that would be al…" There was a rustling sound and then Sarah's voice suddenly appeared, filled with rage and terror.

"Vanessa, get over here right now!" she demanded, and the woman flinched just a bit at the desperation in those words.

"Calm down."

"Not until someone explains to me what the hell is going on around here! Why do my friends all end up dead? What happened to Cary and her boyfriend? Who was the man in the sunglasses and why was he at the farm the night Jacob died?"

This last question definitely surprised Vanessa. Apparently, the mental barrier that had kept the memories at bay hadn't been as strong as everyone had believed. The team from that night had agreed that Sarah's loss of memory was probably the best thing that could have happened to all of them. If the child hadn't truly forgotten that night, she was an even bigger target for more than just the Others.

With a weary sigh, Vanessa told the furious teen, "I promise I will answer as many of these questions as possible, but this is not the time. You are much too upset, and I have more pressing issues to deal with at the moment."

"What could be more important than this?" That voice, now thick with tears, was enough to melt even the coldest heart, but it didn't matter. She could not discuss this with the girl tonight. Not with so much else going on. This was a situation that required a great deal of tact and concentration, both things she would also need to deal with the Council. She could not split herself like that right now, especially since doing so would endanger all of their lives.

"I understand how upset you must be, but I *cannot* discuss this with you tonight. Just try to calm down and believe that what I am doing, I am doing to keep you safe."

"Safe from *what*?"

"I love you very much, Sarah, and I will gladly help you straighten out this mess, *but not tonight*."

There was a long pause broken by the occasional sniffle, and when Sarah spoke again she seemed to be much calmer. Fierce emotions still lingered just beneath the surface, but they did not break free.

"Alright," she agreed. "Tomorrow morning at eight."

"I'll see you then. And don't worry too much. You'll be safe tonight."

The girl started to say something, then sighed. "I guess I'll ask you about that tomorrow, too."

She could feel him lingering just behind her in the living

room as she placed the phone back in its cradle and it made her smile. Sarah would definitely be safe tonight because despite his minor injuries and battle-induced fatigue, he was going back out there to keep an eye on things.

"She's safe?" he asked stiffly.

"Yes, but she's terrified. And with good reason, wouldn't you agree?"

"I should get back. They could try again." She knew by the harshness that crept into his tone that he was already blaming himself for the death of the boy, and Sarah was a convenient way of shifting his focus to something else.

"Go," she sighed, turning to face him with a weary smile. "I'll take care of everything here tonight, and tomorrow morning we can tell her everything she needs to know."

He nodded, marching quickly upstairs to change his bloodstained clothes before he went back to work. Before he left, she stopped him long enough to give him a quick hug, which was all he would allow. Things were getting far too dangerous. For them to have made such a bold move as to attack in a crowded mall should have been unthinkable. And yet they had done just that, only proving that they would now stop at nothing to get what they wanted.

"Please be careful," she pleaded, and although her mind argued that he was needed elsewhere, her heart begged for him to stay.

"I'll be back in the morning."

The door closed and she had just enough time to wipe the tears from her eyes before the phone began to ring once again.

Chapter 35

Angela was gone less than twenty minutes after Sarah finished her phone conversation with Vanessa, leaving strict orders to lock the doors and stay inside. Sarah didn't need anyone to tell her that she might be in danger. That much was fairly obvious. Her insides had been twisted in knots ever since she'd spoken to Vanessa.

You'll be safe tonight.

How could she say something like that? How could she know that nothing bad was going to happen between now and eight o'clock tomorrow morning? So many unanswered questions swam around in her mind, and the more she tried to push them away and think of something else, the more questions she seemed to find. She tried watching television, but the pictures of her missing friends seemed to be on every channel. There were chores that needed to be done, like washing and drying dishes and folding laundry. That almost helped for a while, but when she started to open the door to take out the garbage, Angela's warning rang in her ears again.

With a sigh, she tossed the bag of trash into the corner of the kitchen beside the back door and trudged up to her room. If only she had some sort of idea why all of this was happening, she might be able to help the police find Cary. Why wouldn't anyone talk to her? Vanessa had said something about having more important things to take care of, but what could be more important than helping the missing teens? If she knew anything about the kidnapping and she didn't report it to the police, Vanessa could end up in prison herself. So why was she stalling?

"Because you were way too upset," she told herself, flopping down on her bed. "She didn't want to talk about it until you sounded a little less like a homicidal maniac."

Feeling the tears creeping in again, Sarah grabbed the remote control on her nightstand and turned on the CD player that sat on the shelf across the room. The song that immediately began to play brought a slight smile to her face. Anarchy in the U.K. by the Sex Pistols. How fitting. She began to hum along, and then a few moments later, she found herself singing at the top of her lungs. This exercise in silliness managed to ease the tension enough that by the end of the next song, Beethoven's Moonlight Sonata, her mind had begun to journey into the distant land of dreams. Finally, just before nine o'clock, Sarah fell into a deep slumber that lasted until just before the first rays of dawn touched the treetops outside her window. The same tree in which a silent figure crouched patiently, watching for any sign of trouble while she rested peacefully in her bed.

Chapter 36

Dragging her weary bones out of bed, Sarah made her way down the hall to the bathroom. She needed a shower before this nightmare of a day began, but she didn't bother to grab any clothing before leaving her room. Her bathrobe was hanging next to the toilet. That would be good enough. Besides, she was the only person in the house by the sounds of things.

She turned the handles until steaming hot water poured from the shower head, filling the room almost instantly with a thick steam that clung to every inch of every object in the room, including her. Slipping out of the clothing she'd forgotten to change out of the night before, Sarah stepped beneath the soothing heated droplets.

Just as she was reaching for the shampoo, there was a sound from somewhere on the other side of the shower door. The fog that now seemed too thick to breathe also made it impossible to see anything unless it was right in front of her. She shook her head and laughed at how ridiculous she was being. No one was in here, except maybe Amy who would simply be grabbing a hairbrush or giving her teeth a good scrubbing, and even that was unlikely at this hour.

"Calm down," she told herself. "Geez, one little scare at the mall and you turn into Angela, terrified to take a damn shower by yourself."

Even though she knew it was silly, she finished her

bathing quickly. No sense wasting time in here where she felt like she was suffocating. Besides, she was feeling a bit hungry. Not surprising since she hadn't eaten dinner last night. A quick flick of her wrist and the water stopped falling. Still amazed at her ridiculous behavior, she reached out and slid the door open.

And suddenly she was staring into the greenest eyes she had ever seen. The face that held these stunning objects was also quite impressive, with a strong jaw line and a smile that took her breath away. The crowning achievement of this masterpiece in flesh was the hair. Flames reached from the man's scalp down to just above his ears. The color was so amazing, like nothing she had ever seen before.

"Hello, Sarah," he whispered, extending a hand to help her out of the shower, and she took it willingly, her eyes fixed on his.

"Who are you?" she heard herself ask, but her voice was little more than a whisper of air passing through her open mouth.

"For now, all you need to know is that I am a friend. The rest will come later." He helped her step out of the shower, wrapping a towel around her naked body as he did so. And still, she couldn't take her eyes off him.

"How did you get in here? And why?"

"I wanted to see you for myself. You are every bit as lovely as I have been told." His flattery sent shivers all through her body, and although she had just met this strange man who had obviously broken into her home and watched her showering, somehow he seemed to belong here.

"How did you get in here?" she asked, some of her sense finally returning. It only lasted long enough for him to turn up that charming smile a few extra notches.

"What a practical question," he beamed as her legs began to feel like cooked spaghetti. "My sweet nothings usually draw the conversation in other directions."

"Sorry," she started, and then her brain spoke up once again. Who was this strange man and why was he watching her shower? Was he dangerous? Was he here to hurt her? Her defenses kicked in at last, and her tone became much more cold and sarcastic as she managed to pry her gaze from this magnificent creature. "I guess I don't get a lot of guests in the bathroom while I'm naked."

"It is I who should apologize. I suppose I was simply too eager. I let my curiosity get the best of me."

"Curiosity?" Now what was that old saying about curiosity and cats? Oh yeah. It's a killer. Good thing neither of them were felines.

"Some of my colleagues have been talking." His eyes began to drift over her, taking in every inch as he continued to explain. "They say you are quite a trouble maker."

"Me? What did I do?"

"Oh, nothing you need to worry about just yet." The tips of his fingers danced over the bare flesh of her arm, sending a shiver down her spine. "They also mentioned your beauty. I thought they were exaggerating. No creature could be as lovely as they described. Standing here before you, though, it seems their words did not do you justice."

"Liar," she whispered, her voice thick and strained.

"I never lie," he smiled, his eyes catching hers once again.

God, his eyes were so green. They reminded her of Vanessa's eyes, though where hers were soft and warm like summer grass, his were hard and cold. He held her gaze, captivating her with those mysterious emerald orbs. It took everything she had to convince herself that she needed to break away, though the idea made her stomach twist in knots.

"I should probably get dressed," she said, desperately trying to clear the fog that now seemed to be creeping into her mind.

"Yes, I must be going as well. Always something to do these days."

He started to walk away, and the panic in her voice when she called out to him was revolting.

"Will I be seeing you again soon?" She was practically begging now. How completely pathetic.

He stepped closer, reaching up to brush a few stray hairs from her face. Anticipation filled her as he slowly leaned down. He stopped just before their lips met, and she thought she might explode with eagerness.

"Very soon, Sarah." The words were a warm breeze against the soft skin of her mouth, and then he stood and turned to the door. Her heart was racing and her breathing had turned to short, eager gasps, only adding to the lightheadedness she felt. The man stepped out of the bathroom without a second glance at the trembling girl leaning weakly against the sink.

Chapter 37

Sarah awoke at four-twenty-seven the next morning with a start, nearly bolting out of bed before her eyes were completely open. Her pajamas were drenched in sweat and her breath came in short, panicked gasps. A nightmare. That was the only explanation for such behavior. But it was gone now. What could have frightened her so badly? An image of a man with copper hair and cold jade eyes flashed in her mind, but then it, too, vanished.

On trembling legs, she made her way to the bathroom to shower and get dressed. Her insides still twisted anxiously, but at least she knew that soon she would get some answers. As the warm water washed away the last traces of her dream, Sarah began to wonder about the fate of her friends. Had they been located yet? Were they safe at home right now? Or were they still missing, maybe even lying dead somewhere, waiting for someone to stumble upon their bodies? A vision of Cary lying motionless in the old barn, wearing a blue high school letter jacket and staring up at the crumbling loft above filled her head, and she had to choke back the tears that began to rise up.

At six, she had grown restless and could wait no longer. The house had become like a prison, its cream colored walls beginning to close in on her like some sort of funhouse attraction. Maybe a walk would help clear her head and prepare her for whatever was about to come. Instinct told her that leaving the house alone right now was probably a bad idea, but her sanity screamed that if she didn't get out of there soon, her mental health would be seriously compromised.

There was a pad of paper on the kitchen counter beside the phone for taking messages, and it was here that she left a note for whomever happened by. Probably Angela, since she was always the first out of bed, even in the summer when she worked the late shift at the supermarket and there was no school to worry about.

Went for a walk. Be back in a bit. No worries.

The back door was unlocked, which seemed a bit odd since she specifically remembered checking it before going to bed. Maybe Amy had taken the trash out last night. She hadn't been around for Angela's warning about the dangers of the outside world. Silently opening the door, Sarah left through the back, making sure she locked up as she went. She cut across the yard and through the neighbors' yards as well until she reached Maple Street which led straight to the park. Maybe the fresh air and the quiet of a hot summer morning would help clear out the cobwebs, so to speak. Just as long as she was home by eight. The news had predicted quite a nasty day with a significant rise in humidity as well as temperature. By evening, there were supposed to be a few thunderstorms, and hopefully that would cool things off a bit, but until then she wanted to be inside where the air conditioning could compensate for Mother Nature's faults. And besides, Vanessa would be waiting.

Sarah found the park completely empty, just as she'd hoped. The air, though already thick with moisture, was refreshing. She took a series of several slow, deep breaths, closing her eyes and welcoming the stillness. A few birds began to chirp and stir in the nearby trees as she strolled through the soft green grass. If she hadn't been wearing some of her favorite stockings, she might have slipped out of her boots and continued in her bare feet.

"Excuse me," an unfamiliar voice called from behind her, breaking the tranquility of the morning.

Her heart leaped up into her throat as she turned to see who it could be. It was a man, balding and scrawny, probably in his late forties or early fifties. He was wearing red running shorts and a white tank top that proclaimed him to be a member of the Early Risers, a group of older folks who came out here at the crack of dawn to jog and share the latest gossip from various local chains. He was smiling awkwardly as he approached, and she forced her muscles to relax. *Probably just wants to know what time it is*, she thought.

"I'm sorry, did I startle you?" he shook his head. "I suppose with everything that's going on right now I'd be a little jumpy, too."

"What?" she asked, clearly shocked by his words. How did he know what was happening to her? She'd never met this man before in her life.

"The missing kids," he replied. "You know, the police

still haven't found them. If someone could just walk into our mall, shoot up the place and then get away with a couple of teenagers, I don't think anyone is safe anymore. Wouldn't you agree?"

"Yeah, I guess so."

Just a friendly stranger trying to pass the time until his troop of joggers arrived, that was all. Yeah, right. If that was all he was, then why were there a dozen alarms going off inside her head all at once?

"Sorry. Once a gossip, always a gossip." He chuckled, and the sound sent a shiver down her spine. "I was wondering, do you have the time?"

"Uh, yeah, just let me check…" Reaching into her purse to pull out her cell phone, she tossed another nervous glance at the man's face. He was still smiling, but it seemed to be masking something else. Something unnatural.

As her eyes dropped down to the bag at her side, Sarah suddenly went from nervous to completely panicked, and those alarms that had been sounding since she'd first heard the man's voice were now screaming for her to run before it was too late. Trying desperately to pretend like nothing was wrong, she forced her eyes to continue on to their initial destination. But that wasn't as easy as it sounded, because they wanted to linger on their discovery.

"Are you feeling alright?" the man asked, and now there was a wicked sense of excitement radiating from him, as if he couldn't wait for something to happen. As if he couldn't wait to use the object that had magically appeared in his right hand.

"Yeah, I just didn't sleep very well last night," she lied. Could she outrun him if she had to? Maybe if she wasn't wearing these damned boots, but there was no way to take them off now without letting on that she knew what was about to happen. If only she'd given in to her initial instinct earlier and gone barefoot. "It's six-thirteen."

"Lovely," he replied, and she met his gaze once again, barely able to keep her eyes from drifting to the enormous knife with the serrated edge that would no doubt tear through her flesh in a matter of moments. And she was all alone with this psycho, so there was no hope of rescue. *Should have listened to Angela for once.*

"Well, I really should get going," she smiled, hoping that she could just walk away like nothing had happened and everything would be okay. Maybe she had just imagined the blade. Yes, that was it. Paranoia had taken control and now she was hallucinating. Nothing a few months in an institution couldn't clear up, right?

As she turned to walk away, all her fears were realized. The man grabbed her arm with his free hand, raising the knife with the other slowly, as if he were savoring every drop of fear radiating off of her in sickening waves. Their eyes met for just a moment, and she watched as his confidence began to falter. The corners of his mouth sagged just a bit, and the weapon trembled in his hand.

"I thought you would be more of a challenge," he laughed, his enthusiasm renewed as his gaze shifted to her neck. "The others spoke of you as being much more exciting."

"Let me go." Although this was intended to sound like an order, it came out more like a whine.

"Come with me, and I promise you won't be harmed." The look in his eyes offered a different promise, this one filled with agony in exchange for defiance.

A moment passed while she considered her options. Running would only end in pain or maybe death. Screaming would be useless, since there was no one here to help her. She could try to fight back, but in the end this man was much stronger than he appeared, as was evident in the painful grip he maintained around her bicep. Her only option, it seemed, was to travel to an unknown destination with the psycho killer.

"Lead the way," she almost sobbed, choking back the tears once again.

He seemed almost disappointed that she should give in so easily, but he did not attack. Instead, he began leading her farther into the park toward a grove of trees where she had once sat and mourned for the lives and the memories that were lost at the old farm. As they walked, she wondered just how much more of this insanity she would have to endure before it all ended. How it would end was clear. She was going to die. It was the events leading up to that inevitable demise that she was worried about.

"What are you going to do to me?" Her voice quivered, but she kept the tears back just a little longer.

"That depends."

"On what?"

"On you." His grip tightened and anger edged its way into his words. "I'm just a lowly messenger, so I don't have all the details, but I do know that the big players are interested in you. If you accept their proposal, you could go a long way."

"Big players?" Now she was slowing down, trying to stall in the hopes that someone might show up and help her. He didn't go for it.

"You'll see soon enough. Keep moving." Something sharp pressed into her right side, and there was the sensation of warm liquid trickling down her skin. Surprisingly, her only reaction was a small cringe, though her mind screamed that she should run or try to fight back or *something*. Preventing any of these natural reactions from actually taking place was one of the most difficult things she had ever done, but she pulled it off. Barely.

They were almost at the edge of the woods now. Once hidden by the trees, this man could do almost anything he wanted to her without being seen. There was a chance that other visitors might hear her if she began to scream, but there were ways of dealing with that. Like slicing open her throat.

The pressure on her arm suddenly disappeared as the

morning stillness was broken by a loud, breathy whistle. She turned her head to where the man had been standing, and saw him lying on the ground at her feet. A large chunk of the side of his forehead was now missing, including his right eye. And looming over him with a silenced pistol in each hand stood the man in black. He was still wearing the same shades that had hidden his eyes at the mall.

Shuffling sounds in the trees drew their focus to four more would-be assailants, all carrying weapons of some sort. The man in black seemed not at all surprised, but she was a wreck. Her legs shook violently, and once again she found herself regretting her choice of footwear. How had she gotten wrapped up in all this? Here she was, standing in the middle of what appeared to be a Wild West shoot-out, but why were they fighting? The answer was obvious. They were fighting over her. The real concern was why. What was so special about her? Again, more questions for Vanessa to answer, assuming she made it to the question and answer portion of the show.

In a series of lightning fast movements, the man in black dropped the two attackers on the left, a short blonde woman and an old man with a crooked nose who didn't look as though he should even be able to walk without assistance, let alone fight to the death with someone. He then proceeded to blow holes in the heads of the other two, taking out the woman on the far right first.

After it was all over, he rushed to the final victim, a

lovely young woman with shoulder length chestnut hair and ruby red lips untainted by cosmetics. The guns slid mechanically to their hiding place beneath his long black coat, and when his right hand emerged, it now held a blade that resembled the one which had punctured a hole between her ribs, although this one was about twice the size. Three quick chops and the woman's head was severed from her body. The man turned to her, moving with quick deliberate steps as he spoke.

"Cover your eyes," he ordered, but before she could react there was a blinding flash of light and then nothing at all.

Chapter 38

As Amy stepped back into the kitchen, moving to the sink beside her mother to wash her hands, the man made his move. He had been watching Angela from the top of the stairs, anxiously awaiting the young girl's return. Now they were all in position, the older woman within his reach and the younger far enough from the phone and both exits that he would have plenty of time to react in case of any possible escape attempts.

"So, do you think she's okay?" Amy asked her mother, and Angela smiled.

"Don't you worry about Sarah. She always has a few tricks up her sleeve."

As the woman began to take a step away from her daughter and the stairs, the crouching figure finally attacked. Grabbing the woman by her throat, he swung her around so that her back was pressed tightly against his chest. The blade he pulled from his belt was very similar to the one Sarah was seeing at that moment, though this lunatic was much younger and more handsome than the one in the park. When the cold metal touched his captive's neck, she let out a tiny yelp that made his pulse quicken. This was going to be more fun than he'd expected.

"Stay right where you are, and your mommy won't get hurt."

Oh, how he'd waited for this moment, planning every

second out in his head so methodically that he was prepared for anything. But to actually be here making history! To feel this woman's heart racing or hear her daughter begging for their lives. To know that in the end, all of his hard work had paid off, and now the entire world was going to know about what he had done here today. These were things that no one could prepare for.

"Adam?" the young one gasped, suddenly recognizing him from his old life. "But...we all thought you were dead!"

"Not dead," he grinned. "Reborn. And now, I have come to reclaim that which was taken from us eighteen years ago."

The woman stiffened in his arms as she heard these words, and a tingle of excitement raced through him. This one was going to fight. Maybe not yet, but soon. She was a mother, after all, and her child was being threatened.

"She isn't here," Angela growled, and he felt the anticipation growing inside of him until he thought he might burst. Any minute now.

"Of course she isn't. But you are. So, how can I be sure that our little cupcake finds those she doesn't know she lost? By making sure she finds the ones she knows are missing."

"You're kidnapping us?" the girl exclaimed, obviously shocked that anyone would do such a thing to someone like her. After all, she lived in a quiet little neighborhood that was a part of an even quieter little town, and nothing bad could ever happen here. Apparently she hadn't been watching the news recently.

"I would love for both of you beautiful ladies to take a little ride with me, but if you both leave, who will be left to tell The Child what happened?" The girl looked puzzled for a moment, and then understanding finally dawned on her face.

"You're going to kill one of us…" Her voice was thin and airy, as if she didn't have the strength to back it up. All the color had drained out of her face, and he was pretty sure she was going to black out.

"Hmm, perhaps. Or perhaps I'll leave another kind of message. One that some of her friends will recognize."

The man watched as Amy suddenly bolted into the living room, but that's as far as she got. Her mother's screams made her turn around, just as he'd planned. The blade was lodged deep in the woman's shoulder, a harmless wound that could surely be repaired by a gifted surgeon. The pain it inflicted, however, was much more interesting.

"I suggest you stick around and see what happens next," he called to the girl in the other room.

And fearfully, she did just that.

Chapter 39

The Girl hit the ground with a sickening thud, and for a moment the world stood still. She was dead. She had to be. Even he had felt the incredible pounding just behind his temples as the creature's energy had escaped and tried to find its way back to its master. She had been given a lot more power than most, leading him to believe that this attack had been planned for a very long time by some very serious enemies.

He'd overheard the one with the knife telling her that she had attracted the attention of some "big players," and now it wouldn't matter because she was dead. He had killed her, just like he had killed the boy and his father, and any number of others throughout the years.

A soft moan escaped The Girl's slightly parted lips. The air that had been trapped in his lungs for the past few moments finally escaped in a loud sigh of relief. So it wasn't quite as bad as he'd thought. She wasn't dead, but she was probably never going to regain consciousness. Rushing to her side, his focus immediately centered on the tiny trickle of blood flowing from her nose. Definitely some sort of hemorrhaging, and it was very likely there was nothing that could be done to reverse the damage. But then, just a second ago he had been certain she was dead. Maybe it wasn't such a silly idea to hope for the best this time. Optimism had never been his strong suit, but something about this girl made him want to believe that everything could still be okay.

Grabbing his cell phone from his coat pocket and putting the knife away, he couldn't help but notice how steady her breathing was. Her skirt had slipped up as she collapsed, revealing the tops of her stockings, and he gently tugged the material back down into its proper place. Things would be awkward enough from this point forward. No sense making her feel even more self-conscious at their first meeting.

Maybe positive thinking wasn't so hard after all. At least he was entertaining the idea that she might wake up eventually.

"Hey, man. What's up?" Thomas's voice sounded just as it always did, friendly and cool as if there wasn't a thing wrong in the world.

"I need a cleanup crew at Maple Park. Maybe a doc, too."

"For you or someone else?" No need to ask who that other might be. Thomas was fully aware of the events that had led up to this encounter, just as the rest of the locals were. Thomas also knew that the time to let The Girl in on their little secret was approaching.

"The Girl."

"Thought so. How many bodies?"

"Five. Make it quick. The joggers will be arriving soon."

"We'll be there in ten."

They were there in six. The van pulled up and two individuals, one man and one woman both dressed in police uniforms, began sealing off the entrance to the park. Thomas hoped out from behind the wheel, smiling cheerfully at the man still kneeling beside the unconscious girl. That smile began to falter a bit as he approached and started to get a closer look at the scene. Five bodies, just like he'd said, but by the looks of things they might have to add one more to the list of casualties.

"What happened?" Thomas asked, joining him on the ground.

"She didn't cover her eyes fast enough," and he was disgusted by the thickness of his voice. The other man placed a comforting hand on his shoulder.

"I'm so sorry," Thomas shook his head. "I guess I can call Vanessa and tell her not to worry about the doc."

"She's still alive."

The words seemed to shock Thomas even more than it had shocked him when he'd realized that she had survived what no other human could have. His lifelong companion sat for a moment in silence, watching The Girl's chest rise and fall in a steady, normal rhythm as though she were only taking a quick nap in the soft green grass.

"This is incredible," Thomas whispered. "I mean, no one has *ever* survived the flash without some sort of protection…"

"She was looking right at the body when it happened."

Thomas shook his head once again, still unable to believe that this story could be true. "You have to take her to the

Council. There's no way they can say she isn't the one. Not after this."

"Don't bet on it. And besides, she still has no idea what's going on. Vanessa was supposed to speak with her this morning…"

His words were interrupted by a bone chilling blast as an explosion rocked the entire neighborhood. The men instinctively drew their weapons and moved into a defensive position around The Girl. The concussive blast blew out all the windows in houses and cars for nearly half a mile. Dogs began howling in fear and pain, alarms pierced the otherwise peaceful morning air, and people began to drift out of their homes, their faces a mixture of confusion, anger, and horror as they surveyed the damage.

"What the hell was that?" Thomas might have been the joker of the group, but he knew when to get down to business. This was definitely not a time for foolishness. The team began fanning out, looking for the source of the explosion while the two men remained crouched beside The Girl.

Suddenly, she bolted up into a sitting position, sucking in a deep gasp. For a moment, no one moved. Her protectors wanted to be relieved. She was alive, after all. But the horrible vacant stare on her face told them they weren't out of the woods, yet. Then, she screamed. It was the most horrible, ear popping, blood curdling sound either man had ever heard, and both dropped their guns so that their hands were free to cover their ears. It didn't help. The sound seemed to come not only her mouth but from somewhere inside their heads as well.

Just as suddenly as it had begun, the wailing stopped. With ringing ears and watering eyes, the men regarded each other and then The Girl with an uncomfortable sense of puzzlement. Her eyes searched their faces frantically, recognizing them almost at once which seemed to frighten her all the more. Her voice shook as she spoke, and her words were dripping with fear.

"Please, don't hurt me," she begged, and Thomas reached forward to take her hand in his. She drew away instinctively at first, then gave in once she realized he meant her no harm.

"We won't hurt you."

The man's voice was soothing, and the other hunter found he was jealous of Thomas's ability to comfort. He also discovered he was jealous of The Girl's reaction to this man. Her face relaxed and then crumbled in despair as she threw her arms around Thomas's neck, bawling hysterically and shaking so violently he was afraid she might be having some sort of seizure. They were still locked in this unusual embrace when Vanessa pulled up a few moments later with her favorite doctor in tow.

As Vanessa and her companion arrived on the scene, Thomas began trying to pry The Girl's arms from around his neck, chuckling, "Get her off of me."

Vanessa stepped up and tried to help, but The Girl

refused to let go. After a few soft whispers and some gentle coaxing didn't work, the woman turned to the hunter for help.

"You try," Vanessa told him, stepping aside. Not entirely sure what it was she expected him to do, he moved forward and placed a gentle hand on The Girl's shoulder.

He touched The Girl, and the scar on his arm instantly felt as if it was on fire. His training kicked in as his hands immediately went to his pistols, pulling them from beneath his jacket. There was an instant to reflect on how often this action had been performed in the past hour before his thoughts quickly turned back to the task at hand. Somehow, he had to deal with this situation without hurting The Girl, though the odds of her still being alive if one of these things had taken her body were so small that he should not have hesitated.

She survived the flash, so maybe she can pull through this, too.

The doctor said something, but he was too focused on the situation to much care about anyone else's input, especially this man's ideas. The thing had Thomas, and if there was no other way, he would kill The Girl to keep the body count at a minimum.

"Let him go, or I'll put a few new holes in the back of your skull."

Something tickled at the back of his mind, like a pesky fly buzzing around that he couldn't quite manage to swat away. It distracted him long enough that his eyes involuntarily drifted to those of the creature standing in front of him, where they were caught in a trap that could only be escaped through death.

"Silly boy, put those away before someone gets hurt." The voice was The Girl's, but the words were accented with a hatred that could only come from one of the Others.

Vanessa suddenly stepped forward, trying to speak to The Girl who was probably gone by now. His peripheral vision caught sight of her just as she hit the ground, silently screaming in torment with her arms wrapped around her stomach.

"What did you do to her?" he demanded, and in those horrible eyes he watched organs being ripped to shreds by invisible hands. Wanting to scream with revulsion and anger but completely unable to do more than stare into those dark pits, he was struck with the realization that if he didn't end this now, they were all going to die here in the park.

And then he was free. The pistols sagged a bit as his gaze shifted to Vanessa, still lying on the ground and writhing in pain. Then, forcing himself to maintain control, he tossed a nervous glance at The Girl. Her face was contorted in a strange mixture of fear and determination as her gaze focused on some unseen object just in front of him. Finally, the muscles in that face began to relax, the eyes closed, and The Girl dropped to her hands and knees, gagging as if she were about to vomit.

"Okay," she choked. "I don't know what just happened to me, but somebody had better start explaining all of this, and I mean *now*."

Chapter 40

There was no smooth transition this time from sleeping to waking. One moment there was only darkness, and the next she was screaming, staring into familiar faces that seemed to always signal danger. The moment she realized the horrible shrieking that pierced the morning air was coming from her, she silenced the sound, grateful to be rid of it. The men sitting beside her seemed to share her relief.

"Please don't hurt me," she heard herself saying, but somehow it wasn't her at all. She wanted to question these men, find out who they were and why they kept popping up in her life, but the words would not form. There was something in her head that was blocking all attempts at communication, and it scared the hell out of her.

"We won't hurt you," the large man, Thomas, replied, and she watched as her arms suddenly wrapped around his thick neck. The other man, the one she had saved at the farm, regarded this scene with little interest at all, or at least that's what it looked like on the outside. From her place trapped deep inside her mind, she could feel the conflicting emotions of jealousy, anger, pity, and a strange sort of longing that pulsed from every inch of the man in black.

A car was pulling into the gravel parking area beside a familiar black van. It was Vanessa, and she had someone with her. He was an older gentleman with bits of white streaking his pale brown hair and carrying what appeared to be a gym bag. Frustrated and terrified, Sarah found herself wishing for a better view of the mysterious man.

Instantly, she was split in two, one piece moving along beside the old man as he approached while the other remained entangled in an emotional fit that was scaring the hell out of everyone nearby. The bag was definitely just an old gym bag, but incredibly, she found that even though it was zipped up tight, she could see what was inside. It looked like medical supplies of some kind, although nothing like you'd find in a normal first aid kit. There were hypodermic needles and syringes, vials of strange liquids, and all the materials needed to create an IV. These were the kinds of things you might find an EMT carrying, not some little old man. But then again, hadn't she just been attacked by some elderly joggers?

They arrived back at the scene, which was the only way to describe it, and the old man began trying to separate her from Thomas.

"Get her off me," the man laughed nervously, but the ball of panic growing in the pit of his stomach manifested as a swirling mass of red and black as she watched Vanessa trying to coax her into releasing the poor man. It was no use. Her arms were locked in place as though the muscles had forgotten how to relax.

"You try," Vanessa suggested to the man in black. He hesitated for a moment, then reached down with an awkward attempt at both comfort and tenderness. When his hand met her flesh, he recoiled immediately, drawing his weapons and pointing them directly at her head.

"What are you doing?" the old man cried, trying to knock the guns away. The man in black didn't budge.

"Let him go, or I'll put a few new holes in the back of your skull." His tone was flat but firm, and she watched in horror as her arms unwrapped themselves from the man's neck, turning to face the others with a malicious smile.

"Kill me and kill The Girl." Her voice was cold and distant, not her voice at all but rather that of something dark and slimy and wanting nothing more than to kill the man who believed himself to be in control of the situation.

Don't shoot! I'm over here!

She tried to scream these words, but found she could only watch as this twisted play wound its way into the final act. The man seemed to hesitate for a moment, glancing first at Vanessa and then at Thomas who was scurrying to his feet. He must not have found anything helpful in those faces, because when he turned his eyes back to her face, the part of her that had broken away could see the tension rolling off of his muscular frame.

Something. There must be something she could do. Focusing all of her attention on reuniting with her body, Sarah found herself transported to the tiny space between her body and the man with the guns. Neither one seemed to notice her.

"Silly boy," she heard herself saying, but there was no time to focus on that. She had to do something before she ended up dead. "Put those things away before someone gets hurt."

"Sarah," Vanessa cooed, taking a step forward. Sarah watched in horror as a bolt of jagged white light shot from her fingertips, hitting Vanessa's chest and stomach. That lovely porcelain face suddenly twisted in pain, and the woman dropped to her knees, holding her middle with shaking hands.

"What did you do to her?" the man demanded, but the face staring back at him only grinned wickedly.

Okay, so when one finds oneself possessed by some unknown entity, what does one do? Why didn't she pay more attention to those damned horror movies? The thought brought with it memories of Jacob. Sitting in Jacob's living room while his parents discussed the events of the day in the kitchen. Making dinner with Jacob's father as he cracked some string of really lame jokes. Making out with Jacob in the science lab after school when they were supposed to be studying. Waking in the dark with Jacob's dead body lying next to her. Gazing into the dying eyes of the man who stood before her now and somehow calling him back from the edge of death.

Something flashed in the back of her mind for just an instant, and then it was gone. A clue of some sort, but what had it been? Trying to track it down was useless. It had come and gone as quickly as one of Cary's boyfriends.

Cary. Was she okay? Sarah realized that she'd been so

wrapped up in her own business that she hadn't bothered to call and check up on Cary's parents to see how the search was going. If she made it out of this alive, that was the first thing she was going to do. These crazed killers seemed to be drawn to her like pyromaniacs to a bonfire, and so it must have been her fault that someone attacked the mall to begin with. Or maybe it was some sort of gang war between the old folks who walked the mall and the Early Risers and she just happened to get caught up in the middle of it. The woman whose head had been hacked off, however, didn't strike Sarah as the kind of person who would be found hanging out with either group.

Cover your eyes.

The eyes. That was it. Something about the eyes. Turning her attention to the familiar face that she should have only seen from this angle in a mirror, she finally found it. The hint she needed to fix this mess was right there in front of her. The eyes that should have been dark brown were glowing with some unnatural shade of crimson, as if they were filled with blood. Did the others see this? Probably not. Even if they did, they were so focused on ending the confrontation that it probably wasn't a big concern.

Something that felt a bit like a hand but more like a strong breeze started batting at her, trying to keep her away. Sarah realized that her body had been saying something, but it stopped short, never finishing the thought that had seemed so important to it just seconds before. Summoning every ounce of will in her being, she pushed forward until the force that had opposed her finally disappeared. There was a strange sort of sensation, almost like the feeling that comes with riding in a descending elevator, and then she was on her hands and knees, choking and shaking as though someone had just tried to strangle her to death.

"Okay," she gasped, tired of being left out of the loop and ready for some answers. "I don't know what just happened to me, but somebody had better start explaining all of this, and I mean *now*."

Chapter 41

"I'd say it's safe to put those away now," Vanessa sighed, swaying as she tried to stand. The man hesitated for a moment and then holstered his weapons.

"You're hurt," the man in black stated flatly, tossing a quick glance at the red-haired angel before bringing his focus back to the trembling girl on the ground before him.

"I'll live," the woman told him, but the look of misery stretched across her face said otherwise. The old man Sarah had noticed earlier seemed to be very aware of Vanessa's discomfort as well.

"Let me help you back to the car," the old man offered, leading the injured woman away from the rest of the group. She stopped him long enough to give one last order.

"Bring her to the house," she told the man in black. "We have much to discuss."

After she was gone, Thomas reached down and helped Sarah to her feet. The expression on his face was an odd blend consisting mostly of disbelief with a healthy dose of awe. Rather than being amused by what she saw, the girl's defenses immediately shot up, and as usual, her mouth was the primary weapon.

"What are you staring at?" she demanded. "Never had a girl's arms around you before?"

"Never one quite as amazing as you," he replied,

seeming to pull himself together once again.

"Yeah, well, I hope you enjoyed it because it's never going to happen again."

"I wouldn't be so sure of that. Besides, you were the one who didn't want to let go." And for once, Sarah seemed to be speechless.

"Enough," the man in black bellowed angrily. The stress of the morning must have finally gotten to him, though he recovered quickly from the tiny outburst. "We need to get out of here."

"Agreed," Thomas nodded as one of the other team members came running up to them. She seemed a bit winded, as if she'd just run a marathon.

"You need to see this," she panted, and Thomas tossed a nervous glance at the other man before dashing to the van. The rest of them followed quickly, piling into the vehicle as the scout gave Thomas directions. Very familiar directions.

The vehicle drove a few blocks, then took a sharp right and all within sat in shocked silence at the chaos before them. Smoke hid some of the damage, but it was clear that the explosion heard earlier had come from this region. Thomas slowed to a crawl, but even that soon became impossible due to the debris in the road. Pieces of wood, shingles, furniture and odd bits of cloth littered the street, but that wasn't the worst of it. The worst was the sound. Crackling flames made the hot morning air even more unbearable, but the sound of screams that sliced through the confusion made Sarah's blood run cold.

They stepped out of the van, the three strangers moving quickly towards the sounds. Sarah, however, did not follow. Her attention was focused on something else. Something lying on the nearby lawn of Mr. Arnold Hayes, a long time neighbor who had shared some of his favorite cookie recipes with her when she was a little girl. Now that neighbor was gone, probably with the others who had fled in the wake of this disaster, and his lovely lawn, which he took such pride in keeping weed free and emerald green, was littered with odds and ends from someone else's home.

The object that had drawn her attention was nothing very spectacular. She probably never would have seen it had they not stopped at exactly this spot. Now, stepping up onto the curb and into Mr. Hayes's yard, she suddenly felt the heavy smoke-filled air beginning to gather around her, suffocating her with its toxic moisture. Sarah dropped to her knees, running a hand over the cracked glass that protected the photo within the little gold frame. Her mother had taken the picture just before the two little girls had left to go trick-or-treating. Andy always hated Halloween, but the rest of the family loved it. Candy, costumes, and scary movies...what was there to hate?

She couldn't have been more than eight at the time the photo was taken, and that put Amy at right around five or six. The younger girl was wearing a white robe with a halo and feathered wings. Sarah was dressed as a vampire, with fake fangs and a black cape. She could remember very little of that night, but she did remember that Amy had been sick with chicken-pox just days before they were supposed to go out, and no one thought the poor dear was going to be up for so much walking. Somehow, though, Amy had found the energy and the sisters were still stalking through the neighborhood long after most of the other children had given up to begin taking inventory of their sugary riches.

With her mind locked in the past, she didn't notice the glass slice through her palm as she picked up the frame and slid the picture out. Nor did she realize she was moving again until a hand wrapped around her upper arm. When she finally looked up from her treasure, she saw the woman who had led them here. Her mouth was moving, but Sarah couldn't hear her. She was still lost in memories too happy to escape.

The woman pushed past her, running back to the place where the van sat, empty and waiting to be needed once again. Sarah began to wonder if maybe she was projecting, and then the cries of pain tore through the stillness once again, only this time they were much closer. Ripping herself from the tranquil memories of happier days, Sarah realized that she was standing at ground zero, and the home from which the blast had originated was the same home where she had returned on that cool October evening with her sack full of sweets.

The two men who seemed to have a much better grasp of what was going on appeared to be cutting something out of the tree that had served as an escape route from her bedroom window since she was nine. It took her a moment to get a good view of the object, but when she did her heart crumbled. That dangling, limp thing in the tree was Angela.

Dropping the photograph, she rushed to help them. Howls of pain echoed throughout the neighborhood as the man in black tried desperately to cut the electrical tape that was wrapped around the woman's wrists and a very thick tree branch, using the same utensil he had used to chop off another woman's head not even an hour ago. Thomas stood on the ground, lifting the pathetic creature in the hopes of easing some of the tension on both the tape and her arms. His body hid most of hers, but Sarah was pretty sure she was naked. Blood dripped from the tips of her toes, forming a dark red pool at the base of the old oak. And her face. Twisted and ghostly white, it was the face of a zombie in one of those old horror films that Jacob used to love so much.

The thought of Jacob brought a frightening image of his body lying in a casket. It was quickly replaced by the body of her mother as the lid of the coffin slammed closed, forever separating the girl and the woman who had put up with her outrageous behavior for the past eighteen years.

Sarah tried to help Thomas support the lifeless body, but the sight of all that blood was making her queasy. It was everywhere. All over her, all over Thomas, all over the ground, in her hair, on her hands… Would it ever wash off? Finally, there was a tearing sound from above and the woman's arms flopped down to her sides. By now, she was too weak to do much more than moan. The man in black dropped down beside them just as the other woman returned with a duffle bag and a blanket.

"I thought I told you to get her out of here," the man scolded the woman, although his eyes were distant and his words lacked any real force.

"I tried," the woman replied. "Do you think she'll be alright?"

"There's a lot of blood. If we can get her to a hospital in the next ten minutes, she might make it."

"She's gone," Sarah whispered, feeling the tears starting to gather as they had done so often in the last twenty-four hours. She had seen her mother's eyes, and there was nothing there. It was too late to save her, too late to call her back as she had done for the man standing beside her now.

"Not quite, but if she doesn't get help soon…" Thomas began. Sarah finally snapped, releasing the hurricane of anger and tension that had been building up inside of her since her trip to the mall.

"Don't you get it?" she screamed in a furious voice that was made more miserable by pain and fear. "My mother is dead! She's DEAD! No doctor or magician or goddamned miracle working faith healer is going to change that!"

Sirens were approaching. Someone must have

contacted the fire department or the police. Of course they had. This was the biggest disaster the community had ever seen. The first thing the refugees would have done once they were out of danger was call for help. The EMT's pulled up to the silent group still crowded around the dying woman. The man in black seemed to be lost in his own thoughts, and Thomas worked with his female partner in a desperate attempt to stop the bleeding from Angela's many wounds. Her torso was littered with cuts and gashes, as was her back, and a deep stab wound ran across both shoulders just above the collar bone.

"She'll be taken to the hospital," the man in black took her by the arm and led her away from the mutilated corpse-to-be. His face was calm, and so was his voice, but she sensed that he was fighting hard to maintain the cool exterior. "They have to try to save her as long as she still has a pulse."

"Then I should go with her. She shouldn't be alone. What if the person who did this comes back to finish the job?"

"She'll be dead before she gets to the hospital. You said so yourself."

Yes, she had said that. But she wasn't a doctor. How could she be so certain that there was no way to help her mother? She started to tell the man this, to say that she had just been upset and she didn't really *know* that Angela was going to die, but the man's face stopped her. For an instant, he lost control and the agony she saw was unmistakable. Whatever lack of experience she wanted to use as an excuse to hope, that look said he could counter it with his own painful memories.

"I still want to be there," she choked. "It's the least I can do for her."

The man considered this for a moment as Angela was placed on a stretcher and loaded into the emergency vehicle. Firefighters raced around frantically, surveying the scene for injured people and potentially dangerous situations. The community would be cleaning this up for months, and they may never be able to repair the psychological damage of such a direct attack on their sense of security.

"Alright, we'll go to the hospital. I can call Vanessa on the way."

"We?"

"I'm not letting you out of my sight until this mess is finally resolved. You go with me or you don't go."

Absolutely not used to being told what to do, especially by a strange man who didn't appear to be much older than her, Sarah's stubborn side emerged. Pulling her arm roughly away from this arrogant man and balling her hands into fists at her sides, she planted her feet firmly in a stance that screamed disobedience.

"I'm not going anywhere with you," she growled. "For all I know, you'll take me out to the middle of nowhere so you can rape and murder me!"

"Do I look like a murderer to you?"

"As a matter of fact, you do. I just watched you chop

some woman's head off with a knife, for Christ's sake! And if I did decide that you weren't going to torture me to death, I still wouldn't go anywhere with you."

"Really?"

"Yes, really. You may not have any heinous acts in mind at the moment, but you're still male and by the look of it, you're the dominant control-freak type. Guys like you see an opportunity to take advantage of a girl and they take it."

"You're not my type." His complete lack of interest stunned her into silence. "If you want to go, now would be best. Otherwise, I believe Vanessa is waiting for us."

For a moment, she only stood there, trying to decide what to do next. She could continue this argument, but it would get her nowhere and it might mean missing her last chance to say goodbye to her mother. Still, her bullheadedness refused to give in. A compromise was finally reached.

Rolling her eyes, she told him, "Fine, you can give me a ride to the hospital, but that's it. Once I'm safe and sound in the waiting room, we're done. You go your way and I take care of Angela. Deal?"

There was a long pause as he considered her offer. His face said he wasn't thrilled at the idea of leaving her alone, but she gave him her own defiant glare. She would not be bullied by this stranger, no matter how creepy he was.

Eventually, he gave a sharp nod and said, "Alright."

That was it. Just one word, but it was said with such a

feeling of contained frustration it almost made her smile. Victory, though small in this case, was usually a reason to celebrate. However, given the circumstances, she simply couldn't bring herself to gloat.

"We should hurry," she choked. "My mother won't last long."

Chapter 42

The trunk was suffocating. The smell of old motor oil, sweat, and blood mingled in her nose, the last of these odors radiating from her own quivering body as she tried to clear her head and think of a way to escape. It was no use. This was an old Cadillac with enough trunk space for a girl like her if she kept her legs pressed tightly against her chest. Unfortunately, it did not have a safety latch for an occasion such as this, a standard feature in most new cars. It didn't matter, though, because her hands and feet were bound behind her, making it nearly impossible to move at all. There seemed to be no hope of breaking free from this dark and overwhelming prison.

The car traveled for what seemed like hours, but it was probably closer to ten or fifteen minutes. Her thoughts kept drifting back to her mother dangling from that tree as the kidnapper stuffed her into this tiny space. The sounds of her mother's agonized screams still echoed in the prisoner's ears.

Why them? Why this family? Why Sarah? Adam had told them that her older sister was the cause of all this, but he hadn't told them why. Or maybe he had. She remembered something about how he was trying to recover what had been stolen from him. Maybe he was part of Sarah's biological family. Could the Cannons have been Sarah's real family? If he was related to Sarah, then maybe Sarah could talk some sense into him before he did something awful to her poor adopted sister.

Then again, this guy was obviously not acting reasonably, so logical arguments might not help much. Either way, waiting around for someone to come rescue her seemed like a very bad idea. There had to be a way out of here, and she was going to find it.

Before she could, though, the car slowed and finally stopped. When the engine stopped, her heart sped up. He was coming. Any minute now, he would pop the trunk and she might have a chance to break free. Groping around blindly, she searched for a weapon. Anything that could be used to defend herself or buy enough time for her to get away. In the movies, there was always something, like a screwdriver or a tire iron. But this was not a movie. The man's trunk was empty except for her cramped body.

Metal scraped against metal as the key slid into the lock. Things seemed to be happening in slow motion now, the key turning, the trunk lid slowly rising, blinding her with the day's brightness. A dark shadow loomed over her, blocking some of the brilliance from her bloodshot eyes.

"So, you survived the trip here," the figure chuckled. Strong hands reached in and grabbed her roughly under the arms. "I figured you would suffocate back there in this heat. You're tougher than I thought."

Adam dragged her out of the vehicle and up to a set of concrete stairs. She couldn't see exactly where they were because she was too busy wiggling and trying to fight off this crazed killer. He ended up pinning her to the ground on her back and nearly dislocating her shoulder in the process. Rolling his eyes, the kidnapper began pulling her along behind him as he marched up to the large glass doors at the top of the stairs. Finally, they reached their destination, though the distance to get there seemed to double in length as the stone scraped at her back and legs, tearing through her clothing and into her flesh.

A wave of relief washed over her when they entered the building and the rough surface beneath her was replaced with cool gray linoleum. The relief disappeared the moment she realized where they were.

"You seem to be having fun," another man's voice echoed throughout the silent entrance. It was a deep, silky voice that reminded her of a used car salesman pitching a great deal. "I trust that the woman was dealt with."

"Just like I planned it," her captor reassured the voice, dropping her battered body roughly onto the hard tiles.

She was able to twist around enough to see past the murderer for a clear look at the other person in the room. He was tall and very handsome, with hair the color of flames and eyes that sparkled like emeralds. This new man was dressed in a very expensive pinstriped suit, and he was positively beaming with delight as he tossed a wink down at the girl on the floor.

"I have other arrangements to make," the Suit said, stepping past Adam to hunker down beside the girl. The smell that radiated from him was a nauseating blend of cologne and used matches. He reached out and brushed a lock of damp, matted hair from her eyes. "Such a lovely little thing. But much too weak, I'm afraid. Use her as you can and then get rid of her."

He stood, straightening his jacket before exiting through the swinging glass doors. The other man took hold of her legs just above the ankles and began dragging her down the hall to another room, obviously pleased by his new gift.

The girl, bound and gagged and stinking of her own sweat and fear, could only hope that he would kill her quickly. But in the end, even that was too much to hope for.

Chapter 43

"She isn't answering." The muscles in his jaw tightened and began to twitch frantically as he sat down in the chair next to her.

They had been trying to reach Vanessa for hours now with zero luck. Angela was still alive, but only because the doctors had hooked her up to a roomful of machines that now performed all the functions her own body could not. The surgeon that Sarah had spoken to said no one expected her mother to survive much longer than a few hours this way, and definitely not past tomorrow evening. She had been waiting for Vanessa to arrive, to help her face the difficult challenge of saying goodbye to the woman who had raised her, but it seemed as if she would be facing this challenge alone after all.

"So much for that little deal of ours," she pouted. The idea of him leaving her here alone was absolutely nauseating now, considering the circumstances. Still, she tried to play tough guy and keep a straight face. What good would it do to give in to that voice inside just dying to scream and break down in a quivering heap?

"Where could she have gone?" The man shook his head, and she noticed him shift slightly in his seat. He was worried that someone had taken her, just like they had Cary. Or worse, that they might have done to Vanessa what they had done to Angela.

"She'll be alright. We just have to take this one step at a time. Vanessa is MIA, but so is Cary. I can tie up this loose end and then we'll go look for them."

"No." The finality of that statement hit her like an eighteen wheeler. They were dead already, and as far as he was concerned, going after any of the missing individuals would only get the search party killed.

"How can you just give up like that?"

"This is a trap. Those cuts on your mother's body were clues. If we follow those clues, we will die."

"Or maybe we'll find Vanessa and Cary alive, rescue them, catch the bad guys, and be the heroes. Did you ever think of that?"

"Vanessa wasn't taken."

"You don't know that. And even if that's true, Cary still needs help. We have to find her before it's too late."

"It's already too late." As he got angrier, she could feel him growing more still, more distant and cold. It only enraged her that much more.

"Stop saying that!" she spat through clenched teeth. If he kept pushing, she was going to start screaming, and once she lost that last thread of control, she might never be able to stop. He broke first, though.

"This is not a fairy tale!" he snapped, clearly tired of the conversation. "Things do not always end in happily ever after. Your friend is dead, and there is nothing we can do about it."

The man's phone rang and he jumped up, running outside to answer it. If he wouldn't help her, then she would find a way to save the people she cared about without him. Besides, she had no idea who this guy was. From what she had seen and heard so far, he seemed to know Vanessa, and his concern for the woman's safety implied that he cared about her, but other than that what did she really know?

Elijah. His name is Elijah.

She knew that he had been worth saving that night at the barn, and that she had risked her own life to give him his. Wasn't that all she really needed to know?

With a sigh, Sarah brushed the hair back from her face and pulled out her own phone. Amy needed to know what was going on here. She was probably at her boyfriend Seth's house. Giving bad news over the phone didn't sound like much fun, but she needed someone here with her. The idea of facing what was left of her mother alone made the tears inch that much closer to the surface, but she choked them back with the idea that her sister would arrive soon. Amy would be there by her side when the world crumbled. She had to be.

Chapter 44

Outside, the man in black paced anxiously in front of the emergency room entrance, his cell phone pressed tightly to his ear.

"I know you're worried, and I would have called sooner, but…"

"But you were too busy with Raymond to bother." There was no inflection in his voice, no hint at the rage that was trying to break free. Still, she sensed his anger. She always did. And to his surprise, she responded with all the fury he refused to show.

"How dare you!" Vanessa spat into his ear. "I would never do something like that to you, and for you to even think for one instant that I would makes me seriously question your judgment!"

"My judgment is just fine, but I think maybe yours is a little off." It was getting harder with every word to control his temper. Soon, this would escalate into a full-scale verbal war and things would be said that neither party could take back. Things were too crazy right now to lose one of his closest allies.

"Dr. Trubal took me to see a few friends of his because that thing that was inside of Sarah managed to tear open a few organs before it left. If we hadn't arrived when we did, I most certainly wouldn't be talking to you right now."

Speechless, the man stopped moving and allowed his

mind to fully digest this new information. Vanessa had been injured when she left the park, they all had seen that. But there had been no external manifestations of her wounds, and so he had just assumed she was fine. If Trubal hadn't been there, he would have just sent her home to rest.

"Are you still there?" Now her anger had faded into annoyance. Soon, it would disappear altogether.

"But everything is okay now, right?" There was a sigh of relief from the woman who had come so close to death just under an hour ago.

"I suppose it will be soon enough. Ray said that it was bad, but they're pretty sure the bleeding has stopped. With a little rest, I should be back to my old self in a few weeks." Choosing to ignore the fact that she called her savior Ray rather than Dr. Trubal as she normally did, he focused his attention on the tiny tremble in her voice as she said it.

"Can I speak with him?" There was a slight hesitation, which told him that she was hiding something from him. This suspicion was further reinforced by her response to his request.

"Oh, I don't think that will be necessary," she chuckled, but the uneasy sound was all the confirmation he needed.

"Put him on the phone. Now."

A moment later, Raymond Trubal was on the phone asking, "How are things going on your end?"

"Peachy. How bad is it?"

The sound of the weary doctor's sigh made his stomach

clench. Such a sound could only mean very bad news. When next he heard the doctor's voice, it was thick with unshed tears.

"We've done as much as we can here, but the odds of her surviving much more than a few days are pretty slim. Every time we stop the bleeding in one place, something else breaks open. In short, she's bleeding to death, and there's nothing we do can stop it."

"Take her home." The doctor was clearly shocked at first by this idea, protesting immediately.

"Moving her will only make the problem worse. She has to stay here."

"She's going to die either way. The least we can do is make her comfortable, and the best place for that is at home."

"I just…I can't…" Then, with another heavy sigh, the doctor caved. "I'll see to it she's taken home right away. Will you be there when she arrives?"

"I have some things to take care of here, but I'll be there as soon as possible. Would you stay with her until then?"

The doctor was once again stunned into silence by this request, eventually agreeing just before handing the phone off to Vanessa.

"So now you know."

"Yeah."

How had this happened? How had he failed to protect so many people so many times? Maybe this was the wrong career path for him. Something a little less dangerous might be a welcome change for him. Something where he didn't have to carry around an arsenal and go for days without sleeping or eating. Something where he didn't have to worry about becoming emotionally attached to others for fear that they might end up dying slow, agonizing deaths. Unfortunately, this was a career where quitting was not an option. The only people who lived to retirement age were members of the Council, and even their life spans were significantly shorter than most.

"…taking all of this?" His attention wandered back to the voice of the woman lying in a hospital bed on the other side of town.

"Sorry, what?"

"I asked how Sarah was taking all of this. She must be out of her mind trying to sort everything out."

"Right now she's focused on Angela. The docs say she'll be gone by morning."

"Oh, the poor dear! She must be so upset! And Amy…"

"Amy is missing."

"Missing?"

"She wasn't at the house. Thomas swept the area twice, but there was no sign of her."

"Does Sarah know?"

"Not yet," he answered flatly. "I'm not the greatest at delivering bad news."

"She's going to figure it out soon," Vanessa told him in that familiar motherly tone. It would have been almost comforting if his mind wasn't plagued by her approaching death. "Do you have any idea where she might be?"

"Yes," he answered curtly. His slight change in tone was all the hint she needed.

With a sigh, Vanessa asked, "How on earth did it all go so wrong so quickly?"

There was a long thoughtful silence when he thought he might have lost the signal, and then Vanessa spoke again in her serious I'm-giving-orders tone that always meant trouble. "Elijah, listen to me very carefully. Sarah is going to need someone she can trust, and I can't be there. With Amy, Angela, and Cary gone, that leaves one person."

"I'm probably the last person on Earth you should be asking to help comfort her right now."

"It doesn't matter. If she doesn't have someone to talk to, she'll go find someone. And we both know who, or rather what, that will be."

"I suppose you're right. Maybe I could call Thomas."

"Thomas doesn't have a clue what's really going on here, and you can bet that will be one of her first questions once things begin to settle." She was right, of course. This was a perfect opportunity for the Others to accomplish their primary objective.

"Fine," he agreed, rubbing absently at the back of his neck with his free hand. "I should go. The sooner things are settled here, the sooner we can talk in person."

Refusing to let his last goodbye to this woman be said over the phone, he ended the call and put the tiny bit of technology back in his coat pocket. The air was still thick with moisture, but storm clouds had begun to form off in the distance. It would be best if they could get back to Vanessa's before the rain hit.

Then again, would rushing back to the dying Vanessa really make a difference? If Trubal had taken her to his doctor friends, it would be twenty to thirty minutes just driving back to her home. Add to that the fact that moving her would take longer than usual given her delicate state and suddenly, there was time for The Girl to say her goodbyes to Angela. Besides, fighting The Girl about staying at the hospital for any length of time would only waste precious moments when he could be with Vanessa, saying his own goodbyes.

As he turned to go back inside, he noticed a very attractive young blonde woman stepping out of a flashy red sports car. She was wearing a matching strapless red dress that hugged every curve of her body, leaving nothing to the imagination. While her face was attractive, it was also a bit overdone. He preferred a more natural look, and besides, blondes didn't do much for him anyway. Still, something about her had caught his attention, and it was best to trust his instincts when it came to suspicious characters.

His fears were confirmed as he suddenly realized why she looked so familiar. She had climbed out of the passenger side, but now the driver was slowly emerging. Not quite able to believe what he was seeing, he stood motionless just beside the sliding glass doors. The driver was an older gentleman, wearing khaki pants and a red button down shirt that matched the woman's dress. His hair had been chemically altered to add highlights since the graduation, but it was the same old Andy.

"I really think we should have brought flowers or something. You know, to look more sincere." His words seemed to annoy the woman, who shook her head in disgust as he met her at the rear of the vehicle.

"She's practically dead already," the woman sneered. "Why pay good money for something she's never going to see?"

"Yeah, but if we're trying to play nice, shouldn't we do something as like a…a peace offering?"

"You saw her reaction to you at the graduation ceremony," the woman rolled her eyes. "Do you really think a few flowers will fix that?"

"You're probably right," Andy shrugged. "So, how would you go about this?"

"Just toss some jewelry at her. No woman could ever resist that kind of bribery."

Clearly, neither of them knew The Girl at all. Just the presence of this man in Angela's hospital room would be enough to infuriate her. The fact that he'd brought his girlfriend along for the ride would only add fuel to the already uncontrollable fire. He needed to get her out of this place before all hell could break lose.

    The couple stopped long enough for Andy to lock up the car and activate the alarm using his handy keychain remote. The man in black took this opportunity to slip inside the building unnoticed by either. Sarah would be furious when she saw him, and with good reason. The trick would be to get her out of the hospital before she realized he was here.

Chapter 45

She stepped into the room and was greeted with the sounds of the life support machines. The one that monitored the patient's heart let out a soft beep every few seconds, while the machine that was doing the work of lungs too mangled to function gave a long, slow hiss as it pumped air in and out through the tube running down her mother's throat. Other gadgets surrounded the bed as well, but she wasn't sure of their purpose. Probably it was best she remained ignorant in this area. If she truly knew how little the woman's body was capable of, it might make this seem a bit too real. At the moment, she felt as if this was all just one big nightmare from which she should be waking any moment.

There were no chairs or other pieces of furniture on which to sit, and the edge of the bed was surrounded by the terrible beeping, hissing machines that seemed to be taunting her. *Where were you,* they wheezed. *Where were you when your mother needed you? She told you not to leave the house, but you didn't listen. Now look at what's happened. Your mother is dying and your sister is gone and it's all your fault.*

"My fault," she whispered, squeezing through a tiny gap in the sea of equipment. "I should never have left."

"And what would you have done if you'd been there?" The deep, toneless voice startled her and she slammed an elbow into one of the gadgets that looked like it might be in charge of the bags of fluid dripping down into her mother's veins. The man in black stood in the doorway, lingering as if he wasn't quite sure he wanted to cross the threshold of this death room.

"What do you want?" she snapped, immediately regretting the bite in those words. The man seemed unimpressed by her rudeness.

"I told you I'm not going to let you out of my sight until the situation is dealt with."

"Why?" And now the questions came. There were a million of them floating around in her head, but they all seemed to boil down to this one simple word.

"Because you need me," he replied, and she knew somewhere deep inside that it was true. She needed someone to yell at, to interrogate, to trust. With Vanessa gone and her mother dying, who else was there?

"You hardly know me," she argued.

"I know more than you think." So much sorrow in those dark chocolate eyes. Maybe he really did understand. Maybe this mysterious man who seemed an omen of evil really did know how she was feeling as she stood in that cramped, sterile cage, surrounded by the cacophony of approaching death.

The man stepped into the room, offering his hand to the frightened girl, and she took it gratefully. Though she still knew almost nothing about him, and he did always seem to pop up when there was trouble, he also seemed to be one of the few people in her life that hadn't lied to her. Throughout this entire, miserable day that had been filled with nothing but misfortune for a whole lot of people, only he had been willing to lay it all out on the line for her. True, he had aimed two loaded pistols at her head back in the park, but then again, he had been the only person who sensed that something was wrong in that situation, and his actions had probably saved the lives of a lot of other people as well. And he had hesitated even though it was clear that he should not have wasted a moment in deciding what to do. He should have killed her.

    For the first time, she seemed to truly see this man. He was tall, though not as tall as his companion from the park. The dark, heavy clothing disguised his frame, making him seem lean and without any curves, though she doubted this was the case. Based on his clean cut, freshly shaved appearance, she was guessing military, and military men liked to stay in shape, especially if they were gearing up for battle. Besides, the way he'd dealt with those creeps at the park was all the proof she needed of his physical prowess.

    His eyes, though…There was such heartache in those eyes. Such wisdom and regret. Most people spent a lifetime racking up that kind of pain, but he seemed to have done it in just a couple of decades.

    As she studied his forlorn face, something silver and gleaming caught her eye. A delicate chain dangled from his neck, and on it hung two wedding bands. One was clearly a man's ring, though rather than the typical gold, it was made of something less yellow. Silver, maybe. Beside it was a daintier matching ring with several small diamonds embedded in it. They were simple, yet elegant, and completely captivating. Where had they come from? Who did they belong to before he found them? Had he taken them from someone? Were they a symbol of his own lost love? The possibilities were maddening.

Before she could bring up the enthralling bobble, though, he spoke up.

"We need to go," he said softly, though his words remained flat and emotionless.

"I can't leave her. Someone should be here for her when she…" When she dies. That's what she had meant to say, but the last word got caught in her throat. He glanced at the bed, then the door, and then his eyes fell on her face.

"I know how much she meant to you, but there's nothing that can be done for her now. There are other problems that must be dealt with, and quickly."

"That's right, dear. Run along and play with your new friends."

Both Sarah and the man in black turned their shocked faces to the woman lying in the hospital bed. She was sitting up, grinning hideously at them with the tube that had been shoved down her throat just moments ago now held tightly in her hand. The whites of her eyes had turned dark red, and tears of the same color oozed slowly down her cheeks. Sarah's grip on the man's hand tightened as the thing that looked almost nothing like her mother now stretched out its other hand and beckoned to the girl.

"Don't you want to give your dear old mom a kiss?" it cackled, causing the skin on its lips to crack open and bleed which only added to the hideousness of the scene.

"It's time to go," the man coaxed her gently, tugging on her arm. But she could not move. Her feet were stuck right where they were, as though the soles had been coated with superglue.

"Dear little Sarah," the monster wheezed as more blood began to drip from its nose and mouth. "If only you had listened to me. If only you had stayed home like a good little girl, none of this would have happened. How does it feel to know you killed your own mother?"

"Don't listen to it," the man whispered, and the creature shot an angry glance his way.

"Perhaps you should ask your friend here. He knows all about murdering parents. Isn't that right, Elijah?"

"What is she talking about?" Sarah asked, sounding as if she'd just woken up from a long afternoon nap.

"It's a trick," the man answered quickly, refusing to look at the creature on the bed. "Please, you have to trust me."

"Yes, trust this strange man who tried to kill you at the park today."

Hearing her own thoughts and fears coming from that horrible mouth was almost more than she could bear. The sheets were now stained crimson, and the monster's skin was beginning to burst open in other places as well. Deep gashes ran along its cheek bones. A series of horrible gory cracks raced across its forehead. And beneath the hospital robe, every cut that had been stitched by desperate surgeons was breaking free. Soon, the guts of this stolen body would be lying on the bed for all to see.

"She does not belong to you!" the man finally blurted out. His grip on her hand remained firm, but he took a step towards the creature on the bed this time instead of trying to drag her away. She tried to pull him back, but he stood his ground, barely noticing her efforts.

"I think our little Sarah will come around, once she discovers the truth about you and your organization." There was a sound that reminded her of a champagne cork being popped, and the front of the creature's robe was soaked in a variety of fluids, most of them very unpleasant in both sight and smell.

"She will not become one of you."

The sound of these two beings arguing over her future triggered something inside of Sarah's head. Something stronger than either of them could have anticipated. Something only headstrong teenage girls like Sarah possessed. In an instant, her feet were free to move again, and they did so with a fierce determination that caused the creature's smile to drop down into a sneer. She moved forward with every intention of beating some answers out of the thing that had disguised itself in her mother's body, but the man maintained his hold on her hand, preventing her from getting too close.

"I think it's about time someone started making sense around here." Alternating waves of anger and fear rolled through her body, and the monster shrank back much like a dog that's been kicked shies away from an approaching boot. "Let's start with answering a few questions. Who are you and where is Cary?"

"That pathetic creature is not your friend, just as this woman was not your mother."

"Enough with the question dodging! Tell me something useful!"

"Of course, dear," and now its voice was a deep gurgling sound as if it were trying to speak while gargling a mouthful of dish soap. "I'll tell you everything you want to know. But not now. This body will not last much longer, and it would be best if we could be alone for our little discussion. Hunters tend to be easily excited."

Hunters? What was that supposed to mean? It was clearly referring to the man standing just behind her, but any deeper meaning was lost on her. She started to speak up and voice her confusion when suddenly all of the alarms on the machines began to sound in a deafening chorus of bells and chirps that blotted out any thoughts that tried to emerge. The man gave her arm a sharp tug, pulling her tight against his body and pressing her face into his chest. At the same time, he pulled an arm up to shield his own eyes from the bright flash that ended up knocking them both sprawling across the floor. The man did not lose his grip on her, though, and she landed on top of him, still cradled in his arms.

For a moment, they laid there in silence. There was time for Sarah to notice how strong this man was, and how absolutely perfect he smelled. No cologne, no strong aftershave, just the smell of some softly scented soap. Then she noticed that he hadn't moved. Neither had she, though. Could he be laying here thinking about the same things she had been? Pressed tight against his chest, Sarah could feel his heart beating steadily and the soft in and out motion of his chest as he breathed. She realized she was holding her breath and let it all out in one large gust of air only after his eyes slowly began to drift open.

"You alright?" he asked, not pushing her away but clearly distracted in his attempt to survey the entire room for possible dangers.

"Fine," she answered breathlessly.

Slowly, Sarah managed to pull herself up to her feet and off of the man lying beneath her. The man refused to take her hand when she offered it, but she simply shrugged it off. Maybe he was a bit too focused on keeping them both alive to worry about being polite.

"So, time to go?" He nodded a quick reply, and they crept out into the hall where they were nearly run over by a team of doctors and nurses on their way to Angela's room. *Must have finally realized there was a problem*, she thought bitterly.

They managed to push past the mob and make it to the stairs just as the elevator doors were opening. By the time Andy and the blonde stepped into the hall, arguing about where they were going to eat dinner, Sarah and her protector were halfway to the lobby on the first floor.

Chapter 46

"Alright," Andy shrugged nervously, "so the hospital didn't quite go as planned."

"Damn right it didn't!" Jessica planted her perfectly manicured hands on expertly sculpted hips and spat, "You were supposed to talk her into joining the club, Andy."

"Well, what was I supposed to do? She took off before we could get to her!"

"You are such an idiot!"

"Children!" Adam barked, startling the two bickering baboons into silence. "The problem is not that she left the hospital before you. The problem is that we have no idea where she has gone or with whom she is traveling."

"Where could she go? Her house is gone, her mom is gone, her sister is gone, Cary is gone. Who's left?"

Sadly, the mongoloid had a point. He had destroyed every tie she had to this place. There was nothing left for her except Them. So where was she?

"Keep racking your tiny brains until you come up with an answer," Adam told them, giving Andy a condescending pat on the shoulder. Then, grabbing his coat, he told them, "I await your call."

"Where are you going?" Jessica demanded, and he grinned wickedly.

"I'm going to go ask Amy for some advice."

"Whoa," Andy began to protest, but his argument was interrupted.

"Relax," the boy reassured the nervous father. "I'm not going to hurt her. I'm just going to ask her a few questions.'

"And if she doesn't give you answers?"

"She will." Without another word, Adam marched out the door to the car waiting at the curb. Very soon, the Child would be Theirs, and then things would really start to get interesting.

Chapter 47

Raymond Trubal was waiting for them at the front door in his wrinkled dress shirt and gray tweed pants. There were a few small blood stains on those pants, leading his thoughts in directions he could not allow. Now was not the time for dwelling on things he could not change or things he should have done differently. The Girl had questions that must be answered before it was too late.

"Thank God you're here," the man in the doorway said, his voice quivering with exhaustion. "I wasn't sure you'd make it in time."

"Where is she?" His voice was flat, and although he knew it would make her proud to know that even now his training was second nature, it still felt wrong to act as if there was nothing wrong when Vanessa was inside dying.

"In her room. The trip here was hell, and I'm not sure how much longer before…"

He pushed past the old man, The Girl following close behind. They marched quickly upstairs to Vanessa's bedroom, the only sound to announce their approach being The Girl's big clomping boots. When he pushed open the door, he was met with a wave of sweet cinnamon, and tears threatened to rise up. Swallowing a few times seemed to force them back down where they would wait for a better time. He lingered in the doorway as The Girl entered the room ahead of him, rushing to the dying woman's side the moment she saw those sunken cheeks and dark ringed eyes.

"What's wrong?" The Girl demanded, looking to Vanessa first and then turning to him. A frail, ghostly hand reached out to the confused face, stroking her cheek with almost motherly affection.

"I'm dying, Sarah." The sound of those words, spoken so matter-of-factly, tore at his heart. He turned from this emotional scene, trying to keep his own grief secret even from himself. She wouldn't allow it, though. "I want you both to hear what I have to say before I go, so get over here."

After a slight hesitation in which he actually considered just running back down the stairs and out the door, he crept over to the bed, standing just behind The Girl. Vanessa smiled gently at them, seeming very pleased with herself.

"Your father always said I would have made the perfect drill sergeant." Her face twisted in pain for a moment, and then she took a deep breath and continued.

"Sarah, I have a lot to tell you, and I'm getting weaker by the moment, so please listen carefully. No interruptions, understand?" The Girl nodded, tears streaming down her cheeks as she sat on the edge of the bed. "Good. Let's start with your parents.

"Your mother and I grew up together in Montana. Her family wasn't wealthy by any means, but they did own a small farm which she inherited after her parents died. No brothers or sisters, just her left to run the place. I lived just down the road about a quarter of a mile, and we used to get together every Friday night for a girl's night. Nothing too spectacular, just sitting around watching old movies and eating popcorn or chocolate or whatever happened to tickle our fancy.

"Anyway, I showed up one Friday, I think it must have been nearly October, and she told me she wasn't really feeling up to seeing anyone. After some serious coaxing, she finally let me in and I managed to pry a rather ugly story out of her about how some man had showed up at her door a few days earlier, forced his way into the house, and raped her. The poor girl was covered in bruises and cuts, so I didn't doubt her story. I tried to convince her to go to the police, but she seemed dead set against the idea. So, I decided that her living out there all alone wasn't safe, and I packed my things, moved out of my parents' house, and started helping Abigail take care of the farm.

"About six weeks later, Abby found out she was pregnant. Her first instinct was to go to the local women's clinic and get rid of the baby, but I convinced her to keep it, at least until it was born. Then, if she wanted to give it up for adoption, fine. She agreed, and in June she gave birth to a beautiful baby girl whom she named Sarah Grace Kallie.

"Abby loved that little girl. Spoiled her rotten, some might say, but then again, I was just as guilty in that respect. We had a blast for the next eleven months, just a happy family on a beautiful farm. You used to love the ducks. We would spend hours on the edge of the pond watching them and feeding them breadcrumbs. And then They came.

"One night, we were all sound asleep and suddenly the baby woke up screaming as if she was absolutely terrified of something. Abby and I had just enough time to make our way down the stairs before the trucks pulled up. There must have been somewhere between ten and fifteen people dressed in black with masks that covered their faces, and when they broke into the house, there was nowhere for us to go. They had the place surrounded.

"Abby grabbed one of the baby's stuffed animals, wrapped it in a blanket, and led us all upstairs. She pushed us into a closet and ran back down to meet the intruders. When she bolted out the back door and into the fields, they followed, giving the baby and me a chance to get to my beat up old pickup and just barely escape. I remember hearing a lot of gunfire, and Abby's screams, and that's all. I never went back to that place. I was too afraid someone might be waiting there for me, and once I discovered what I was up against, I knew I'd made the right decision.

"I arrived in Wisconsin three weeks later, broke and exhausted with a hungry baby and a truck whose engine had finally given out. A lovely couple happened to be passing by and noticed us along the side of the road. They offered us a ride and a place to stay for a few days, which was nothing short of a miracle as far as I was concerned. They told me about how they were trying to adopt but there was a two year waitlist for anything other than troubled teens. I gave the baby up to them, knowing that she'd be better off with this loving family than with a jobless, homeless girl barely considered an adult in the eyes of the law.

"I met Elijah's father, Michael, while I was waitressing at the Old Blue Diner. Eventually, I moved in here. Once I had become an indispensable member of the household and Michael knew he could trust me, he told me what it was that kept him so busy all the time.

"There are things in this world that most people never see. Dark, ugly things that must be stopped from growing too powerful and taking over our world. Michael worked with the people who are trying to stop these dark forces, what we typically call the Others. There are different ways of halting the activities of the Others, one of which is very direct, as you saw Elijah do today in the park. The man downstairs is a doctor who specializes in research that is trying to discover how some of their poisons work and how to combat the physical damage they cause to our people. Michael was a scholar, and his specialty was studying human myths about these creatures to find useful methods for defeating them.

"In his research, Michael discovered an ancient prophecy dating back nearly two thousand years. A Nubian holy man was apparently shown a vision of the future that drove him mad, but before it did, he was able to write down what he saw.

The trouble is, anyone who tries to decode this document ends up suffering from the same madness. Michael managed to translate enough, though, that a handful of bells went off inside my head. I believe it was talking about you, Sarah. It mentions a child who will be sent to end the reign of evil on Earth. It also specifically mentions that the child will be born in the center of a new land, and that she will carry the mark of light."

He watched The Girl's hand drop to her stomach, the place where a single white dot about the size of a grain of rice marked an otherwise flawless complexion. Despite her many attempts at tanning, and even her handful of attempts to cover it with makeup, the mark always managed to shine through like a bright beacon, drawing the attention of anyone who saw it. Needless to say, The Girl rarely left that portion of her body exposed.

Vanessa nodded, again stiffening as another spasm rocked through her withering body. "I have kept an eye on you as best I could since this discovery. You were still just a toddler then, and I didn't think it would be wise to rip you away from yet another family just because of a few coincidences. You were happy. Things seemed safe enough. It wasn't until the Others suddenly took an interest in you as well that our suspicions were confirmed, and by then you were almost sixteen years old." Her voice was weakening, and her eyelids had begun to droop. Time was nearly up.

"So, you think I'm some big hero who's going to save

the world, huh?" The Girl sniffed, wiping at her tear streaked face. "And all this time I thought you liked me for my charming personality."

Vanessa managed a weak smile. "I love you, Sarah. Since before you were born, in fact. I realize that losing yet another loved one is going to be difficult, for both of you, but you must trust that all of this has happened for a reason. You must be strong for each other, and you must trust each other. Elijah knows as much as I do about all of this, so if you're smart, you'll stick with him. He won't let you down. And as for you," she turned to him, her eyes swimming with pain as she spoke, "take care of this girl. She doesn't have the training you have, but she will be a valuable ally if you just let her help. Understand?"

He nodded, feeling one renegade tear escape down his cheek and land on his mud-caked boot. Vanessa returned the nod, relaxing a bit as she did. He couldn't take much more of this. If he had to stand here and watch her die…

The Girl's head suddenly spun around, her eyes meeting his. Strangely, those eyes were full of hope, not fear or sorrow. Something about that made him feel a little better about this situation. Maybe she had another ace up her sleeve.

"Vanessa, I think you're right," The Girl said excitedly, jumping up off the bed. She placed one hand on the dying woman's abdomen, eliciting a cry of pain, and the other she rested on the woman's forehead. "All of this has happened for a reason. I never would have believed such a crazy story a few days ago, but now I think I know what I have to do."

Vanessa struggled to meet the intense gaze of The Girl, but when she did something extraordinary happened. The woman's face went slack and he watched as her body began to change. The bloated mess that had been her abdomen slowly shrank as pallid skin became a flush pink once again. Vanessa's cheeks lost that sunken in look, turning bright and rosy. At the same time, the pain he had seen in her eyes was amplified a hundred fold, and a horrifying sound began to issue from the woman's mouth. It almost sounded as if she were trying to scream underwater.

The Girl collapsed onto the floor, and Vanessa began trembling like an autumn leaf in the breeze. As soon as The Girl hit the carpet, nature released its fury outside, unleashing a torrent of rain and shooting bright bursts of lightning across the blackened sky. The doctor came racing up to see what was happening, surely thinking the end had come. Instead, he found a perfectly healthy, albeit exhausted, Vanessa sitting up in bed, too shocked to speak.

"What happened?" the doctor asked. He waited for the deafening crash of thunder outside to die down before answering.

"She just saved Vanessa's life," the hunter told him. Scooping The Girl up into his arms as if she weighed nothing at all, he left the stunned couple to sort out the details while he put their savior to bed in his room.

Chapter 48

So dark. And cold. Her tiny body trembled as she tried to press farther into the corner of the cramped cell that was now her home. Time had ceased to exist here in the shadows, so it was impossible to tell how long she had been here, huddled away from the bars and the drafts that blew between them. The crazy man had brought her here and locked her in this cage. At first, her biggest concern was that he might be considering rape. He'd done a lot of awful things in the short time since he'd appeared in her mother's kitchen. Such a heinous act would not have surprised her at all. But instead, he had simply left her in the dark room where she was certain she could hear the sounds of something skulking around just on the other side of the metal poles that could not keep out the cold.

No blankets, no bed, no way to keep warm, but she didn't think it was cold enough to worry about hypothermia. Still, her hands and feet were numb, making any escape attempts even more ridiculous. There had been no warning that anything like this might happen when she awoke that terrible morning, so she was still dressed in just the shorts and tank top she'd slept in the night before. But if she caught pneumonia in here, she would become much too weak to even consider trying to run. He seemed to have thought of everything.

A harsh creaking sound startled her out of her thoughts, and a bright sliver of light greeted her aching eyes. The crazy man had beaten her around a bit in the struggle to shove her into this cell, and one eye was beginning to swell. Still, she could see the brilliance growing until it became a large radiant rectangle. It was so bright, it almost hurt to look at it. And standing in the middle of this beautiful light was a shadowy figure. It had something in its hands, but her eyes refused to focus enough for her to see what it was. Feelings of hope started to blossom deep within. Rescued at last. A smile began to form on her lips as she tried to stand. The grin dropped off her face, though, the moment she heard the figure speak.

"Hungry?" It was him. He was back, and in his hands he carried a tray of food.

As he approached, she noticed his skin was even paler than it had been when he'd brought her here. In fact, he looked like a walking corpse now. Whatever had twisted his mind and convinced him to do these things was now twisting his body to match.

"Please let me go," she begged once again. It hadn't worked the other dozen times she'd tried, but at the moment there really wasn't much else.

"Eat up." Nothing fancy, just some lumpy oatmeal and a Styrofoam cup of water. He slipped the tray through a small opening at the bottom of the bars just big enough for the bowl. The cup he handed to her through one of the vertical spaces between the cold steel rods. "Your sister will be here soon. We wouldn't want her to think that we mistreated her poor little

Amy, would we?"

"Adam," she begged, but he shook his head and smiled wickedly.

"You know," he said softly, pacing slowly around the metal bars that held her captive, "things would go so much faster if we just knew where The Child was hiding. You could be out of here by morning."

He was baiting her. The thing that had once been a friend was now trying to talk her into giving up her sister for a chance at freedom. Ridiculous, right?

"How should I know where she is?" Amy mumbled, leaning miserably against the cold metal. "I've been trapped in here with you, remember?"

Adam's face twisted in rage, and she honestly thought he was going to kill her in that moment. So much hate and anger seemed to be locked behind those big, blue eyes. If he unleashed that fury on her, then escape would suddenly go from unlikely to impossible.

Amy took a step back, trying to put as much distance as possible between her and the lunatic, but it didn't seem to matter. His eyes were burning a hole in her brain, searing away all intelligent thought and leaving only pain in its place. She tumbled to her knees, barely aware of the cold, hard concrete as it scraped away flesh. With her hands on her head, she closed her eyes and screamed.

"Adam!"

That deep, commanding voice shattered the boy's concentration, and the pain was instantly gone. It was like someone had flipped a switch in her brain. Sobbing and even more terrified than she'd been before, Amy scurried over to the corner of her cell, pressing her back to the only solid wall available. Turning her attention to the door once again, the hysterical girl found the salesman with the bright red hair storming towards them, and she couldn't stop herself. Panic took hold as furious green eyes locked on the boy outside her cage, and Amy began to scream once again.

"Look what you have done!" the man barked, and Adam cringed. "If Sarah comes here and discovers that you have broken her sister…"

"I'm sorry," the boy pleaded, tears in his eyes. "I was trying to find out where The Child is staying, and I just got a little carried away."

"No harm may come to this girl!"

Turning from the boy, the man shook his head. Those horrible green eyes fell on a new target, and Amy stopped screaming in the hopes that he would lose interest. Maybe if she was completely silent, he would forget she was there and those eyes would go back to blazing through whatever soul Adam had left. Anything to make him stop staring at her.

"Amy, dear," the man smiled, and some of the fear she'd felt just a moment ago began to melt away.

He wasn't going to hurt her. He wanted to help her. Of

course he did. She was Sarah's sister, after all. This strange man was only trying to help Sarah discover the truth and reunite with her family. Amy suddenly realized that they had taken her prisoner because they needed to keep her safe. With all of the kidnappings and death that seemed to follow Sarah around, these men were desperate to make sure both girls remained alive and together, no matter what.

"There's a good girl," the man cooed, and Amy couldn't help but smile. "Why don't you get some rest while Adam and I have a little chat?"

She was pretty tired. Curling up on the floor, she barely even noticed how cold or uncomfortable she was as he eyes slowly slid shut. The last thing she heard before she finally drifted into a deep slumber was the man's voice commanding something to follow him. At first, she thought he was talking to Adam, but then she heard a horrible scraping sound that would haunt her dreams for the rest of her life, and she shuddered as she felt something large pass through the room. The door closed, and then, there was only darkness.

Chapter 49

She was standing beside the swings at the park where the morning had suddenly taken a turn for the worse, and she wasn't alone. The angel with the magnificent red hair was standing beside her, shaking his head.

"You shouldn't have done that," he lectured, and there was a sense of fierce rage hidden deep within those words. "You've left yourself weak and vulnerable. That man you call your friend could do any number of terrible things to you while you recover."

"She was dying."

"Good riddance!" With a sigh, he dropped his head and rubbed his temples in frustration. "Sarah, I know you think you can trust these people, but they are not your friends. They think they know what's going on, but they have no idea what you are or what you will become."

"And you do?" These words which would have been spoken in anger with anyone else had lost their sting in this place. Instead, they seemed to be a soft plea for help from the handsome stranger.

"Yes, I do." His hands wrapped around hers and she felt that same kind of anticipation she had felt the last time he'd touched her. It was just a dream, but it felt so real when his skin met hers.

"Then tell me." She stepped closer to the mysterious

man, but he shifted his grip from her hands to her shoulders, preventing her from moving any farther.

"Not now," he shook his head. "There isn't enough time. Besides, I want to make sure I get to meet you in person." A wicked little grin lit up his face, and she felt her own mouth doing the same.

"I can't wait," she told him with a playful wink. "So, when will this meeting take place?"

"Patience, dear. First, you must get rid of these horrible people you've been spending your time with. There is no place for them in our world."

"What exactly do you have against them?"

"It's nothing personal, dear. They are simply misinformed, and I am afraid their ignorance may put your life at risk." She wanted to believe him, to trust this lovely man with all her heart, but something about the tone he used made her doubt his sincerity. Emerald eyes stared coldly into her soul, almost amused as she questioned his motives.

"But they saved my life," she argued with a nervous laugh. "They've saved me more than once."

"Sarah, please try to understand. The boy is a hunter. He will do whatever he is ordered to do. And that woman…"

"Vanessa," she interrupted, growing more frustrated with each condescending word.

Did he really think she was so stupid and naive? Did he honestly think she would just blindly follow a stranger, especially in a ridiculously impossible situation like this, without a good reason? She had known Vanessa her entire life, and while she still wasn't quite over the whole adoption secret thing, she trusted that everything the woman did was in the best interest of the people that mattered. Who was this guy to imply anything else?

"Yes, of course," he sighed, bowing his head for just a moment. At first, she thought her reaction had angered him in some way. Her mouth did have a tendency to cause trouble. When he looked up, though, his eyes sparkled with amusement. "Vanessa, then."

"What part of this is funny to you?" she demanded. "You stand there, lecturing me about how desperate things are and how the people I'm with are incompetent jerks that could care less what happens to me, and now you're making fun of me? At least Vanessa and Elijah take this whole thing seriously. And the take me seriously, too."

"Now, Sarah," he soothed, trying hard to hide the laughter bubbling up inside. He came very close to somber, though there was still a hint of that patronizing tone in his words. "I know what they've told you, about how the situation is life and death, but it simply isn't the case. No one wants to kill you. No one would dare."

"Why not?"

"Again," he sighed, pulling her close, "this is not a discussion we need to have just yet. For now, just know that you are safe. Amy and Cary are still alive, and will be for at least another day. There is no need to rush."

"Wait, Amy? She's not with her boyfriend?" Her stomach sank as she realized she'd been so caught up at the hospital and then with Vanessa, the idea of her sister being in any kind of danger had never even crossed her mind.

"She was with Angela when they were attacked. The poor child is being held prisoner. She's bait."

"Bait?"

"Do you mean to tell me this topic has yet to come up with your beloved Vanessa?" There it was again. His attitude was really pushing her buttons.

"Can the sarcasm and tell me where she is," she spat, pushing him away roughly. He just shook his head and chuckled.

"As you wish," he shrugged. Placing the palm of his hand against her cheek, he whispered, "I do love a girl who knows what she wants."

Pain tore through her head, forcing her eyes closed in an effort to keep them from popping out of their sockets. When she looked up again, the man was gone and so was the park. Instead, she was surrounded in darkness. It was so cold here. She could feel the hard concrete floor beneath her and the chill from the walls pressing against her back and shoulders. Her head ached, she felt her right eye swelling shut, and her extremities were growing numb as the seconds ticked by.

But that wasn't the worst of it. Somewhere in that

darkness, she could hear a soft scraping sound. It was awful, like fingernails on a chalkboard, and it seemed to come and go in a very familiar pattern. A chill ran up her spine as she realized what it sounded like. It had the same rhythm of an animal pacing in a cage at the zoo. Tigers moved with that same slow, deliberate pace, back and forth as they watched from behind the bars of their prisons. Waiting, watching, dreaming of a day when nothing stood between those razor sharp claws and the people who had trapped the beasts in the first place.

Beside her lay a bowl of uneaten oatmeal, much too lumpy and cold for anyone who wasn't starving to look twice at. An empty white foam cup lay on the floor beside it. And somewhere next to her, she could hear the sounds of sobbing.

Chapter 50

"How is she?" Vanessa asked, stepping silently into the room.

"Still asleep." She had been asleep all night and half of today. And he had been here, watching over her the entire time, afraid to sleep in case her condition suddenly changed. Silly, since there was nothing any of them could do if something did happen to her. She was on her own, and that made him nervous. It wouldn't be impossible for the Others to get to her in such a weakened state. They were notorious for popping up in people's dreams.

"We could have left her in my room." Vanessa sat at the foot of the bed, her gentle green eyes watching somberly as The Girl's chest slowly rose and fell.

"It's fine," he answered shortly. Truthfully, he was relieved to have her here. At least he knew she was close, and he didn't have to worry about trying to keep his existence a secret as he fought to protect her from the monsters.

"So, still no word from the Council," Vanessa sighed. "What are they waiting for? They know she's with us. Why don't they just call us in?"

"They'll call," he replied, though the idea was far from reassuring.

She gave a soft chuckle and said, "Maybe they're waiting for fuel prices to come back down before they all try to fly in for a meeting. The news says things are getting pretty nasty in the Middle East again. Probably another war, more inflation, politicians with crazy ideas getting the rest of us into trouble."

"At least you don't have to worry about me going off to war."

Shifting the weight of those eyes to him, she smiled sadly and said, 'You're already there."

"Vanessa..." he began the age old argument on whether or not he should really be doing any of this, but she shook her head. Taking a deep breath, she forced the tears back.

"She's been out for a while," she changed the subject. "Do you think she's okay?"

"She's fine." He didn't really know that, but his gut told him it was true. Instinct hadn't led him astray yet, and hopefully, this would not be an exception.

"Well, I'm sure she'll be awake soon. In the meantime, why don't you get some rest? You've been up for almost three days and you're starting to doze off anyway."

"What about her?" Never once during this conversation had his gaze left the sleeping girl until now. Turning his tired, bloodshot eyes to the woman who had been on the brink of the abyss just hours ago, it was almost impossible to imagine her as anything but the vibrant lovely young lady before him. "I can't leave her alone."

"I'll sit with her for a while. You need to sleep."

"But the doctor said..."

"Raymond means well, but he doesn't know any more about what happened than the rest of us. I feel fine. Now go."

He hesitated a moment longer, but in the end, she was right. Trying to go much longer without sleep would be putting all of their lives in danger. A fresh eye and a clear mind would be necessary to combat the things that would be coming for them soon. And a good dose of luck couldn't hurt either.

Dragging himself from his perch at the edge of the bed, he crept out to the hall and down the stairs. Too tired to make it all the way to his room in the basement, he flopped down on the couch instead. His eyes closed and in a few seconds he was sound asleep.

Chapter 51

When she finally pried open her puffy raccoon eyes, it was almost six in the evening. The sun was getting ready to set, and the rest of the world was performing its evening ritual before turning in for the night. At this rate, she was never going to get back onto a normal sleeping schedule.

Clearing her throat, she managed a weak chuckle which startled the woman sitting in a wooden chair beside the door. Vanessa. Relief washed over her as the woman approached the bed. At least that was alright. Now, to find Amy. Her dream returned for a moment, and it was so real she actually thought she was still sitting in the cold room. Brushing that world away, she managed to push herself up onto her elbows.

"Feeling better?" Sarah smiled, and Vanessa returned the gesture with a sigh of relief.

"Much," she nodded, her smile growing until it stretched almost the entire width of her face. "And you?"

"Oh, I'm swell, thanks. One question, though."

"What's that?"

"When do we eat around here? I don't mean to be picky, but starving the kid who saved your life seems a bit rude."

Vanessa laughed, wrapping her arms around the still weary girl in a grateful embrace. Sarah managed to stand on shaking legs with a little help from her friend, and they found their way down the stairs in no time. When they reached the first floor living room, Sarah had finally regained most of her balance and was walking just fine on her own. Both ladies shook their heads at the sight of the man in black, passed out on the sofa in a very deep sleep. Vanessa pressed a finger to her lips as they slipped silently past him and into the kitchen.

"He's been asleep for maybe six hours," Vanessa whispered once they were safely out of earshot. "I'm sure the smell of food will wake him, since he probably hasn't eaten since I fed him breakfast two days ago. Poor dear. It's been almost as long since he's slept, though."

"What was he doing all that time?"

"Keeping an eye on you, of course. Since his father died six years ago, Elijah has kept you safe.'"

"You mean he's been following me?" She wasn't sure if she should be grateful for everything he had done for her or outraged at the idea of someone stalking her. "For six years I've had someone tagging along behind me like some creepy stalker?"

"Actually, longer than that. Like I said, Elijah took over the job when his father died. We've been keeping a close watch on you since you started preschool. It's only been recently that we had to call in some extra help, and let me assure you, Elijah wasn't too fond of the idea that your life was in someone else's hands. Even if it was just for a few hours a day."

Stunned into silence, Sarah seated herself at the table with a rough thud. Fourteen years. They had been trailing her for fourteen years. How had she missed it? Easy. They were good at what they did, and she wasn't looking for them. Any of them. But if they had been following her, then wasn't it reasonable to assume that whatever they were trying to protect her from had been doing the same?

"I can't believe any of this is actually happening. It just seems like some kind of bad dream." Her voice was weak and cracked frequently, but she wasn't going to cry. She couldn't cry. There were no more tears left in her.

"I know this is difficult," Vanessa cooed, placing gentle hands on her shoulders.

"No, I don't think you fully appreciate the situation." The panic edging its way into her words was more frightening than anything that had happened recently. Losing control now might mean a complete breakdown, and then what would happen to her sister? Still, she couldn't shake the feeling of sinking into a deep, dark pit of nothing.

"Let's recap, shall we?" she sneered. "First, my friends disappear because some nuts show up at the mall and kidnap them. Then, I get attacked by crazed joggers at the park, and the next thing I know I'm having some sort of New Age, hippie, out of body experience. Next, I discover that my house has been blown to bits, my sister is missing, and someone decided to turn my mother into a modern art sculpture. When I get to the hospital, the doctors tell me my mother is going to die, so I go in to say goodbye and find out that my body wasn't the only one with an unwanted guest. And then we come back here where you're in the process of dying as well, you tell me this insane story about how I'm supposed to save the world, and I end up saving you for practice. Now, you tell me, how am I supposed to believe that any of this is real?"

"It has been an awful lot for two days, hasn't it?" The woman eased herself down into the chair next to Sarah, taking the girl's hands in hers. "We will get through this, I promise. Everything is moving so quickly now, and I want you to be as prepared as possible when the time comes for you to do whatever it is you're meant to do. It won't be easy, but at least try to remember that your sacrifices will lead to the salvation of billions of others. And Elijah and I will do our best to be here for you for as long as we can."

"Yeah, well, Captain Friendly in there is probably the last person you want on Sarah watch right now. If he does his robot impression one more time…"

"Elijah may not seem like the kind of guy you're used to hanging out with, but he really does have your best interests at heart. And once you get past the tough guy act, he's a very sweet young man."

Sarah laughed. "So, if I keep working at it, I might be able to chip away that icy exterior in say, a decade or so?"

"Something like that," Vanessa smiled and patted her hands. In one graceful motion, the woman stood and opened the refrigerator, beginning the work that they had come here to do. "How does a ham and cheese omelet sound?"

"Like heaven."

And the woman began preparing the meal while Sarah silently reviewed the facts as she knew them. Her mother had lived in Montana on a farm. Her father was a rapist. She had not been given up willingly by her birth parents, but rather by Vanessa who had been a close, personal friend of her mother's. Vanessa and her employer, Michael, had been watching over her since she was three, and when he was old enough, the man in black had joined the stalker club as well. There was some sort of ancient prophecy that seemed to point to her as the planet's only hope in the fight against some strange, scary critters called The Others. Her adopted mother was dead. Her adopted father was an abusive jerk. Her sister and her best friend were missing. And there was some mysterious man with breathtaking red hair and gorgeous green eyes that kept coming to her in dreams, promising to tell her the truth just as soon as she left the only people who seemed to be helping her at the moment.

How much more could possibly go wrong?

Chapter 52

The smell of food woke him rather abruptly from a very sound sleep which dreams had not been able to penetrate. Crawling off of the couch, he found that most of his body had grown stiff and sore over the past few hours. Not really surprising, considering he had spent the night before perched on the edge of his own bed while The Girl slept, and the night before that he had watched her sleeping in her room from the tree just outside her window. And of course, there had been fighting. Nothing dramatic, just a few really nasty ones whose flashes had been extremely strong.

Stiff legs carried him out to the kitchen, stretching and trying to regain some of his normal limberness. Vanessa was just placing a steaming plate of food in front of The Girl, who was seated at the old oak table. Fully expecting some witty greeting from either female as he dropped down into the chair opposite The Girl, the thoughtful silence that followed instead was unnerving. The Girl devoured her food ravenously, but her mind seemed to be miles away. It only made sense that she should be sorting through the crazy mess that was her life now. Such a dramatic change from high school graduate to target of a world-wide organization as well as the supernatural monsters it was trying to stop.

Vanessa sat a plate in front of him as well, and he hardly took time to taste whatever it was he was shoveling into his mouth. The woman shook her head as she walked away. By then, he had half the plate cleared.

"I swear I could feed you dog food and you'd never know the difference," she sighed, but her eyes were distracted. She kept glancing over at the phone, as if she were waiting for it to ring with a strange sort of anticipation. It dawned on him as he tossed the last bit of food into his mouth.

"Still nothing?" The Council should have made contact by now. The moment he showed himself to The Girl in the park, it had become impossible to stall the meeting any longer. The entire clean-up crew that arrived had seen her, and she had seen several of them, including Thomas.

"Doesn't matter," she replied, filling the sink to wash the dishes. "We can't put it off any longer. She has to go to them."

"You are aware that *she* can hear everything you're saying, right?" The Girl's attention finally drifted back to the conversation taking place in the kitchen.

"Yes, we are." Vanessa's eyes never left the sink. "There are some people you need to meet before things go much farther. Now is the perfect time. If we wait too long, things could start to get a bit chaotic, and trying to meet with the Council will be hard enough while they aren't distracted by other events."

"The Council?"

"The Council is our governing body. They set forth the

rules by which we live, give orders when necessary, and generally take care of the legal and political aspects of our world." Still, Vanessa wouldn't look at the frightened girl gnawing fiercely at her fingernails. It was a sure sign that she was really upset, and although it was a terrible habit, he would never say anything to The Girl about it. Not now, at least. No reason to focus on such trivial details when the big picture was so terribly overwhelming.

"So why do I have to meet them?"

Sorry, kid, but there's no escaping this one.

"They need to know if they can trust you. Paranoia has always been their greatest defense, I'm afraid."

"What if I'm not what you think I am, Vanessa? Then what?"

She had cut right to the heart of the issue, as usual. What did any of this matter if she turned out to be a decoy, put in place by the other side to distract them from the real Child of the Prophecy? The thought had occurred to him a few times, but to dwell on such ideas would only lead to madness. The Girl obviously had some sort of superhuman powers, but where they came from was anyone's guess. The fact that she had never actually used these powers until recently, after the Others had taken an interest in her, could be seen as proof that she had been given her powers by one of the bad guys to distract their only opposition.

"I don't think we really have to worry about that right now," Vanessa smiled nervously, glancing back at The Girl just for a moment in an effort to comfort without revealing her own fear. It was not successful in either aspect.

"What about Amy? And Cary? Are we going to go look for them?"

Once again, she knew more than he thought she did. Her sister had been missing since the explosion. Maybe she'd put the pieces together, realizing that Amy never stayed away that long. She should have called or something by now. Or maybe there were other factors at work here. Could the two girls be connected in a way that didn't require a phone for communication?

"Sarah, now is not the time for this discussion," Vanessa sighed, placing the last of the dishes in the drying rack.

"So we should wait until we know they're dead before we discuss it?" The Girl's own fear showed through, but it was edged with anger. Never a good sign with this teenage girl whose rage usually led to acts of great stupidity.

"It's a trap. They want you to come after the girls because then they don't have to come after you." Vanessa was trying to remain calm, but it was becoming obvious that her own frustration was mixing with exhaustion in a dangerous combination. "I know you care about them both very much, but we cannot allow ourselves to take the bait."

"So that's all they are to you, then. Bait."

The Girl slammed her chair back, knocking it to the ground as she assumed her most menacing pose. He stepped between the feuding females, determined to keep the peace even if that meant tying one or both of them to these lovely wooden chairs until the situation was resolved. And by the looks of things, that might not be much of an exaggeration. Vanessa had turned to face her would-be attacker, and now they were locked in a battle of wills, waiting to see which would back down first. He had seen Vanessa angry, though not often, and he knew that behind that loving, cool exterior burned the heart of a warrior. Still, if the fire in The Girl's eyes was any indication of her own passion, he was willing to bet that Vanessa would be the one to cry uncle first.

"We are going to help them," The Girl growled from deep in her throat, and it reminded him of someone else he had met once. The memory was so strong, he could almost smell the stench of the rotting bug carcasses in the hot desert sun as he and Thomas stood facing the two young fugitives, engaged in a very similar form of negotiations. That girl had been headstrong and determined to survive as well, but in the end, her life had ended just like a million others.

"You are being completely unreasonable!" Vanessa's patience finally vanished and she took a step towards The Girl. He managed to restrain her, but she wasn't really the problem.

The Girl was moving in as well, looking as if she meant to kill this woman who had done so much for her since before she was born. Spinning around, he caught the furious teen by the shoulders and was surprised at her strength. For such a fragile looking girl she certainly was powerful. Her anger was deflected for a moment and redirected at him.

"Let me go." Her words were like needles digging into his brain. Refusing to be intimidated, he held tight.

"Sarah, that is enough!" Vanessa shouted, and he could hear the fear in her voice. She felt it, too, but she had no idea what it was. He, though, had felt this kind of tingling anticipation before, gnawing at his mind and pressing upon him until he thought his head might implode.

"Tell him to take his hands off of me, now!" As The Girl's voice rose, so did the energy in the room. It was exactly the kind of thing that happened just before one of the Others unleashed all the powers of hell.

"Calm down and I will." The first words he had spoken since things had gotten out of hand, they seemed somewhat absurd. It didn't take a genius to figure out that this thin, frail looking girl could probably hurt him in ways he couldn't even imagine, but maybe she was too upset to see that she had the advantage. If not, he was in for a serious stomping.

There was a tense moment when he thought she might try to fight, and then her shoulders slumped as all the strength suddenly left her. If it hadn't been for his grip on her shoulders, she would have crumpled to the ground in a heap of defeat. Instead, he led her to the couch in the living room and let her collapse onto a softer surface. Vanessa followed, her arms wrapped around her chest as if she had caught a chill.

"What's happening to me?" The Girl mumbled more to herself than either of the individuals now sitting beside her. "What's happening to my life?"

"It's been a very difficult forty-eight hours, and I think we're all still a little shaken up by the recent tragedies. At this point, the best thing we can do is put all of this behind us and deal with the problems we face right now." Vanessa brushed a lock of hair from The Girl's face, but there was no response. The vacant look in her eyes was enough to tell him that she had reached her limit for now, and trying to force her to think about her situation any further would be fruitless.

"Come on," he said, gently guiding The Girl back onto her feet. Vanessa gave him a quick glare as her silent way of demanding that he explain himself, but he ignored it. There had been enough arguing for one night.

He took her to his room, helping her slide off those big, uncomfortable looking boots. Most of the work fell to him, as she was still much too dazed to even realize what was happening around her. In his closet, he found an old t-shirt, and Vanessa entered the room a few moments later with a pair of her sweat pants. Apparently, she'd finally realized what he was doing and agreed. The best thing for The Girl right now was a warm bed and a good night's sleep. Though the clothing they'd gathered definitely wouldn't be the best fit on her small body, it would be more comfortable than the miniskirt and strapless top she was wearing now. Besides, her current attire was caked with mud and blood.

As he reached up to help her out of her shirt, he came to the sudden realization that she was not wearing a bra. While that normally was not a concern when helping a wounded hunter, it left him in an incredibly awkward position now. Not only was he uncomfortable with her being topless, but he was afraid he might react in a completely inappropriate way. Every other female he'd undressed had been wounded, and it had been all business. This time, though, it was different. Very, very different. Thankfully, Vanessa noticed his hesitation and stepped in to help.

"I can help her change," she volunteered. Grateful for being relieved from the task, he nodded and started to leave the room. The Girl's sudden and completely unexpected reaction as she finally realized what was happening startled everyone.

"NO!" she screamed, jumping off the bed to grab his arm. His muscles instinctively tensed, and it took a serious effort to keep his hands from their familiar routine of reaching for the pistols hanging just under each arm.

The expression that he discovered upon turning his head towards The Girl was far worse than anything he could have anticipated. Extreme fear, bordering on hysteria, desperately battled grief and exhaustion for control of what was typically a very beautiful face. Her eyes, puffy and red, shed not a single tear, choosing instead to simply swell and take over as the dominant feature. Quivering lips begged for reassurance, but he had none to give. Why wasn't she begging Vanessa for comfort with that terrifyingly familiar expression?

"Please, don't go," those tiny trembling lips begged, and he looked to Vanessa for help in this, his area of greatest weakness. The woman slipped her hands gently around The Girl's wrists, trying to lead her back to the bed so that she could rest. The Girl's grip on his arm tightened, her fingers digging into his flesh in a desperate attempt to keep him from stepping outside the room.

"He's only going out to the hall for a moment while you change," Vanessa coaxed, and while the hands didn't let up for a second, the face of the frightened child began to soften. Her eyes never left his, though.

"I'll come back." On the outside, he was perfectly calm and in control of the situation. Inside, however, he was a mess.

Seeing her like this brought back a flood of memories. His mind flashed back to what it had been like when his parents died. And then there was his first big mission when the orders had come directly from the Council. All those nightmares made flesh, and yet he had survived. This girl was strong, maybe even stronger than he was, and she would find her way through just as he had. Still, her entire life was gone, including most of her emotional support. The people she trusted most were all gone, except for Vanessa. But that had been enough for him. Maybe it would be enough for her as well.

Pulling his attention back to the panic-stricken face

before him, he said again, "I will come back."

"Promise?" And now she sounded like a scared little girl on the first day of school, begging her parents not to leave her alone in a strange place with strange faces that all seemed to be spouting new ideas and rules. Maybe that wasn't so far from the truth.

"I always come back."

"He's right, you know. I've tried a million times to get rid of this eating machine, but he just keeps showing up on the doorstep asking when the next meal will be."

Vanessa's attempt at humor seemed to fall on deaf ears. The Girl didn't laugh, didn't even smile, but her hold did finally weaken until Vanessa was able to pry her away from the man who had been by her side through the past few days of chaos. The eyes lingered on him until the door finally swung shut, and the immense weight that seemed to be resting on his chest was suddenly lifted.

Stepping back until his body rested against the wall behind him, the tough demeanor melted and he breathed a sigh of relief, mixed with frustration and a hint of his own fear. If this girl got attached to him, which already seemed to be the case, he wasn't certain he could handle the responsibility of being her confidant as well as her protector. It was difficult enough to keep things completely professional when he was still just a figure lurking in the shadows behind her. Now that she was so close and becoming closer with every moment they spent together, it was going to be almost impossible. And if the Council decided to reject this potential candidate as well? He would never be able to stand that kind of loss again. Not if they continued down this path.

After a few moments of rustling around inside the room, Vanessa poked her head out and gave him a weak smile. Her eyes told him that she was just as worried about The Girl as he was. She stepped into the hall, leaving the door open but keeping her voice low enough that they would not be overheard.

"Be careful with her," she mouthed as he met her halfway. "She's hurting and scared out of her mind."

"We'll both be fine."

She smiled, running a hand across his brow and down his stubble-covered cheek. "Yes, I think you will." Her hand quickly moved to her mouth, covering a timid yawn. "Time for bed. Where will you sleep?"

"I'll stay with her," he replied as if sleeping anywhere else had never been an option.

"Alright," she grinned, raising her voice just enough that The Girl could hear as well, "but no monkey business." With a quick wink to The Girl sitting on the edge of the bed who appeared to be still slightly dazed, Vanessa made her way down the hall to her own room and the man in black stepped into his.

Chapter 53

The world she had been trapped in for unknown hours, maybe even days, was suddenly shattered with the sound of screams. So far, the only break in the silent, pitch black world since her arrival had been the delivery of a single meal that still sat on the cold concrete floor beside her. She was hungry, practically starving in fact, but no amount of hunger could ever persuade her to eat the food he gave to her. It wasn't death through poisoning that Amy feared, but the possibility of other weaker drugs that would render her helpless and unable to even attempt an escape if a plan could be devised.

When she first heard the piercing cry, she thought that it must have been her own. The whole situation was finally starting to get to her, making it difficult to distinguish her voice from the ones inside her head. More than once, Amy had caught herself thinking out loud, talking to no one but herself. Still, this cry had seemed muffled somehow. Not hers, but someone else's. Someone outside this cold, lonely place. Sarah? The man had already told her that she was being used as bait to trap her older sister. Maybe the trap had worked.

A burst of brilliance tore through the nothing that had held her prisoner for so long, followed by the loud crash of the door slamming into the wall behind it. For a moment, she found herself blind and deaf and completely helpless. Panic gripped her, locking every muscle in place as she choked on her own fear.

    When her senses began to clear, she saw two figures struggling in the doorway, their silhouettes framed in a beautiful white light. One was Adam, his tall, lean shadow a familiar sight to her as it had haunted her since she had witnessed the murder of her mother. The other she did not recognize by sight, but as soon as she heard that ridiculous nasal whine, there was no question who this other captive was.

    "Let me go you stupid pig!" And now she could see the glint of gold as the light reflected off of that normally perfect head of hair.

    "It's nothing personal," the man sneered, pushing his prisoner towards another set of bars next to the already occupied cell. "Just following orders."

    "Impossible! He would never order you to do this to me! I want to speak to him, now!" Cary seemed unafraid of this lunatic who had slaughtered countless innocent people in the past few days, and who knew how many more before that. Her haughty attitude seemed to amuse the man, who grabbed her arm and practically threw the outraged captive into her cage.

    "Hope you enjoy your stay," he chuckled, swinging the door closed. "I promise you won't be here long."

    He left the room after giving both of the girls a wicked grin. The door closed once again, leaving them together in this place of shadows and misery. The presence of another lost soul gave Amy hope to counter the fear, and her joints finally unlocked. Creeping towards the wall of bars that faced the other cell, she could feel her heart beginning to beat a little slower. With the two of them working together, perhaps they could make it out of here alive after all.

"Cary," she croaked, her voice resembling that of a bullfrog with a nasty head cold. She was hoping for a reaction that included relief, hope, maybe even a little bit of excitement. What she got was anger and dismay.

"Leave me alone, Amy." Shrinking back as if she had been struck, the already confused girl became even less sure of the world around her. It had been Cary, she was sure of that. Except this didn't sound like Cary, because even she could never be that ignorant.

"I just thought that we could…" she began, but the person in the neighboring cell stopped her.

"You thought I would help you escape, right? Well, forget it."

"I don't understand." The tears were close again, but she managed to push them away for a little longer. Hopefully until she found out what was going on here.

"Of course you don't. You never do. You have no clue what is happening around you, and you never will because neither of us will ever see the outside of this prison again. At least not alive."

"But how do you know that? How can you be sure? Someone might come to rescue us."

"The only person stupid enough to come rescue us that isn't already dead is Sarah, and since that's the whole idea anyway, I'm pretty sure the crowd she's hanging with now won't let that happen."

Amy slowly crawled back to her corner, wrapping her arms around her knees not only to keep warm but as a way to protect her trembling self from anything that might be lurking in the dark nearby. Cary was wrong. Someone would come looking for them. Someone had to come. The good guys didn't lose, and the innocent were always protected by someone. If nothing else, she could count on her sister. Sarah would never leave her here alone. She would find someone to help track down and rescue her frightened sibling from this monster that had already killed their mother.

Huddled in the corner, trapped in a world she had no part in, Amy waited anxiously for help to arrive. Though the next few hours were terrifying and miserable, Amy soon found that her faith in her sister was well founded. And it nearly cost all of them their lives.

Chapter 54

"I'm sorry for the way I acted earlier."

It was the first thing she'd said since he'd left the room for her to change. She'd been so quiet for so long, he thought she must already be asleep, and he had begun to drift off himself despite the ache in his back from the hard floor below. The sound of her timid apology jerked his mind back from its wanderings near the border between sleep and waking.

"Get some rest," he mumbled, unsure of what else to say. There was no need for her to apologize to him. He understood exactly what had happened, and it was perfectly normal. Not to mention, it felt kind of nice to know that she wanted him around, even if it was just for protection.

"I can't," she replied, shifting around until her head popped into his view from the floor at the foot of the bed. "I'm worried about Amy. And Cary. Do you really believe they're dead?"

"If they aren't, they will be soon. There's nothing that can be done about it."

"I don't believe that, and you shouldn't either. Please, you have to help me find my sister. Maybe it is too late for Cary, but I *know* Amy is alive and she needs help. Please, Elijah."

The sound of his name, spoken by The Girl whom he never believed would even know of his existence, let alone remember such a detail, made it difficult to refuse. When coupled with the desperation in her eyes and the knowledge that if he didn't help her, she might end up resenting him as well as Vanessa, or worse, go out and try to find these captives on her own, it was nearly impossible. Still, logic argued against such a risky endeavor. To walk right into the trap that had been set specifically to lure The Girl into their lair would almost certainly mean his own death, if not hers.

"You don't realize what you're asking," he argued, also aware that if the Council found out that he had risked letting such a valuable asset fall into the hands of the enemy, he would be dead even if he did manage to escape the clutches of the Others.

"I'm asking you to help me save someone's life. Someone who happens to be very important to me. If the tables were turned and it was Vanessa that had been kidnapped, wouldn't you want someone you trusted to help get her back?"

She was going to do this, no matter what he said. It was settled. They were going into the lion's den, whether he liked it or not. With a sigh, he pulled himself up off the floor, extending a hand to The Girl to help her off the bed. She tossed an uncertain glance at the boots sitting beside the bedroom door, and he shook his head. Those definitely would not do. A few quick steps brought him to his closet, and after some digging, he found an old pair of his boots, too small for his fully grown feet now but perfect for the girl sitting anxiously on the edge of the bed.

He was amazed at how swiftly her fingers moved, lacing up the boots with surprising grace and speed. Once they were tied, The Girl stood and he led her down the stairs, saying a silent prayer that Vanessa would not wake until they had returned. No need to worry her any more than was necessary. If she knew what they were doing, she'd try to stop them, and the last thing they needed was another fight. Best to avoid any further conflict by simply sneaking out.

The Girl was quite stealthy, though he should have expected as much. This wasn't the first time she'd snuck out at night. In fact, she was an old pro at this. He let her lead the way, silently admiring her nimbleness as they stalked out the front door and down the driveway.

Once outside, The Girl asked, "Where do you think we should start searching?"

"Searching won't be necessary," he replied, pulling open the driver's side door of the black sedan. "We already know where they are."

"We do?" She slid into the passenger seat, softly closing the door behind her as if she were afraid of disturbing Vanessa even now. It would be too late for her to stop them at this point, and since the woman asleep inside would have no way of knowing where they were going or what they were doing, she couldn't send anyone else out after them.

"They left a message, complete with map."

"I didn't see any map."

"Yes, you did. You just didn't know what it was" The car pulled out of the driveway, speeding off down the streets and closer to the downtown area. The Girl still didn't have any idea what he was talking about. That much was clear from the look on her face.

"Do I even want to know what that special method of communication was?"

"It was carved into your mother's body." The Girl's face instantly went from slightly pale to ghostly white, and he honestly thought she was going to be sick. "Should I roll down a window?"

She shook her head, speechless even after everything she had seen over the past few days. He wasn't convinced, so he slowed the car and pulled over in the closest parking lot. It was some little furniture store, just preparing to close up shop for the evening. The face of an older woman, maybe late forties, early fifties, peeked out from behind the white lace curtains hanging over the front window. The look she gave the vehicle was one of contempt and frustration. *Probably thinks we're last minute customers*, he thought.

The passenger window slid down a few inches as he pushed the power window control button, and the cool night breeze drifted into the tiny compartment where they sat. The Girl leaned into the wind, taking a deep breath to steady her nerves. Clearly, she had not seen any hidden meaning in the markings carved into her mother's flesh. Until now, that is. Why hadn't he been gentler in breaking the news? To be so blunt about such a violent, disgusting crime without even a hint of sympathy or compassion was more than insensitive. It was downright mean. Hadn't she been through enough already? Why was he forcing her to relive those memories of her mother being cut down from the tree in what had once been her front lawn, or the sight of that same woman a few hours later, attached to a myriad of machines via a tangle of tubes and wires?

"I'm sorry," he muttered awkwardly, not really sure what to say or do to make the situation better, if it was even possible to do so.

She surprised him once again, placing her soft, warm hand over his in an odd gesture that seemed to offer comfort to *him*, not her. Her eyes met his, and it was clear that she was fighting back a flood of tears. But that wasn't what shocked him. Tears were normal for someone her age that had been put through all the tortures of the damned in just a few short days. What wasn't normal and impressed him more than anything else this girl had said or done in the entire time he had known her, was the lack of fear hiding in those big chocolate eyes.

"I'll live," she chuckled, her voice thick and shaky, but still calm. "The back was the map, wasn't it?" He nodded, and she did the same. "I knew it looked familiar. Should we go back to the hospital for a better look, or did you already see everything you needed to see?"

"There's no need to go back there." A relieved sigh

escaped through her parted lips as she leaned her head back against the headrest.

"Lead the way, then."

"Are you sure you're up to this?" One last chance to back out. One last chance to turn around and forget this whole crazy idea. One last chance to decide that their lives were more important than those of the prisoners and just go back to their safe, warm beds.

"Positive. Let's get moving before there's nothing left for us to save."

"How do you know it isn't already too late?"

With a shrug of her shoulders, she told him, "I just know. Now quit stalling and drive."

Without another word, he drove out of the parking lot and headed for the police station. The trap was set, she had taken the bait and so had he. Now the only thing left to see was how this little drama would end. Though his heart hoped for the happily ever after scenario, his gut told him it wasn't going to be quite so clean and cheerful. He was really hoping his heart was right.

Chapter 55

Something was definitely off here. Despite the increasing number of crimes in the area and the continuing search for the missing children, the parking lot was filled with police vehicles. True, it was late, but there should still be one or two on patrol, shouldn't there? Yet it appeared that there were no empty spaces in the area reserved for official police parking. But that wasn't the only thing wrong.

The moment she opened the door and stepped out of the vehicle it hit her. The smell was outrageous, and for a moment she honestly thought the omelet she had eaten just hours before was going to make another appearance. The world began to blur and darken, her senses too overwhelmed by the stench surrounding her to take in anything else. Vaguely aware of a firm pressure on her arm, she managed to steady herself and clear her head enough that she was no longer afraid of passing out.

"Alright?" Elijah's concern was not found in his voice, but rather in the way his arm wrapped around her waist, trying to help her balance on wobbly legs. So much tenderness and yet it was clear he was trying to hold back as much as possible. Once again, she found herself wondering about this man and the chain of events that had led him here.

"Do you smell that?" Of course he did. How could he not? Something that awful was impossible to miss.

"Smell what?"

For a moment, she was speechless. Maybe this was it. Maybe the situation had finally gotten to her. Refusing to follow this trail of lunacy any farther, she shook her head and took a step forward. The man at her side, however, didn't move.

"We should leave before they notice us," but they both knew that it was too late for that. Events had been set into motion, and now no force in the universe was going to stop her from going into that building to find her sister.

"I think it's a bit late for that." Whoever had set this trap was expecting them, and the odds of them not being noticed the moment the car pulled into the parking lot were about the same as the odds of the bad guys inside being eaten by a group of wandering gnomes.

"There's still time to change your mind." No hint of fear in his voice, but his posture had grown rigid and menacing as they stood there beside the car as if he were expecting an attack right there in the open. Of course, there didn't seem to be much to stop such an incident, especially since there were no police in sight at what should have been the base of operations for the search teams still looking for Cary and Joseph.

"I'm not leaving without Amy," she replied stubbornly, expecting him to continue his argument until she either caved in or the enemy finally made a move and it was too late to turn back. Instead, he gave a small nod and began marching towards the building, pulling his pistols from beneath his coat.

"Stay behind me and do exactly what I tell you," he ordered softly as they began climbing the stairs to the doorway of the building. "No arguing. Understand?"

"Yeah, sure," she answered, tossing nervous glances around at the seemingly abandoned area surrounding them. He didn't seem convinced.

"This is serious," he hissed, finally breaking that cool exterior for just a moment as his frustration got the better of him. "One mistake could lead to a lot of deaths, including yours."

"I get it, okay? Let's just get this over with."

They reached the top of the stairs, discovering that the front of the building was made of large glass windows. They could see everything in the lobby, and anyone who might be waiting in the shadows that filled the room could see them as well. Feeling a bit too vulnerable out here in the open, Sarah moved in closer to the man with the guns. He paused long enough to study the door and its frame, then reached behind his back, handing her one of the firearms.

"I don't know how to use this," she said, pushing the weapon back at him. He tossed an annoyed glance at her, then went back to the door. With a sigh of defeat, she wrapped her hands around the cool metal and tried to make sure the business end was pointed in a safe direction, away from the man who was trying to help keep her safe.

Using his free hand, Elijah grabbed the handle of the

door and pulled. Given the state of things so far, she almost expected it to be locked, but when he tugged it gave no resistance. Hesitantly, they stepped through the main entrance to the building and into the lobby. A desk sat against the wall opposite the door, creating a perfect hiding place for an attacker. The only other furniture in the room consisted of rows of chairs along the walls to either side of them. At first glance, most people would assume there was nothing wrong with this scene, but as Sarah followed behind the man in black who was clearing the room with swift accuracy, it became apparent that things were not as normal as they looked. Especially once they got to the pool of blood behind the desk.

"What do you think happened here?" she whispered, running her fingers along two large slash marks in the office chair lying behind the massive oak structure.

"People died," he answered, turning away from the grisly scene and focusing his attention on the hall to the right.

She didn't reply. How could anyone find a decent come back for such a horrifyingly simple statement? When he began moving towards the hall she followed, staying just far enough behind him that they weren't actually touching, but if he stopped suddenly they were both sure to crash and burn. There were no lights, and the inability to see the man just inches in front of her face would have been enough to induce panic in any other situation. The only thing keeping her mind from snapping at that moment was the thought of her sister, huddled in this same darkness, feeling the same terror without anyone there to comfort and protect her.

A hand grabbed her elbow and she barely managed to suppress a scream before realizing it wasn't the boogeyman. Elijah's deep, strong voice soothed her frazzled nerves, but his words chilled her to the bone.

"We're going back to the cells," he whispered. "It looks like there's a light in this room, so we have to be extra careful. Stay close, be quiet, and get ready to run."

"Roger," she answered breathlessly. Never before had her heart beat so fast or so hard.

A few more steps and she could see the silhouette of a door on her left. Dim yellow light surrounded the heavy wooden slab, but it was a welcomed change from the visual void through which they had been traveling. Elijah slowly turned the door knob, careful not to make a sound. Their greatest advantage here would be the element of surprise. If they could keep everyone in this building from realizing they were here, of course.

The moment the door slid open, they almost lost that edge. A fresh wave of putrescence hit her like a tsunami. Gagging and trying desperately to maintain control over her body, Sarah found the dizzying stench too powerful to fight. Her knees buckled just as her stomach finally ejected her partially digested meal. Elijah was there in an instant, sweeping her hair out of the way and silently comforting her simply by being near. When at last a few moments passed with no further incident, she looked up at the man whose face showed no hint of disgust or anger at such a girly reaction. Instead, she found understanding and perhaps a bit of amusement flickering in those big brown eyes.

"Alright?" he asked, but before she could reply, she saw what terrors awaited them beyond the doorway for the first time. Clearly, he saw the shock and moved to block the scene from her view. It was too late. Visions of that night would haunt her for the rest of her life.

This must have been the dumping ground for bodies, because there were corpses stacked everywhere. Three stacks of bodies lined the wall to her left. Though she wasn't really counting, her initial estimate was something close to thirty bodies. Many wore the uniforms of local police officers and the sheriff's department. Others, however, seemed to be prisoners. She saw at least two paper name badges proclaiming their wearers as visitors. All of the victims seemed to be just tossed casually into these piles without any rhyme or reason.

Many of those near the bottom of the piles had clearly been here for a while, their flesh already bloated and oozing a variety of fluids. Wounds had been given a chance to coat nearly the entire floor with a thick, gummy mess that would undoubtedly make a sound like mud sucking at the bottom of her boots when she tried to walk across it. And she would have to walk across it. The only other door was on the opposite side of the room.

Aside from the mutilated cadavers, there was broken furniture and bloodstained paperwork scattered everywhere. Bullet holes were apparent even in the faint glow of the overhead emergency lights. One wall was missing a large round chunk of drywall, and based on the weapons that littered the ground nearby, she was guessing it was the work of a shotgun blast. Whatever had happened, it must have been a surprise to the people working here. Who would ever expect someone to walk into the police station and start murdering people? More importantly, though, what kind of monsters would be capable of such a thing?

The same monsters that had tried to kill her at the park. The same monsters that had sliced up her mother and left her hanging from the tree in her front yard as bait to lure her to this very place. The same monsters that had her sister right now, doing God only knew what to her as they waited patiently for their prey to arrive. And she had done just that, hadn't she? She had walked into a trap set just for her in the hopes of saving Amy's life. Now, given the scene that lay before her, it would seem there had really been no hope at all.

His hand shot to her mouth as soon as he realized what was about to happen, barely keeping her fear from giving them away. His eyes met hers, drawing her back from the edge of insanity. They crouched there for what seemed like an eternity as she fought to maintain control over her emotions. Only later would it occur to her that he had been risking his life at that moment in order to spare her any further trauma. With his focus solely on her, anyone or anything could have crept right up to them and killed them both. He could have waited long enough for her to get a grip on reality, and then taken her back to the car and driven back to Vanessa's. Instead, he gave her a chance to steady her nerves, and then helped her to her feet, always keeping her eyes focused on his.

"She's not in here," he reassured her, leading her through the clutter of corpses.

Her foot slipped in something wet. Her entire body froze and her muscles seized up as her mind began to edge its way back towards panic. Images of what might have been down there beneath her boots made her stomach lurch once again. His grip shifted from her hands to either side of her face, firm but not angry or rough.

"Best not to look," was all he said, and she found that she had the strength to keep moving after all.

Once they passed through the doorway on the other side of the room, he finally pulled his gaze away to survey the area around them. A single fluorescent bulb lit the tiny hall with sickly yellow light, flickering occasionally as if it might finally succumb to the same fate as its neighbors at any moment. There were three doors, one on either side of the hall and one at the end farthest from them. The one directly beside them was labeled Janitor and was obviously not big enough for anything other than a few custodial supplies. The other two, however, were made of heavy steel and gave no real indication of what might be waiting on the other side.

"Which one?" The words came out as little more than a sigh, but the man seemed to hear her just fine. He nodded to the last door in the hall. Of course. This was a trap, and the best place to set a trap was as far from the exit as possible.

They made their way to the door, Elijah in the lead but still trying to keep an eye out for attacks from behind. By this point, Sarah was beginning to feel the wear on her nerves. The adrenaline rush she had felt coming into the building was beginning to fade, leaving her beyond exhausted. When this was all over, she was going to go find a nice warm bath and a soft bed where she would sleep until it was time to head off to college.

The door swung open easily, but she could hear it long before Elijah even reached for the handle. It was faint, but it was there. Someone inside this room was crying, and not just a few silent tears but a flood of hysterical sobbing. It was difficult to say whether her protector had heard it as well, though if his lack of reaction upon opening the door was any indication, the bawling must have been just as audible to him. The noise stopped as they stepped into the room, replaced instead by something much worse in its familiarity.

"I swear to God, Adam, if you don't let me out of this cage right now, you'll be lucky to see the sunrise!" The indignation in that voice was impossible to mistake, and as soon as she heard it, Sarah felt her heart begin to pick up speed.

It was Cary.

She started to race forward, hoping to find her friend and set her free before anything bad could happen, but Elijah grabbed her arm. There was no way to see more than a few feet into the room because that was as far as the light from the hall illuminated. The idea of running farther into the blackness where anything might be waiting was ludicrous, and yet it still infuriated her that he would stop such a futile and potentially dangerous action. The look on his face halted a rather nasty stream of profanities from bursting forth. Something was wrong here. The clenched muscles in his jaw told her that he felt it, and now she could feel it too. Creeping into her thoughts was the overwhelming sensation that they were being watched from somewhere in the shadows surrounding them.

"Adam!" Cary shouted again. "I don't know what he promised you, but I can guarantee it's not worth the hell you'll be put through if you don't get over here and unlock this door RIGHT NOW!"

"Stay here," Elijah breathed so softly she almost didn't hear him. Side stepping into the darkness, the man in black faded away into the background.

"I know you're there! You can't ignore me forever!" The sounds of enraged screams filled the air as Cary's anger finally got the best of her. Sarah covered her ears, wincing in pain as the sound echoed through the room almost as much as in her head. "He won't keep his promise, Adam! Once he has The Girl, your job will be done and he'll do the same thing to you that he did to me! Do you want to be the one trapped in this cell?"

Before she had time to think about what she had just heard, another shadow filled the doorway from behind her. A deep, masculine voice made the air around her tremble.

"Hello, Sarah."

At the sound of her name, she instinctively turned. Standing in the doorway was a man. His pale, thin face and dark rimmed eyes made him look more like a walking corpse, and still, Sarah recognized those impossibly blue eyes, as well as the blue letter jacket with the red stains on the chest. Jacob's jacket.

The last time she'd seen it had been that night at the farm when everything had first begun to unravel. Now, it was draped over the skeletal frame of Jacob's missing brother, Adam.

"We've been waiting for you. I was beginning to wonder if you would actually show up. Your sister, however, never doubted you."

"Where is Amy?" Sarah growled, surprising even herself as the shock she felt turned to rage.

"She's safe," the ghoul replied, stepping closer to the angry girl. "You can visit with her in just a bit if you like. But first, there are some things we need to discuss."

"You kidnapped my sister and killed my mother! What

is there to discuss?"

Most people might have felt intimidated by such a man, especially given his history of violent behavior. Even Sarah would have been terrified by this situation if the creature hadn't been so familiar. She had been there when this boy got his driver's license. She had watched as the boy and his older brother wrestled playfully on the living room floor of their family home, back before the entire family had been killed and the house sold to pay hospital bills. Well, maybe it hadn't been the entire family after all. Instead of doing the logical thing and taking a few steps away from this monster, Sarah found herself advancing towards him.

His initial reaction was one of surprise, halting in mid stride as he considered the actions of the girl standing before him. The shock wore off in a matter of seconds, and a smile began to form at the corners of his mouth.

"You are either very brave or you have no clue what is happening around you. I'd like to think it's the former." He extended his hand to her, waiting for her to accept it and be led away from the darkness, away from the thick stench of decay that filled the air around her, away from the man in black and Cary's angry screams. He could lead her into the light, save her from this life, give her the knowledge she needed to take control of her life once again. He could give her Amy.

The sound of metal scraping against stone drew the attention of both Sarah and the kidnapper. Someone, or something, was moving around in those shadows, and it was highly unlikely that whatever it was would turn out to be harmless. After the past week, Sarah was beginning to believe that nothing in this world was harmless.

"Show yourself, hunter!" The booming voice of the creature in the doorway made Sarah jump just like all those silly teenage girls she had watched at the movie theater with Jacob.

The thought brought back a flood of memories, things she never wanted to think about again. A blue letter jacket soaked with blood. The same jacket that now hung loosely on this monster's fragile frame. The feel of a gun in her hand. The sight of a woman's brains being scattered as bullets tore through her skull. The man in black dying in the grass. A balding man in red running shorts lunging at her with a knife. The only comfort she had was the knowledge that somewhere in here Elijah was lurking, waiting for someone to make a move. But how long would he wait? Would it be too late?

There were some shuffling sounds and a muffled yelp, followed by whispers too faint to decipher. Sarah took little notice of these things, too wrapped up in her own thoughts to care much about the events taking place around her. She had to do something. Somehow, she had to find a way to get herself out of this mess, because the chances of someone coming along to rescue her were growing smaller with every passing moment.

The world was drenched in a blinding white glow as the overhead fluorescents suddenly flickered to life. Sarah's arm instinctively moved to her face, trying to shield her eyes from the glare. The unusual weight of the hand at the end of that arm startled her out of the daze she had been trapped in. She still had the gun.

"You didn't honestly think you could just walk in and rescue the damsel in distress without any resistance, did you?" The man looked even worse in this light, as though he should be lying in a hospital room somewhere instead of stepping past her towards the cells on the other side of the room.

Elijah stood just inside one of the cells, a small, trembling figure huddled against him for strength. Though the girl was dirtier and definitely more terrified than the last time Sarah had seen her, there was no mistaking her identity. In the cell just beside the one that held Sarah's sister stood Cary, her eyes blazing with fury as she glared at the man moving towards her.

"Sarah, run!" Amy screamed, but they all knew she wouldn't do it. Sarah had come all this way to rescue her baby sister, and she wasn't about to run away now that she was so close.

"There's nowhere to run," the crazy corpse chuckled. "No one leaves this room unless I allow them to. Seems as though you're all trapped here until after Sarah and I have our little talk."

They were all so focused on each other that none of them noticed Sarah raising the gun to eye level, carefully taking aim at the beast that had destroyed her life. None, that is, except Elijah. She caught his gaze for just a moment as Amy began pleading with the madman, and what she saw there gave her hope. He thought they still had a chance of making it out of there alive.

Convinced that if he thought they could do it then it was still possible, Sarah drew in a deep breath, steadied her nerves, and squeezed the trigger. The loud bang that tore through the air and silenced everyone in the room was enough to shatter eardrums. Amy let out a squeal, hitting the concrete floor as Elijah moved to shield her with his own body.

Sarah stood in silent wonder as the unthinkable happened. All prospects of escape melted away as she watched the bullet slow and then stop just inches from its intended target. The maniac that she had once called friend turned around slowly, knocking the slugs to the ground with a brisk sweep of his arm. Any hint of amusement that might have been lingering on his face was gone now, replaced by a growing fury that would soon become a raging inferno of hatred.

Suddenly, the clump of metal pressed tightly in her hands began to grow hot, burning her flesh until she simply couldn't hold it any longer. It fell from her grasp, turning red and then bright orange as it began to melt on the concrete below. Blisters began to form on her palms and fingers even before the monster spoke.

"Stupid girl!" The ghoulish figure seemed even less

human with his hateful sneer and unnatural growl. "Your weapons are useless against one as strong as I!"

"You are not strong." Elijah's voice rang clear, stopping the other instantly. It turned on the man in the cage, demanding an explanation.

"I am stronger than any other that has served the Great Ones."

"And yet your body suffers from the power they have given you. Our kind was never meant to carry such a burden." Elijah stood as he spoke, not bothering to help Amy off the floor as he did so.

"What do you know? Only what that stupid Council of yours wants you to know. I know the truth."

"And what is the truth?"

"That I am stronger than ten hunters! That I can destroy you and bring The Child to those who will give her everything she needs to grow in strength and knowledge!" The ghoul was advancing on the cage once again, but this time she knew it was an intentional distraction. Elijah was trying to buy time for her to escape, despite what the beast had said about them all being trapped. Amy seemed to catch on a moment later, taunting the creature as well in an attempt to focus its rage on those who had no real hope of escape.

"Have you looked in a mirror lately?" Amy rasped, her voice a dry brittle thing after her time spent in this damp, cold room. The poor girl would be lucky not to catch pneumonia.

Then again, would it really matter if her life ended here in this prison?

There had to be something she could do. They had come here to save Amy, not to add to the list of casualties by leaving both her sister and Elijah here with the bad guys while she ran away. The gun had been a bad idea because the creature had expected it. If the others could take his attention away from her for long enough, though, perhaps he would not expect another attack.

Not really knowing what she was planning until she had done it, Sarah lunged at the monster, knocking them both to the ground. She was quick and he had been taken by surprise, yet he still managed to get the upper hand. Twisting his fingers into her hair, he flopped her onto her back and climbed on top of her. His free hand wrapped around Sarah's neck, squeezing just hard enough to make speech almost impossible but not hard enough to crush her trachea, though she was certain he could accomplish such a feat without breaking a sweat.

"He has filled your head with lies, Sarah." The thing's breath in her face brought the same stink that had made her vomit just moments before in the room down the hall. "We can help you. We can make you strong. We can fix this mess and give you your life back. Isn't that what you want?"

"What I want is for you to get out of my face. Haven't you ever heard of breath mints?" Her response brought a smile to the creature's thin lips.

"Such wit," it chuckled.

Before it could say anything more, though, a big, heavy boot came sailing out of nowhere, colliding with the thing's left cheek. The grip on her throat disappeared as the creature fell backwards, but its other hand was still tangled in her hair, giving it the leverage it needed to catch its balance and prepare for the next attack. Waving its free hand in the direction from which the boot had come, Sarah was vaguely aware of a loud thud as something large hit the wall next to her. The creature seemed to be having a difficult time as it tried to keep track of the girl beneath it and the assailant to its left.

"You cannot have her!" it screamed, and the walls trembled with the fury of those words. Gunshots tore through the air, and while the beast was busy deflecting the bullets, Sarah managed to pry herself out from beneath it. With a cry that was beyond anger or surprise, it fell to the ground in a pile of cloth and flesh stretched over bone. The rings around its eyes were now almost black. Blood trickled from its nose. It looked like a cancer patient just before the doctors shut off the life support.

Sarah had a flash back to her mother, lying in a hospital bed, blood pouring from every opening in her face. Did this thing that used to be a man know what was happening to its body? Did it know that it was dying?

"Sarah, get Amy out of here," Elijah commanded, snapping Sarah out of the dreadful memories that had begun to consume her once again. She glance around the room, found

Amy huddled in against the wall near the door, and immediately ran to her sister.

"We can't get out," Amy sobbed as her sister grabbed her arm and tried to drag her through the open door. The moment they hit the edge of the concrete that made up the floor of this room, the girls froze. It was as if they had simply lost the ability to make their legs move any farther. Try as she might, Sarah could not push through the exit.

Taking a step back, Sarah turned her attention back to the kidnapper, who was currently slamming Elijah's head into the wall. It had said that no one could leave without its permission. So, they would just have to get its permission. More determined than ever to make sure they all left this place alive, Sarah marched over to the monster.

"Hey, asshole!" The creature stopped bashing Elijah's skull in and turned to her. "Let's get a few things straight. First of all, if you want to convince me to chat with you, killing the people I care about is definitely not the way to do it. Secondly, it seems as though you aren't feeling too well, so maybe now isn't the best time to be threatening others."

"I'm feeling fine." Blood oozed down the creature's face from its nose and mouth, although from the looks of things, Elijah had yet to get a hit in. "And I didn't plan on killing them. Yet."

"Funny. That hole in the wall says otherwise." Elijah was lying on the floor, dazed but not dead. Amy stood beside the doorway, still unsure of what to do next.

"If I promise to let the others go, will you stay and talk?"

"How can I say no?"

"Fine, then they're free to go." The monster took a few steps forward, grasping her shoulder with a fragile hand. "They should probably go before we begin our discussion anyway. People like them cannot possibly understand what it is to have our strength."

"You can't do this, Sarah." Elijah was on his feet again, though still a bit shaky.

"Stay out of this," the creature hissed. The man in black took a step forward, but she shook her head.

"He's right," she agreed. "Take Amy and get out of here."

"What about me?" Cary finally spoke up. "Aren't you going to get me out of here?"

"Sorry, but the boss has other plans for you." The beast's eyes locked on Sarah's, and she began to feel herself losing her grip on reality once again. Her thoughts drifted to a distant memory, blurry and without much substance. Cool glass pressed against her forehead, the smell of engine oil and bile filled her nostrils, and somewhere Cary's voice carried a message to her ears that chilled her soul.

I think tonight might be a good time to take Sarah out to the farm. It's very quiet, and private. Perfect for a couple of teenagers looking for some time alone.

Cary was one of them. She had set up the attack at the farm. She had set up the attack at the mall. She had been responsible for the death of Sarah's mother and the kidnapping of her sister. And now she was begging for someone to save her.

"Sarah, you can't leave me here," the girl pleaded, and deep down, Sarah felt a piece of her begin to grow cold and hard. How could this girl, who had been there with her through so many things over the years, who she had shared all her most intimate secrets with since kindergarten, just turn around and betray her like this?

"Shut up, Cary," she hissed, not taking her gaze from the other monster in the room.

"You can't do this to me! I'm your best friend!"

Her anger finally grew into a blaze of fury which she intended to unleash on the vile betrayer still imprisoned in this wretched place. She started to turn her eyes to the cage, but the creature would not let her.

"They are not your friends, Sarah." His hands wrapped around hers and she found that she could not escape. Even if she wanted to run, she couldn't. He had control over her eyes, her body...even her thoughts were his. "Come with me and I will show you a world you've never dreamed of."

He was leading her to the door, and she was following without a fight. This was not right. She had to do something, but it was impossible. This thing was going to take her to some other things and they were all going to sit around and chat about the wondrous things that she could do and how powerful she was and wouldn't it just be too cool if she could help them do whatever it was they were planning to do and then what a time they would have as they flaunted their superiority over the rest of the world until the end finally arrived but it wouldn't matter because...

"You're going to kill me," she whispered, and the creature that had once been known as Adam grinned, his lips splitting and oozing red liquid down his chin. Was this what they had planned for her? Would she look like this before she died? Or worse, would she even care that she looked like this before she died if she became as powerful as this poor boy?

"You will live until it is your time to die, and until then, we hope to make things as interesting as possible for you." Not quite the reassurance she was hoping for. Panic clouded her vision for just a moment, and suddenly the creature's hold over her began to weaken. She could feel him struggling to maintain control, but it was no use. The spell was broken. Sarah was free.

Its hands tightened around hers, but most of the physical strength had already left the creature. When she gave a sharp tug, the bones in its wrist crackled and crunched like dried autumn leaves. It wailed in agony and she bolted down the corridor back to the room of death where the world suddenly began to dim as the waves of nausea returned. The creature caught up to her quickly, cackling madly with its limp, useless hands dangling in front of its chest.

"You cannot escape. It is too late for that. He will be here soon, and you will see just how ridiculous it is to run."

"Guess what! I don't want to join your little bad guys club! Now why don't you just go back to your girlfriend in the cage and let me go back to what's left of my life? Fair enough?" Her voice shook, but not from fear. The smell that brought back memories of dinners left half-digested on the concrete floor and the puddles of blood and gore that she seemed to be sliding around in were much too strong for her to focus on anything else.

"It doesn't work that way. You are one of us, whether you want to be or not. And if you are not working with us, then you are a liability."

"If you think I'm going to go along with your little plans and end up looking like a walking corpse just like you, then you must be crazy." Her nervous laughter bounced off the walls, cutting through the tension in sharp, jagged slices. The creature was not amused.

"You're crazy if you turn down his offer. Imagine, Sarah. Anything you could ever possibly want or need for as long as you live!"

"Do you really want to know what I want more than anything? I want my mother back!" It stopped advancing and stared at her in amazement. Apparently it hadn't been expecting such a request. "Can you give me that? Are you powerful enough to bring my mother back? You were strong enough to kill her, why not bring her back from the dead?"

"Even he can't do that," the man whispered, clearly struggling with some intern conflict.

There was a brief glimpse of the boy he used to be in that moment, and Sarah immediately recognized his anguished expression. She knew more in that one moment than she ever wanted about how the other team got to its victims. Grief and pain were their tools, and they used them to manipulate anyone they could. But it hadn't worked with her. Instead of becoming weak and vulnerable when they took her mother and sister, she'd grown stronger. More defiant. And now, if they couldn't find a way to change that, they would kill her because she was as strong as this boy without their help. She always had been.

"But there are so many other wonderful things he can do for you," he finally recovered, turning back into that monster whose only goal was to make her pay for what she had done to his family. "You don't need that woman, just like you don't need the hunters or that girl you called sister. All you need is him." He was stalling, and if she didn't get out of there soon, it would be too late. Whoever he was planning to hand her over to would be here any minute.

Refusing to let this beast win, or any of his friends for that matter, Sarah finally found her footing and turned to run again. She hadn't taken more than two steps before some invisible force knocked her feet out from under her, sending her sprawling face first onto the sticky, blood soaked floor.

"You are beginning to try my patience, Sarah," the thing said, and each word brought it one step closer to her as she scrambled to her hands and knees. "Stay where you are."

"Oh, God," she moaned, an idea suddenly beginning to form in her head. Pushing herself up from the gooey mess beneath her, she forced a few weak gagging sounds from her throat. "I think I'm going to be sick."

She began crawling backwards, away from the stench and towards the enemy. He chuckled softly as she approached, apparently not noticing as she palmed a piece of broken chair in her right hand. When she felt her feet bump up against his, she let out a tiny yelp of terror, and something jerked her up off the ground to face him. Gripping the sliver of wood tightly, she waited for an opening.

"They must have the wrong girl," the thing laughed, spraying blood and bits of gore all over her, and for a moment she thought she really might puke.

"I'll make you a deal," she offered, trying to take his attention away from her actions by making him focus on her words. "Let me go, and I'll drive you to the airport myself. Plane tickets to anywhere you want, my treat."

"Why would I want to run? I have everything I could ever want here."

Almost. She almost had him.

"Once the cops find out what you've done..." He burst

out in deep, gurgling laughter at the thought, giving her a perfect opportunity, but she hesitated just a moment too long.

"I've killed all the locals, and as far as larger organizations, my friends will protect me."

"Just like your friends protected your brother?"

A broken hand collided with her cheek in a powerful blow that should have shattered her jaw. Instead, it simply bruised her cheek and knocked her to the ground once again. The invisible hands yanked her back up to her feet before the stars had faded.

"Don't open your mouth again until you're told, or I'll show you what pain is."

Knowing that this could be her last chance, she lunged at the creature, wooden weapon aimed directly at his face. He deflected the blow, but it clearly surprised him. The weapon caught his upper arm, ripping open the flesh beneath his jacket without damaging the material. Blood poured from the wound as the creature's face grew paler with each passing moment.

With a growl that was part fury and part agony, the beast used its invisible appendages to once again attack. This time, it pinned her to the ground, immobilizing her as he scanned the room for a weapon of his own. It found what it needed lying just behind one of the overturned desks. The silver letter opener hovering in front of its chest, it crept slowly over to the trapped girl, leaving a streak of bright crimson to blend into the almost black goo on the floor behind it. Based on the creature's ghostly appearance, she guessed it wouldn't be long before it died from blood loss. Long enough, though, to finish her off. Or at least cause some serious damage.

Kneeling over her, the metallic object raised above its head by an unseen hand, it grinned wickedly.

"I wonder how much your little hunter friend would like you without those pretty brown eyes," it sneered.

The room was suddenly filled with three loud explosions, each accompanied by a bright spark of light from the other side of the room. It was too dark in the hall outside to see what had caused the flashes, but it wasn't necessary to see the source. All that really mattered was that the monster that had been trying to keep her here was now covered in its own blood and missing most of its chest. Behind the beast was a fresh crimson pool littered with bits of flesh and bone. It gave one last gurgling shriek before its body came crashing down beside her, spraying her with things she didn't want to think about.

She could remember screaming, though in her mind, it seemed to be coming from someone else, and then the next thing she knew, she was lying with her face buried in sweet smelling cloth. The floor was still beneath her, but there was something lying beside her, pressed tightly against her body. Thoughts of the thing that had once been a boy but was now just a mutilated carcass filled her head, and she immediately leapt to her feet, backing towards the exit as quickly as possible. She had to get out of here. She had to find Amy and...

"Elijah?" It hadn't been a dead body that was pressed against her after all. Elijah slowly pulled himself up off the floor, dragging weary limbs as if every moment he remained conscious required more energy than he had left. She hesitated for a moment, not sure how to help him or even if she could help him. The question of whether or not she *should* help him never even crossed her mind. He had more than proven his devotion to protecting her. Now it was her turn.

"Amy's in the car," he grunted, putting a hand to his temple as he staggered towards her.

Not entirely sure she could actually do it until she did, Sarah wrapped the man in black's arm around her shoulders and tried to steady him as they stumbled out into the hall. With a great deal of effort, they managed to make their way out of the building and down the front stairs to the car. By then, all parties were exhausted and more than ready for a good night's sleep. Amy saw them coming and hopped out of the car to help, Elijah's big black coat wrapped around her tiny frame. Sarah volunteered to drive, since the car's owner was obviously in no condition to do so. The entire car ride back to Vanessa's was silent, as everyone was still too stunned by the events of the evening to say much of anything. The silence ended abruptly when they reached the driveway of their destination.

Chapter 56

He had known the boy would not last much longer when they had talked on the phone earlier that morning. Still, he had not realized just how badly things might go until now. The Child was strong. That was good. The Child was also traveling with a hunter, and that was bad.

Squatting down next what was left of the thing that had once been Adam Cannon, he could not help but smile. She had surprised him yet again. Somehow she had managed to evade his grasp despite the extra bit of power he had given to the boy. By the looks of it, Adam had not even managed to slow her down, or at least not enough for it to matter. The only way she could have impressed him more was if she had done it alone.

The shouts picked up again from the cells at the rear of the building, bringing his attention back to the task at hand. He had to tie up one last loose end before he went back to finding a way to win over The Child. In the end, she had shown incredible bravery and loyalty to her family simply by coming here tonight. That meant intimidation was out of the question, and using her loved ones to bring her out of hiding would not work a second time. He would have to find another way.

But then, he had already known that. It was why he had begun sneaking into her dreams, telling her all the things she wanted to hear and providing a sensitive shoulder for her to lean on. His backup plan had already been set into motion, just in case they ever met unexpectedly. If she already knew him as an ally from her dreams, she would be less likely to question his actions when she met him in reality. It was a standard practice when trying to attract a potential protégé, and now it had given him the edge he would need to finish this.

"Adam!" she screamed as he stepped through the doorway, gliding silently to her cell before she had a chance to react. The dim lighting made the terror on her face as she suddenly realized who he was that much more pronounced. "I...Why..."

"Shh," he soothed, reaching between the bars to run a gently hand over her cheek.

"You promised me," she sneered, but her eyes told him that she knew what was coming. He could even smell the slightest hint of fear beginning to ooze from her perfect curves. "You said I'd be a star."

"And you said you would deliver The Child."

"I tried! It's not my fault you and your goons are too stupid to..." Her words turned into a dry, rattling gasp as he wrapped a hand around her delicate throat and squeezed. Her trachea snapped like a sapling, bringing a smile of satisfaction to his face. He had wanted to do this for a long time. Since she had signed on almost four years ago, in fact.

The body fell to the ground with a sickening thud as he stepped away from the cell. So much for getting any information out of this one. Then again, she had never been very useful in gathering intelligence. Sad, really, considering how much access she had to The Child. Even The Child's adopted father had been able to provide more valuable details about the target than this pathetic creature.

Leaving the mess to be sorted out by the authorities who were already on his personal payroll, he made his way back to the car waiting outside. This plan had not worked out quite as well as he had hoped, but he had gained some valuable insight into the mind of his prey. Soon, he would have what he wanted. The Child would come to him without protest, because now, he knew exactly what she needed.

The car slipped silently off into the night as he began making the necessary preparations.

Chapter 57

Vanessa was sitting on the porch when they pulled into the drive. The moment she saw the car, she leapt up from her seat beside the rosebush and was nearly run over as she rushed the vehicle. Anger flared in her eyes, though to Elijah, her fear was much more obvious. He sighed the moment he saw her, making Amy chuckle softly.

"Let me guess," she croaked. "You didn't leave a note." The Girl met her sister's gaze as she turned off the ignition, and both girls burst into fits of relieved laughter. The furious red-head threw open the rear passenger side door, her green eyes blazing.

"What were you thinking?" Clearly, Vanessa was not amused.

Elijah brushed off the questions as if batting away a pesky insect as he stepped out of the car. Sarah and Amy were too busy hugging and laughing and crying to notice what was happening outside their windows.

"You took The Girl and walked right into their trap, Elijah! How could you be so irresponsible? You know how important she is!" Vanessa's shouts were beginning to draw the attention of neighbors, though the girls still seemed oblivious to her rage.

"I know it was stupid, and I know you're disappointed, but..."

"Disappointed? I think that's a bit of an understatement!" This was a fight he was not going to win, no matter what how sound his reasoning. He had never seen her this upset about anything, not even when his father died or when the Council ordered him away on a suicide mission. Not even when she had been on the verge of death.

"Leave him alone." The Girl was climbing out of the driver's side door, rubbing her cheeks in an effort to wipe away the tears. She only managed to smear the filth that covered her hands onto her cheeks, and though Vanessa managed to reign in her shock almost instantly, there was a moment when her face was filled with absolute terror at the sight of all that drying blood. "It was my idea. If you want someone to yell at, I'm your girl."

"Don't think I've forgotten you," Vanessa pointed an accusing finger at The Girl, but only for a moment. Then she turned her attention back to him. "Of all the stupid, reckless things you've ever done, this is by far the worst. I can't believe that you would endanger not only your life but Sarah's as well."

"We had to save Amy," The Girl demanded, but Vanessa ignored her.

"I told you to stay put and let the others deal with it. Why would you do something like this, Elijah?"

"I said leave him alone!" The Girl shouted, and this time, everyone listened. "I talked him into it. This was my fault, and I'm sorry if we worried you, Vanessa."

"You have no idea what we are up against, Sarah. Hopefully you never will. But it is our job to protect you from them. A job that Elijah usually takes very seriously." The accusing glance she shot him was almost comical.

"He was protecting me! Unlike you, he realized that I wasn't about to just sit around while a bunch of psychos killed what's left of my family. I would have gone after Amy, with or without him, and if he hadn't been there tonight, I probably would have died."

"I know it's hard for you to understand right now, but Amy is not our responsibility. You are."

"So you would just let her die? If it came down to saving just one of us, you would let Amy die?" Amy seemed to be shrinking back against the car, her face rapidly losing what little color had returned since they found her at the prison.

"Yes," Vanessa replied coolly, although he knew it would not be quite so easy for this woman to make such a decision. Standing here in the driveway, she could claim that logic would prevail in such a situation, but if it really came down to a choice, there would be a rather vicious battle between her brain and her heart.

"So what makes me so special? What is it about me that makes my life worth more than the lives of the people around me? Explain to me why I'm so important, and maybe I won't think of you as a heartless witch anymore."

"I've already told you..." Vanessa began, but The Girl

cut her off.

"That I'm your savior, right? Do I look like a superhero to you? If it hadn't been for him, I wouldn't be here right now!" She tossed an angry wave at him, redirecting Vanessa's attention once again. Before the barrage could begin all over, he ended the discussion with a few simple words.

"It's late," he replied, pushing past her towards the house. "I'm going to bed."

"We are not finished here!" Ignoring her cries, he made his way up the porch steps and through the door, certain that she would come racing after him any second. He breathed a sigh of relief when he reached his bedroom door without any further incident. Maybe tonight hadn't been a great idea, but he had saved a young girl's life. That had to count for something. Didn't it?

Not even bothering to take off his coat or boots, the exhausted hunter flopped down on the bed, his head full of questions, though one seemed to stand out against all the others. Why had she defended him? Vanessa was right, it was his fault that she had nearly been killed. So, why did she volunteer as the scapegoat? Wouldn't it have been easier to just go along with the angry woman outside? There were very few people in this world that he could count on when it came to backing his decisions, and he had known all of them since his childhood. All except this girl, who had only known him for a few days. Why did she keep trying to help him?

Eventually, he drifted into a restless sleep where the events of the past few hours seemed to play in a never ending loop of chaos and fear. Each time the dream ended, he would awaken to find that only an hour had passed, and once he finally settled his nerves enough to rest again, it would start all over with the scene waiting for them as he pushed open the doorway to the police headquarters and found all the mutilated bodies. Eventually, after the fourth replay of The Girl helping him out of he building and into the backseat of his car, he decided it was time to find something else to do. Sleep was highly overrated, anyway.

Grabbing a towel and some clean clothes, he made his way to the bathroom down the hall with the idea that maybe a nice hot shower would relax him. He definitely needed it, whether it helped him sleep or not. When he arrived at his destination, he discovered that someone else had already beaten him there. From behind the closed door, however, he did not hear running water or any other typical bathroom sounds. Instead, he heard the sound of muffled sobs echoing from within.

Though the sound was one he'd heard before, especially after his father died, he was certain that it was not Vanessa behind that door. Taking a peak downstairs, he found Amy sound asleep on the couch. That left only one other possibility. Trying not to wake the rest of the house, he gently rapped his knuckle against the door. Inside, he heard her begin to scramble. Maybe he shouldn't have bothered her. Maybe he should have just gone back to his room until she fell asleep.

"Just a sec," she replied softly through a stuffy nose. There was a bit more shuffling and then the toilet flushed. The Girl stepped out of the room, rubbing her eyes as if she'd just woken up. "It's all yours," she smiled weakly, her hair hanging damp and limp around her pale face.

She had changed her clothes, borrowing one of Vanessa's tank tops and a pair of sweat pants that weren't covered in gore. The black top made her skin seem almost translucent in the dim light, and it hung loosely on her tiny frame, hiding all of the curves she normally chose to accentuate. It was completely not her style. The hunter found himself fighting the urge to smile at The Girl, who looked like a child playing dress up in her parents' closet, and that desire terrified him.

For a moment, he considered just letting her go back downstairs without ever acknowledging what he had heard. It might be better for both of them in the long run, especially since he was terrible at comforting others. And then he remembered the look on her face earlier that evening when he had told her that he was stepping out into the hall so that she could change clothes.

He reached out and caught her arm as she tried to move past him.

"Do you like pancakes?"

She looked at him as if he were completely insane, finally laughing as she replied, "Yeah, sure. Who doesn't?"

"Meet me in the kitchen in fifteen minutes then." And though she still seemed completely dumbfounded, she nodded her head and continued on down the stairs. He went into the bathroom and quickly showered, changing out of the filthy clothing he had been wearing and into some fresh laundry. Fifteen minutes later, he made his way down to the kitchen.

Chapter 58

"You know, you're pretty handsome without the shaggy beard and the layers of filth. And you can cook. Better be careful. A girl could definitely get used to this."

The Girl's words startled him, making him nearly drop the searing hot griddle as he scooped the last few pancakes onto a plate. It was the first thing she'd said since he found her sitting here at the table, waiting for him. But that's not why her words had surprised him.

He put a plate of food in front of her, as well as a glass of orange juice, then sat down beside her to eat as well. His plate was clean in a matter of moments, while she chose to take her time and taste the breakfast he had prepared. When he was finished stuffing his face, he began trying to think of ways to approach the inevitable conversation that must follow. Of all the people available, why did he have to be the one she seemed to trust? This would be so much easier for someone like Vanessa. She knew how to deal with people.

"I'm alright, you know." Well, that solved the problem of getting started at least. Obviously she had known why he invited her to dine with him this morning. Now, what should he say or do to get her to open up a little more?

"You didn't sound all right," he answered, immediately regretting his choice of words. Now he sounded like he was lecturing, and that's not at all what he wanted.

"So maybe things are a little overwhelming right now, but I think I'm handling it all pretty well. Don't you?"

"Better than I did when my parents died." Where did that come from? This was about The Girl, not him. He had to keep his focus here.

"Same bad guys?" He nodded, not really sure how much of his life's story he wanted to share with this girl, but finding it easier than he could have ever imagined. "Well, then I guess that's one thing we have in common. Of course, they didn't burn your house to the ground. And they didn't try to turn you to the dark side."

"You're half right." An image of a small, thin woman with raven hair flashed in his mind. Long before the Others had tried to kill him at the farm, they had used a much more sinister tactic to try recruiting him. The thought of the look in her eyes when he finally chose his side still made his muscles tense, as if he were preparing for an attack.

"Which half?" The Girl's voice brought him back from that scene in the desert just a few short years ago. He had to stop this discussion. It was making him very uncomfortable. Somehow, he had to turn it back around to focus on her, not him.

"Does it matter?" Not the most sensitive reply, but then, he'd never been known for his sensitivity.

"Sorry I asked." She stood, leaving her half-eaten pancakes on the table. "Thanks for breakfast." She was leaving and he still hadn't convinced her that she was with friends.

"Wait." Rising from his seat as well, he found that he had no idea what to say next.

"Look, I know you and Vanessa think you're helping, but you aren't. Maybe there is something to this superhero bit, and then again, maybe not. Either way, I'm not interested. You've all been doing fine in your little war without me. Why is it so important for me to join in now?" She still didn't understand. This wasn't just some game they were playing. The fate of the world was at stake. And recently, the bad guys had begun to win more battles than they lost.

"Things are out of our hands now. No matter what you decide, the Others will not let you get away from them."

"And neither will your Council."

He'd been thinking it, but to hear her say it only reinforced the helplessness that he felt. How could he go on protecting her if the Council decided she wasn't worth saving? And if they gave the project a green light, if they told him that she was the child they had been searching for? How could he alone fight off the hordes of demons that would inevitably attack?

"Be honest, Elijah. Are they going to kill me?"

"No, the Council doesn't kill anyone."

"But you do." Again, exactly what he was thinking. Except this time, there was something she hadn't been able to pick up on. He had defied the Council on plenty of occasions, and though it might mean his own life in this case, he wasn't about to kill an innocent girl.

"This is a war, and I am a soldier. I will do what I have to in order to survive, and I will fight for what I believe in. But I am not a murderer."

"Even if the Council orders it?"

"It wouldn't be the first time I went against their orders."

There was a tense moment as she studied his stony face, and then her features softened. Dropping her shoulders and her head, The Girl began to sob once again, though there was no door for her to hide behind this time. Unsure of how to respond but knowing that he should do something, the weary hunter placed a hand on her shoulder in a weak attempt to comfort. He was not expecting the reaction that followed.

The Girl threw her arms around his chest, burying her face in his shoulder and trembling like an autumn leaf in a strong wind. Such affection was completely foreign to him, and he wasn't sure he knew what to do.

"I'm so sorry," she mumbled into his shirt, and the defeat he heard in those words broke through his emotional defenses like a tank through a brick wall. His arms wrapped around her and they stood just like that until The Girl finally ran out of tears.

When she finally started to pull away from him, there was a strange sort of reluctance in him that at first shocked the hunter. This was exactly the kind of thing he'd been trying to avoid. Getting attached to someone like this was probably the worst thing that could happen right now. Still, he understood the feeling of being trapped, and those nights spent drying puffy red eyes were pretty familiar, too.

"You should try to get some rest," he told her, finding his own voice a bit ragged around the edges. She nodded, turning to head back into the living room where her sister still slept. He started to gather the dishes when another thought occurred to him. "Why don't you take my bed," he called softly. There was a moment of hesitation as he watched The Girl tossed a nervous glance at the still sleeping Amy. "I'll stay down here with her."

"What about you? Where will you sleep?"

"It's almost morning. Besides, I've had more than enough sleep for tonight."

That was a lie. He was still horribly exhausted. But he was used to such deprivation. This girl was not. Besides, she could use a break, especially since things could start getting crazy again at any moment. The Council was sure to call about their little adventure last night, which would mean a meeting between them and The Girl. The idea twisted his stomach into a terrible knot which was only made worse by the thought that the Others would be around shortly to tie up loose ends as well.

"Elijah?"

"Hmm?" he grunted absently, his mind still on the

future.

"Thank you." He stopped halfway to the sink, his hands full of dishes. Why was she thanking him? What had he done for her in the past few days besides create more problems and make things more complicated?

"Go get some rest." He held his breath until he heard the door to his room close, and then the brave knight went to the sink to finish the dishes. Just one more reason for the ladies to fall madly in love with him, right?

Just as he was putting the last dish back in the cupboard, a timid knock fell on the back door. He probably wouldn't have heard it at all if he hadn't been downstairs, though with his fragile nerves, his ears might very well have picked up on it. Only one person ever came to the back door, but it never hurt to be cautious, especially now. Drawing a knife from the drawer next to him, he crept silently to the door and peeked past the tiny curtain in the window.

Thomas waved cheerfully back at him. They had been friends for long enough to know and anticipate certain actions, so it was no surprise to the giant when Elijah tossed the knife back into the drawer as his friend stepped into the kitchen.

"Nice to see you're still alive," Thomas joked, though there was an underlying tension in his words. "After last night, the crew and I had bets going. I won, naturally."

"So you've heard."

"Everyone has."

Including the Council.

The unspoken words seemed to fill the distance between them, reinforcing the idea that the time for The Girl to join their society or die had finally come.

"How angry are they?" The grave look on Thomas's face was all the answer he needed. "I'll take her to see them as soon as she wakes up."

"Oh, it's gone way beyond that. The Council is taking you off of this assignment. They feel that you've lost your objectivity."

"They can't do that." But they could. And they would. He had crossed the line, endangering the very thing he was supposed to be protecting. They would not give him the chance to do it again.

"It gets worse. They're sending you on a thinning raid in Chicago. Apparently, there's been a huge influx in the area, and the Council wants to make sure the Others can't take over the entire city."

"They're sending me on a pop drop?" His outrage was beyond control, and both men immediately checked the neighboring room to be sure that his shouts hadn't woken any guests. A few moments later, they were back in the kitchen, neither quite sure what else to say.

"You can't go, man," Thomas finally spoke up. "It's bad out there. I have a buddy that I talked to this morning. He's right there in the thick of it, and he said that these aren't your average minions coming into the area. They're the real deal. Every team member that goes into a raid in that city dies."

"I'm not going anywhere. They can't take me off of this assignment. Who will watch over The Girl?"

"That's not our problem anymore." And in that statement, he heard a thousand other things. Thomas could care less what happened to The Girl. All he wanted was reassurance that the boy he'd grown up with wasn't about to go on a suicide mission. Even if he did care, it wouldn't matter, because the Council had already made a decision about this particular candidate.

"They don't think she's the one, do they?"

Thomas's patience finally snapped as he shouted, "Forget the damned Girl! They're sending you off to die, Elijah!"

"Keep your voice down," he scolded, but his words lacked any real force. How had so much gone so wrong so fast?

"I think it's time you left town. Take a vacation, see the world..."

"Hide from the Council?" He shook his head, thinking of all the new problems such actions would create. "We both know that won't work."

"Then talk to them. Make them understand why you did what you did."

"How can I when I don't even know why I did it? Besides, they've made their decision. It's over."

"So you're just going to give up?"

"What else can I do? If I go against their wishes again, then I'm terminated. If I follow orders like a good little soldier, then the Others will kill me."

Things were definitely not looking good. And then there was The Girl. How could he just stand by while they murdered her? She had been through so much, and she trusted him with her life. How could he hand her over to the Council when he knew it would only end in death for her?

"If you're smart, you'll run. The worst thing that can happen is getting caught, and so what if they kill you then? You're gonna die if you stick around here. Trying to escape would at least give you a fighting chance." Thomas had a point, although it wasn't a very convincing argument. Why waste the time and money in an effort that would inevitably end with the same results?

"I think I should wait and discuss it with Vanessa." She would know what to do. She always did. Thomas frowned and shook his head.

"No time. The Council is flying in right now. They'll be here tonight, and they want to speak with both you and The Girl as soon as they arrive."

Perfect. So now he was faced with one of the biggest decisions of his life, and he only had a few hours to make it. Why couldn't he wake up and start a day without knowing that it was going to be one of the worst days of his life?

"Fine," he sighed, rubbing his eyes wearily. "I'm going

to go tell Vanessa what's going on and start packing. Keep an eye on things down here."

"No problem."

But there was a problem. In fact, there were lots of problems with this plan. If he tried to run, they would catch him. And if he left, he would be abandoning Vanessa. And The Girl. What would happen to them once he was gone? What if the Council found out that Vanessa knew about his plan to flee? Would she suffer the same fate he faced? And then there was Thomas. Surely they would terminate him as well for his involvement in all of this.

Upstairs, he skipped Vanessa's room and immediately went to his own where he found The Girl fast asleep on his bed. Should he wake her and tell her what was happening? Would it matter if he did? She couldn't protect herself from them. This poor creature who had suffered so much already was about to find an end in all of this madness, though he wasn't so sure it was the end she hoped for.

Rather than disturb her, the man in black crept silently across the room to the closet where he began packing the duffle bag that had accompanied him on so many other journeys these past few years. It had seen him through many difficult times, this dirty, scuffed old scrap of leather and nylon. How fitting that it should be with him on this last trek. The world melted away as the memory of his first trip out of Wisconsin on Council business transported him back in time. Everything was different then. Vanessa had been so worried that he wouldn't come back. And he almost didn't. If it hadn't been for the California project and her amazing superhuman abilities, his entire team wouldn't have made it out of that desert alive. And how had he repaid that generosity? He had killed her and her boyfriend, leaving their bodies to rot in the desert.

This time, though, he would not allow the Council to use him as their instrument of death. If they wanted The Girl dead, they would have to find someone else. Slinging the tattered bag over his shoulder, he marched silently downstairs, determined to make this situation end in something other than death.

Chapter 59

Home.

Staring at the beige vinyl exterior that her mother had spent months of overtime money on because Andy refused to repair the flaking paint brought a sense of vertigo. Was this real? Had she only dreamed all of the chaos of the past few days? Could it be that she was home once again and that things were exactly as she remembered?

The smell of lavender filled her nose as a warm breeze drifted out of the garden. The same garden that she had worked to create with Amy and her mother just a few short months after Andy had left. This must be real. She could feel the gentle wind lifting the hair from her neck, smell the damp earth beneath her feet, hear the neighbor's dog barking frantically as the mailman approached the mailbox.

Relief washed over her as she finally accepted that this was not just a dream. This was her life, not that tattered mess she had been trapped in a few hours ago. Any minute now, her mother and sister would walk out of that door and ask her what she was doing out at this time of morning.

But why was she standing outside her home, staring at it from a distance instead of lying huddled beneath the covers on her bed? If the mailman was making his rounds, then why wasn't she still in bed? It wasn't as if she had to go to school. And why were the neighbors' cars still parked in their driveways?

Shouldn't they be at work? Maybe it was a weekend, but if that were the case, then there would be people out mowing their lawns or kids out enjoying the summer before the noon day sun became too much for even their young bodies and they retreated into the coolness of their homes.

"This is wrong," she whispered, and the moment the words left her mouth, she knew them to be true. She began noticing little things, like the fact that the flowers planted in front of the house were pansies, and her mother only planted begonias. Or the way Mr. Robertson's car was parked in the driveway, when he always put it in the garage unless he was washing it.

"Well, it's not perfect, but I wanted you to feel like you could at least live a normal life in your dreams." Spinning around, she found the stranger with the red hair standing just behind her.

"You did this?"

"It seemed like you could use a bit of an escape. I am sorry if I upset you."

"No," she shook her head, tears beginning to fill her eyes. "It's wonderful. Thank you."

"How are you?"

"I'll live," she chuckled, and the man shook his head with a smile that made him even more handsome than she remembered.

"Of course you will," he agreed. "I never doubted your

ability to survive such a situation. Still, it must be difficult to lose so much so quickly and without any explanation."

"Oh, Vanessa gave me an explanation. I just don't buy it."

"She did? And what exactly did she tell you?" He took a few steps closer as he spoke, stopping just inches from her. While his words were distant an uninterested, his eyes told another story, burning with curiosity. It was frightening and incredibly attractive, all at the same time.

"She says I'm some sort of superhero who's supposed to save the world. There was mention of a Prophecy, and something about a mob that killed my biological mother back in Montana. It was pretty crazy." Part of her wanted to tell him more, tell him everything she knew and even some things she only suspected, but there was another part of her that was screaming such an action would only make things worse. She chose the middle ground.

"Yes, well, I think Vanessa is a little confused." While his words echoed her greatest fears, that the woman who was trying so hard to protect her was also completely insane, his eyes burned with a strange intensity that she at first mistook for anger. When she noticed the slight curve at the corners of his mouth, it became apparent that he was not furious. He was practically giddy with anticipation.

"Who are you?" she blurted out, and immediately regretted it. Maybe she didn't want to know who he was. Maybe it would be better for everyone involved if she never knew the identity of this stranger who seemed to keep invading her dreams at some of her most vulnerable moments.

"I am a friend." Somehow, she wasn't convinced.

"If you're my friend, then how about some answers. Tell me what you know about this mess, and then maybe I'll consider trusting you."

The man laughed and shook his head, saying, "You are definitely a fast learner. I would love to tell you everything, Sarah, but unfortunately, I made a promise to some very important people."

"I know all of my other friends' names."

"I can't break my promise." Before she could argue any further, he reached out and placed a gentle hand on her shoulder. "What I can do is promise you that I will be waiting for you at the bar on Chestnut this afternoon."

"And you'll tell me everything?"

"I will tell you as much as I can, which is more than those other fools will do."

"Alright," she agreed, stepping closer until their faces were just inches apart. "Let's seal the deal with a kiss."

"I'm afraid that would be cheating."

"Cheating? What does that mean? Besides, who's going to know?" she teased, running a finger gently down his stomach. He reached down and stopped her before things could get interesting.

"You are clever, but I am afraid that information is classified. Besides, it is time you returned to the real world. You have missed some very interesting details."

"What details?" She took a step back, but the man didn't move.

"Ask the hunter. If you can find him."

And suddenly her home was gone, replaced by the barren white walls of Elijah's room. It was a stark contrast to her own room, with all her band posters and walls lined with music, movies, and books, or her wildly mismatched sheets and pillows on a slightly modified canopy bed that she'd had since she was ten. Staring at the neutrality around her brought back the tears that seemed to be so near the surface these past few days. Pushing herself out of the strange stiff bed, she barely managed to chase them back into their hiding place where they would wait for the next opportunity to burst forth.

There were voices coming from downstairs, one female and obviously upset. Creeping out into the hall, she finally recognized the voice as Vanessa's, though the second voice was not as familiar.

"…can't believe you didn't come to me first. And you let him leave! What were you thinking?" Well, sleep didn't seem to have improved her mood any.

"I thought he talked to you upstairs," the other voice replied. She knew that voice, but from where? "If I had known what he was up to… Oh, hell, you know him as well as I do. He was going, no matter what anyone else said."

"You don't know that. Maybe I could have reasoned with him. It's not like Chicago was a death sentence."

"Obviously you haven't been to Chicago recently." That tone…

Nice shootin', Tex.

Thomas.

"No one makes it out of a raid in that city alive these days. It was better for him to run."

Run? Who was running?

Ask the hunter. If you can find him.

Elijah was gone. She knew it not only from the conversation below but also from the knot that had begun to form in her stomach. Something was horribly wrong with this situation.

And there was something else. Though it was difficult to say exactly what, there was something gnawing at the back of her mind. Something bad.

"We have to go find him, before he does something stupid." Vanessa was right, but where would he go? The airport? The bus station?

The Council.

The tiny voice that whispered inside her head was almost too soft to hear. If she hadn't been so wrapped up in her own thoughts, she might never have noticed it. And the strangest part was, it sounded like Elijah's voice.

Where is this Council of yours? she asked herself, but there was no reply. She had to find him. If he was in as much danger as the arguing couple downstairs seemed to believe, then he had to be warned. But where to start looking...

Vanessa's room, of course. Elijah had a cell phone, that much she could remember. Vanessa had to have the number somewhere. If she could find that number, then she could contact the man who had risked his life for her more times than she cared to imagine.

Another thought occurred to her. Where was Amy? Why wasn't she saying anything? She couldn't possibly still be sleeping with all the arguing downstairs.

No time. Once Elijah was safe, then she could focus on her sister. Moving swiftly and silently, just as she'd seen the man in black do the night before, she found her way into Vanessa's room and began rummaging through the nightstand drawers. Hundreds of numbers awaited her inside, but none of them were labeled with recognizable names. There were jumbles of symbols, some of which looked like an actual alphabet while others just seemed to be squiggles on paper. Unfortunately, there were more of the latter in the drawer. The second problem seemed to be that none of the numbers were recognizable. There were pieces missing, since some of the sequences were only four or five numbers long, and some of the strings of characters included members who were reversed or upside down. Clearly, there was no information here that could be risked leaking into enemy hands.

Okay, Sarah, think! This is just like one of those crazy brain puzzles you loved back in grade school. Find the key, break the code.

But that was the trick, wasn't it? The key. There had to be a pattern, some sort of method to this madness. It might help if she knew what some of the other symbols were, but there was clearly something to the reversals and upended numbers. Could she find it in time? Difficult to say for sure, especially since she had no idea how much time she had before things fell apart. If the queasy feeling in the pit of her stomach was any indication, it wouldn't be too much longer.

Spreading the collection of paper scraps across the floor in front of her, Sarah took a few deep breaths to steady her frayed nerves and began looking for clues.

The more she stared, the more jumbled and confused her thoughts became. Time was running out. She had to hurry. What if she didn't figure it out? What if this encryption proved to be too difficult? Never once had she met a code she couldn't break, but what if she'd finally met her match?

Give up. You'll never figure it out.

It had been a long time since she'd heard that voice. The voice of Andy. The voice of her mother. The voice of a dozen teachers, all telling her she'd never amount to anything because of her clothes, her income, her attitude. And she hadn't given into that voice yet.

I have to keep trying. He'd do the same for me.

Letting her eyes lose their focus a bit, she watched as the numbers and symbols began to blur together.

Stay calm. Relax. Breathe. Let it come.

And then, it happened. Like a river suddenly breaking free of a dam, the system fell into place. Though she had never actually seen many of the symbols before, Sarah managed to pick through them and assign a letter to each one, realizing quickly that some were actually representing sounds rather than single letters. The numbers were simple after that. Two reversed threes meant read the number backwards. A reversed six and an upside down seven meant that the first three letters should trade places with the next three. The backwards four was a little tougher, but after a few moments and a quick glance at the phone beside the bed, she realized it must mean shifting each number up one on the number pad.

Finally, she found a slip with what was clearly a cell number and what she thought was Elijah's name, or at least a form of it. Before she could dial the number, there was a knock on the front door downstairs. The queasy feeling she had noticed earlier suddenly became a sharp, twisting pain in her gut, and she quickly moved away from the scattered papers for fear that she might ruin them with the pancakes she'd eaten just a few hours earlier.

Now or never. Call him and warn him before it's too late.

She had the phone in her hands and was dialing the number before she had a chance to question it. There was an answer on the third ring.

"I don't have time for this right now, Vanessa," the man in black answered in a stony voice. "You aren't going to talk me out of it."

"Running off without me? I'm hurt, Elijah." A long pause followed as the shock of hearing her voice instead of Vanessa's slowly wore off.

"How did you get this number?"

"Found it in Vanessa's room," she answered casually. Then, back on topic, "So, suicide is the only option, then?"

"It's not suicide. I have to speak with them. It's the only way to convince them of the truth."

"And what truth might that be?" Another pause, but it answered her question. "They think I'm just another dud, don't they?"

"I have to go talk to them."

"But it won't help. We both know that." Sighing, she asked, "So where does that leave us?"

"Just stay there with Vanessa and Thomas until I get back."

"And if you don't come back?"

"I always come back." Was that a hint of amusement she heard in his voice? "Just make sure your bags are packed in case we need to leave in a hurry."

"I'll tell Vanessa."

"Tell me what?" Spinning around, she found Vanessa

standing in the doorway of the room. The frown on her face as she glanced at the floor told the younger girl that she was not amused.

"Speak of the devil," she mumbled.

"Who are you talking to?" the woman asked, stepping into the room.

"Elijah. Wanna say hi?"

"No," the man in black responded quickly. "Just be ready when I get there."

"I'd love to speak with that boy," Vanessa smiled, but it seemed a bit strained.

"Sorry, he says he has to go." Then, into the phone, "Hurry back, cause I think things are about to get pretty interesting around here."

There was a soft click as he hung up on his end just before Vanessa snatched the phone from her hands. She reached down and started gathering papers as the elder woman discovered that the connection had been severed. The woman placed the device back in its cradle, shaking her head.

"You almost had me convinced," Vanessa chuckled.

"Of what?" she asked, sliding open the drawer beside the bed once again.

"Let me guess, he gave you his number in case you ran into trouble when he wasn't around."

"Something like that." Every fiber of her being was filled with the rush of her accomplishment, begging her to tell

Vanessa how she cracked the code. Still, if these past few days had taught her nothing else, it was that caution was the key to survival. Rather than bragging about how brilliant she was, perhaps this was a secret she should reveal later, once she was sure it wouldn't cause more problems. With the luck she'd been having, the CIA would probably find out about her amazing abilities and kidnap her to work as their own personal secret decoder ring.

"Your mother's lawyer is downstairs. He says he needs to speak with you and your sister."

Perfect. Things weren't crazy enough, now there was a lawyer involved.

The weary girl made her way out into the hall and down the stairs. Vanessa caught up to her at the bottom where they found Amy whispering softly to Alan Grove, the man who had dealt with all of Angela's legal matters since the divorce. Thomas stood nearby, leaning against the wall with his hands in his coat pockets.

"Sarah," Alan greeted her, extending a hand for a friendly yet solemn handshake. "I'm so sorry about you mother."

"Thank you," she responded automatically, somehow managing a soft smile as she said it. "It's so good of you to stop by."

"Well, I wanted to make sure that you girls were safe. The police said something about you being missing when I talked to them after the explosion."

"As you can see, we're fine. Vanessa has been kind enough to lend us her home until we can figure all of this out." On the outside, she was everything the world expected of a girl that had just lost her mother and her home. Inside, however, she was full of questions about how this man had found her. Could he be one of the bad guys? He said he had talked to the police, but all of the local law enforcement had been killed. Maybe she was just being paranoid, or maybe this guy was someone she needed to keep an eye on.

"That's the other thing I wanted to discuss with you. Is there somewhere we can go to talk privately?"

She tossed a glance at Vanessa, who immediately moved to usher Amy and the giant out of the living room. Amy refused to go quietly, though. Desperation in her eyes, the panicked girl broke free of Vanessa's grasp and raced to her sister's side.

"Sarah, don't," the girl pleaded, her tiny fingers wrapping around her big sister's bare bicep.

"It's okay, Amy," Sarah tried to reassure her, placing a comforting hand over Amy's icy grip. "I'll be fine. Go with Vanessa and get some breakfast."

Amy gave the lawyer one last questioning look, then allowed Vanessa and Thomas to lead her away to the next room. She kept casting worried glances over her shoulders, though, despite the soothing whispers of the charming auburn beauty.

Thomas seemed rather nervous about leaving as well, though he hid it much better. It was nice to know he was nearby, just in case.

Once they were gone, Alan and Sarah sat on the couch, side by side with his briefcase on the coffee table in front of them. There was a long silence as the man unlatched the case and pulled out a folder full of paperwork.

"Angela loved you girls both very much," he told her in a thick, crackling voice. Clearing his throat, he managed to continue without shedding the tears that had welled up in his eyes, though it was clearly a challenge. "She wanted to make sure you were taken care of if anything ever happened to her. She also wanted to make sure your father was not an issue. She succeeded in at least one of those areas."

"Andy is not my father," she corrected, but there was no strength in her words. Looking into those big gray-blue pits of sorrow, she simply couldn't feel anything but an overwhelming sadness.

He handed the stack of papers to her, his hands trembling slightly, and said, "These are copies of your mother's insurance policies, bank account statements, and her will. In that folder, you'll find that you have been named executor of the estate and you are the beneficiary of every policy. You have also been given custody of your sister until she turns eighteen. Angela made sure Andy had no claim to either of you girls or your money."

"I don't think I'm ready to deal with all this yet." But she had to deal with it. She was the executor, the beneficiary, the oldest daughter. This was her responsibility.

"Of course," the man nodded, running a shaky hand over his mouth. "I'm sorry, Sarah. I know this is hard for you, but I'm afraid it has to be done. If your father tries to contest the will..."

"He is *not* my father." The sudden fierceness of her words shocked both of them into silence. The overwhelming sorrow had finally begun to fade in the face of her growing rage. But he didn't deserve this. He was trying to help, to do what her mother had wanted. No matter how she felt at that moment, Alan Grove should not be her target. Taking a deep breath and fighting the tears that once again lingered just below the surface, she apologized. "I didn't mean to yell. It's just been a really emotional couple of days, you know?"

"Yeah." He didn't seem completely convinced that she'd pulled herself together, but he let her push forward with the conversation.

Forcing a smile, she said, "Okay, so why don't you explain to me what all of this says in plain English?"

"It says, minus taxes and funeral expenses, you're now worth about six million dollars."

Sarah's jaw dropped as she turned her attention to the papers in her lap. Impossible. Why would her mother have always been so financially frantic if this much money was available to them? Then again, it was all tied up in insurance policies.

"I'm sorry, I must have just hallucinated. What did you say?"

"Angela was always paranoid about money," he quickly explained, "so she tried to make sure that you had nothing to worry about if she was suddenly unable to take care of you. She took out several life insurance policies, plus there's the insurance for the house and the cars…"

"This is crazy." She stood, shaking her head and staring at the papers in her hands. Never once in the past forty-eight hours had she considered what they would do about money or food or shelter. Now, suddenly, she didn't have to.

"I've already taken care of funeral arrangements. I hope that's alright with you. It's just that I had no idea where you two were until just a few hours ago, and none of the other relatives wanted the job…"

"Thank you," she interrupted. There was no need for him to explain. She was actually glad to have someone else take on that responsibility. Truth was, she didn't think she would be able to look at her mother without seeing that bloated, seeping monster from the hospital. Desperate to finish this conversation and get back to sorting through the mess that had become her life, she added, "I'm glad she found someone like you to share the past few months with."

Was that true? Was she truly happy that her mother had

been seeing this man, doing many of the same things she had punished her eldest daughter for? Excessive drinking, staying out all night during the week, ignoring those she supposedly loved? Still, none of that was truly this man's fault. He had obviously loved Angela, and he was trying to comfort her daughters, despite his own grief. To punish him would be horribly unfair.

"The funeral is today. Two o'clock at Willow Ridge Cemetery." Alan stood, collected his things, and headed for the door. Sarah's attention once again settled on the folder that contained the last of her mother's legacy. It was still difficult to believe that she was gone, let alone that she'd left her children millionaires.

"Sarah?" Alan lingered in the open doorway, holding a small scrap of paper in his right hand. "If you or Amy need anything…"

"We'll be in touch," she smiled, hoping it didn't seem too strained. He placed the card on the plush green chair beside the door and left. A few moments later, Amy timidly entered the room from the kitchen, followed closely by the others.

"The funeral is this afternoon," she sighed, tossing the folder on the coffee table and heading for the stairs.

"What's in the folder?" Amy called after her, but she was too emotionally exhausted to stay here and explain everything. Instead, she found her way to the bathroom where she began the grueling process of preparing to bury her mother.

Chapter 60

How had this happened? A week ago, The Girl was getting ready for graduation, the Others had practically disappeared, and the Council was discussing the idea of finally revealing everything to her. Now, The Girl's family was in shambles, the Council was demanding her presence and discussing her inevitable termination, and he was facing a death sentence as well.

Twenty minutes ago, she had surprised him once again with a call on his cell phone. The only people who had the number were Vanessa and Thomas, and neither would have given it out without a good reason. But The Girl claimed she'd gotten it from Vanessa's room, not Vanessa. Yet another impossibility, since all of Vanessa's documents were written in some secret code that had been developed by his father. It had been a hobby for Michael, and despite an extraordinary effort, his son had never been able to understand. That made it a perfect way to keep any confidential information from falling into the wrong hands.

Now, after spending the last fifteen minutes in this tiny room with its white walls and deep red carpet, sitting in a plush red chair and listening to the ancient grandfather clock tick away the seconds until the Councilor arrived, he couldn't help but wonder what The Girl was doing at that moment. Was she safe? She had mentioned things getting interesting. Was that some kind of code? Maybe they really would need to make a quick getaway. Had she given Vanessa his message? There was a very good chance that this meeting was going to end in bloodshed, and if he made it out alive, they would all have to run.

Damn the Council! How could they do this to him? He had given so much, and now they were going to punish him for one mistake? Okay, so it wasn't the first time he had defied the Council, but every time he had gone against their orders, it had turned out for the best. Their cause had always benefited from his actions. So why were they suddenly ready to ditch him and terminate his assignment?

The door behind the black marble desk that stretched in front of him finally opened and the only Councilor to arrive so far stepped in. Councilor Claire Marcum glided silently to the leather office chair behind the desk and sat, her eyes never leaving his face. Though she was almost fifty years old and appeared to be about the size of a twelve year old girl, he knew she was not someone to provoke. Only the cleverest, toughest individuals survived long enough to become Councilors, and though she may not look it, this woman could hurt him in ways he could never imagine.

"I assume you're here about the little stunt you pulled last night." Not a hint of emotion was present in her words or her expression. If she was as furious as Thomas claimed, she must have some amazing self-control.

"I came to talk about The Girl." His tone matched hers,

coaxing a hint of movement at the corners of the Councilor's mouth. Whether it was amusement or anger, he couldn't say, but he had triggered something in this woman. Her next statement clarified things for him.

"Such dedication. I have to wonder if that same kind of devotion to your work would be present if the assignment was something other than an attractive young lady."

"You can't terminate this assignment yet. You haven't even met her."

"After last night, it is clear to us that she is not the one we seek."

"What do you know about last night?" His words remained calm, but inside he was a jumble of fury and fear. Had they sent someone to spy on him? An extra hand in this mess would have been welcome, but the idea of someone lurking in the shadows just behind him was ridiculous. It suddenly occurred to him that this must be how The Girl had felt when she'd found out about him.

Then again, such things were expected from the Council. They were notorious for their intricate spy network and their ability to know everything that happened within the Society because of it. The Girl had been completely blindsided by the news that she'd been followed for most of her life by strangers. He, though, had always known he was being watched.

Before he could consider the implications of such well-founded paranoia, the Councilor pulled him back to the conversation at hand. Her words were a harsh reminder of why he was here in the first place.

"I know that if you hadn't been there to rescue the damsel in distress, that pathetic excuse for a minion would have taken her to his master. The child we are looking for would never be overpowered by such a lesser being."

She had a point. The child from the prophecy was supposed to be incredibly powerful. Powerful enough to send the Others back to their own world. Powerful enough to defeat even the fiercest of the enemy's warriors in this world. Defeating one little minion should have been like a stroll through the park. Then again, The Girl's last stroll through the park had nearly ended in her death.

"She's been sheltered from this world for her entire life. How can we expect her to use abilities she doesn't know she has? Besides, shouldn't you at least meet her before passing final judgment?"

"Why are you so concerned about this girl? Even if we do let her live, she's no longer your assignment. Once we find The Child, the Council will take over the responsibility of training and protecting it. Your job is over." The Councilor's icy stare told him that she was expecting him to argue. His response clearly surprised her.

"Is that why I'm being sent on a suicide run in Chicago?" There was a moment of silence as she considered what to say next, though he suspected she also needed that moment to compose herself. He allowed her all the time she needed, refusing to give up any information about his source for this information, either intentionally or accidentally.

"Did your friend Thomas tell you that?" she prodded, but silence was his only reply. "Alright, I suppose it wouldn't hurt anything to meet with this girl. Bring her here at eight o'clock tomorrow morning. Afterwards, we can discuss *your* future."

When the Councilor rose, he did the same, bowing slightly as he did so. She didn't seem to notice, but he knew better. She saw everything. Once she was out of the room, he turned and waited for one of the Councilor's flock to escort him out through the door beside the big wooden clock.

A few moments passed before Councilor Marcum's newest guard, a short but muscular young woman named Mona, entered the room. Her pale blond hair slid over the shoulders of her black coat like streaks of paint. The thick, red gunk on her lips only served to make her fair complexion almost sickly as she approached with the hint of a sneer at the corners of her mouth.

"Time to go," she ordered in a thick, gravelly voice. Only women who were long time smokers and steroid users had voices like that. Given the size of her, he was guessing the latter.

Refusing to argue and cause even more problems, he followed the woman back through the maze of offices, past the giant board room that would serve as the meeting place to discuss his future. Again, a sharp sense of rebellion spiked deep in his gut as he tried to decide what to do next. How dare these people treat him like a dog to be put down on a whim? Who were they to decide who had earned the right to live? And why was life something that had to be earned to begin with? Shouldn't it just be a given?

"She worth it?" He didn't look at the burly woman, nor did he answer her question. Instead, he played dumb in the hopes that it would keep them all alive a little longer so that he could sort out this mess.

"I have no idea what you mean," he answered flatly, but she obviously didn't believe him.

"She's gotta be one hell of a girl to make one of the Council's favorite hunters consider going rogue."

"She's an assignment," he told her, refusing to admit or deny the accusation. Lying to the Council would get him killed for certain, but in this case, the truth could be just as deadly.

"Well," Mona said, holding open the outer door to spill sunlight into the sterile office building, "all I know is she's got enough magic to make you face off against the Council. That's pretty impressive, even if she isn't what they're looking for."

Refusing to acknowledge the woman's observation, he made his way down the concrete path to the parking lot where his car sat waiting. The sun was already approaching its peak, leaving the air thick and sweltering. It was a huge change from the controlled environment where he'd me the Councilor. The inside of the car was worse, though, and he immediately flipped on the air conditioning the moment the engine began to hum.

Well, he had bought them some time at least. The question now was, should they wait and meet the Council, or should they just run?

Chapter 61

The funeral was outdoors at the grave site where the woman that had raised her would spend the rest of eternity buried beneath layer after layer of dirt and rock. It wasn't fair. What had Angela ever done wrong, besides making a few bad choices like the adoption of a certain baby girl? This wasn't right. Her mother shouldn't be the one lying in that casket, too grotesque for anyone to lay eyes upon. Sarah felt the guilt bearing down on her, making her chest ache under the pressure. If anyone should be dead right now, it was her. Everything that had happened to her tiny family over the past year had been because of her.

Alan was there, and so were some of Angela's coworkers from both the grocery store and the real estate office. Many of Amy and Sarah's classmates showed up, though they appeared to be more interested in catching up on all the latest summer gossip than they were in comforting the girls. Probably making fun of the ridiculous outfit she'd borrowed from Vanessa. On its rightful owner, the black dress was simple and elegant, reaching to just above the knee and hugging her body in a tasteful yet flattering way. On Sarah, it looked completely ridiculous as it hung on her scrawny shoulders as if she were a closet hanger. And the shoes…well, she'd never really been one for heels, and pumps were generally out of the question. Today, though, she'd had little choice in her attire. At least Amy was taller with more curves. She actually looked almost normal in the blouse and skirt combo she'd snatched from Vanessa's closet.

The pastor's words provided her little comfort, and the guilt began to edge its way into paranoia. Did any of these people know the truth about what had happened? Did any of them know that she was to blame? They all seemed to be staring at her, accusing her of so much without saying a word. Any minute now they would turn on her, those reproachful eyes glaring, screaming that she was a murderer, that she had killed her mother and now they were going to kill her.

"Sarah," Alan whispered from beside her, pulling her out of the horrible world her mind had begun to drift towards. "You okay?"

"This is my fault," she answered softly, not really sure why she was saying it at all. This man could never understand. He had no idea how crazy her life had suddenly become, with people chasing her around, trying to kill her or protect her or recruit her. Still, she had to tell someone. Maybe she could just leave out the parts that would make her sound like a raving lunatic.

"What could you have possibly done to change things?"

"I could have listened, taken Angela's advice for once and stayed home instead of going for a walk in the park that morning. Things would have been very different if I'd just listened."

"You're right," he replied, and her stomach twisted

sharply as she waited for the rest of the crowd to turn and agree as well. They would make her pay for what she had done, make her give her life for the one that was taken from them. Instead, he nodded to the slowly descending casket and said, "We could be putting three of those in the ground instead of just one."

"You don't understand…"

"If you had been there, then they would have either killed you or taken you like they did Amy. Either way, none of you would have survived."

"How did you know about Amy?"

"She told me earlier while you and Vanessa were upstairs. I can't believe you went head-on with a mass murderer. My buddy at the crime lab showed me pictures of the station. You were very brave, but also very stupid."

"What was I supposed to do? Wait for the police to find her?" Amy stepped up to the casket, Vanessa at her side, saying her last goodbyes to what was left of their mother. "She needed me."

"And you needed her."

"I have to go." The man grabbed her arm before she could take the first step.

"She mentioned someone else. I think she said his name was Elijah."

"I have no idea what you're talking about." Despite her waning apprehension about this man, she refused to discuss any of the complete insanity that had taken hold of her world over the past few days with him. Whether it was caution or simply a refusal to acknowledge that any of it had happened, it just seemed wrong to talk about such things here. Even if he believed her stories, someone else might overhear. Someone a bit less understanding. The thought sent her eyes darting through the crowd again, looking for anything suspicious. Could one of the monsters be here? Or maybe a Council spy? Without Elijah, she was a sitting duck.

"Relax," Alan smiled. "I don't care who he is or what he was doing there last night. But if you happen to see him again, tell him I said thanks for making sure you both got out of there safely."

"I doubt he'll be back, but if he shows up, I'll give him the message."

Honestly, she didn't think Elijah would care much about this man's thanks, but she was hoping she'd have the chance to deliver the message personally. Not only would that mean the man in black had survived his meeting, but she'd have yet another excuse to spend some time with him. And, though she never would have believed such a thing when they first met, she was beginning to like the guy.

"Oh, and I almost forgot. Your mother knew how much you love to snoop and find gifts early, so she gave me this for safe keeping." He handed her a small purple envelope that could only be meant for one thing.

"Money?" The man shook his head as he walked away.

"Better," he called over his shoulder. "Happy birthday."

Not quite ready to look inside, she slipped the envelope into her borrowed purse and turned her attention to Amy and Vanessa. Thomas had joined them from his observation point in the car, clearly ready to leave before things got crazy. She felt a bit of the tension ease from her body as she realized they weren't quite as vulnerable as she'd first thought. Amy was a mess, barely capable of breathing, let alone speaking through the hysterical sobs that had taken control of her body. Could she go back to that? Could she be strong for Amy until things settled down a bit? Could she trust the woman who had lied to her for so many years about so many things?

She glanced down at her watch. Almost three. A man with hair the color of flames was waiting for her at a bar with answers to her big questions. Despite the voice in her head screaming for her not to go to him, she knew she was out of options. Staying here with Vanessa and Amy would only end in more death. Even Vanessa had no clue what was happening. Maybe Thomas had given up a few details, but if Vanessa knew the whole truth about the Council, she would never have allowed them all to waste this much time saying goodbye in a big, open cemetery. They would have been on a plane to Siberia by now, not parading around like huge bullet magnets. No, the only way any of them would survive this disaster was for her to find the missing pieces of the puzzle that was now her life. For that, she needed him.

    Pulling out her cell phone, she quickly called a taxi to take her to her destination. The rest of them were so busy consoling one another and trying to calm the hysterical Amy, they barely noticed her presence anyway. Without a word to the any of the grieving individuals around her, Sarah slipped away from the crowd and silently exited the cemetery.

Chapter 62

His phone rang just as he was pulling back onto the main highway. Thankfully, news of the Council's displeasure hadn't had time to infiltrate all of his contacts. His weapons dealer had been more than happy to supply the extra gear now stashed in the trunk. Daryl was a loyal Council flunky, but because he was so isolated at his tiny farm in the middle of nowhere, he was usually the last to hear any news from the big shots. Unfortunately, his isolation also made it difficult to stop by for supplies without someone finding out. If the Council discovered this unscheduled visit, they would definitely suspect that something was up.

Choosing to ignore the cloud of doom that seemed to linger over all of them, he steadied his nerves and tried to prepare for even more bad news. The name on the display said it was Vanessa calling from her cell, but then, the last time he'd expected to hear Vanessa's voice, he had gotten a very big surprise. If The Girl had Vanessa's mobile phone, things may have just gone from bad to nightmare.

"Hello," he answered flatly, and the response he got was not at all comforting.

"She's gone!" Vanessa nearly screamed into the phone. "We were at the funeral and she disappeared! You have to find her, now!"

"Calm down." Two words he never thought he'd have

to use when talking to this woman. "Tell me what happened."

There was a pause as she took a few deep breaths, and then she explained, "We all went to Angela's funeral. Amy was having a really hard time with everything, so I stuck close to her. When the service was over, Sarah stepped aside to speak with Angela's lawyer, and the next thing I knew, she was gone."

"Did you see any other vehicles nearby?"

"Nothing unusual, just the other people at the funeral. They were all still there when she disappeared."

"Did you check with the cab company?"

"No, not yet." He caught a hint of a sniffle in the background. It didn't sound like Vanessa, so he chose to ignore it and focus on the bigger problem.

"Get everyone back to the house. I'll take care of The Girl."

Pulling the car into a convenience store parking lot, he called the local taxi service.

"Big Yellow Taxi. How may we help you?" a woman greeted warmly. He did not return the sentiment.

"Patch me through to dispatch," he commanded.

"Is there something I can help you with, sir?" Some of the perkiness had faded from the voice, but the woman still seemed to be working to keep the customer satisfied.

"Sorry, I just really need to speak with Bill in dispatch. It's an emergency."

"May I ask who's calling?"

"Tell him it's his old hunting buddy."

There was a moment of silence as she checked with the dispatcher and then there was the click as he was transferred.

"What can I do for you?" a familiar voice answered.

"I've got a little problem I thought you could help me with."

"What kind of problem is that?"

"I'm trying to find someone, and I think she may have taken a cab from the cemetery."

"Well, I haven't gotten any calls for pick-ups at any cemeteries," there was a pause as the man flipped through some papers, "but I did get a call from a girl at the dry cleaners down the street from Maple Ridge."

"Did she give a name?"

Please, let it be her.

"Nope, said she was paying in cash. There was a car just one block over, so I sent the driver to pick her up. Sounded like she was in a hurry."

"Any idea where she was going?" If this guy didn't give him some information he could use, he was stuck canvassing the entire city, looking for some stupid girl that couldn't manage to stay out of trouble for a few hours while he was out trying to save her life.

"Let me talk to the driver. Hang on." After what seemed like an eternity that was probably closer to ten minutes, there was a click and the dispatcher finally proved himself useful. "The bar on the corner of Chestnut and Pine. I think it's called…"

"Brew Moon. Thanks."

He didn't even give the man a chance to say goodbye before hanging up the phone and peeling out into the street. They would never serve her alcohol and she knew it. She'd tried enough times to realize this town was too small to get away with fake ID's. So why the bar? And more importantly, why *that* bar?

Everyone in the Society knew that Brew Moon was a hot spot for the Others. There had been frequent raids on the place since it's opening in 1972, at least until the murder of Michael Crawfton.

That night was still etched into his brain, its pain burning bright in his memory. He'd gotten the call at just past ten. Vanessa had been downstairs in the library working on research while his father checked in on The Girl. There had been so little activity in the area, the Council had been on the verge of sending him back to the Academy and terminating the assignment.

All of that had changed in the blink of an eye. The voice he'd heard as he'd answered the phone was not that of his father, though it had clearly been Michael Crawfton's agonized screams echoing in the background.

"Put her on the phone," it had commanded, and before he could protest, Vanessa had been at his side, snatching the receiver from his hand.

"Who is this?" she'd asked. He had watched in horror as all the color drained from her face and she continued, "I understand. Please, just let him go."

He'd started to grab the phone, to demand an explanation, but it was too late. Slamming the earpiece back into its cradle, the woman had bolted to the front door. He'd been right behind her, taking the wheel despite his youth, and she had given him strange, erratic directions as they'd raced through the dark, empty night. It had almost seemed as if even she didn't know where they were going.

Any strength she'd managed to cling to vanished the instant they'd pulled onto Pine Street. Even from a block away, it had been obvious something horrific lay just ahead. He remembered the sound of her flopping back against the seat, defeated and alone, but his eyes had been locked on the grisly scene outside the bar.

As Vanessa had begun to sob hysterically, he'd slowly pulled the car up to the curb, the headlights illuminating what was clearly the mutilated corpse of his father. A thin cord had been wrapped around his neck and used to dangle his bloody body from the light post outside the bar. The weight had been enough that even with the short time between the phone conversations and their arrival, the line had begun to tear through the flesh of the man's throat. Soon, he would be decapitated as well as eviscerated.

The body had been stripped of all clothing, and into the

chest was carved a message. A single word that would haunt his dreams until the day he died.

If she was at that bar, then the reason was obvious. The same thing that had lured his father there had also managed to attract The Girl as well. The Others were notorious for being creatures of habit, which meant that the very same beast could be waiting for her just as it had been waiting for Michael. But would she meet a similar fate, or did the Others have something else in store for The Girl?

Things had just gone from bad to worse, and if he didn't get to her soon, there would be no hope left for any of them.

Chapter 63

He was waiting for her at a corner table with a margarita and a smile. Finally meeting him was more incredible than she could have ever imagined. He was even more charming in person, standing to pull out her chair as she approached and even taking her purse for her. His eyes were the deepest green she'd ever seen, making her believe that if she stared at them for too long she could get lost in their vast beauty. And his hair…just as it had been in her dream, though more vibrant and alive even in the dingy light of the bar. Her stomach fluttered in anticipation at the sound of his deep, haunting voice.

"I thought you might need a drink after such a difficult morning." He slid the beverage across the table, allowing the tips of his fingers to brush gently against hers. It sent a tingle up her arm and to her spine, where she just barely managed to suppress a shiver.

Christ, I'm acting like some cheap romance heroine.

"Thanks," she replied, finding the sound of her own voice grating and unattractive compared to his.

But then, comparing any part of her to this glorious creature was absurd. He was a marble angel, every detail chiseled by some divine power and given a spark of life so overwhelming, it seemed she might suffocate in his presence alone. Sitting here, her mousy brown hair with its shock of faded purple hanging limply across her shoulders as her dull brown eyes stared in awe at his magnificence, seemed almost insulting. Even more ridiculous was the idea of romance blossoming between them. What on earth could he ever see in a silly teenage girl?

"Well, I suppose we should get down to business. There is much to discuss and little time before your companions realize you are missing."

"How do you know I didn't tell them where I was going?"

"Because if you had, the hunter would be trailing along behind you."

Hunter? He had used the same word once before to refer to Elijah. In fact, even Vanessa had labeled the man in black with this odd term. The sound of it rang in her ears, echoing through her head ominously.

He seemed to sense her discomfort, reaching out to wrap her hand in his. That one touch sent a wave of longing coursing through her veins, casting out any sense of foreboding. All she knew in that moment was that he was miraculous, and that radiant smile on his face was meant just for her. Desperately trying not to seem like the goofy girl with a crush, she did her best impression of casual.

"And how can you be sure he's not?" She took a sip of her drink, amazed at how perfect this moment was. There were no other patrons in the bar, only a bored bartender in the back watching television. Alone with an angel.

"Because you are. But that is another discussion. You

have questions, and hopefully, I have answers."

"Hopefully?" He shook his head and tapped the expensive watch wrapped around his wrist. Yes, her questions were limited by time, so why waste any with ridiculous flirting? "Alright, why am I so special?"

"My, that is a bit more direct than I expected," he chuckled. "I assume what you really want to know is why everyone is so interested in you. The answer is your lineage."

"You mean my parents?"

"And grandparents and their parents…"

"I don't understand."

"Generations ago, a very powerful young man had a daughter. She had a daughter, and then came another daughter, and after several generations have passed, we arrive at a young woman in Wisconsin who had a daughter of her own. The father of this child was also incredibly powerful, and when the two bloodlines mixed, something amazing happened." He paused, and she realized she was sitting on the edge of her seat, just inches from him.

"What?" she asked breathlessly.

"You," and his smile was so radiant at that moment she thought she might go blind from staring at it.

"Wait," she shook her head, a nervous laugh escaping in the process, "Vanessa said my mother was from Montana."

"Did she?" he asked with a knowing smile. "That is interesting." She waited for him to elaborate, but he just sat there, grinning at her. Eventually, she sighed and let it drop. She could always try again later. Perhaps a different line of questioning would lead to some more information.

"Alright, so I'm the daughter of two powerful bloodlines. Which ones?"

"I am afraid I cannot answer that right now, but I know someone who can. Would you like to meet him?"

"In a minute. First, tell me who you are."

"Again, not the question I expected. You are full of surprises today."

"After what I've been through these past few days, I'm not going anywhere with anyone I don't know." Obviously, this response impressed him.

He leaned in until their faces almost touched and whispered, "But you would kiss a stranger?"

"In a dream, yes," she replied, trying to keep her cool even though her entire body seemed to be on fire at his very touch.

"What about in a sleazy bar where no one is watching?"

He's trying to dodge your question.

"I don't kiss anyone until I at least know his name." This time he didn't seem as amused, and the edges of his brilliant smile dimmed a bit.

"Why is my name so important to you?"

"Why do you keep trying to avoid telling me?"

With a sigh, he leaned back and said, "You may call me

Ethan."

"No last name?"

"Sarah, we do not have time for these games!" His anger seeped through, making each word sting like an angry wasp. When he saw her cringe, his tone immediately softened. It was different, though, as if something dark and ominous was hiding behind that heavenly façade. Almost as though the anger was real and the rest was some sort of mask.

"If you want more answers, you will have to come with me. They will be here any minute to take you away, back to that mess they have created."

"I don't know if I should…"

"You have to come with me," he demanded. "You have to meet him."

My, that sounded familiar. Hadn't Adam said something similar?

There are so many other wonderful things he can do for you…

Something was definitely wrong. Maybe this man wasn't the shining angel she thought he was. Even as she thought this, she found some of the wonder seeping from her vision of him until finally, she was looking at what lay beneath. He was not angry or desperate like Adam had been. He was empty. Cold. Cruel.

"Who do I have to meet?" It took a great deal of effort, but she managed to keep herself from backing away from this man that now looked more like a demon than an angel.

"Your father."

"My..."

The man turned his gaze, smiling warmly at someone behind her. When she turned to see who it could be, she found herself face to face with the most intimidating man she'd ever seen. Thin but muscular, this man had the same dark molasses eyes she saw every morning in the mirror and the same jet black locks of hair trimmed neatly around the neckline of his outrageously expensive suit. His thin, pale face was handsome yet sinister. And he had found his way into the building, crossing the room until he was standing just inches behind her without ever making a sound.

"It seems we will not have to travel far," Ethan stood, giving the other man a brief nod of greeting.

"You have done a fine job," the stranger told him, his gaze fixed firmly on her the entire time. "There is one last problem out in the parking lot for you to solve."

"It would be my pleasure." Winking at her, Ethan quickly grabbed his jacket and headed for the front door, leaving her all alone with this other terrifying man.

"What do you want from me?" she whimpered, disgusted at her inability to hide her fear.

It hadn't been until just now that she realized Ethan might be dangerous. He had convinced her that he could help her. This man, though, was clearly a threat. He made no attempt to hide the callous tone in his voice or the calculating look that seemed to see through to her soul. This man was a nightmare made flesh. He was the boogeyman in her closet. And here she was, alone and afraid, facing off against this being of pure evil.

"You are lovely," the man replied, reaching out to sweep a strand of purple hair behind her ear. "Even prettier than your mother."

"I have to go." She tried to stand, but he placed a firm hand on her shoulder and guided her back to her seat.

"They have kept us apart for long enough. It is time for me to finally meet my daughter."

"Don't call me that," she spat, shocked by the anger she suddenly felt towards this man. The fear was still there, but the idea that this stranger would come in after everything else that had happened to her family and claim to be her long lost father? Outrageous!

"Quite a temper," he frowned. "I can see this will take some time."

"I thought we didn't have any time."

"That situation is being handled right now."

There's one last problem in the parking lot…

They'll be here any minute…

"Elijah is outside, isn't he?" The man's smile was nowhere near comforting.

"Ironic that he will be killed outside the same bar as his father, and both of them because of you. I love how circular life can be."

She jumped up from her seat and was immediately tossed to the floor by the lightning quick movements of the stranger. The right side of her head hit the floor hard enough to make her ears ring and her vision darken for a moment.

Great. Now I have a concussion.

"If this is your way of trying to make friends, it's not working." A well-polished shoe collided with the side of her chest, knocking all the air from her lungs.

"You will come with us. Conscious or not, it makes no difference to me."

"Some father," she laughed, and immediately thoughts of Andy began to race through her head. He'd nearly killed her, would have if something hadn't happened to stop him. Now it was happening again, but this time there was nothing to save her.

"You would be a valuable asset if you had a little more discipline. Unfortunately for you, I can get what I need without your permission if necessary."

Another kick landed squarely in her arm, creating an audible crack that twisted her stomach into a knot. Pain raced from the point of impact up her arm and into the rest of her body, bringing tears of pain and frustration to her eyes. If the goal was to make her pass out, this guy wasn't wasting any time.

"I thought..." she moaned through clenched teeth, but the man interrupted by leaning down and wrapping his strong, slender fingers around her throat.

Get her to a hospital.

Elijah's voice. Even then he had been protecting her, rescuing her from whatever forces were working to destroy her. And she had doubted him. She had come here looking for answers because she thought Elijah and Vanessa were the bad guys, hiding information from her to keep her away from those who really wanted to help. All those dreams of the man with the red hair. All those times she'd wanted to tell him everything but something in her gut told her to hold back.

What if that's what they had wanted all along? What if the only reason she was alive right now was because these things thought she would lead them to valuable piece of intelligence? Granted, she had no idea where the Council might be, but Elijah and Vanessa did. Would they use her to get what they wanted from her protectors?

"Such a shame," the man growled, squeezing until there was no air flowing to her lungs at all. Pain and asphyxiation blurred her vision, but the emptiness of his eyes was clear even now. "If only we had gotten to you a few years sooner."

She was being sucked into the emptiness. Gasping. Falling. Dying.

Cover your eyes.

No. Closing her eyes or looking away would only end in death. But staring into those unending pits of death wouldn't get her much further. Or maybe it would. She had brought Elijah back by looking into his eyes. She had saved herself from the thing that took her body in the park by staring it down. Maybe the same thing would work with this guy. What was the worst that could happen? It could *not* work and she could die?

Focusing what strength she had left, Sarah returned the intense stare of the man before her, hoping that such an action would at least startle him enough to make him let go. All she needed was a chance to break free, and if she didn't get it soon, it really wouldn't matter anyway.

Even through the red-black haze that had begun to coat her vision, she witnessed the change in the man's face. His snarl began to falter, his grip on her throat loosened, and the man lost his balance, tumbling to his back on the floor beside her. The moment his hand released her throat, she began gasping for air and crawling towards the door. Elijah was in trouble. She had to get him and get the hell out of here.

A hand wrapped around her ankle, and without looking, she kicked as hard as she could. There was a harsh, meaty thud as her foot collided with flesh, and suddenly her foot was free. Her vision was slowly clearing, and with a little effort, she managed to climb to her feet. Stumbling out the front door, she found Elijah and Ethan engaged in a heated battle.

If this fight was being scored based on number of injuries inflicted, Ethan was definitely winning. Elijah's head was bleeding, coating half of his face in the thick, scarlet liquid. His left cheek was already bruised, his nose was clearly broken, and one arm was wrapped around his chest as he struggled to keep the pistol in his free hand trained on his target. Ethan, however, wasn't even dirty. It looked like he had never touched his victim while inflicting all of this damage.

"Your father would be proud," Ethan laughed.

Elijah wiped a wad of blood from his left eye. Ethan just laughed harder.

"You have lost, little hunter. Be a man and admit defeat. Besides, I think I might just let you survive this one. Sarah is ours now, and I am sure the Council has more time for torture than I do."

There was a car sitting just outside of the bar. Elijah's car. And the engine was still running. Without further thought of what she was about to do, Sarah dove behind the wheel, slammed the door shut, and pressed the accelerator to the floor. A flick of her good wrist and the vehicle was suddenly pointed directly at the red-headed monster. The look of disbelief on his face was more gratifying than anything she had ever experienced in her eighteen years.

When the car crashed into the unsuspecting man, there was a horrible thumping sound just before the body was drug beneath the front wheels. The man screamed, turning her blood to ice.

I just killed a man. I'm a murderer.

The passenger door flew open and her arm immediately stiffened, her hand still tightly clenching the steering wheel. Before she could stop it, she was screaming and sobbing, certain that this was the end, that the hands reaching into the car were aiming for her neck once again. But this time, they wouldn't be stopped. This time, she would die.

"Easy," her attacker said softly, and then she noticed the silver chain with the wedding bands dangling before her. Elijah.

"They were going to kill me!" she shrieked, still unable to let go of the wheel.

"He wasn't alone?"

The question seemed almost ridiculous to her at the moment, considering her injuries, until she realized that Elijah hadn't been inside. He hadn't seen the other man, so he probably assumed that Ethan had done this to her before he had marched outside into the battle.

"We need to go, now." He grabbed her wrist and gently pried her hand from the wheel. Then, he helped guide her to the passenger seat as he took the wheel.

Backing over the body resulted in another set of agonized screams and more grinding noises before they sped off down the street. The tiny twitch of his shoulders made her wonder if he'd meant to do it, but she was too terrified to ask. Silence filled the car for a few moments as both individuals tried to sort through the details of what had just happened. Elijah was the first to speak.

"How badly are you hurt?"

She had been expecting a lecture, questions as to why

she had run off or what she was doing at that bar alone. She was prepared for a reprimand, but his concern caught her completely off guard.

"I think my arm is broken," she croaked, wincing at the swelling in her throat.

"Vanessa can set it once we get back to the house."

"We can't go back there! They'll find us! They'll kill us and Amy and Vanessa…"

"We have to go back long enough to gather supplies. Besides, we can't leave them behind." Of course he was right. Still, what if they didn't get out fast enough? What if those monsters came after her again?

"I'm sorry," she whispered, choking back the tears. "I shouldn't have gone there. It was a trap. I should have known better."

"Why that bar?" Once again, the question shocked her. She had expected a lot of questions, but this was not one she was prepared to answer. She hesitated, not certain of what to tell him, or if she should tell him anything. Her gut had told her not to tell the red-headed demon anything about Elijah. She had trusted the man in her dreams anyway, and it had nearly gotten them both killed. There wasn't that same feeling deep in the pit of her stomach this time, but maybe caution would still be her best option.

Elijah was different, though. Ethan had been too good to be true, and the moment she'd questioned her view of him, the illusion had crumbled. The truth was that he and his bar buddy were bad news. All they wanted was to use her and then toss her aside. She hadn't let the high school football heroes do that to her, and she certainly wasn't about to let a couple of strange older men get away with it, either. Elijah, though, didn't seem to have that same fake exterior. Sure, he played the hard ass, but it wasn't covering up the ugly, dark hole inside where his soul should be. It was more like a barrier to protect the humanity left in him.

It made perfect sense. If this was the kind of thing he dealt with every day, he had to be guarded. Anything else and these monsters would eat him alive. His genuine concern for her, though, implied that with almost no effort, she had slipped past his defenses. He trusted her, and now, it was time she trusted him.

"I've been having these dreams lately. The man with the red hair, Ethan, he's been in them. He told me if I met him at the bar this afternoon, he would give me answers to all my questions."

"Hmm," the man replied thoughtfully, and for a moment she thought the real lecture was about to begin. Instead, he said, "They promised you answers, huh? For me, it was safety." She just stared at him for a moment, not fully understanding what he had just told her.

"This happened to you, too?" The words were deep and throaty, but the surprise remained quite obvious.

He nodded, "The one I spoke with promised to keep me and the rest of my family safe if I met with her. Played the seduction card, too."

"Did you go?"

"Considered it. In the end, my training won out. I told Vanessa what had happened and she helped organize a raid on the meeting location. It was the first big raid I'd ever been a part of, and it went off without a hitch."

"You probably think I'm an idiot, then, don't you?"

"Not at all. I knew exactly what I was dealing with and it was still hard to resist their charms. Can't expect you to do something I almost couldn't. Seems a bit unfair, if you ask me."

She shook her head, not really certain what to say next. Finally, she turned to him and blurted out the first thing that came to mind.

"Of all the people in my life right now, I think I trust you the most." He didn't respond, but she saw the muscles in his jaw tighten. "You're the only one who hasn't lied to me. You haven't tried to kill me yet. And you're the only one who seems to be trying to see things from my perspective. So, Elijah, when this is all finished, I think I'm going to buy you a drink. Just to say thanks."

"I don't drink."

"Well, then I guess you'll have to make an exception."

"I don't think so."

"Why not?"

"Because I've seen what you look like drunk, and I'm definitely not interested."

"Alright, fine. Coffee then."

"No caffeine."

"Jesus Christ! Tofu and bottled spring water? A rice cake? What the hell do you eat?"

As she tried to raise her voice, a huge bolt of pain tore through her chest. Gasping, she found herself barely able to breathe as a spasm in her lungs left her choking and wheezing. Elijah was instantly back to business, pulling the car over to take a look just as the coughing began to die down.

"What happened in the bar?" he demanded, pulling her arm out of the way and gently unzipping the side of her dress to inspect her ribs. The left side of her body had turned an alarming shade of purple, much like the side of his face.

"Some jerk kicked my ass," she wheezed. The next few coughs left her palms spattered with blood as the harsh, metallic taste of it filled her mouth. "Some team we are."

"You just survived a demon attack," he told her calmly as he pressed on the bruise. "Very few people can say that."

With a tiny, pathetic whimper, she told him, "I can't believe you actually do this for a living. You'd have to be completely insane to choose this lifestyle."

"Nice to see you being so open-minded." He reached over and brushed a strand of bright violet hair behind her ear, then quickly retracted his hand before things could get too awkward.

"I'm sorry, but this is just insane. Never being safe, always afraid of the shadows…"

Quickly changing the subject, he pulled back out onto the busy street and told her, "There are more important issues at hand, like how to hide from the Others and still make it to our meeting with the Council tomorrow morning."

"Meeting?"

"I spoke with one of the Councilors. She agreed that no judgment will be made about you until after you meet with the Council."

"And you? Are they still sending you off to your death?"

"My punishment has nothing to do with you." They were going to kill him. After everything he had done for this stupid Council, for the world… For her.

"What if I talk to them? I could explain what happened, that it was my idea and you were just protecting me."

"It wouldn't matter. This would have happened eventually even if I wasn't given this assignment."

Assignment. She was someone's assignment. The idea was strange and uncomfortable, like a new pair of boots that were a size too small. Didn't they realize she was a person and not just some name on an old piece of paper?

"What will you do?" There was no reply, and the rest of the drive was spent in an awkward silence as they raced past the

The Others

first hints of rush hour traffic.

Chapter 64

They had been gone for over an hour. Anything could have happened to them. Pacing nervously across the living room, she didn't even notice Thomas leading Amy out into the kitchen. If only one of them would call. Not knowing what was happening or where they were or if they were safe...

The sound of a car door slamming shut jarred her out of her panicked thoughts, and she rushed through the front door. It had to be them. Something bad had happened, she just knew it. They would need to call Ray. He would know what to do.

But it wasn't them. The gaudy red sports car made her heart ache with disappointment. The driver, however, brought on a whole new set of feelings as he climbed out of the vehicle.

"What are you doing here?" she demanded, but the man just shook his head as he approached the porch, his hands hiding in the pockets of his gray cargo shorts.

"Is that any way to greet an old friend?" he asked with a smirk. If she hadn't been so worried about the kids, she might have lost her temper and punched out a few of those expertly sculpted teeth.

"You are not welcome here."

"I beg to differ. My daughters are here."

"Sarah is not your daughter."

"I have legal documents that say otherwise," he replied

smugly. Stepping up beside her, she felt the urge to hit him slowly begin to grow as he told her, "Now that their mother is gone, it's my job to look after the girls."

"They are perfectly fine here," she answered, barely able to maintain her calm.

"But you aren't their legal guardian, are you?" There was a short pause as he waited for a witty retort or some other form of attack. When she didn't react, he continued. "I am taking Sarah and Amy back to Phoenix. They'll be safe there with me."

"Why are you suddenly so interested in playing dad?"

"I'm not playing dad. I'm accepting my responsibility as a single parent. The girls are to be packed and ready to leave at eight a.m. tomorrow. We have a plane to catch at eleven, and I hate to be rushed."

"They aren't going anywhere with you."

"They're my children!" His cool finally cracked, and she saw the old familiar Andy once again. He didn't want to be a father. Too much work involved and not enough payoff. Something else was going on here.

"You tried to kill Sarah," she continued, hoping to upset him enough that he gave away his real reason for being here.

"I would never have killed her."

"Really? Because the bruises on her throat said otherwise."

"Listen to me," he hissed, pushing his face towards hers until their noses practically touched. She held her ground, despite the overwhelming cloud of alcohol-scented breath that suddenly engulfed her. Must have needed a little liquid courage to get up the nerve to come visit. Elijah and Thomas had clearly made an impression. "I put up with those brats and their neurotic mother for sixteen years, and I'll be damned if I don't get something in return."

"Is that what this is about? The inheritance?" Laughing in his face, she told him, "Angela's lawyer stopped by just this morning to discuss that very thing with Sarah."

"I'm their guardian. He should have discussed it with me."

"No, you aren't." The look of shock and confusion that lit up Andy's face brought forth another tiny giggle. "Sarah is eighteen, which means she's an adult. And guess what? Angela left everything to her!"

"That's not possible," he mumbled, but he had clearly lost all the smugness that had accompanied him here. The booze must have worn off, leaving only uncertainty and disbelief.

"It's very possible. Even more interesting, though, was the fact that Angela just had all the paperwork updated a few weeks ago, making your favorite daughter Amy's guardian." He took a step back towards the stairs, glaring at her with an intensity and rage that would have frightened most. Not her, though. She took a step forward and continued to taunt the furious man. "Looks like you lost big on this one, eh, Andy?"

"You did this," he hissed, pointing an accusatory finger at her as he backed down the steps and stumbled towards his car. "You did this, but it doesn't matter. I'll get what I came here for. I'll get all of it, and you'll be the one who loses."

Andy had never intimidated her, and even now at his most menacing, she refused to let him scare her. Still, she couldn't help suppressing a tiny shiver as she thought about what he might be capable of doing. He'd nearly killed a child he'd raised for almost eighteen years. The life of a woman he barely knew would mean little to him. Angela had once told her that this man was one of the most ruthless she'd ever met when it came to money. If he believed she was the only thing standing between him and millions of dollars, she didn't think he would hesitate to do whatever it might take to get rid of her. And with things as complicated as they were right now, how long would it be before one of the Others caught up with him and gave him the opportunity he was looking for?

Taking a few determined steps toward the car, she called, "Are you threatening me, Andy Goode?"

"We should have never taken that miserable little brat from you!" he cried, still backing away. Coward. "This is your mess! If you hadn't gone and spread your legs for a demon…"

"Get off my property!" she commanded, her anger seeping out as she pointed stoically into the distance. She knew that what he saw was the fury of a goddess, and she didn't care.

Let him see. Let him understand that to feel her rage was to feel the wrath of heaven and hell. Maybe it would keep him away long enough to get the girls out of this place.

Jumping into the car, the engine roared to life and he sped away into the sunset. The outraged woman took a moment to compose herself, closing her eyes and sucking in a few slow, deep breaths. It took a great deal to make her lose control like that, but after everything he had done, she was surprised she hadn't snapped sooner. Add to it the stress of not knowing where Sarah and Elijah were, and things were bound to get ugly.

Stepping back inside, she was greeted by two worried faces. They were just as terrified about the kids as she was, and all the shouting out on the porch must have drawn their attention.

"What's up?" Thomas asked in a tone that was just a bit too awkward to be considered casual.

Flashing him her most comforting smile, she replied, "Nothing to worry about. Any news?"

And though she'd successfully managed to turn the conversation back to the big worry of the moment, she wouldn't be able to avoid Andy forever. While she joined in the discussion on what to do about the missing teens, her conversation with the man who had once convinced her that he was worthy of fatherhood continued to lurk in the back of her mind. He was definitely going to be a problem that would have to be dealt with before he got out of hand. As soon as Elijah got

back, she would discuss it with him.
    As soon as he got back.

Chapter 65

The look on the red-headed beauty's face changed from unimaginable fury as she stormed through the front door to meet the car to pure panic the moment he stepped out of the vehicle where she could see his bloody face. Any concerns he'd had about a lecture vanished in an instant.

"Please tell me you didn't drive with that head wound."

That was her way of scolding without sounding like she was attacking him. Vanessa was no fool. She knew that immediately after battle there was still plenty of adrenaline pumping through his veins to make even the smallest jab turn into something deadly.

"I've had worse. Check The Girl. She's in pretty bad shape."

Nodding, the woman moved swiftly to the passenger side door. Sarah climbed out cautiously, limping a bit and cradling her left arm against her body as the older woman softly cooed familiar comforting phrases reserved for the really bad injuries. Based on The Girl's dazed expression, her swollen throat, and the rattling sounds she was making as she struggled to breathe, Vanessa's reaction did not surprise him. Nor did her next order.

"Call the doctor," she whispered as they hobbled past him to the porch where Amy watched in horror. Thomas was already on his way down the front steps to help with the injured girl.

Trudging along behind them, he pulled his phone from his pocket and dialed the number he should have called the moment they'd left that bar. His conversation with the doc lasted less than a minute, but it was long enough for Vanessa and Thomas to get The Girl settled on the couch. Without a second thought, he went to the hall closet and grabbed Vanessa's emergency kit, dragging it into the living room with arms that felt like rubber.

"Sit down and let Thomas take a look at you," the woman commanded, never taking her eyes from The Girl.

"I'm fine."

"You don't look fine," Thomas shook his head, guiding the weary hunter into a nearby chair. "It'll only take a sec."

"I don't need your help!" he snapped, completely unable to hold back the fear he was feeling at that moment.

"Easy, tiger. I think you must have hit your head pretty hard. Looks like you really got pounded, man."

"It was the one from the mall, I'm sure of it. Outside the bar, Brew Moon on the corner of Chestnut and Pine. She went there to meet him."

"Wait, are you telling me you two were up against one of them? Alone? She must be something special if you managed to survive that kind of attack."

"Look, I already told you, I'm fine. Go help Vanessa with her until the doctor gets here." He tossed a sloppy wave at the body on the couch, but Vanessa shook her head.

"I don't think there's anything any of us can do for her. There's massive internal damage, not to mention severe head trauma. How she's still conscious is a mystery to me."

The woman's words brought an odd tingling sensation to his eyes and his vision began to blur. At first, the feeling was so foreign that he wondered if he was getting ready to pass out or vomit. As the first tears began to trickle down his cheeks, he finally realized what was happening. He was crying. He hadn't cried since the day he'd watched them lower his father's casket into the ground.

"She can't die," he choked out, barely able to fight of the hysteria that threatened to take hold of his mind.

"I'm so sorry, sweetie," Vanessa whispered, turning to him as she gave up all hope for The Girl. Wrapping her hands around his, she filled the space between them with empty words meant to comfort. Instead, it brought out a fury that had been locked away deep inside the hunter since his training had begun almost fourteen years ago. "She just wasn't what we thought she was. It's not your fault, you did your job."

"My job was to protect her, and now she's dying!" The woman frowned but did not pull away. Thomas jumped in, trying to help and only making things worse.

"Listen, man, she was just an assignment."

"She's not an assignment! She's a person! And she's not dead yet!" Pushing himself out of the chair and past the two stunned individuals, he stood silently beside the couch. "We're supposed to meet with the Council tomorrow to straighten this mess out."

"I think the Council is the least of her concerns right now." Those words were the last straw. Vanessa might be the expert on the Prophecy, but she obviously knew nothing about this girl, who had already lost so much because of them.

He closed the distance between them in one step, towering over her with his most intimidating sneer.

"She is not going to die. Not tonight. Not for a long time. Now, you can either stay here and help her, or you can run to your little doctor boyfriend and leave her with someone who gives a damn."

"I do give a damn!" she barked in return, and he could see her desperately grasping at what little control she had left. Perhaps she was trying to hide her own feelings of fear and anguish to spare him, just as she had when his father died. It didn't matter, though. She couldn't give up on The Girl. Not yet. Not until they knew for certain that she was beyond their help.

"Elijah, you need to calm down," Thomas stepped in, trying to pry the two of them apart. He held his ground, forcing Vanessa to take a step back.

"You're not thinking clearly," Vanessa argued.

"My thinking is just fine. Go find a way to help, or get out. All of you." His gaze flicked to Thomas just in time to catch a hint of movement in the doorway of the room. The doctor had arrived, ushered in by a very frightened little sister.

"Thank goodness." Vanessa breathed a sigh of relief, running to the man in the doorway.

"Sounds like I got here just in time." The doctor's flat tone conveyed his disapproval, but at this point, the hunter didn't care. If the rest of these people were so willing to give up on this girl, then he would just have to find someone else that would help her.

"She's in real trouble. I don't think there's anything left for us to do." Vanessa led the old man to the girl on the couch whose breathing suddenly didn't seem quite so labored. "I found signs of massive internal hemorrhaging as well as some pretty serious head trauma. Hospitals are out, and the Council would never let us use the private facilities."

"From what I can see, she looks like all she needs are a few bandages and a good night's sleep."

The rage was instantly replaced by shock and then relief as he slowly made his way back to the sofa. Even as the doctor spoke, he saw that the injuries she'd sustained that afternoon were quickly fading. Had his tired mind distorted the world that badly? Perhaps the blow to the head had been as bad as Thomas said.

"She has some minor bruising around the neck, but that appears to be from days ago, maybe even weeks. Looks like her arm is pretty banged up, but nothing that won't heal in a day or two." The doctor pulled out his stethoscope and listened to her lungs, shaking his head. "No fluid. Regular heartbeat. Everything seems fine."

"You're joking, right?" Thomas interjected. "Doc, I saw her when she first got here and she was practically dead. Now you're telling us to just slap a bandage on her and let her sleep?"

"Sometimes, in stressful situations the mind tends to make things seem worse than they really are."

"I examined her myself," Vanessa interrupted. "You know me, Raymond. I don't exaggerate."

"Well, I don't know what else to say."

The doctor had taken his eyes from The Girl, but the hunters had not. While Vanessa argued about what she knew was true, they watched as the bruises around The Girl's neck and the swelling in her arm slowly faded away until there was nothing left.

"Uh, Doc?" The disbelief in Thomas's voice was enough to turn everyone's attention to the events taking place in the living room. Even Amy finally took a few timid steps into the room.

"What's happening?" her tiny voice asked from behind the crowd, but no one responded. They were all still too shocked by what they were witnessing to find the words.

"Call me crazy, but that's not natural, right?" No one even noticed Thomas's sarcasm.

"She's one of them," the doctor whispered, grabbing hold of Vanessa's arm in an attempt to pull her away. She shook him off with an exasperated grunt, and then turned back to The Girl.

"Amy, you stay here with Sarah. We'll be in the kitchen if anything happens."

With an obvious effort, Vanessa managed to pry herself away from the miracle before them and exited the room. The others followed shortly after. He stayed for a moment, still trying to convince himself that she hadn't been alone with those things long enough for them to turn her, but knowing that it was entirely possible. If their little debriefing led the others to believe that she might be an enemy spy, then she really would die tonight.

"I'll watch over her," Amy whispered softly, wrapping her tiny trembling hands gently around one of her sister's.

"If anything changes…" his voice cracked. One soft, tender hand found its way to his shoulder.

"Go. We'll be fine."

He nodded and started to step away, pausing as the pressure on his shoulder increased just a bit.

"Thank you."

"You know where to find me." He quickly made his way to the kitchen where a sea of frightened faces anxiously waited to discuss this strange turn of events.

Chapter 66

"I thought you said this little plan would work. I'm supposed to be rolling in dough right now, and instead, I hear that little bitch is getting it all!" The enraged man's cheeks were so red with fury that it seemed they might burst into flame at any moment. Secretly, the demon hoped something so dramatic would happen. Anything to shut him up.

"Calm down," the red-haired beast ordered, giving the man no indication of how irritated he was at the entire situation. He stepped around the desk and closer to the ranting mortal, straightening his crumpled suit. "You will get your money. All you have to do is tell us where she is, and we will take care of it."

"She's staying with that whore, Vanessa. God, I can't believe she laughed at me! Right in my damned face!"

"Are you certain?"

"Where else would she be?"

It had been nearly an hour since the incident at the bar, and if he had been in their shoes, he would have immediately run off to an unknown destination the moment he hopped behind the wheel of that car. But not The Child. She had risked her life to save her sister, she had left herself vulnerable in order to heal the red-headed woman, and now she had attacked a very powerful adversary head-on to rescue her pet hunter. Of course she had gone back for the others before leaving town. It was the most natural thing for her to do. Even so, he did not like having it rubbed in his face that he had missed something so obvious.

Placing firm hands on the man's shoulders, he smiled and said, "I will take care of everything."

"Yeah," the man nodded, a bit unnerved by his touch.

The demon nodded in return, patting the man's back gently. This ridiculous creature had given them as much useful information as it could. Now, it was time to get rid of it before it interfered with future plans. Reaching into his coat, he pulled out a large blade and plunged it into the man's abdomen before he had a chance to realize what was happening. The look of shock as the metal penetrated flesh was priceless.

"Those who deal with devils must be ready to pay the price," he whispered in the man's ear as he pulled the weapon from its human sheath and plunged it into a new location, this time somewhere in the left side of the chest. He missed the heart, but that made it all the more interesting.

Repeating this act almost seventeen times in various non-fatal areas, he found himself sad to see shock setting in. By number twenty-two, the man was dead and his only outlet for the rage he felt was gone. After letting out a shrill cry that summed up the frustration and anger of a beautiful plan foiled by a simple underestimation of the prey, he finally managed to pull himself together and make a few phone calls. He was about to put together a team that even a hundred skilled hunters could not evade, and in a matter of hours, he would collect what was his.

Once he was finished gathering his army, the demon glanced at the edge of the desk where he had dumped his belongings upon entering the office and seeing The Child's adopted father. It had taken quite a bit of energy to heal from his little chat. Being run over by a car might not kill a being such as him, but it certainly did make for a miserable day. By the time he had gone back into the bar and discovered The Master nursing his own wounds, he had been too exhausted to worry much about the bag sitting beside the table.

Now, though, he was curious about its contents. It certainly did not seem the kind of thing that The Child would carry around by choice, meaning that it was probably borrowed from that woman, Vanessa. Borrowed hand bags rarely yielded valuable clues about their temporary owners, but any insight into the way this girl's mind worked would be helpful.

In one graceful motion, he spilled the contents onto the desk. As he suspected, he found very little inside. Some lip gloss, a wallet with the girl's driver's license and a few dollars, some keys that undoubtedly fit the lock on a house that no longer existed…and a purple envelope. The last item intrigued him, and he quickly pulled a silver letter opener from the drawer beside him. As he sliced open the delicate paper, he felt his pulse quicken.

It was a birthday card, complete with sappy sentiment scrawled inside in some arrogant computer font. However, beneath the prewritten message was a much more personal one.

Sarah,

I may not know much, but I know I love you. Always and forever. Have fun at college, but don't drain your bank account dry for booze!

Angela

XOOXXOXOXO

Interesting...

He slid the card back into the envelope and tucked it away in one of the drawers. This clue was worthy of further investigation, but for now, he had a kidnapping to plan.

Chapter 67

"They got to her in a dream. Told her to go to the bar for answers. She had no way of knowing…"

"What did you find when you arrived?" Vanessa interrupted, clearly irritated by the entire situation. Her frustration, however, didn't hold a candle to his own as he sat here, telling them everything he could without putting The Girl in more danger.

"The place looked empty. I left the car running in case we needed to make a quick exit, got out of the vehicle, and was intercepted on my way to the door by the same one Anthony and I engaged at the mall."

"Where was Sarah?"

How could he answer that question when he didn't really know where she was at the time? She'd come out of the bar during his confrontation with the demon, but where she had been up to that point was a mystery.

They tried to kill me!

"I don't know." And that was the truth. Until he could get more details out of The Girl, he didn't know anything about what she'd been through.

"You didn't see her when you arrived?" Vanessa was beginning to sound like a damned interrogator.

"No."

"So you engaged the enemy. Then what?"

"He attacked me, I fought back, and I got my ass handed to me. If she hadn't plowed into him with the car, I wouldn't be here right now."

"So the next time you saw her, she was behind the wheel of your car."

"Yes."

"Then it is possible she was alone with one of them either before you arrived or as you were engaged in combat, correct?" At that moment, he hated this woman more than anyone else in the entire world. Thankfully, he had managed to regain some of his self-control, because without it, he would have lunged across the table and choked the life out of her.

"Yes." His tone was flat, but his teeth were clenched so tightly it came out sounding more like a hiss.

"But you didn't see her speak to anyone."

"No."

"Alright. Let's hear what Raymond has to say." She turned to the doctor, who cleared his throat nervously.

"Well, I've never actually seen the repair of damaged tissue that the Others are capable of, but I can say for certain that no human being can do what she just did. It's impossible."

"Kind of like Jesus walking on water, huh?" Thomas chuckled. Vanessa shot him a serious scowl, and then turned back to the doctor.

"Then again," the old man smiled, "I said the same thing about your recovery."

"But I thought she did that, too." Thomas seemed to know exactly what to say to make Vanessa even angrier than the moment before.

"This is very serious, Thomas," the doctor cautioned. "If those monsters are using her as a decoy, then all of our lives are in danger."

"She's not a decoy," Thomas argued. "We all know that regeneration is the one power they never hand out to minions of any level. It's the only way to maintain control. Anyone who could recover from injuries as quickly as they do wouldn't be intimidated by physical threats."

"Perhaps it is that assumption that they are counting on," the doctor replied.

"Isn't this prophesized savior of yours supposed to have some fancy powers, too?"

"The Council has already said…" Raymond began, but was interrupted by yet another antagonistic comment courtesy of Thomas.

"The Council hasn't even met this girl. How would they know?"

"I think you've been listening to Elijah again."

"Yeah, well, he may be a little nutty at times, but he also has some valid points. The Council doesn't have all the information we have. They haven't been dealing with this kid for half their lives, nor have they spent the last few months just waiting for those things to attack her. I think we should leave this decision about whether or not she's a bad guy to the people who've been with this assignment the longest."

"Elijah and Vanessa may have the most information about the situation, but they have become too close to the target," the doctor argued. "The Council is much more objective."

"Are you sure about that? I don't know if you've noticed, but Elijah is not exactly their favorite hunter. They've just been waiting for an excuse to get rid of him, and now they've got it. If she's a phony, then someone must not have been doing his job."

"That's ridiculous." The look on Vanessa's face mimicked rage, but he saw it for what it really was. Fear.

"Is it? They could care less whether or not this is the right child. No matter what their decision tomorrow, Elijah is going to Chicago. Isn't that right?" And suddenly three sets of nervous eyes fell upon him, searching his face for answers.

"The Council has chosen to keep their decisions on my case and The Girl's separate." His reply was as diplomatic as it could be, and completely vague. Still, Vanessa understood exactly what message he was trying to convey, and it stunned her more than any words of anger could.

"I say we at least give The Girl a chance to explain herself," Thomas suggested, breaking the awkward silence that hung around them like some dark, ominous cloud ready to release a torrent of emotion.

"I agree," Vanessa chimed in. The doctor considered it a moment longer, then nodded.

The hunter stood, gave a slight tilt of his head as a sign of his approval, and then quickly left the kitchen. Once he was through the doorway, his hard composure crumbled, and the young hunter breathed a sigh of relief. When she woke up, she was going to have some serious explaining to do. Thankfully, that wouldn't happen for quite a while. The Girl was safe, at least for a few more hours.

Chapter 68

A desert. She was standing in the middle of a desert. To her right, she could just make out the edge of some sort of lake, but something about it felt wrong. This place was poisoned, and if she stayed here very long, she had the feeling she would be, too. The sounds of some unnatural creature screeching in the distance slowly trickled back to her ears, sending a chill down her spine.

"It is not really so terrible." The sound of that silky smooth voice spun her around until her eyes landed on the brilliant red hair of a familiar figure. On his face was a bitter smile that chilled her even more than the howls she'd heard earlier. "Miss me?"

"I'm dreaming again," she breathed in a whisper that was barely audible to her ears. "This isn't real. You can't hurt me."

"If that was my intention you would never have known I was here until it was too late. No, Sarah, I am here to enlighten you."

"More of your tricks? Well, guess what? I'm not playing your little games anymore. Get out of my head and get out of my life."

Shaking his head, he asked, "What do you know about your hunter friends?"

"I know that they haven't tried to kill me yet, which is

more than I can say for you." She was trying to reign in her curiosity, but it was no use. No matter how much she fought it, she wanted to hear what this monster had to say. Even though she knew that was exactly what he wanted, even though it was clear that he could not be trusted, she needed to listen.

"Just a few years ago, those same hunters that are supposed to be protecting you gunned down two innocent children. I was not there personally, but a very close associate of mine stood right here at the edge of this lake and watched it happen."

"I don't believe you." And she almost convinced herself that she was telling the truth. Almost.

"Believe what you will," he shrugged, stepping past her to the edge of the water. "The smell of their deaths still lingers in the air. Sickening, is it not?"

"I don't smell anything," she muttered, but that was a lie. She did smell something. Something that reminded her of the prison and the hospital. Something that turned her stomach into a knot of anxiety and weakness.

"Hmm," he smiled knowingly. "Perhaps you are right. Perhaps I am lying to you. Then again, what if I am not?"

"I already told you, I'm not playing your stupid games." But it was too late now. The seeds of doubt had already been sown.

He turned to her, still smiling. The condescension and pity she saw in his face made her want to tear his throat open and add him to the list of casualties in her life. When he stepped up and tucked a lock of her hair behind her ear, she nearly did just that.

"Ask him," he whispered wickedly, a twisted sort of glee in his eyes. When she knocked his hand away, he chuckled softly, making her that much angrier. Then with a wink, he brushed past her and disappeared into a swirling cloud of dust that surrounded her. The sounds of those strange animals were closer now, almost on top of her. The world faded into shadows as the brown cloud blotted out the sun. Feeling completely helpless, she desperately tried to get her bearings in the mysterious sandstorm, but it was no use.

Crumbling into a heap of exhaustion and fear, the sounds of voices echoed in her ears. Some she recognized, but some were as foreign to her as this lifeless landscape.

You cannot save her. She must choose. Damnation or death.
Her choice is my choice.
Elijah, put the gun down. They're kids, for Christ's sake!
Yes, Elijah. Let them come to me. I will care for them as if they were my own.
Shut your yap, lady, before I slice off that pretty little head!

She could see them now, shadowy figures facing off in the fading cloud of debris. Thomas was easy to spot as he barked at the tall, slender woman with jet black hair that trailed down her back to her waist. She was dressed in a black pinstripe business suit and wearing stilettos, which seemed quite odd given the setting. Beside her cowered two frightened teens, one male and one female. He was short but muscular and had a hardness that made him seem older than he looked. The girl, though, was lean and had the same unnaturally dark hair as the woman in the suit. Her eyes, though…

Thomas suddenly doubled over and a cruel smile spread across the woman's face.

"Watch your tongue, hunter," she hissed, "or you may find it lodged in your throat."

"Let them go!" the girl with the strange alien eyes cried, taking a step towards the woman. The boy pulled her back, but this reaction seemed to please the woman in the suit.

"Men," she rolled her eyes, a playful grin on her face. "They say we are free to decide, that they will follow us to hell and back, but when the time comes, they simply crumble under the pressure."

The boy's hands shot to his temples as he cried out in agony. At his side in a flash, the lavender eyes of the girl looked on in horror as blood began to trickle from his nostrils.

"Please," the girl pleaded, tears twisting the light that touched those beautiful eyes to make her look even less human. "I'll come with you. Just leave them all alone."

"Of course, Zoe." Offering a hand to the girl, the woman smiled and said, "Come quickly. There is much to do."

"Zoe, no!" the boy cried, but it seemed it was too late. The strange girl had made her choice.

Shots rang out, tearing through this heart-wrenching scene and turning the world into a sea of chaos and carnage. Bullets ripped apart the head and chest of the boy, leaving little more than a mess of mangled meat. The woman was next, her body blown to bits as lightning fast lead blew holes through her as well. There was just enough time for those big, lavender eyes to take in her killer before she met the same fate, her corpse collapsing as the final shots still echoed through the empty air.

For a moment, the man in black just stood there staring as if even he couldn't believe the brutality of this attack. Then, slipping his pistols back into their holsters beneath his coat, he calmly marched over to the bodies and began removing their heads with the same blade she'd seen him use at the park. He started with the boy, moving with cold precision until he was left with the severed head of his victim dangling from blood-soaked fingers.

"Jesus Christ!" Thomas finally shouted, but the man in black didn't flinch. He simply moved on to the next body, that of the girl with the lavender eyes, without a hint of emotion on his stone cold face.

Thomas raced over and grabbed his shoulder just as the second decapitation was complete. With her head dangling between them, the two men faced off, Thomas furious while his companion remained indifferent.

"You didn't have to kill them!" the giant barked, but his booming voice did little against his friend's granite will.

"The Council ordered us to terminate the project," the man in black answered calmly.

"Do you hear yourself? I thought we agreed that the Council doesn't always know what's best! They aren't here! They can't see that these were just a couple of kids who didn't know any better!"

"They were going to join the Others. That makes them the enemy." Turning towards the woman in the suit, he tossed the severed head to the ground and started to kneel. Thomas grabbed his collar and yanked him back around before the task could be completed, though.

Getting within inches of the killer's face, the giant spat through clenched teeth, "They were kids, Elijah. They were not projects or assignments or enemies. They were just kids."

"If I'd let them go, the Council would have killed our entire team." Ah, there was a spark of humanity left in him. She could see the slight twitch in his jaw and the flash of anger in his deep, brown eyes. "I did what needed to be done. This blood is on my hands, no one else's."

And there it was. He had weighed his options. He knew that the only way to protect Thomas was to follow the Councils' orders, but he had taken on the responsibility of performing the deed himself. Why? Because he knew this task was too much for the soft-hearted giant. Rather than put his friend in such a difficult position that could result in a very heavy conscience, he had taken on the burden himself. And he'd been carrying it with him all this time.

"How touching." Both hunters spun around to find three men approaching. The setting sun left their silhouettes difficult to see, but the leader's accent was definitely Deep South. Alabama, maybe?

The hunters drew guns and began backing away, but they seemed much too tense. After watching Elijah take out three targets without blinking, she thought nothing could intimidate him. Clearly, she was wrong.

"Oh, what's the matter little hunters? You scared? Maybe we just ain't young enough for ya, huh?" As he got closer, she could see he was wearing faded jeans with an old t-shirt and cowboy boots. On his head was a ridiculous looking cowboy hat that matched the boots and a grin that nearly cut his face in half.

"Thomas," Elijah ordered, and Thomas seemed to know in just that one toneless word what he needed.

"Roger that," the giant nodded. With his guns still trained on the trio, Thomas slowly began moving away from Elijah.

"You boys are so sweet," the cowboy chuckled. "How long you been together? Maybe you're just soul mates, is that it?"

"I thought your kind was suave and sophisticated," Thomas sneered, all the while moving away from the crowd while Elijah crept in the opposite direction.

"Well, I may not be the smooth talker you're used to, hunter, but by the time that sun pops back up I guarantee you'll be wishin' you were."

Just as the tension reached its apex and the threesome prepared to strike, she felt strong hands wrap around her biceps. Suddenly the blowing sand and old western shootout scene vanished, replaced by something much more familiar…

Chapter 69

They both looked so small and fragile there, one huddled on the floor beside the sofa, the other a mess of blood and rumpled clothing that wasn't hers tossed casually across the deep green velvet cushions. Maybe he should take them upstairs to make them more comfortable. Then again, they looked pretty content as they were.

"You've really got a thing for that girl, don't you?" Thomas whispered from just behind him. Vanessa was still out on the porch, saying goodnight to the doctor. With as cozy as those two had become over the past few months, they would probably be awhile.

"Not now," he whispered, refusing to turn around. The last person in the world he should have to explain himself to was Thomas. They had grown up together, best friends since they started training at the age of five. If they didn't know each other by now, after dozens of battles and years of instruction, then they never would.

"Listen, Elijah, I'm not trying to lecture. We both know I'm the last one who should be giving advice in this field. Just promise me you won't do something crazy. At least not until we're sure where things stand. After tomorrow's meeting, if things still look this bad, I will personally drive the two of you to the airport or bus station…wherever you want. Deal?"

"Yeah, sure," he responded absently, not really wanting

to think about tomorrow or what it could mean for all of them.

"There's another problem. Andy was here earlier, and he says he wants both the girls to move out to Phoenix with him."

"Amy might go."

"Not without her sister," Thomas grinned, "and we all know how she feels about her daddy."

"Andy's just a control freak with a big ego. I can handle him."

"I don't know. Have you seen his girlfriend? There's no way that moron got a chick like that without some help. Besides, he rolled into the driveway in a car that costs more than most houses, yet his big concern seemed to be the girls' inheritance."

"You think he's with Them?" The idea that Andy might team up with the bad guys was not new. Any other time, he wouldn't be an issue. However, if he decided to make a move now, when things were already so out of control, that could change.

"All I'm saying is watch your back."

"Thanks," he replied, rubbing weary eyes that felt as if they might pop out of their sockets at any time.

"You want me to stick around tonight? Help keep an eye on things?"

"No, you should get going. Things will be fine until morning." A hand landed on his shoulder, and he felt a hint of a smile creeping across his face.

"You know my number. And if things start to get too intense with her, remember, I want details."

"Keep dreaming," he grinned.

"Hey, I gotta get my thrills when I can."

There were footsteps, then the sound of the back door softly opening and closing. Quietly, he crept into the room where the girls rested peacefully, squatting down next to the younger, less damaged teen. She jumped the moment his hand touched her shoulder.

"So what did you decide?" she asked sleepily.

"We'll figure it out tomorrow, after she has a chance to tell us her side."

The girl nodded thoughtfully, saying, "At least she gets that much."

"You can thank Thomas for that. He convinced them to wait. For now, though, you should head upstairs and get some sleep."

"What about Sarah?"

"I'll take care of her," he replied, trying hard to keep any emotions out of his voice as well as his body language. He'd already gotten too close to The Girl. Better to keep his distance from this one and avoid any further problems.

"Yeah," she smiled, getting to her feet and stretching. "I know you will."

With a soft pat on his shoulder, she made her way to the stairs and up to his room, leaving the young hunter alone with her older sister. He watched her go, waiting until he heard the door upstairs close before gently plopping his weary body into the plush emerald chair next to the girl.

Perhaps it was a bit too soft and comfortable. The moment he sat down, his eyelids began to droop. It had been a very long week, and he'd had next to no sleep. The level of exhaustion he was feeling was not surprising under such circumstances. However, until he was certain things were settled between all sides, there would be no time for sleeping. Someone had to stay awake, to keep an eye on things in case…

"In case what?"

He bolted up out of the chair, finding himself face to face with a creature he never thought he'd see again.

"You're dead," he told the tiny raven-haired imp. The last time he'd seen her, he'd been decapitating her in the sweltering heat of the Australian outback. "This is a dream."

"Is it? The Girl should be dead right now, but she isn't. Maybe you were wrong about me too."

"I wasn't wrong."

"Of course," she sneered, taking a few slow steps toward him. "The mighty hunter is never wrong. Especially when there are lives at stake."

"Stop where you are, or I'll kill you again." But could he? His entire body seemed to be made of lead, weighing him back down until the softness once again surrounded him. The phantom clearly sensed his indecision and ignored his threats.

"This girl does not belong to you. She is one of them. Kill her now. Redeem yourself in the eyes of The Council. End this ridiculous game before more innocent lives are lost."

"She is not one of them," he argued, watching as the child crept ever closer and knowing that there was nothing he could do about it. His body was paralyzed, and he was beginning to believe there might be a supernatural element to it.

"You don't understand what's going on here," she hissed, now just inches from him. And from the couch. She wasn't heading for him. She was heading for The Girl.

"Leave her alone."

"I already told you, she isn't yours!" the child screamed. The Girl began to stir, and the raven haired beauty placed a gentle hand on her forehead. Then, with a soft smile she whispered, "Such a lovely young thing. Sad that her life had to end this way."

"I won't let you hurt her."

"I'm not the one you have to worry about." Tossing a wicked glance at the window, the sound of Vanessa's laughter trickled into the living room. "She is very loyal to her Council. How long before she turns on this poor child?"

"Vanessa would never hurt her." If he could just get to his guns.

"Just like you would never hurt an innocent young girl?" So bitter, this child with the hauntingly beautiful lavender eyes.

"Last chance," he warned. "Get out."

"Ooooh…" She feigned fear, but she did take her hand off The Girl. That was a start. "Alright, Mr. Scary Hunter. I'll go. But not until you promise to clean up your mess. Finish this, or they will do it for you. And I can guarantee the death they give her won't be nearly as clean and painless as the one you're capable of dealing."

"I said GET OUT!" he screamed, leaping out of his seat with such ferocity that he feared he might send the chair toppling through the large window behind him.

And suddenly, she was gone. The room was empty except for him and The Girl, who was now moaning and thrashing around violently on the couch beside him. It had been a dream after all. A nasty nightmare that was either his subconscious trying to tell him that they were all screwed this time, or the Others trying to trick him into doing their dirty work. Either way, he could definitely live without such messages.

Turning his attention to the restless teen, he knelt down beside her, coaxing her gently to wake from her nightmare. It worked. The Girl's head shot up from the couch, taking her entire upper body with it and knocking him to the ground. Panting frantically with eyes as wide as some cheesy anime drawing, her face jerked around in panicked leaps, slowly taking in the reality that surrounded her. Eventually, her gaze fell on him, and there it lingered as understanding finally dawned on her weary mind.

"What happened?" she gasped, using trembling hands to rake back chunks of purple and chestnut hair from her damp brow.

"You were dreaming," he answered, pushing himself back up to a sitting position.

"Yeah," she replied absently. "I guess I was."

"Want to talk about it?" She shook her head quickly, and he decided to let it drop for now. If it was important, she would tell him.

"Where is everyone?" she finally asked, but her thoughts still seemed distant.

"Amy is upstairs sleeping," he answered, "and Vanessa is outside with the doctor."

"Who needed a doctor?" The question was so innocent it caught him a bit unprepared.

"Uh…you did." He stumbled over the words like a nervous cadet on exam day.

"Really? How bad?"

"We'll talk about it later with Vanessa."

"That bad, huh?" She sighed, pulling her tiny legs up to her chin. "Are you alright?"

"Just a little bump on the head," he answered, but her concern touched him in a way that was frightening. She had nearly died, yet her first concern was his well-being. It was completely the opposite of what he'd expected.

"Good," she smiled warmly. "I'd hate to hear you were seriously injured because I did something stupid."

"Wouldn't be the first time," he answered, and she surprised him again with a deep, hearty laugh.

"I guess I am the queen of bad decisions, huh?" she chuckled, and he was glad to see that any signs of injury had been completely erased from her delicate features. "So, I guess this is our chance to chat about what's happening before the rest of the world tries to butt in again."

"There's nothing to discuss." He couldn't tell her what had happened while she was asleep. How she had miraculously healed all the wounds that would have killed any other human being, or how the rest of the people around her were slowly starting to wonder if maybe the Council was right about her not being the Child of the Prophecy.

"More for Vanessa to tell me, huh? Alright, then why don't you tell me about that interesting trinket around your neck? You don't strike me as a jewelry kind of guy."

"I don't think so."

"Come on," she prompted, but he just sat there on the floor beside her with his best blank stare.

He had already gone too far with this girl. She had gotten past his defenses, and no matter how hard he tried, he couldn't seem to keep her from digging deeper. This had to end. He had to get his objectivity back before something else happened. If he couldn't make quick, logical decisions when the time came, they would all die.

"You know, trust works both ways." God, it was like she was inside his head. Refusing to show how much she'd shaken him, he continued to cling to his stony façade.

"I don't trust anyone," he replied, knowing that his words were pushing her away but also knowing that it was necessary to protect both of them. She didn't give up easily, though.

"Except Vanessa." She tossed the words at him so quickly he had no time to respond. "Or is it *especially* Vanessa?"

"In this field, no one can be trusted."

"Wow," she shook her head, leaning over on her elbow until her face was just inches from his. "No wonder you have no friends."

"Friends are a luxury I can't afford."

"Must be nice to never get lonely."

He had to get out of here. Once again, she had found just the right buttons to push to make him feel both cornered and comfortable at the same time. There was no time to discuss his past or his feelings now that they were targets of both the Others and the Council. Right now, they needed to rest and then run.

"I should go check on Vanessa," he answered, quickly pulling himself to his feet. He heard her shifting around behind him as he approached the window, but he didn't dare look back.

Vanessa was standing on the driver's side of the

doctor's car, just out of his line of sight. All he could really see was a slight bob of her head from time to time as the faint sound of her laughter drifted up from the driveway. The image of the raven haired ghost girl flashed in his head, and he fought the urge to look back at the living room. The room where he knew a far more dangerous girl was waiting for some answers.

Maybe she was right. Maybe a friend wouldn't be such a bad idea right now. Maybe this girl could help him make sense out of a life built on chaos. Glancing down at his hands, he found himself fiddling with the chain around his neck again.

Without turning, he finally spoke up, afraid of what she might say or do if she saw his face. If he was going to tell his story, he wanted to do it quickly and with as little detail as possible. After all, this wasn't something he did often, and it was one of the most uncomfortable things he'd ever chosen to endure.

"When my mother died, my father gave me her wedding ring," he said to the window, his voice just barely above a whisper. "When he died, Vanessa gave me his ring as well. I've worn them around my neck ever since. Satisfied?"

"You must miss them a lot," she answered, standing just behind his right shoulder.

His reflexes took over and he spun around to face her, reaching for his guns in one fluid motion. Before his fingers had fully wrapped around the weapons, her hands seized his. He'd always prided himself on his speed, had even received formal recognition from the Council for it. This girl was not only faster, but she seemed to know what he was going to do before he did.

"Sorry," she smiled, but it did nothing to help him regain his composure. She scared him more than he would ever admit.

"I think I should go get some sleep," he said, his voice cracking on the last word.

"Where? This place is packed, and I think all the beds are spoken for."

"I guess that means you get the couch." Stepping past her, he made a dash for the kitchen. She followed close behind. When he pushed the refrigerator out of the way, revealing a door to the basement, The Girl's jaw dropped.

"How long has that been here?" she asked.

Opening the door, he told her, "Since the house was built. Tell Vanessa I'm working in the library."

"No way," The Girl shook her head, inching her way closer to him. "I'm not leaving your side for a minute."

"Go check on Amy," he ordered. It came out much harder than he'd intended thanks to his own anxiety, and for a moment he thought she was going to cry. That's what scared little girls did, right? But she didn't cry. She did something far more redeeming in his eyes. She stood her ground.

"Amy is fine. Now, are we going down those stairs or what?"

There was a moment when he tried in vain to intimidate

this girl who still had no clue who he was or what she was caught up in. And she knew it. She knew that she had no idea what to expect. Her actions earlier that evening had proven her ignorance. Yet here she stood, not even flinching as he attempted to stare her down.

"Alright," he finally cracked, and in doing so, he let her into more than just the cellar.

She stepped back onto the porch and caught a glimmer of movement from the corner of her eye. Before the smile could even form, Thomas was standing at the bottom of the steps, hands in his pockets as he waited for her.

"You and Ray are certainly friendly," he winked, and she just shook her head.

"Raymond and I have been friends for a very long time," she told him, though he didn't seem convince.

"Sure," he shrugged. "Not my business. You're an adult, right?"

"Absolutely," she agreed.

"What is my business," the giant continued, "is that boy in there. Your little Sarah has her hooks in deep."

"Yes," she nodded, "she certainly does. He's not acting like himself at all. That stunt at the prison and now this…"

"Well, it's about damned time he found someone like her."

Stunned by his words, she stared in silent wonder at the

giant. Elijah was taking too many foolish risks because of his interest in Sarah. She had been eager to discuss this with Thomas in the hopes that he might help her convince the boy to take some time away from this assignment. If she could just get him to leave before…

"Look," Thomas interrupted her thoughts, " I get it. You don't want to see either of them get hurt. I can respect that. But that girl is the best thing that's ever happened to him and we both know it."

"She nearly got them both killed!" she hissed, trying not to draw any unwanted attention.

"She makes him human," Thomas countered, and she couldn't find the words to argue. "He's been marching around like a robot on autopilot since his dad died. Every decision he's made has been based on Council directives and cold, hard statistical advantage. Until now."

"The Council in angry…"

"Oh, the Council is furious!" he spat. "The Council hates it when its puppets become real boys! I say, if she makes him happy, then to hell with the Council!"

"Thomas…" she began, but he cut her off again.

"He showed more emotion tonight than I've seen in years. The Elijah I saw in there was the Elijah I used to sneak into the girl's dorm with on panty raids. That's the boy who called me friend when no one else would. That's the guy who took a bullet for me, who sold his soul to the Council to spare me the nightmares. She brought him back from the dead, and I'll be damned if I'm gonna let anyone take him from us again."

There was a long pause as she considered how to respond. He was right. Elijah had never truly recovered after his father's death. It had seemed that only three people in this world had kept him anchored in this life. She and Thomas had been there to sort through the initial aftermath, but it had been Sarah that truly brought him back from the abyss. Without her, they would have certainly lost him to the despair and rage.

With a deep sigh, she told Thomas, "I know you're right, but they cannot be together."

"Because the Council says?"

"Because it's too dangerous. I am taking Sarah away tomorrow. Raymond will help Amy hide. He has some connections outside the Society. You have to help Elijah find a place to lay low until the Council loses interest."

"That's insane! No one hides from the Council!"

Shaking her head, she told the hunter, "You don't understand. If they stay together and he finds out the truth, it will kill him."

"What truth?" Thomas demanded. When she hesitated, he asked more sternly. "Vanessa, what truth?"

"That Sarah is my daughter," she answered softly. But that was only part of it. Her father was the real concern, but again, that was not knowledge she was ready to share with anyone in the Society. As it was, Thomas was the only person she had ever shared this secret with.

"Really?" he asked, clearly stunned.

"Yes, but if he finds out…"

"He won't," Thomas reassured her. "Not from me, anyway."

"Thank you." Then, taking a deep breath, she managed to choke back her tears before she said, "I should go check on them."

"Lovebirds are in the library," the giant grinned. "Amy's upstairs."

"So much for keeping them apart," she rolled her eyes.

"I'll hang around to keep an eye on things. I think the rest of you could use a little break."

"That would be lovely," she agreed as he turned towards the street.

"Sweet dreams," he called over his shoulder.

With a weary sigh, she made her way into the house and upstairs to check on Amy.

Chapter 70

"So, this is your place, huh?" She ran a delicate finger along the edge of the computer desk, inspecting it for dust. Finding none, she gave her nod of approval. "Small, but clean. I like it."

"The bed is over there," he motioned to another smaller room just behind her. "Get some sleep."

"I thought that was your plan. Besides, I think I might do a bit of reading before bed."

"No."

Once again, his tone was a lot harsher than he'd intended, but he was more reluctant about letting her sift through the dozen bookcases that filled the tiny space than he had been about sharing details from his past. Those were his father's books. The same books that held top secret information about the history of the Society, the Council...and, or course, the Prophecy. He didn't want her to know what was in those books. Not yet. Not when they were so close to convincing the Council to let her live. If anyone other than he and Vanessa knew she'd been down here, they were all as good as dead.

"More of your secrets. I find it fascinating that the more time I spend with you, the more mysterious you seem to become." The Girl moved closer to him, her arms crossed in front of her chest and a playful smile on her face. "Come on. You know everything there is to know about my life. Shouldn't I be privy to that information as well?"

"Not now."

"Not until your Council says it's okay?"

"Exactly."

"The same Council that's planning to send you off to die? Doesn't it bother you that someone who knows nothing about you is going to decide your fate?"

"It's their decision to make." He turned to the closet and began digging around for some extra blankets.

"Well, if you want to just roll over and let them take control of your life, good luck. I'd much rather take matters into my own hands and try to stall my death until the ripe old age of ninety."

"This discussion is getting old." Grabbing the bedding materials, he stormed off towards the tiny alcove where he would most likely be spending the night on the floor. He didn't make it more than a few steps before she took hold of his arm once again. "Stop doing that."

"What?"

"Touching me," he grumbled.

"Oh, I forgot. You're the big scary hunter and *nobody* touches the big scary hunter, right?"

"Just go to sleep. Things will seem clearer in the morning."

"Things are clear enough now. This is my last night in this town, no matter what the Council decides. And Amy is as good as dead. There's no way your Council will let her live after what she's seen. So, what will I have left, even if I do make it out of tomorrow's meeting alive?" And the desperation in her voice was the final nudge that broke through his defenses, striking his very core.

Staring into those big brown sorrowful eyes, he promised, "I will not let them hurt you."

"They already have."

"They're strong, but you're stronger. That's why they're scared. It's why we're all scared."

"So they don't know anything more about me than I do? Is that what you're telling me?"

"What I'm telling you is that all the information they have doesn't matter. You are the unknown. Use it."

"Alright," she nodded, a strange sort of determination in her eyes, "I will." Snatching the bedding from him, she quickly made the bed and curled up beneath the heavy woolen blanket.

There were more blankets in the closet and one last pillow which he grabbed thankfully. If he was going to sleep on the cold concrete floor, at least he was going to have a soft place to rest his head. And that was the last real thought he remembered until he awoke a few hours later to the sound of her collapsing as she discovered just how dangerous the Prophecy could be.

Chapter 71

He started snoring before his head even reached the pillow. Even so, she waited until she was certain he was completely out before she slipped from the bed and back to the rows of books that had first caught her attention. The truth about who she was and why the entire world seemed to be interested in getting rid of her was here. She could feel it calling to her from among the stacks.

Tossing one last wary glance back at the sleeping hunter, she couldn't help noticing the deep, dark circles that ringed his eyes or the soft stubble along his jaw. Half of his face was so swollen and bruised, he was barely recognizable. This week had been hard on her, but she hadn't even stopped to consider how the people around her were taking it all. Was Amy upstairs alone, bawling her eyes out over their dead mother? What about Vanessa? She'd lost a friend and nearly lost her own life. How was all of this affecting her?

And of course, there was Elijah. How many sleepless nights had he spent just keeping her safe? How many missed meals or trips to the ER had he endured for her? In just the short time she had known of him, he had rescued her from so many crazies, she'd almost lost count, and those were just the encounters she'd actually witnessed. How many more times had he risked his life for her without her knowledge?

Well, this was it. This was her chance to do something,

to stop all of this from getting even more insane. She was going to get to the bottom of all this tonight. Turning her attention back to the tiny library, she began searching for a clue about this Prophecy and maybe her past, too.

"Where are you," she whispered, creeping silently past the hundreds of texts that lined the walls.

Her eyes scanned quickly over them, catching titles that sent shivers down her spine. The dingy, yellow light from the two hanging bulbs cast eerie shadow on the walls around her. From the ceiling hung ancient cobwebs that danced across her skin as she passed by them, leaving her flesh crawling with the sensation until she wanted to scream. It wasn't difficult to imagine the owner of this library sitting down here for hours, driving himself completely mad in his search for answers. Would she do the same if given the opportunity? Would she waste her life down in this dark, cold room sifting through old, musty books until she'd entirely lost touch with reality?

"I know it's here somewhere," she muttered. There was only one thing she wanted to read, and if she didn't do it now, she might never get a chance. Fortunately, it wasn't difficult to find once she stopped looking at the bookcases.

Lying on a desk in the corner of the room was a dusty old manuscript. By her estimates, it looked to be about a zillion years old. The yellowed pages were frayed and warm to the touch, which surprised her. Down here, everything felt cold and damp. Everything except this book, that is. It was stacked on top of two other volumes that looked almost as ancient, though they held little interest for her. She had found it at last.

Tossing back the cracked leather cover with slow anticipation, she started to smile. The world had been lying to her since the day she was born. Now it was time for facts. Her smile disappeared the instant she saw the clearly handwritten pages. Definitely not English. In fact, this didn't look like any language she'd ever seen before. Where the hell had this come from? Strange symbols danced past her eyes as she flipped through the pages, and any hope she'd had about the future melted into defeated exhaustion.

So that was it then. It was over. She would have to put her life in the hands of strangers who seemed to only be concerned with their own continued existence at this point. And as long as the survival of the entire world depended on her, it was in their best interest to keep her alive. But then what? Could she continue down this path, following them blindly until it got her killed, never really knowing why any of this was happening?

No. She wouldn't give up that easily. It wasn't her style. Besides, translating a foreign language was sort of like decoding a secret message. She'd broken Vanessa's code in a matter of moments. And though it was true that this would probably be much trickier, she was confident that she could do it.

Staring at the pages before her, she felt her body relax as her mind kicked itself into overdrive. There was a distinct pattern to the grouping of the symbols. Words, perhaps, or maybe sentences? Hard to say just yet.

Stop thinking so much and let it come.

Yes. She just had to relax. The answers would come, but she had to stop fighting them. She felt the familiar sensation of falling into the page, of becoming the text. This was a part of her somehow. These symbols that filled her senses felt comfortable, like slipping into a favorite pair of jeans.

The groupings were words. Yes, words, but not like the words she heard every day. These were foreign sounds. Growls and moans and unimaginable noises that most humans would never hear. And in those sounds came a voice that she didn't immediately recognize. It, too, was a part of her, whether she wanted to accept it or not.

The Child shall come and with It bring the end.

Her father.

The doorway sealed for eternity with the life of The Innocent.

The Master.

Peace for all time comes at a price.

The man in the suit, the one with the black hair and the empty eyes…That man was her father. Andy was nothing. Angela was nothing. Amy was nothing. He was her family. And he was calling to her. Waiting for her to answer.

My daughter. My life. Come home to us. Come to the ones who can give all that you desire. Come…

The image of Angela's mutilated body dangling from the limb of the same old oak she had used as an escape route on numerous occasions filled her mind. So much blood pouring from that butchered body, pooling at her feet until she was drowning in a sea of scarlet death. She wanted to scream, to call for help, but how could she? This was her fate. Destiny had chosen her to be here at this moment, consumed by the chaos that surrounded her as she was carried away to a new life of destruction. The voices instantly stopped as she hit the ground, trembling and gasping for air. For a moment, everything stopped, and she found herself alone in darkness.

When her head hit the desk, she didn't even notice. Nor did she feel the cold of the ground beneath her or smell the dusty odor of old books. She was no longer caught up in the ancient words of a prophet no one had ever heard of, but that didn't mean she had found her way back to the dreary basement where her body resided. Her mind was left drifting through the space somewhere between here and there. Between life and death. Between real and fairytale.

Suddenly all those old stories came rushing back from her childhood. The Gingerbread Man had always been one of her favorites, along with Little Red Riding Hood. Angela had spent so many nights reading and re-reading these tales until the young Sarah had finally fallen asleep. Now, she was the girl in the red cloak, and she was running as fast as she could from the Fox with the beautiful red coat. Behind him was the Big Bad Wolf with thick black fur and empty eyes. Before her stretched a terrible, gnarled grove of trees that seemed to be reaching out, pulling her in with their dark, twisted limbs that resembled the long arthritic fingers of a dying grandmother.

She could feel the panic welling up inside of her as she faced the inevitable. There was nowhere to go. It was either run into the evil trees ahead or let the vicious predators catch up. Neither option sounded pleasant, but she knew she didn't want to be eaten by the monsters behind her. So, rather than allow such a horrible idea to push her anxiety farther and possibly incapacitate her, she charged into the creepy woods.

Just as she had feared, branches instantly twisted into her cloak, ripping it to shreds as the forest tried to strangle her with the crimson cloth. Refusing to be defeated by a bunch of plants, though, she forced her way forward until she found a dark, menacingly quiet clearing. She was bleeding and sobbing and completely exhausted, but at least the trees weren't trying to tear her apart.

All around the edge of the tiny meadow, the branches beckoned. The sound of whispered wails and comforting sighs filled her head until she thought she would go mad. Covering her ears, she tried to find a path out of this place, but there was nothing. Even the way she'd come had been consumed, leaving only more gnarled claws urging her forward.

"Run, run, as fast as you can." Spinning around, she found the Wolf staring at her from the edge of the woods. At his side was the Fox, who snarled, "We've already caught the gingerbread man."

"Please," she gasped, clutching at the tattered remains of her hood as they slowly approached.

Snapping its razor-sharp, white teeth at her ankles, the Wolf seemed to be enjoying her fear with a twisted sort of satisfaction. The Fox snarled, and she jumped just as the Wolf sunk those fangs into her calf. With a cry that was half pain and half panic, she dropped to the ground as he shook his head. Flesh tore, and the sound made her stomach clench long before the agony reached her brain.

Sarah…

The voice was flat and hard, and it made the entire world tremble with its power. Wolf and Fox both stopped as the ground beneath them began to shake. Snarling in surprise and anger, the two beasts seemed to be waiting for an explanation. The trees, meanwhile, began to sigh and moan in frustration.

Sarah…Can you hear me?

The terrible nightmares began to shriek as the very sky tumbled down around them. The earth below began to fracture as well, leaving huge fissures that now separated her from the beasts. She wailed once again as a tremendous bolt of pain shot through her head. Closing her eyes, she let her body collapse into the cold dampness of the ground beneath her, hoping that this might be the end and knowing that it wasn't.

"Damn it, open your eyes." The frustrated mumble came from just beside her, and now she really could feel strong hands gently brushing the hair from her face. The smell of an antique library filled her nostrils once again, but beneath it was the scent of something much more familiar.

The basement. She was in the hidden basement of Vanessa's house. The man beside her was the same man who had saved her life at the mall and the park and the police station and who knew how many other places. Those other things, the Fox and the Wolf and the dark forest, they weren't real.

And when she opened her eyes, she knew this was true. She found herself staring up into deep brown eyes full of concern. Her trembling hand found its way to her forehead where a knot the size of a golf ball was beginning to form. Wincing, she forced herself to sit up, though she welcomed the assistance offered by the man beside her when she tried to stand.

"So that's the prophecy you people keep talking about," she chuckled. "Well, it certainly packs a punch, doesn't it?"

"I told you, these books are off limits." It was clear that he was trying to reprimand her, but his distress took the edge from his words.

"And I told you, I'm not going to just roll over and let everyone else decide my future for me."

"Yeah, well, I guess that hard head of yours came in handy tonight," he sighed as he took a closer look at the welt on her head. "I'll go get some ice for the swelling."

"No," she shook her head. "Not necessary."

"It'll only take a minute…" he started, but she wrapped both hands firmly around the nearest bicep and held on tight.

When he turned to her, she could see the strain of repressed reflexes as he made a conscious effort not to reach for a weapon once again.

"Really," she whispered, and he picked up on her anxiety instantly.

Placing a comforting hand over hers, he told her, "You're hurt. I need to go tell Vanessa…"

"Vanessa has more important thing to worry about than a little bump on the head. Please, just let it go."

"If you have a concussion…" he tried again, but she cut him off.

"I don't want to be alone," she whispered, stepping closer to the man in black. The man who had once again rescued her from the clutches of some unknown enemy. The man who was now looking at her with a mixture of concern and understanding.

Rising up on the tips of her toes, her lips met his without a moment of hesitation. And to her surprise, he didn't pull away.

Chapter 72

Before he knew what was happening, her lips were pressed firmly against his. Every ounce of training flew straight out of his head as those lips began to part, and he pulled her closer, wrapping her in an awkward embrace. He found himself returning the kiss with such ferocity he was afraid he might hurt her, but when he tried to back off, she reached up and wrapped her fingers in his hair, as if she wanted more, not less.

Her mouth broke away from his, moving instead to his neck and making control that much harder. This wasn't happening. This had to be another dream. There was no way she was really here, no way those were really her lips pressed against his flesh, no way those were her hands traveling down his shirt, caressing his belt buckle, making him forget how wrong the world was right now.

"Elijah," she breathed into his ear, and he decided control was overrated. Spinning her around, he pressed her back up against the wall trying not to hurt her and using up what little willpower he had left in the process. She cried out softly, though whether from pain or pleasure he couldn't say.

You have to stop. What if Vanessa walks in? What if the Council finds out? What if…

"We should stop," he panted, surprised at how quickly his heart was racing.

"Why?" And though he'd had a million reasons just a

few seconds earlier, he couldn't remember a single one of them the moment she pressed her hips against his.

With a low, agonized moan, he returned the gesture, making her gasp. Guiding his hands until they were resting on two perky little mounds beneath the stiff black material of her borrowed dress, she reached up and pulled his face down to meet hers once again. The absolute torture of touching without really touching was tearing apart his sanity one second at a time. He let her pull his shirt out of his belt, slipping her hands underneath. The feel of her soft skin caressing his bare chest was heavenly.

If only this could last. If only they could stay here in this bliss. No worries about life or death or loved ones. Just the two of them like this forever. He wanted to tell her all of this, wanted to share how truly miraculous this moment was for him. He'd been dreaming about it for years, after all. But when he opened his mouth, the words wouldn't come.

"Sarah," he finally whispered as her mouth met his neck once again.

And that was all he managed to get out before the sound of the back door opening caught his attention. His hands immediately dropped as he took a step away from The Girl, finding his weapons still exactly where he'd left them.

"What's wrong?" she asked breathlessly.

"A noise upstairs," he replied, quickly marching back to the staircase.

"What kind of noise?" she questioned, but he didn't respond.

He reached the kitchen to discover that his fears were well founded. Though his mind was still a bit fuzzy, it didn't prevent him from noticing that the back door was slightly ajar. He quickly decided that The Girl shouldn't go unprotected. Handing her one of his guns, he motioned for her to follow. She started to protest but stuck close when he began moving through the kitchen.

They stepped into the living room, stumbling upon three men with black ski masks and matching assault rifles creeping toward the stairs. None of them noticed him or The Girl as they approached. The Girl was inexperienced and jumpy, but she would shoot when the time came, of that he had no doubt. And if there were more upstairs? The gunshots would undoubtedly notify anyone in the house of their presence. Could he take out three before any of them could get a shot off?

These questions disappeared as one of the figures caught The Girl in his peripheral vision. Before the enemy soldiers had time to react, he began firing, and all three of the intruders' foreheads exploded in a spray of gore. She stood there in complete shock, staring at the bodies as they tumbled to the floor. The look of absolute panic he saw beginning to take hold sent him racing into action. The last thing they needed was for her to have a complete meltdown.

"We have to go," he whispered, grabbing her arm with

his free hand in an attempt to pull her towards the front door.

He was losing her. That blank stare as he tried to get her out of harm's way was the same one he'd seen the night she talked him into helping her rescue her sister. The same lost hopelessness she'd exhibited as Vanessa tried to help her change was taking hold again, but this time, there was no way to talk her through it. He couldn't reassure her that things would be alright in the middle of a damned battle. If he didn't keep his mind clear and focused on getting out of here alive, they would end up on the floor with the three corpses at the base of the stairs.

At that moment, another flood of masked figures burst through the window, spraying glass and bullets across the room. With a hard shove, he knocked The Girl to the ground, covering her tiny body with his own. She shrieked as bits of metal tore apart the wall beside them, but she didn't seem to be hit. The firing slowed as one of the figures stopped to reload, and he took that opportunity to yank the frightened child to her feet, dragging her up the stairs to find some cover and maybe even a way out of this mess.

His room was at the top of the stairs, so it was the first place they managed to duck into before they became as perforated as the living room wallpaper. He didn't take time to thoroughly inspect the room, choosing instead to make a quick sweep with his eyes as they stepped inside. No bad guys in sight. With his back to the room, he secured the door as best he could, pulling a large chest of drawers in front of it to buy some time.

His hand slipped on something warm and wet smeared across the smooth, polished surface. He knew that feeling. That was fresh blood. A glance at his palms confirmed his suspicions. But why would there be blood on his dresser?

The answer was lying between his bed and the window, two twisted faces drenched in crimson staring blankly at the ceiling. The Girl's face was completely expressionless but for a tiny hint of a smile at the corners of her mouth. Knowing that the Others had almost succeeded in their goal of breaking her, he forced his own emotions down into some deep recess of his soul to be dealt with later and focused his attention on her.

Chapter 73

No.

It wasn't them. It couldn't be them. She was dreaming again. That had to be it. There was no way some crazy people in ski masks had just broken in, shot up the living room, and then left Vanessa and Amy here like this.

Just a dream. They aren't real.

The thought brought relief and comfort, though she knew it was a lie. Embracing the deception, she let her mind begin to drift away, hopefully to something more pleasant than this. Unfortunately, the thoughts that filled her head were far more frightening.

"He's waiting," she grinned, sensing the edges of her sanity becoming just a little more frayed as the words whispered through her.

"Who?" the hunter asked, and the sound of his voice was almost enough to wake her from this trance.

"He's always waiting. If I go to him, he'll make it quick. Painless. If I fight…"

Blood. So much blood. And pain. It was dulled by distance, but even so, it brought her to her knees. Worse than the pain, though, was the cold emptiness that filled her as he crept inside, trying to take control of her body and mind.

"Sarah, who is waiting?" And the feel of his hand on her elbow brought with it the agony of knowledge. He was going to die here, just like the others. The sound of his screams echoed through her soul as thick, acrid smoke filled her nose and stung her eyes.

You have done this, Sarah. You have damned them all.

"Fire," she gasped, gripping him tight as she struggled to maintain control. "Run."

"I'm not going anywhere without you," the man in black told her, and she knew it was true. He would not leave her side, especially not when there was so much danger surrounding them.

"Please," she pleaded, and though her companion obviously thought the comment was directed at him, he was the last thing on her mind at that moment.

Begging already, dear? At least wait for the real torture to begin.

"Tell me what to do to help you," Elijah's voice commanded, never losing any of its strength despite the waves of fear that radiated from his body. If only she were that strong. Then maybe she could break free from the monster in her head.

So much. Too much. Baby crying in a closet. Mother lying nearby in a ruby puddle. Father hanging from a lamp post. CHOOSE. A girl with lovely lavender eyes and only half a skull.

How much do you know about your little hunter, Sarah?

"Stop," she moaned, but it was no use. The images, the smells, the tastes, the sounds…They all came in a jumbled heap that her brain barely had time to process before the next wave hit.

He is a killer, make no mistake. Once he knows who you are, he will put a bullet in that empty head of yours.

"Sarah!" the hunter called, but she was too far gone. She barely noticed her body being lowered gently to the ground, her left cheek grazing the scratchy carpet below.

What will you tell him before he slits that delicate throat? Will you beg for his mercy as well?

They were coming in. Elijah couldn't stop them. The monsters would take her and do awful things to both of them until they no longer filled a need. The dark man was trying to show her, trying to give her a glimpse into the hell that waited beyond this room. But it wasn't just her.

I will protect you from him, daughter. I will save you from your own humanity. But you must do something for me in return.

They had already taken everything she'd ever known. Now, they were going to take the one man who was trying to keep her safe. The one thing that was keeping her sane. She had to fight them, before they took the only thing she had left.

Pushing past the pain and grief, she barely managed to climb up to her feet once again. Past, present and future still overlapped, but she was at least beginning to recognize the differences between them. They had a different taste. Past was bitter and aged. Future was a mixture of coffee and stale beer. And present…present was silky sweet like thick, rich cocoa.

Using what strength she did have, she focused her attention on this, the present. Elijah was desperately trying to push more furniture in front of the door, while those on the outside were pounding their way through despite his efforts. They wouldn't last much longer like this.

Grabbing his wrist, she croaked, "Window."

With a quick nod, he bolted to the closet, removing what appeared to be a rope ladder. As they raced to set it up, she stumbled over the lifeless limb of her sister. For a moment, the world faded and that voice consumed her thoughts once again.

She was not your sister. These people were nothing. They have served their purpose, and now you must serve yours.

Pushing these thoughts away, she stumbled over to the window where Elijah waited patiently. How could he be so calm right now? The world as they knew it was falling apart, and here he was, waiting for her without a single hint of impatience or panic. Hope swelled up in her, followed by something else that she refused to identify. All that mattered was that it was warm and comforting, the exact opposite of what she had just experienced.

"You go first," he whispered, helping her onto the ladder. "I'll be right behind you. And if you run into trouble, use this." He handed her his cell phone. "Thomas and Gregory are both trustworthy. They'll help you."

Lowering herself down onto the first rung, she looked up into those deep brown eyes one last time and the truth finally sliced through her like a knife in her heart. He wasn't coming with her. He might try, but they both knew what was going to happen here. The sounds of the men outside the door grew louder as the barricade finally collapsed, and the man in black took his attention away from her long enough to fire a few shots into the madness rushing in.

Scurrying down the ladder, her foot slipped halfway down and she hit the ground a moment later, back first. The wind was immediately knocked from her lungs as the world swam in darkness. Before her vision cleared, she smelled it again.

Smoke.

When the world returned, she had managed to hobble to the street. She didn't even remember standing, let alone moving. Looking back, she saw the flames beginning to leap from the kitchen windows. He was still in there somewhere, fighting for his life and hers. She should go back and help him. That's what he would do for her, though whether out of responsibility or honest affection, she wasn't sure.

You aren't serious, are you? Have you forgotten what happened in the basement ten minutes ago?

It seemed like an eternity since that shared moment in the hidden library. And if his response to her advances was any indication, there was a whole lot of honest affection hidden behind that stony exterior. Not to mention a wicked wild side to that man.

"No sense wondering what could have been."

Him. The red-headed demon from her dreams. At first,

she wasn't sure if he was really standing there or if he had just crawled insider her head like the other one. Then he smiled, and it didn't matter if he was real or not.

She broke into a sprint down the deserted road, trying to escape him and all the while knowing that she never could. It took only seconds for him to catch up to her, and when he did, he wasn't even winded.

"Come now, Sarah," he laughed from just over her shoulder. She pushed that much harder, but it made no difference. "Give yourself up before someone else gets hurt."

Her foot caught on something, and she tumbled to the ground in a heap of sobbing, panting hysterics. If she didn't calm down, she was going to hyperventilate and pass out. Since that would leave her completely vulnerable, it was definitely not on her list of good escape plans.

Pushing back onto her feet, she forced her nerves to steady as she faced down the enemy. As he approached, a smug smile stretched across his face, she tried to think back to any kind of self-defense knowledge she might have picked up over the years. Unfortunately, she came up empty handed.

"There is no reason to be so frightened, dear," he cooed, and she felt her stomach twist into a knot. "I'm not going to hurt you."

"Save it for the next conquest, psycho." Wow, she sounded pretty brave, especially considering how much her hands were trembling.

"Oh, there is no other conquest, Sarah. There is only you." Okay, so just when she thought things couldn't get any creepier, this freak says something messed up like that. Fantastic.

"Look, I'm not interested," she snorted in disbelief.

"You were quite interested a few hours ago," he replied with a sly smirk.

"You mean when I ran over you with a car?" she cried in horror. "Jesus, you are nuts!"

In a flash, he was standing right in front of her, his hands wrapped around her elbows. As he pressed her body to his, she tried to land a kick anywhere that might at least distract him, but it was no use.

"You are my destiny," he growled fiercely, his eyes digging into hers with such intensity it felt like her head might explode. With a sharp cry, she felt the urge to push him away growing until it was unbearable.

And suddenly, she was on the ground, panting in relief as the madman gripped his head in pain. Before he could recover, she was scrambling to her feet. She couldn't escape, but maybe she could find something to help her fight back. There was an open garage door across the street. Maybe she could find a weapon…

Something that felt like a polar bear slammed into her back, knocking her face first to the asphalt below with a sickening groan. There was enough force to send her sliding into the curb, and her vision blurred as her forehead slammed into the concrete lip. The taste of blood filled her mouth, and there was enough time for her to consider how familiar such a thing had become over the last few weeks before her mind cleared enough to realize how much trouble she was truly in.

"Seems as though you're not much of a challenge without all your little hunter friends to protect you." He was standing over her, holding something in his right hand. It didn't look like a weapon, but what else would he be holding? The shadows of evening concealed its identity for a while longer as he continued scolding her. "Aren't you even going to try to fight back? After your little lecture about how the hunter shouldn't just lay down and give up, here you are, lying on the ground at the feet of your enemy."

"Thought you weren't going to hurt me," she muttered through swollen lips.

With a wicked grin, he bent down and brushed a soft hand over her untouched cheek as he whispered, "This is just a scratch compared to what I'll do if you run again."

Perfect. Not just a nut job, but an abusive, control freak nut job. Could this get any worse?

Gunshots rang out in the still night air, and the monster's chest exploded in a spray of scarlet chunks. Ethan stumbled sideways, dropping the bundle of twine he'd been carrying to reveal his attacker. Standing behind the beast with the beautiful red hair was Thomas, his guns drawn and prepared to fire another volley into the monster.

"Move!" he screamed, firing two more shots as it lunged at him. Without another thought, she scurried to her feet and bolted from the scene, pushing herself past the limits of exhaustion until she reached a tiny convenience store in the middle of nowhere. Never once did she even consider looking back.

Chapter 74

Stepping out of his rusted blue pickup, his faded brown leather cowboy boots clapping noisily on the pavement beneath, he tossed the remains of his cigarette to the ground. A series of deep rattling coughs followed, reminding him of why the doctor kept hounding him about quitting. Then again, he was a fifty-seven year old divorcee with no children. What reason did he have to quit?

Inside, he tossed a quick nod to the clerk, a man who looked much closer to death than he did. Shawn Richards was no spring chicken, and after several messy divorces and putting two kids through college, he was probably more likely to have health problems than a man who'd smoked a pack a day for the past thirty years.

"Usual?" Shawn asked with a sly smile, and they both laughed.

"Yep. Just a six-pack and a carton."

"Killin' the liver and the lungs both tonight, eh?"

"One stop shoppin'," he replied, grabbing his beer from the cooler beside the register. Shawn reached behind him and pulled out the white and green box that would soon join others of its kind on his kitchen counter. "Anythin' goin' on tonight?"

"Same old bullshit," Shawn laughed. "Saw on the news tonight stock market took another dive. Prices're through the roof on everythin'. And some sorta fire burnt down a whole buncha houses south of here."

"World's goin' ta shit, man," he agreed, shaking his head.

"Only good thing is that guy out inna Middle East. Says he's got a way to deal with terrorists. Says he's gonna get them countries ta sign some kinda treaty, end a buncha bullshit tween 'em."

"Bout time."

"I say, he can end them terrorist attacks, I'd vote for 'em. Any office!"

Both men suddenly grew completely silent as three teenage boys pushed their way through the glass doors. They went straight to the back of the store, headed for the munchies.

"Probly stoned," he whispered, nodding towards the rowdy group.

"An' drunk," Shawn agreed in equally hushed tones. "Kids 'ese days don't know howda have a good time w'out that crap."

"Yeah," he laughed, picking up his beer and cigarettes. They really did sound like a couple of grumpy old men. Shawn couldn't help but chuckle as well, though he still kept a close watch on the boys in the back.

"See ya next week," the clerk smiled. Tossing a quick wave, he headed for the front doors.

As he pushed through to the parking lot, something

slammed into his right shoulder. Beer cans burst as they hit the concrete below, and he found himself struggling to keep his balance as he grabbed whatever had hit him with both hands. Finally finding his footing, he discovered a trembling girl in his arms. She was covered in blood, sweat, and mud. Where she had come from or what had happened to her was a mystery, but it was clear that she needed medical treatment right away.

He scooped her up and carried her inside, noticing for the first time that the blood seemed to be coming from a nasty head wound. Poor thing probably had a concussion. Based on her weight, he'd say she was suffering from some serious malnutrition as well. She was light as a feather.

"What the hell...?" Shawn demanded as he stepped back into the convenience store with the tiny bundle.

"Found 'er outside," he grunted. "Better call an ambulance."

Shaking his head, Shawn picked up the phone and dialed the operator. The girl began to mumble something softly, but it was difficult to make out.

"Can ya hear me?" he asked, placing her gently on the floor just below the register.

Shawn came around to help in any way he could, though there didn't seem to be much any of them could do until the squad arrived. The boys were huddled nearby, silently watching this dramatic turn of events play out before them.

"I saw on one a them TV shows you should ask 'er

questions. Help keep 'er awake or somethin'." Shawn gave him a pathetic shrug.

"Yeah, okay," he agreed, turning back to the girl. "Hey, what's yer name? Can ya tell us who ya are or where yer from?" The only response he got was a series of mumbles and a few stray giggles as she stared blankly up at the ceiling.

"Keep tryin', I guess," Shawn coached.

"Can ya hear us? The ambulance is on the way, okay, butcha gotta try to answer some questions. Can ya do that?"

"Run, run, as fast as you can…" she chuckled. "Never trust a fox with red fur."

"What is she talking about?" one of the boys asked, but they all ignored him.

"Do ya live round here? Is there someone we should call fer ya? Parents, relations, friends? Anyone?" His questions were getting them nowhere, and her cryptic answers were beginning to creep all of them out.

"Dead…dead…all dead," she smiled. "The red fox and the big bad wolf ate them all up."

"Jesus, she's a nut!" Shawn whispered, running a shaky hand over his damp brow. They could all hear the sirens approaching now, and it was only a few moments before paramedics were bursting through the door to collect the child.

"These men're gonna help ya," he tried to reassure her, but it didn't seem to be sinking in. The moment she saw the medics, her eyes grew so large they consumed her entire face, making her look like some ridiculous caricature.

Grabbing his hand, she looked him dead in the eyes and sent a chill down his spine. There were things in those eyes…dark, horrible things that would haunt his dreams for the rest of his life. Years down the road, he would wake from forgotten nightmares, dripping with sweat and remembering nothing except those eyes.

"It won't hurt long," she murmured, and his lungs filled with fire. He began coughing and wheezing, struggling to breathe as she told him, "He's coming. The Big Bad Wolf is coming. He wants his pup. Don't let him take me."

Pulling away, he huddled beside the counter, covering his mouth as he continued to hack and gasp. The medics finally pushed their way in, sedating the frantic girl so that they could finally get her the help she needed.

Shawn raced to his side, trying to make sure he was alright, but he wasn't able to respond. As the fire began to burn out inside of him, he felt his stomach gurgling in a strange sort of bubbly nausea. Before he could warn anyone, a wave of slimy dark goop spilled out of his mouth, coating the floor in a putrid film.

"What the hell?" Shawn gasped, stepping back out of the way.

"Sorry," he apologized quickly. "Musta been the blood."

"Yeah, well, yer cleanin' it up," Shawn lectured, but he

seemed far less concerned with the mess on his floor than he was with the loon being strapped to the gurney.

Everyone in the store watched as she was wheeled into the ambulance. As the red lights flashed off towards the hospital, he couldn't help but wonder again where she had come from. He knew everyone in town, and he'd never seen anyone like her before. That streak of purple hair would have been a dead giveaway. The only other place even close to here was almost twenty miles away. In her condition, she never would have been able to walk that far. That meant she must have either driven here or caught a ride with someone else. Maybe she had been in a car accident. That would have explained the injuries. And what had she done to him? Now that the initial shock and pain had vanished, he actually felt like he could breathe. For the first time in years, he could take a deep breath and fill his lungs with air.

"Come on," Shawn told him. "I'll getcha some fresh beer an' a new carton a cigs. You've earned 'em."

"You know what?" he told Shawn. "I think I'll just head home. Been a rough night."

"Yeah," Shawn agreed, watching him step out into the fresh night air and take a big, deep breath. He never bought another pack of cigarettes again.

Chapter 75

"So this is where you've been hiding." She stopped packing her things, frozen by fear.

Slowly she turned around, expecting a pack of men in black to be waiting. Instead, she found only one hunter, his enormous body blocking most of the exit.

"Elijah said I could trust you," she breathed, barely even capable of that in her current panic. If he wanted to take her to the Council, she couldn't stop him. He was so much bigger, so much stronger.

"Relax," he smiled sadly. "Officially, you died in the fire along with the others."

"All of them?" The tears came again, but she didn't bother to stop them. The giant wiped at his eyes as well before taking a few steps toward her. His hand was fishing around in his pocket, and she took a step back, expecting him to pull out a weapon of some sort. This was the part where he told her that she had to be dealt with before more innocent people died. And he would be right. She was dangerous. Anyone around her quickly became a target. But it wasn't a weapon. It was much worse.

"I thought you should hold onto it." He extended a closed fist, and from it dangled a silver chain with three wedding bands.

"I can't," she mumbled, the tears turning into

anguished sobs.

Shaking his head, he laughed, "I can't wear it. I haven't got the wardrobe."

Trembling fingers grasped the necklace and slipped it over her head. When she tucked it into her shirt, she could smell the smoke again, feel the heat of the flames. It almost seemed to be burning her skin.

She would never take it off.

"Thanks," she smiled, brushing away the saline streams running down her cheeks.

"No problem, cowgirl. So what are you gonna to do now?"

"College," she answered without a second thought.

"Still?"

"It's what my mother would have wanted. Though how I'm going to fund such an adventure is yet to be determined."

"You're a millionaire. Tuition shouldn't be a problem."

"You said the world thinks I'm dead."

"Well, let's just say I have a friend who took care of it. Speaking of which," he reached into his jacket and pulled out a small piece of pink paper, "here's all the information you'll need. He can hook you up with fake documents and such as well, if you still think hiding is your best option."

"Why did you do all this?"

"Because any friend of Elijah's is a friend of mine." Then with a shrug and a wicked grin, he added, "And you've got a nice ass."

The hunter was startled as the tiny girl suddenly threw her arms around him in a thankful embrace, but he welcomed it. Unlike Elijah, Thomas wasn't interested in shutting out the rest of the world. And even if he had been, resisting the charms of the desperate creature now in his arms had proven impossible to even the toughest souls.

"Told you I'm irresistible," he chuckled. Then, more seriously as she broke the embrace, "Stay out of trouble, okay? And if you need me, my number is on that paper, too. Just don't go writing it on any bathroom stalls. The last thing I need is some big trucker calling me at two in the morning looking for some phone sex."

"No bathroom stalls, I promise. What about newspaper ads?"

"Well, those are okay as long as you remember not to include my love of hunting." Slipping a pair of sunglasses over his puffy red eyes, he told her, "It's been a pleasure protecting you, Sarah Goode."

"You've been a good friend, Thomas the Giant."

"If you only knew how well that nickname fits." Sliding the shades down to the tip of his nose, he tossed her a quick wink before leaving the room.

It was over. She was finally free. After all she'd been through, after all the pain and loss, she was actually going to walk out of this disaster still breathing. But for how long? Would the Others find her? Where could she run that they wouldn't eventually track her down? And what about the Council? Thomas had said they weren't looking now that she was officially listed as dead, but what if they realized she wasn't?

It didn't matter. This was her only chance at a normal life. Well, as close as an orphaned half-demon freak could get, anyway. Besides, what choice did she have? There was no one left to protect her. There was nothing here for her, no reason to stay in a place where people would recognize her and possibly blow her cover. Grabbing her bag and tossing it over her shoulder, she left the hospital room without a second glance.

Time to start over.

ABOUT THE AUTHOR

Brandy Morehouse is an educator living in Newark, Ohio. She lives with her husband, Jeremiah, and four children, Hatshepsut, Alexander, Boudicca, and Octavian Morehouse. When she isn't helping students of all ages learn about learning, she enjoys reading, writing, and designing curriculum for a hypothetical school that will be on the cutting edge of education…whenever she gets around to starting it, anyway. Oh, and ice cream. She absolutely LOVES ice cream.

Made in the USA
Charleston, SC
24 April 2012